18
days

18 days

Cory Blystone

This book is a work of fiction. Names, characters, places and incidents are either products of the author's imagination or are used fictitiously. Any resemblance to actual events or locales or persons, living or dead, is entirely coincidental.

A Kwirk Publishing Original

Published by
Kwirk Publishing
Vancouver, WA

Kwirk Publishing Paperback Edition ISBN: 978-1-945931-00-0

Kwirk Publishing Hardback Edition ISBN: 978-1-945931-03-1
Kwirk Publishing Kindle eBook Edition ISBN: 978-1-945931-01-7
Kwirk Publishing EPUB eBook Edition ISBN: 978-1-945931-02-4

Cover art by Cory Blystone

Published in the United States of America

First Printing March 2017

Ravenwood Series #4

Why are you reading this? There is nothing of importance here! Nothing at all! Unless, of course, you want to be one of those people who literally read a book from cover to cover, then, I suppose, you are forgiven.

This is a book. Duh.

For Greggy. Don't kill me.

18 days

< < <   > > >

September 3, 2002

Hey Princess Diarrhea,

Today I know two things for certain. One: I might be way over my head in some of the classes I'm taking senior year, and Two: I think I am completely and totally in love with this new guy in school named Joel. Fuck me.

< < <   > > >

Earlier

The dark ominous clouds that usually hung over the small town of Ravenwood, Washington decided to go on a rare vacation one quiet September morning. For most, this was a confusing time. What was this strange glowing orb of warmth and light invading their normally gray and gloomy sky? "The sun!" a child cried before running into the house out of fear. Okay, so it wasn't that bad. Well, maybe it was since it happened on the first day back to school after a rather depressingly gray summer.

"Balls," Nikki Boloski said aloud as she walked hand–in–hand with her boyfriend to school that morning, dodging classmates driving down Song's End, the sidewalkless street they lived on. "All summer long there was nothing but clouds, clouds, clouds! I call bullshit."

"C'mon, Nik, you should be happy the sun even decided to come out this year!" Chad Walker joked, cracking open a slight smile that barely revealed his bright whiter–than–white and perfectly straight teeth. Almost perfect. That summer had seen a slight alteration in their alignment as his wisdom teeth began crowding his mouth, but it would take a professional to notice… for now.

Nikki glared at his baby blues with her menacing reds, and forced herself to look away as the sunlight made them twinkle like glitter. A warm breeze blew in from the south out of the nearby town of Chancellor, rustling her hair she spent all morning perfecting for that ever–dreaded first day of the school year, causing stray strands to latch themselves onto her mascara-caked eyelashes, annoying her to no end.

Even though Chad had a car, they decided to walk. Something about tradition.

"This is our third school year since we've been together, can you believe that?" Chad asked without expecting an answer.

"I know, crazy, right?" Nikki asked back with the same assumptions.

Before turning onto Main Street towards the school, they both looked north towards Ashley Heights, the yuppie neighborhood of multi–million dollar estates where Nikki's family used to live before her father divorced her mother and moved to the Philippines to be with his boy toy he'd been screwing for years prior while away on business trips. He left her mom a handsome sum of money, enough to stay, but she opted to move to Ravenwood where she grew up, buying a house on Song's End to raise their four kids and two grandchildren born out of wedlock. The Russian Orthodox Church was furious. The scandal drove her away.

"Sometimes I miss it, living up there," Nikki said, voice dripping with nostalgia, staring at the area normally out of view from low–lying fog that usually blankets the hill leading up to Ashley Heights. "I miss being pretentious and ignorant and a complete stuck–up bitch."

"You still are," Chad told her, his face non–expressionistic.

The punch that landed on his upper arm triggered the reaction he was hoping for. Chad loved the fact that Nikki was so hotheaded and feisty. It made for the best make out sessions that would follow.

"Why so angry, my sweet caribou?" Chad asked.

"Oh gawd, you know I can't stand it when you call me that!" she squealed, punching him again in the same place as before, but with her other hand that had a rather large butterfly ring he'd given her for her sixteenth birthday. Her left hook was heartier than her right.

"Oh no, now I'll have a butterfly bruise," Chad faux-pouted. "Kiss it. Make it better."

Nikki rolled her eyes before Chad swung her around towards him, planting his lips squarely upon hers, kissing her passionately until she practically melted into a metaphorical puddle of goo.

A car stopped next to them and a girl in the passenger seat shouted, "Oh my Buddha, Chad! Enough with the PDA!" It was his ex-girlfriend, Jennifer.

The driver, Sheree, could be seen giggling as she began driving off, her sister Kayla in the backseat barely forcing a grin out, and Jennifer exclaimed loud enough for Chad and Nikki to hear, "I miss those lips."

The car's occupants laughed as it sped off.

"We should probably pick up the pace if we want to get to school on time," Nikki, definitely the more responsible of the two, said.

"Or we could take our time because we are seniors," Chad, definitely the least responsible of the two, said.

"Or we could if we want to graduate next spring so we don't end up being super–seniors."

"Ever the logical one."

"Someone has to be."

"Well, I'm blond. People don't expect much from me."

"Well, I'm not. People expect too much from me."

Chad pulled her in closer as they neared the school. So much so that when Nikki went to move her head, she found her earring caught in his hearing aid.

"Seriously?" she said, trying to unhook herself from his device.

"You know, we could just walk into school like this. People will think we've gotten so close we can't detach!"

She punched his arm again. With the butterfly ring. In the same place as before, but with much less force due to proximity.

"Ow! What the hell was that for?" he yelped, rubbing his arm from the pain he wasn't expecting considering it was a close range shot that didn't have much kinetic force to it which made him realize he remembered what kinetic energy was and suddenly got all gleeful that something he learned stuck with him over the summer. Until he remembered he never took Physics. That was Nikki.

"You know damn well why. Can you take out your hearing aid so we don't look like Siamese twins conjoined at the head?"

"You don't want to look like Siamese twins conjoined at the head? But I thought you loved me?"

"Oh my gawd, Chad. You really are a freak, you know that?"

"The freak who loves you!"

Suddenly they found themselves face to face with a giant Afro stopping them in their tracks. It turned around to reveal Courtney Jones, their mutual best friend. "Da fuck goin' on here?" she asked with an accusatory finger pointing towards their connection point.

"Ugh. Chad's hearing aid and my earring are apparently stuck to one another and Chad's being an asshole and won't take his hearing aid off."

"Gurrrl, what kinda earrings you wearin' that gettin' all caught up in the boy's hearin' aids?" Courtney inspected the culprit. "Dayum! That shit's like barbed wire, bitch! Chad honey, you best be removin' that thing 'fore it takes yo' ear with it."

"I didn't even notice them," Chad confessed.

"Figures," Nikki and Courtney said in unison.

The eye rolls that emanated from the two of them could be seen for miles.

"What?" Chad asked as he removed the hearing aid out of his right ear before adding, "Shit!" as part of his girlfriend's earring pierced his finger. "What the hell, Nik?"

"They were a gift from my dad."

"Apparently your dad wants you to be protected since he bought you earrings that double as weapons. Maybe it's an anti–rape thing. Must be popular in the Philippines. They must rape ears there a lot or something," Chad said before sucking his finger.

"Maybe," Nikki concurred as Chad carefully detached the earring.

A tug on his left shirtsleeve caused him to turn and see who was trying to get his attention. It was Meghan. Courtney's little sister. A freshman.

"Don't forget to meet me during break at the common area in the 300 wing for Prayer Circle!" she shouted before running off, her smile larger than life.

"Anything for you, Meg!" Chad told her with an enthusiastic wave and smile to match.

Courtney shook her head. Her Afro followed suit. "You best be watchin' yo'self. The hell you entertainin' her by joinin' her pathetic prayer thang? You ain't no Jesus freak like her. You don't go to no church. You got no idea what you gettin' yo'self into, boy."

Her words shot out in rapid–fire. His ears heard about every third word.

"Please, Court. It's Meghan. I told her over the summer that I'd be in her prayer circle she wanted to form. It'll probably go away quickly from lack of interest." The smile faded.

"Like you only goin' to youth group with her that one time that turned into the whole goddamned summer?" Courtney's hands magnetically locked to her prominent hips, her face full of disdain.

"That was summer. I've got school and cheerleading to worry about now." He rubbed the ear he removed his hearing aid from with his free hand.

"I don't know. Girl's got it bad for you," Courtney said.

"What?" Chad questioned.

"Put. Your. Hearing. Aid. Back. In," Courtney told him, enunciating every word. "She wants you bad."

"Crap, does this mean I need to keep my eye on you two?" Nikki asked unsuccessfully.

"Huh?"

"Seriously, Chad. Girl's been crushin' on you since she in kindergarten."

"What? She's like my sister. Uck."

"Then treat her like one and blow off this prayer shit 'fore it blows up in yo' face!"

"I'm sure it will be over before it starts."

"Don't be so sure. That girl's got almost as much determination as me."

"Fuck. I'm doomed."

"You beyond doomed." Courtney's face snapped back so hard, Chad thought her Afro might swallow it whole.

"We're going to be late, Chad," Nikki interrupted, something she found she had to do quite often when it came to her boyfriend and best friend talking with one another. *The Chad and Courtney Show* could go on for hours.

"You're right. We'll talk later, okay Court?" Chad said.

"Lunch."

"Yeah, see you at lunch, Courtney!" Nikki said far more enthusiastically than she intended. "Oh gawd, why the hell do I suddenly sound so cheerful?"

"It's from hanging out with us cheerleaders," Chad said, all smiles.

"Crap. I knew it'd rub off."

Chad started cheering through the hallway as they entered the main doors of Ravenwood High School. Nikki tried to cover her head in shame to no avail.

"Okay, cheeseboy, let's get to class. Please. Stop. Really? Oh my gawd."

"Oh, all right… my sweet caribou!" Chad said before running down the hall towards their first period class.

"Chad!" Nikki screamed as she chased after him, readying her punching arm for another bicep pounding.

"Welcome to the wonderful world of Psychology," Mr. Kelsey said with so much enthusiasm it poured out of him like blackstrap molasses. His bald head glistened like Jell–O. He pushed up his wire–rim glasses, a smug smile over his pasty face. "Let's discuss what you already know about this subject and maybe get into the real reason that you have decided to take this course."

First period was going to be hell.

Chad whispered over to Nikki sitting next to him in the double–occupancy desk, "And after that we'll begin interpreting each other's dreams!"

"Shut up, Chad!" Nikki whispered back sharply, giving him a glare that would make a courageous lion cower.

Her whisper carried to the front of the classroom where Mr. Kelsey caught it and promptly paused his discussion and asked, "Is there something that you would like to share with the class Miss…?"

"Boloski, sir. Nikki. I was just curious if we were going to be able to interpret each other's dreams some time during the course of the year. I find the subject of dream interpretation quite interesting and would like to know if the lessons we are going to be learning will give us some basic knowledge to do this," Nikki lied, something she perfected in her youth, and judging from how well her father hid his adultery it was probably hereditary.

The professor smiled with delight, drastically making his markedly unremarkable face appear even less attractive than before. "I don't think I've ever had a student so excited to take my class." He paused, closed his eyes, breathing in the moment and letting it savor on the back of his tongue before continuing. "Don't worry Miss Boloski, we will get into some of the aspects of dream interpretation. In fact, the text itself has a few chapters devoted to such early pioneers of psychology as Freud and Jung, who once spent an entire trip across the sea doing nothing but interpreting each other's dreams, as well as…"

While Mr. Kelsey droned on, Nikki turned toward Chad and stuck her tongue out. Chad gave her the gotta-hand-it-to-you look with a shrug, then focused his attention back to the teacher. Or tried to. They both stared at his glossy head, wondering if he buffed it with Turtle Wax.

"It's just so shiny," Chad said quietly after class let out and they were a relatively safe distance from his classroom.

"I know, right?"

"That was a rather impressive save, too. You're speech about dream interpretation."

"I know, right?"

"I'm serious."

"I know, right?"

"Broken record much?"

"I know, ri-i-i-ight hehehe!"

The giggles took over.

"Lying comes so easy for you," Chad told his girlfriend.

"Well, it is an art form and I have years of practice."

Nikki's next classroom was fast approaching.

"I'll see you at lunch, okay?" Chad said.

"Okay, lunch."

Then they kissed despite it being a forbidden rule in the school handbook (that no one has probably ever read), albeit one that was never enforced by anyone and broken by everyone. Waving as he ran down the hall, Chad watched as

Nikki entered her class and barely made it into his English class at the opposite end as the tardy bell rang.

"Then Lisa told Ryan that Sara liked Matt but Matt had the hots for Morgan who be goin' out with Steve at the time even though she just usin' his ass to get to Michael while Michael be datin' Christine and Jennifer Hoang at the same fuckin' time all the while he tryin' to hook up with me! Like, what a prick!" Courtney spouted the latest gossip, one of two "Gs" she loved discussing. The other was girls. "Besides, Morgan plays fo' my team, she just don't know it yet."

"Yeah," Nikki replied at the only time she felt like she could interject a word to feign interest in the conversation, keeping an eye out for Chad to rescue her from Babble–On.

"Nikki, you hear a word I say?" Courtney asked.

"Of course. Michael's a prick."

"Excellent. Anyway…" Courtney's eyes focused on something just behind Nikki.

"What is it, Court?" Nikki asked, almost scared to find out, hoping it wasn't something about her hair being out of place or something factitious like that Courtney was known for pointing out and mocking, especially in public where others would be enticed and encouraged to join in.

"Oh. My. Gawd," Courtney said before looking Nikki straight in the face. "You've got to check out the hottie at one o'clock. I'm a out an' proud dyke and I'd jump ship for a piece of that ass! Mm hmm."

Nikki turned her head over to the appropriate time then quickly turned it back towards Courtney. "Dark hair, dark eyes, tan skinned, slightly built hunk third seat in from the left?"

"Yep, that'd be the one," she said as she continued staring in his direction, holding her head in her hands as her eyes burned his clothes off.

"Oh my gawd, he's hot!" Nikki said loudly.

"True dat."

"Cool me off, girl, I'm boiling over!" Nikki said, waving her hands to fan her face.

Chad sat next to Courtney and across from Nikki, cheesy ass grin firmly planted on his face.

Nikki changed her hand motion and said, "Go away, fly." *Nice cover up. Not! So much for your lying–is–an–art–form argument, dumbass.*

"So Courtney, who's the stud that has my girlfriend all hot and bothered?" Chad asked quietly out of the corner of his mouth.

"Nik and I were tryin' to figure that out. We ain't seen him before. Ow! Why you kickin' me, Nikki?!" Courtney looked over to Chad. "Oh, uh, hehe." Her enthusiasm dwindled as she made eye contact with her ex–girlfriend, Kayla, who quickly diverted hers into her strawberry blond hair as her hands pushed it over her face.

Chad looked down at his so–called tray of School Lunch Board Approved "food" and began picking at it. "Well, do you know his name or not?"

"Chad!" Nikki screamed between her teeth in a voice just barely audible between the three of them.

Sticking his fork into his mashed potatoes and gravy, Chad put his hand in the air and shouted like a sassy black woman, "Cool me off, girlfriend, I'm boilin' over!" waving his hand in the air to mimic Nikki's recent fanning, but quickly falling apart into hysterical laughter.

Nikki covered her face with her hands to hide her embarrassment and the voluptuous shade of red it had become.

"Oh, my poor little caribou," Chad said in a baby voice. "What's the matter? Are you embarrassed?"

Uncovering her face, Nikki responded with, "No, Chad, I'm fine. Oh gawd, did I really look that stupid?"

"Honey, it was worse!" Chad and Courtney said in unison.

After lunch, Chad and Nikki parted with a kiss straight out of a romantic movie. Seriously, it was a full–on reenactment. Nikki and Courtney walked to their fourth period class as Courtney started chatting it up. Again.

"You know, Nik, you really lucky to have a boyfriend like Chad. He don't get jealous at all. He's so cool 'bout everything."

"Yeah, I know. Still, there are times I wonder though."

"Wonder about what?"

"Well, you know, if he's gay or something."

A crack in the breezeway between buildings caught Nikki's eyes as she stared down while walking with her friend, dragging them towards all of the other imperfections in the concrete walkway she thought was solid.

"What? Chad? You sure?" Courtney said as if she was merely pretending not to understand where Nikki was coming from. "He ain't told me and that boy tells me everythang."

"You're probably right. I'm probably just being paranoid. It's just, you know, some of the things he says and does. Sometimes the way he acts. I don't know. I can't help feeling this way. It's like a gut feeling. I mean, the possibility is out there. Hell, I never even had a clue you are gay until I caught you and Sheree having a heart–to–heart. I mean, do you know how embarrassing it is to walk in on a conversation about how your best friend is in love with you?" she said, avoiding Courtney's eyes and instead focusing up on the rust peaking through the steel beams that have been painted far too many times.

"Nik, you've been goin' out for two and a half years now," Courtney said to change the subject back and avoid the elephant between them.

"Yeah."

"Don't you think if the boy was gay he'd, oh, I don't know, not be datin' the hotness that is you?"

"Hot? Me? Seriously, Court. I don't know if your unrequited love for me has blinded you to the fact that I'm an overweight mostly shapeless frump or what is causing you to think he'd be crazy not to date me, but c'mon. Let's be real here."

"I'm bein' real, girl. Chill. You've got tits and ass that go on for miles!"

"Seriously?"

"Seriously, you ain't shapeless. Honey, you curvaceous!"

The compliment slipped away as quickly as it came.

A wind picked up suddenly, swishing Nikki's hair over her face, tickling her eyes and nostrils, a few strands sticking to the corner of her lips. Courtney's stayed in place.

"Ugh, I don't know where I'm going with this," Nikki said, wiping the hair out of her mouth. "Sorry I brought it up."

"Bitch, please. You two have totally done it, right?"

Nikki turned her face, continuing to avoid Courtney's eyes. "Well, uh, to be honest we haven't."

"What?! You been goin' out for two an' a half years and ain't had the sex?" Courtney shouted so loud a couple teachers and a fair number of students looked in their direction, but seeing that it was Courtney, nobody was surprised. She meant for it to sound surprised, even though she knew the answer. After all, Chad told her everything. "Sorry girl, he gay!"

"Courtney, keep your voice down!" Nikki demanded, trying to hide her face from a teacher who couldn't hold in a smile at this revelation.

"I'm sorry, honey. I just find it really hard to believe." She shook her head over and over while facing the ground and seeing the small pink flowers poking through the cracks in the walkway, spurring a miniscule smile. Her hair stayed in place, defying the laws of physics.

"Well do, because deep down we are both rather traditional people." A certain pride swept over her face as she said it, along with an arrogant smile to represent her superiority complex.

"Nikki Boloski? Traditional? Ha! Well I guess you is compared to yo' sister Natasha! Hell, even I'm an angel compared to that slut!" Courtney's eyes bulged wide and wild, along with the rest of her face's expressions.

"Hey! Leave her alone, she's a good person," Nikki said as if she was almost offended at her best friend's words.

"Good to those who pay her!"

"She's not a whore!"

"You right, she free of charge. 'You get a blowjob! You get a blowjob! You get a blowjob! You get anal! You get the real deal because I wanna have yo' baby!' Ha HAHAHAHA!!!"

Courtney's hair bobbled with so much enthusiasm as she laughed, Nikki wondered how it stayed on her head.

"Okay, fine. But she didn't drop out of school. She finished up on time, so that counts for something."

"Yeah, but not without her two–year–old strapped to her hips at graduation and six months preggo with her second child!"

"For you information, Miss Thang, She's an excellent mother," Nikki said, realizing how pathetic that sounded but quickly running out of options that could possibly redeem her sister. "Besides, can't blame a girl for loving sex."

"You gotta point there, sistuh. I mean, you a virgin and can see that."

"What makes you think I'm a virgin?"

"Bitch, please. You'd have told me."

The bell rang.

"Crap!" Nikki shouted as she ran into the building and to their English class, spotting an empty seat that was unfortunately toward the front, and sitting down.

"Ah, Nikki Boloski. What a pleasant surprise," the teacher stated with a grin over his sickly face and an amateurish attempt at a goatee gracing it as well. "I see I've been"—he paused for a brief-yet-noticeable second—"fortunate enough to have you as my pupil yet again."

Courtney took her time walking into the classroom towards an empty chair in the back, not even caring that she was late, but embracing the fact that she yet again could make an entrance.

"Isn't Mrs. O'Hurley supposed to be teaching this class?" Nikki asked, hoping there was just a mistake on the schedule sheet and she was in the wrong room.

One of the students gawked at Courtney who not so quietly chose that moment to take out a piece of mint chewing gum and stick it in her mouth.

"Originally yes, but we had to switch classes for some reason unimportant to you," the teacher stated with a grim expression, causing Nikki to wonder why someone who obviously hated teaching was a teacher.

"Great." *Just my luck. This guy is a freak. A total lunatic! I don't know if I can handle another year with…*

"Mr. Slutz is my name," the teacher said as he wrote it on the whiteboard, causing Courtney and a few other students to nearly choke laughing at how closely it resembled another word. "However, I hate the whole formal mumbo–jumbo, so if you want to call me Dmitri, I prefer it. Besides, it usually catches my attention better."

Nikki slumped her head over her arms on her desk and listened to what Mr. Slutz, I mean, er, Dmitri, had to say. However, she wasn't paying much attention to the words coming out of his mouth because she was too busy thinking about the dark haired kid in the cafeteria and dreaming about his seductive dark eyes and what she'd like to do with his beautiful dark body. Then Chad popped into the picture and ruined her whole fantasy as he often did in her daydreams and dreams as if her brain was giving her a little reminder that that she was already in a relationship.

"Hey Nikki! Wait for me!" Chad cried, running quite awkwardly toward his girlfriend after school was over.

"Oh gawd, Chad. You run like a girl," Nikki said in a voice that feigned embarrassment.

"Well, chica, you always were the more masculine one in this relationship!" Chad said, his voice reminiscent of a Mexican telenovella actor's thick accent when being interviewed on American television programs.

"Shut up, Chad!"

Pouty lips formed on Chad's face as he said in his puppy dog voice with sad ASPCA eyes to match, "Are you angry with me?"

"No, I'm not mad, it's just that…"

"…kid in the cafeteria?" Chad finished, lowering his head to the weed–covered lawn of the schoolyard, suddenly out of character by looking serious.

"Chad…"

"No, it's okay," he told her. "I mean, don't worry about it. I'd be lying if I didn't do the same."

"You mean you have also…?"

"Had a crush on someone else? Absolutely. A few times, actually," he admitted, knowing that he always felt like he could be honest with her, but even that had its boundaries.

"Oh thank God! I thought it was just me!" she shouted, relieved.

Chad giggled. *Gawd, if she ever found out…*

"You're not going to tell me who, are you?" Nikki asked, face scrunched up as if about to admit defeat early in the game.

"Nope."

"Bastard."

"Well, I am, so…"

"That's not what I meant!"

"I know. Wanna go to The Oasis later?" Chad asked, looking up at the clear blue sky with eyes of the same color and noticing a few fluffy white clouds slowly winding across the great wonder before turning his attention back to Nikki for a response.

"That's over in Portland. Besides, it's a school night. Mom will have a total fit over it!" Nikki stated, fidgeting with a ballpoint pen.

"Yeah," Chad snickered. "I could totally see her freaking out because you went dancing on a Tuesday night. She'd be hysterical and cry about how dancing will get you pregnant!"

Nikki shut down Chad before he had a chance to giggle with a look that could kill. "She might agree to going to Pyro's for pizza, though," a slight grin forming on her Charlie Brown face.

"So it is a date, my caribou queen?"

"It is, Chadwick."

"You know I hate it when you call me that."

"Payback's a bitch, isn't it?"

"A bitch it is. Would you care for company on your way home?"

"I'd love it."

"Well then, take my hand as we meander towards the homestead."

"But of course, my love."

Walking hand–in–hand from school, birds could be heard chirping along Main Street as they walked up the slight hill that led to Song's End where no birds ever chirped and darkness crept over even the sunniest of days.

Later

Chad quickly closed his diary file on the computer when he heard the front door slam shut. "Hey, Mom! I'm taking Nikki to Pyro's tonight, so you're on your own for dinner, 'kay?" Chad shouted louder than necessary as he ran down the stairs, his orange tabby cat, Squeakers, following in hopes of being fed. Or maybe tripping him as he ran down the stairs. Cats are assholes like that.

"On a weeknight?" his mother asked. "And her mother's letting her go, too?"

Ms. Walker knew Nikki's mother all to well, having dealt with her on multiple occasions at the middle school she worked at. She also knew her policy on weeknight outings that weren't school related, as in actually at the school.

Chad walked over to the kitchen where his mom had gone to pour herself an inordinate amount of boxed wine into a glass not meant for such activities. The cat followed, running up to his food dish and waiting as patiently as a feline had the ability to.

"I just got off the phone with Nik a few minutes ago, and apparently she said it was okay."

"Hmm… doesn't sound like the Kelley I know who freaks out when you two are just over here studying." She gulped half the glass in one drink before filling it back up. The refrigerator door never closed.

"Well, it could be because it's only the first day school. Nikki alluded to that possibility." Chad smiled, pulling a can of salmon–flavored cat food out of an upper cabinet and plopping the pinkish goo into Squeakers's blue plastic dish, where he hungrily devoured it. "Maybe she doesn't have any homework or something like that. Mrs. Boloski can sometimes be reasoned with, you know."

Ms. Walker pushed her eyes up to the ceiling and contorted her mouth, moving it from side to side as if she was thinking over the situation when she really didn't care one way or the other, but instead just wanted to watch her son squirm with anticipation over her response. "Fine."

Thanks, Mom!" he said, reaching over and giving her a hug that lifted her off the ground and caused some of the chardonnay to dribble onto the orange honest–to–God real linoleum floor.

"But…" she started.

"But? But? No! No buts!"

"But don't come home before nine, okay? No later than ten, however. You've still got school tomorrow, and have to have some time to fill me in on all the details of your date before bed!"

Her enthusiasm was exhausting. Chad never questioned where his came from.

"Don't worry, Mother. I'll be in the door by ten tops. Promise."

"Good. No earlier than nine still."

"And why is that?"

"Because my boyfriend might be coming over and I don't want you catching us doing anything that you might not be ready to see."

Chad's face contorted. "Oh gawd, mom, why?"

A wicked smile spread over her face.

"Whatever. You ain't even got no boyfriend," Chad said, sassy as can be, headshakes and all.

"A girl can dream, can't she?" his mom asked innocently, batting her eyelashes.

"And a lot of dreamin' you'll be doin' gurrrl!" There may have even been three snaps in a Z–formation during this.

"Chadwick!" she cried with contrived shock.

"Amanda!" he imitated.

"Don't call me Amanda. I'm your mother, and you will refer me to as such," she scolded, trying to remain serious but the wine began hitting her faster than usual.

"Or Mom, Mommy… Mommy Dearest!" he said snootily.

"Don't you EVER call me that! That woman was evil and a bad person and I'm nothing like her!" she screamed, sounding eerily like Faye Dunaway as Joan Crawford.

"Sorry. Geez, Mom. I'm going to my room to throw away all the wire hangers before you beat me with them."

Chad ran up the stairs to his bedroom to read and Ms. Walker stumbled into the living room, kicked off her heels, rewound the VHS tape in the VCR, and started watching her soap opera she recorded while away at work. Squeakers, after surrendering to the fact that his food dish would not be refilled with more delightful overly processed salmon, zigzagged up the stairs to join Chad, squeaking and pawing at the door until he opened it to let him in. He found a spot on Chad's pillow to lick his ass for the next half hour until Chad had to leave to pick up Nikki.

"You're disgusting, you know that?" he told the feline.

Ass licking continued.

Chad tossed the book to his side and ran downstairs, shouting, "Operation Wire Hanger Disposal: Complete!"

"Very funny," Ms. Walker told him, pausing the tape.

"Sorry about the sassiness and no boyfriend thing earlier."

"I'm used to it. Besides, if I did have a sex life, I'd keep it to myself."

"Liar."

"Have fun."

"I'll bring home leftovers."

"Two teenagers eating pizza? There will be no leftovers."

"Okay, well, it's the thought that counts."

"Need money?"

"Already grabbed forty out of your purse while you were nursing that chardonnay."

"You're such a good boy. Now give your mama a kiss and have fun tonight."

"Will do," Chad said, kissing his mother's flush cheek. "See you in a few."

Grabbing the keys off the console table by the front door to his shit brown late seventies model sedan covered in Duck Tape to prevent the moon roof from leaking during the ever popular rainy days the Northwest is known for, he could faintly hear coming from the television the shrill voice of Erica Kane lamenting about her latest failed marriage she was about to sabotage by getting back together with Jack. Again. The car door took some effort to open, and as he pumped the gas while trying to start it, he prayed to no god in particular that it would start. *Third times a charm.* Once running, he drove three houses down and pulled into Nikki's driveway across the street. Not wanting to risk the embarrassment of a stalled vehicle, he left the car running while he went up to the door to grab his girlfriend for their date. There was little to no chance someone would steal his car, just one benefit of many to owning an old rust-bucket.

Nikki opened the door before he could knock or ring the doorbell, and greeted him with a, "Hi, sweetie!" before kissing him and shouting behind her, "Bye, Mom!"

"Nine o'clock, no later!" Mrs. Boloski (she refused to change her name, or stop being called misses, or even acknowledge the fact that her ex–husband was a homosexual) yelled from the kitchen in her low husky voice.

"Oh, Kelley, how about by ten o'clock?" Chad asked, flashing a toothy smile and letting the hall light catch his eyes so they twinkled. "That's when Mom said I could be out until."

Blushing, Mrs. Boloski asked, "I have your word?" stirring some foul–smelling concoction with a large wooden spoon.

"Yes, ma'am."

"Need money?"

"No, ma'am."

"Well, have good time then."

She waved them out with her free hand.

"C'mon, let's go. Quickly," Nikki told him quietly, pushing him out the door, closing it behind her.

"What are you in such a hurry for? That hungry?" Chad asked.

"Ugh, no, it's that smell," she told him, an overtly sour look upon her face as they got into the car.

"You mean that stuff she was stirring?"

"Gawd, yes. It smells terrible!"

"What the hell was it anyway?"

"Leftovers."

"What'd she do? Put everything together into some kind of sick stew?" Chad asked jokingly, laughing at the thought.

"Yes."

"You're kidding?"

"The woman is mad." Nikki's face sincere and serious.

"You're not kidding, are you?" Chad's face in pre–vomit stage.

"Can you believe it? I'm telling you, my mom needs to be admitted into a hospital sometime soon before she kills us all! Why aren't you driving, man? I'm starving!"

A Mamas and the Papas song played on the radio as they drove downtown to Pyro's Pizza Parlor, so instead of having a conversation, they sang the song together. When it was over, Nikki started in on how Mr. Slutz—I did it again. Sorry. Dmitri—was going to ruin her senior year. Chad didn't have the heart to tell her his English teacher was Mrs. O'Hurley.

The parking lot looked rather empty, so Chad was able to get a spot right next to the front door. Warning sign number one.

After getting out, Chad ran over to the passenger side door and opened it for Nikki and pretended to be a gentleman as he said, "Allow me, my lady," pulling the door open and taking her hand to help her out. Pretend because the passenger side door only opened from the outside.

They walked into the pizza place and waited for someone to acknowledge their existence for a seemingly inordinate amount of time. Warning sign number two.

"Uh, hellooooo?" Nikki said quietly, barely loud enough for Chad to hear even with his hearing aids at maximum.

While searching for someone, anyone who worked there, a young girl's head popped out of the kitchen area. She quickly wiped her hands off on her tomato sauce stained pants, grabbed two menus, brushed her hair back behind her ear leaving a slick streak of unknown origin, and asked, "Smoking or non?" Warning sign number three.

"Uh, nonsmoking?" Chad said.

"Harrumph," she begrudgingnly responded with as she walked away, leaving Nikki and Chad to wonder if they were supposed to follow or not. The menus dropped onto a table (that she quickly flicked a few crumbs and a straw wrapper onto the floor) indicating they were indeed meant to follow. "You want something to drink?"

"Uh, a Coke?" Chad's uneasiness made his answers sound like questions.

"Water for me." Nikki's bitch–face was in full–on mode.

"[grunt]" the waitress managed as she left to get their drink order.

When she was out of earshot, Nikki said, "Maybe I should have gotten something stronger than water."

"Why?"

Using the menu as a shield, she said, "Let's just say that I'll be lucky if she doesn't spit that loogey she was hacking up into my glass."

"What are you talking about? I mean, sure, she's not got the best customer service skills. What am I missing?" Chad asked, confused and knowing that Nikki would tease him to no end about his hair color being responsible for his lack of understanding in logical matters.

"That whore is my brother's ex–girlfriend. We never got along."

"Why?"

"Uh, because that ho–bag slept with anything that walked, crawled, or slithered on this Earth and probably beyond. And that's just while she was going out with Nureyev! I flat out told Nurey all about it when I found out and she didn't even deny it. Of course, it would have been difficult for her to deny it because he confronted her while she was giving one of his friends a blowjob in our laundry room. Bitch."

"That's a very good reason."

"Tell me about it."

"Danger, Will Robinson! Danger! She's on approach!" Chad whispered.

Glasses landed on the table like they fell from the sky, causing some of the Coke to spill out, snake its way to the edge, and dribble down onto the floor like a tiny brown waterfall as the whore slash waitress pulled out a couple straws that fell onto the matted carpet before she picked them up and wiped them off on her tomato stained pants and threw them on the table and asked sharply, "You ready to order yet?"

"No, but if you give us a chance to actually look at the menu, maybe we will be soon," Nikki said to her with a fake smile full of fake cheer before abruptly pulling the menu into her face so hard it smacked her nose.

"Fine," she said, rolling her eyes and putting the ticket-book between her breasts before adjusting her crotch which released a pungent vinegary odor and walking back into the kitchen like someone who'd been riding a horse all day. She may have queefed as well.

"Nik, I meant for us to have a good time. Let's go."

"Thank God, because there is no way I am letting anything that girl touches get anywhere near my mouth!"

Checking to make sure the coast was clear, they stealthily made their exit.

"Where to? Ravenwood Bar & Grill?" Chad suggested as they drove off.

"We should have just gone there first," Nikki said, her voice full of regret. "But they have amazing pizza and I will be sad because I'm so turned off for pizza for the night. Shocking, I know."

"Maxi's Diner then?"

"I don't know, Maxi's always reminds me of…"

"If you say pads I will punch your face."

"…airplane stickers!" Nikki said as her face lit up.

"Oh my gawd, that's right! Maxi Pads with Wings! My mom was so pissed when she saw that I'd put those all over the front window for all the neighbors to see."

"I think she was more pissed that you were thirteen at the time."

Chad side-smiled his devilish grin.

"Drive!"

A few minutes later when they reached their destination, which was decidedly busier than their first choice, they were surprised to find there was no waiting when they walked in. The red haired attendant asked how many and they told her two and she walked them to a table for four and Chad quietly asked Nikki if she had anything against this one and she punched his arm where it was already bruised from earlier punches and they sat down.

"What can I get to drink for you?" she asked.

"Coke please," Chad said.

"Same here," Nikki said.

"Awesome, be right back with those! Lily will be your server tonight, so she'll be by shortly to take your order."

"Thanks," Nikki said, actually meaning it.

Staring at the menu's burger section, Chad asked casually to himself, "Let's see, what do I want?"

"I know what I'm getting," Nikki stated, closing her menu and placing it on the edge of the table where it almost fell off before she quickly pulled it back.

"That was quick. I haven't even looked at what they have yet," he said as the redhead placed their Cokes on the table. A smile indicated his thanks and a smile from the attendant indicated it was received before she walked off to help the next group that had just walked in the door. "What are you getting?'

Nikki sighed. "As if you didn't know! A Double Monster Burger with steak fries, of course!"

"Of course. Because you've ordered that so many NEVER!" Chad responded. "Ooh! This looks good. A California Chicken Burger?"

"What the hell is that? You on a diet now that cheer season is officially upon us? Seriously, you could stand to gain a few pounds." Nikki's self–consciousness about her weight sometimes caused her to lash out at skinny people, especially during suppertime.

"Hey! I'm not anywhere near as lanky as I used to be!" Chad cried, leaving his mouth wide open.

"True. Puberty did you wonders." Her eyes wandered over Chad's upper body casually.

"Fine. Bacon Cheddar Grill it is."

"Okay, a Bacon Cheddar. And for you, Nikki?" the waitress asked as if she teleported to their table.

"Oh, Lily! Lily! I didn't know it'd be you, Lily!" Nikki squealed, getting up out of her chair and hugging her friend. Lily returned the hug. "Um, I'll have the Double Monster Burger and steak fries instead of those wimpy things."

"Got it. You want the wimpy things?" Lily asked, staring Chad down.

"Yes," Chad responded, head bowed in shame.

"Figures," Lily and Nikki said as they rolled their eyes.

"I know."

"Be right back with those, guys!" Lily said with bubbly personality flowing as she Prancercised (before this became a thing) into the kitchen to put in their order with the cooks.

"I like the wimpy fries," Chad said quietly before sucking Coke out of a straw.

"Because you're a wimp!" Jennifer Hoang said loudly as she brushed past them, followed by Sheree, Kayla, Brendon, and Mr. & Mrs. Hollins taking up the rear.

"Ignore her," Sheree told him.

"Her dad isn't coming home this month and she's taking it personally," Kayla added, sending a chill down his spine he couldn't understand why, but figured it was because she was Courtney's on–again–off–again girlfriend.

"Hi, Chad!" Brendon said gleefully, fabulously gay as ever a twelve–year–old boy could be.

"Hey," he said back with a side–grin.

"Where's Amanda?" Mrs. Hollins asked, her flashy copper hair that obviously came from a generic brand of hair dye found at the supermarket picking up the overhead lights in an unnatural way. They were best friends and worked together at the middle school and have known each other longer than Chad had been alive.

"At home watching *All My Children*."

"Some things never change," Mr. Hollins added before patting him on the shoulder as he made his way towards their booth.

Chad always had a weird and uneasy feeling about the family that lived two doors down from him, but at the same time always fantasized that Mr. Hollins was his dad. Of course, if his mother would ever allow him to find out who his father was, he probably wouldn't need to fill the void with fantasy. Then again, some fantasies…

"Okay, so since we are being honest with one another, I've always thought Mr. Hollins was hot. He's a total DILF," Nikki said, staring at his ass before it sat down, no longer able to be gazed upon. "Especially when he's wearing his scrubs. Washing the car with nothing but swim shorts on. Or…" Her voice trailed off as her hands disappeared into her lap.

"I know what you mean," Chad said before doubling back with, "about hot parents."

"Mm hmm." A bit of drool escaped Nikki's lips. She bent forward to take a swig of Coke. Her hands remained under the table.

"I don't know why Jennifer has been so mean to me lately. It can't just be her dad. She doesn't even like the guy. He just shows up once a month and gives her mom money and leaves again." Chad's voice oozed with melancholy.

"Sometimes it hurts when they don't show up." Nikki had a lot of personal experience with absentee fathers, even before he moved out of the country. Her guilty hands decided to reappear.

"I guess. I just thought we were friends and past the pettiness. Cheer practice this week is going to suck major ass if she's going to act like that."

"If she acts like that, Courtney will put her in her place."

"True that."

"Besides, she was probably just making a funny, okay?"

"You think so?"

"Seriously, she's always joking with you."

"Seriously, she's always joking *about* me."

"Lighten up."

He put on the most innocent face he could conjure. "I just like to make a scene."

"Fine, make a…" Nikki stopped in the middle of her sentence as she spotted the dark haired, dark eyed, beautifully built tan hunk she was drooling over in the cafeteria.

"Uh, Earth to Nikki?" Chad said, waving his hand in front of her face. "Are you having a stroke or something, because I am not prepared to deal with that sort of thing?"

"It's him."

"Who?" Chad craned his neck towards the entrance to look in the direction of her gaze. "Joel?"

"Joel?" Nikki asked. Had she heard him right? *He knows his name?*

"Yeah, the dark haired, dark eyed, beautifully built hunk you were drooling over in the cafeteria today? He's in my Algebra class. We sit right next to each other."

"Joel? His name is Joel? Algebra?" Nikki looked as spaced out and confused as Peppermint Patty when Marcy informed her that Snoopy was a beagle and not just a funny looking kid with a big nose.

Chad, realizing he had no choice but to snap her back to reality, reached over and began to shake her shoulders violently, saying, "Wake up, Nikki! Come back to the light!"

Nikki screamed like she was sincerely frightened, but not loud enough to gather the attention of everyone at the restaurant, just enough to make her feel uncomfortable with the inquisitive glares of those in close proximity. "Gah, what the hell? Get your hands off me you freak!" she yelled, throwing his hands away as her face flushed fuschia.

"Whew, that was close. For a minute there I thought I might lose you," he joked. His facial expression, however, remained stoic.

"Shut up." Her face quickly fading back to her normal shade.

Chad had his famous ASPCA face on as he asked, "Can you forgive me?" melting Nikki's ice–cold heart.

"With a face like that, how could I not," she said, scrunching her nose before kissing him.

"Hey, would you mind if I invited him over to join us?" Chad asked, but sensed her answer would be yes.

"No, of course not. Make him come," Nikki said before quickly adding, "over!"

Using his cheerleading skills, Chad simply cupped his hands and yelled, "Joel!" instead of doing what a normal person would have done: walk over and ask in a regular inside voice.

Joel's head looked up and around, wondering where the call came from. When his eyes spotted Chad, he pointed to himself and mouthed, "Me?"

"Sit with us!" Chad yelled.

Joel walked over to their table and asked, "Are you sure? My dad and I were supposed to go out together but then he said he had a date and I was on my own for dinner and then he left and we have nothing at home because neither of us can cook real food and there are only so many times a boy can eat Ramen noodles."

"No problem! I'll just tell Lily we're having a threeway… I mean, we're adding a third… that there's another person eating with us? Oh gawd," Nikki stumbled over the falling dominos of words spilling out of her suddenly uncoordinated mouth, hiding her face in the palm of her hands.

"Hi, I'm Joel," he said, offering his hand out for a shake.

Nikki took it and shook it before replacing hers in front of her rosy face.

"Shit, that's some grip you've got there! I mean, for a girl. Not that I'm sexist or anything, I just wasn't prepared for that kind of power. Can I wrap my hand around your drink, Chad? The pain!"

Chad pushed his drink toward Joel who gently put his aching hand around it.

Lily almost walked past them when her eyes caught sight of Joel and the Berlin song "Take My Breath Away" started playing in her head, so she stopped and asked, "Who's this?"

"Joel. He's new."

"Hi Joel Heezenew!" Lily said, snorting out a giggle afterwards. "Want me to bring you a menu?"

"Do you have a wedge salad?" he asked.

"Yep."

"I'll take that and a 7–Up."

"Sprite okay?"

"No, it is not okay."

Lily looked like she was about to cry.

"I'm joking! Damn black eyes. People find them so untrusting. Maybe it's because I'm an Indian, huh?"

Now Lily looked horrified.

"Damn, I need to work on my social skills up here."

Chad started laughing, Nikki was busy undressing him with her eyes, and Lily let out a nervous giggle before saying, "I'll go put that salad in and get your Sprite."

"Thanks." He smiled.

After Chad finished laughing, he said to Nikki, "He's got a wicked sense of humor, doesn't he?"

"Yeah," Nikki said back, hoping her brain didn't shut off before she got to the good stuff. "But you don't look like you're from India so I'm guessing Native American?"

"Tillamook Indian. Don't get all politically correct on my account."

"Who's the hot guy?" Jennifer asked out of nowhere, slurring her words as her hands hit the table to keep her steady which caused Chad's nearly full Coke Joel still cupped to spill over a little onto his fingers, her eyes glazed porcelain.

"Joel," Chad said.

"Hi Joel! I'm Jennifer! Chad and I used to date but I dumped his gay ass and this bitch here took him not even thirty seconds later and I've regretted it ever since. Isn't he the cutest thing? Sweet Buddha, those lips are magic."

"Uh…" Joel managed, fingers already feeling sticky.

Chad hung his head down.

Nikki's concentration faltered. The image of Joel in various stages of undress deteriorating rapidly, ruining her mental orgasm.

"C'mon, Jen! Our table's over here, remember?" Sheree said, grabbing her friend and pointing her in the right direction.

"Oh, right! But that guy's so hot, isn't he? I just wanted to say hi, okay?"

"And you've said hi and now you need to eat something. A lot of something."

"Yeah, I want a hot dog real bad."

"It's coming."

Jennifer stumbled back to the booth where the Hollins family sat.

"Sorry about that. She may have had a little to drink before we picked her up," Sheree told them, stating the obvious.

"A little? Is this about her dad not coming this month?" Chad asked.

"That and it's her time of the month."

"Airplane stickers!" Chad said loudly.

"I don't get it."

"I'll tell you the story later. Go take care of her, will you?"

"Will do. Later, guys."

"Poor girl," Joel said sincerely.

"She'll be fine. This isn't the first time," Chad told him.

"That she's been drunk in a public place as a minor?" Joel asked. "Where the hell did I move?"

"No, well, yeah, but it's more that her dad hasn't come home as planned. It's just happening a lot more this last year."

"Well hopefully he isn't carrying on like my dad was!" Nikki said, laughing. Turning to Joel she continued, "He left my mom for a Filipino boy about five years ago. Oh my gawd, I think tomorrow is his twenty–first birthday!"

"You sound far too enthusiastic about your father's boy–toy," Joel said.

"I love ChiChi!" Nikki said in an uncharacteristically high–pitched voice, bouncing in her seat.

"And his name is ChiChi. Of course." Joel bobbed his head up and down.

Before the conversation could spur any further inquiries about Nikki's father's infidelities, Lily swooped in with their food. "Wedge Salad, Double Monster with steak fries, and Bacon Cheddar with wimps. Need anything else other than refills?"

"Nope," Nikki said. "This looks amazing! I can't wait to stuff it in my mouth!"

Lily went to a nearby table that she'd already checked out after the large party had left. Nikki could see the word, "Assholes," escape her mouth as she cleaned up their mess to help out the overwhelmed busboy whose first day was probably going to be his last.

"Poor Lily. Those jerks didn't leave her a tip," Nikki said as she lifted her sandwich to her mouth and took the first of many bites of her glorious cheeseburger.

"What? Poopheads," Chad said with a mouthful, his burger already half gone.

"Ditto," Joel said, still cutting his salad with knife and fork like a gentleman.

After dinner, dessert, and conversations that didn't really mean anything, Chad left the entire forty dollars he'd stolen from his mother's purse, and Joel put down the same for his, leaving a rather generous tip for Lily.

"Hopefully that makes up for those assholes," Chad said.

Before leaving the restaurant, Chad waved towards the Hollins family and Jennifer, who sat slumped against the wall drooling and more-than-likely unconscious. Nikki found Lily and gave her a hug while Chad and Joel walked outside.

Faux–running to catch up with them, Nikki said, "This was fun! We should do it again."

"Definitely," Joel said. "See you in school tomorrow!" before he hopped into his late model BMW.

Chad and Nikki waved from the doors as he drove out of the parking lot before walking to his piece of shit car he bought by scraping every last dime he earned two summers ago mowing lawns and landscaping from a guy who later told him he was going to drive it into a lake.

"He drives a fucking BMW?" Nikki said, shaking her head as she buckled her seatbelt.

"It appears so. Maybe it's his dad's?" Chad said, buckling his seatbelt and starting the car.

Surprisingly it started on the first crank.

"Yeah, maybe. Still, I had fun tonight," Nikki said, looking out the side window as he drove them towards home.

"Me too." Chad kept his eyes on the road, driving with white knuckles, suddenly nervous.

"Yeah, Joel seems like a nice guy…" Nikki's voice trailed off as she began reminiscing the glance she got of his ass as he walked to his car and the way his Levi's clung to his cheeks leaving very little to the imagination. The thought brought quite a bit of excitement to her lady parts.

"Oh, please. Who are you trying to fool? All you want is his body!" Chad blurted, a laugh escaping with the outburst.

"Chad!" Nikki gasped, hand to her chest and feigning shock. "That's not true! I'm a fucking lady!" then added a short moment later, "Well, not entirely true, anyway."

"I knew it."

"Oh, Chad, darling. You know I only want you," she said like one of those British actors in a Jane Austen movie.

"I know. What's looking going to hurt?"

"Nothing, but if I find out what girls you've been looking at, I'm going to kill them!" Nikki grinded her teeth as she spoke even though she was only being playful.

"Hehehe… that shouldn't be a problem," Chad assured her.

Chad walked through the front door of his house at five minutes to ten, just barely making the curfew his mother imposed for selfish reasons. Amanda walked out of the kitchen wearing sweatpants and a loose fitting T–shirt, indicating that at some point during the evening she'd decided to change—a rarity—carrying a heaping bowl of Tillamook Mudslide ice cream in one hand, a spoon in the other, a wicked smile on her face, and a cat trailing her feet.

"Hey," Chad said, trying unsuccessfully to untie his shoes while standing up, managing only one, which he kicked into the coat closet by the front door.

"Hello, Chad. How was your date?" she asked, walking into the family room to watch the local news. She took a bite of her ice cream and produced a look of a woman in desperate need of chocolate whose craving had just been satisfied.

"A little hectic at first, but once we got everything settled it was pretty good." He sat on the loveseat, pulled a lace, got a knot, and uttered under his breath, "Goddammit," as Squeakers twirled around his feet, squeaking and squawking his hellos before Chad told the cat, "I'm not feeding you again!" lightly kicking him away.

Sensing her son's frustration, she debated over getting the juicy details, but curiosity got the better of her. "Okay, spill."

Still working out the knot in his laces, Chad said, "Well, we started out at Pyro's, but Nikki didn't like our waitress because she was apparently one of her brother's ex–girlfriends. She didn't have anything nice to say about her, and what she did say, well, I just don't feel comfortable repeating in front of you."

"Wow, that bad, huh?' she said, knowing that there were very few things off limits verbiage–wise as she spooned another bite of rapidly melting chocolate ice cream into her open and awaiting mouth.

"And honestly, I don't think I could even conjure up anything nice to say about her either after my experience even under threat of torture or maiming."

"Eek! She's worse than I thought. Okay, where'd you go then?"

"Maxi's."

"Airplane stickers."

"Shut up."

"Go on."

"Anyway, while we were there we had Joel join us. Yes!" Chad said as the knot finally loosened, kicking off the shoe and leaving it where it landed in the middle of the room.

"Joel? Who's that?" she asked with intrigue and a mouth full of brown mass.

"Someone in my Algebra class. We sit right next to each other. He's new to town, just moved here during the summer.

Nikki's got the biggest crush on him, it's ridiculous!" he said with a smile revealing his dimpled cheeks.

"And you're okay with that?" she asked, licking the chocolate from the side of her lips. *Joel? I wonder if that's...*

"Yeah, why wouldn't I be?" he questioned, wondering why people made such a big deal about having a crush on someone while going steady with someone else. He was softly stroking his pussy who had made himself comfy in his lap. Without warning, Squeakers leapt off him and ran to the kitchen towards his food dish.

"No reason, just most guys would get jealous about something like that." She took another large scoop of melting brown goo, chunks of chocolate poking through. One escaped and slid down her chin, leaving a chocolate slime trail in its wake. With a quick brush of her tongue, she retrieved the morsel and devoured it. Success.

"Well, we have a looking–no–touching agreement. Like the zoo. She knows that I look at other people, too. Is there anything wrong with looking?" he asked his mom, knowing full and well what her answer would be.

"Not at all. I just know I raised you right."

"As if you had any doubt."

"No, I didn't doubt it, I just like to be reminded I did something right in my life," she told him, spooning the last of her ice cream from the bowl.

"Stop being so down on yourself."

"I can't help it! I'm a single mom!"

"C'mon, Mom. You're the best mother in the world. And I'm your biggest fan," Chad said, reaching out for a hug.

"And that was the cheesiest and most thoughtful thing you've ever said to me," Ms. Walker said, reaching to accept the hug. "Oh, I love you."

"Love you, too."

Yawns escaped their mouths simultaneously as they let go of each other.

"And I think I'm going to go to bed now," she said before another yawn attacked her.

"Me too. I'm a little sleepier than I realized," he said, looking for Squeakers who was already at the top of the stairs letting out pathetic squeaks. "And apparently Squeaks is begging to go to sleep as well. Night, Mom." He kissed her on the cheek, licking up a bit of chocolate.

"Thanks," she said with a bit of disgust, wiping her cheek from excess saliva her son left behind. "Goodnight, Chad."

<   <   <   >   >   >

September 5, 2002

Dear Princess Diarrhea,

Okay, so, perhaps entertaining the idea of joining Meghan's prayer circle during break was a bad idea. I mean really bad. I hate to admit when Courtney's right, but fuck… she's right. Whore.

Meghan is basically trying to seduce me under the guise of saving my eternal soul from hell and damnation. Gawd, this sucks. I really like Meghan. She's always been sweet and funny and happy, but lately she's been clingy and serious and demanding. What gives?

Hormones. It's gotta be the hormones. Ugh, to be a teenage girl with a crush on an older guy. I feel it's important I let her know sooner rather than later that, while flattered, I'm just not interested. It'd be like dating my sister. Ew.

Besides, I'm having another problem. A Joel problem. Without even trying, he's seducing me.

Earlier

"Hey, Chad! You still coming over tonight to study for that asinine Algebra quiz tomorrow?" Joel said, flashing a smile.

"Absolutely. I can't start the year off a failure. I'm gonna need all the help I can get. Had no idea Advanced Algebra was going to be so hard," Chad said, pouting.

"Great. What time?"

Joel wrapped his arm around Chad's shoulder, causing his body to react. To minimize any visualization of said bodily reaction, Chad put his backpack in front of his crotch.

"Uh, about six? Got cheerleading practice now and Mom's making dinner tonight, but we usually eat early."

"Awesome. Remember, Shadowood Apartments. Number J–6."

Another smile.

Arm still around Chad's shoulder.

More than Chad could handle.

"Sounds great! See you there! Gotta use the little boy's room and get to practice! Bye!" Chad yelled as he ran to the boy's restroom where he proceeded to jerk off in a stall, praying nobody would catch him, but just as he ejaculated, Courtney walked in and yelled, "Get yo' ass in the gym now, cracka'!"

"Oh gawd, be right there Court!" he cried. "Fuck."

After wiping up the mess he made, he changed into his practice shorts and ran out of the bathroom where Meghan was waiting for him to exit.

She blinked in rapid succession when their eyes locked.

"Jesus, Meghan, you scared me!" Chad said, dropping his bag.

"Chad, remember? We do not use the Lord's name in vain!" Meghan scolded.

"Sorry."

Her Bible prominently placed on top of her schoolbooks she carried, a cheesy grin over her mouth full of metal, a hairline scratch on her glasses catching the light. She still looked like she was seven. Well, seven with boobs.

"Are you off to cheerleading practice? I saw my sister run down to the gym, so I assume that you would be heading there, too." Her voice full of unquestionable desire and hope and innocence begging to be lost.

"Uh, yeah. Running late, actually. Gotta go."

"Okay, then I will stay and watch!"

Shit. "Okay."

"C – R – O – W – S! Crows [clap clap] are the best!" the team said in unison, finishing a cheer made popular by a cheerleader freshman year during her tryout. She committed suicide a few months after joining the team. Courtney insisted using it in her memory.

Clapping exploded from the bleachers. It was Meghan. Nikki simply stared into her textbook and scribbled Psychology terms down in a notepad beside her. She'd been using cheerleading practice time to study since middle school. Being friends with Courtney and Chad meant living, eating, and breathing cheer. It was just a way of life she had to contend with. Besides, it meant she pretty much had her homework done before even getting home, meaning more time for other activities like watching television and playing violent video games. Meghan, however, was only there to stare at Chad and fantasize.

Chad smiled up to bleachers in both Nikki and Meghan's general direction as Courtney said after turning around, facing him, "Boy, I told you you better watch yo'self. Girl be snatchin' you up and making you her bitch if you keep entertainin' her."

"Not gonna happen. I got this."

"You got nothin'."

"I got one hand in my pocket…"

"…and the other one is giving a high five!" Courtney belted, finishing the lyrics to one of Chad's favorite Alanis Morissette songs, smacking her palm against his face before readying herself for the next cheer.

"Bitch!" Chad screamed, grabbing his nose to make sure it wasn't bleeding.

Courtney smiled.

Chad stuck his tongue out at her.

Meghan yelled, "That was not nice, Courtney! Jesus saw that!"

"Jesus can also see this, cunt!" Courtney yelled, giving her little sister the middle finger.

The coach was not well pleased with hearing profanity, but also didn't really care to stop it. Instead of arguing or scolding or making any sort of reprimands for violating school rules, she simply said, "Five o'clock. Get out."

As the team gathered their things, Courtney said, "So, Nikki says you and Joel studyin' tonight."

"Yep," Chad said, bending over and putting his hands on his knees.

"She's jealous."

"Yep."

"Like, jealous enough to wish she wasn't so good at math so she could be in that low a level."

"Yep."

"Chad?"

"Yep?"

"You hidin' a boner?"

"Apparently not very well. Please for the love of God tell me it isn't that noticeable?"

Courtney glanced, spotting the culprit immediately. "More than you want it to be. Let me get yo' bag for you."

"Thank you."

After grabbing Chad's bag, Courtney shoved it in front of him to conceal his erection.

"I hate being a boy sometimes."

"I love bein' a girl. I can have all the dirty thoughts I want and nobody'd know! Ha HA!"

Chad chuckled.

Nikki asked what was going on.

Courtney told her he was just wiped out as she winked at him.

Meghan was still trying to win over Chad's affection. She looked a bit punch-drunk when he told her he had to get home for dinner with his mom and then to Joel's to study.

"I can take your bag if you're tired," Nikki offered, her own backpack strapped and weighing her down with about a hundred pounds worth of textbooks and notebooks and pencils and pens and an exorbitantly expensive calculator.

"I got it!" Chad said loudly. "I can carry it. Just not on my back, it's sore from holding up Courtney's fat ass!"

"Fucker!" Courtney yelled, punching him in the arm, looking furious.

"C'mon, Nik. Let's go," he said, and they started walking towards the exit closest to the student parking lot. "Thank you, Court. I owe you one," he mouthed as they walked away.

"Anytime, honey," she mouthed back, smiling.

"Eight ex minus four ex equals eight. Ex equals blank. Crap. I don't get it. I should just drop out now while I still have some shred of dignity," Chad said, throwing down his pencil and resigning himself to the fact that he would never be a mathematician. It bounced back into his lap, sticking straight up.

"It can't be that difficult to solve. Hmm… what can you multiply by eight and four that when subtracted equals eight?" Joel asked aloud.

"I don't know. I give up." Chad stared at the pencil, wondering if he should leave it there or pick it up. He opted for the latter for the time being.

"Stop. Okay, so take out the ex from the equation and you have eight minus four which equals four and it's supposed to be eight and four times two is eight and eight times two is sixteen, which when subtracted equals eight! That's it! Two!" Joel exclaimed, giddy something clicked.

"Show off."

"I just worked it out in my head. Only out loud so you could hear my brain thinking. It's kind of amazing in there."

Your head is kind of amazing, only I want to stick my dick in there, Chad thought.

"Were you thinking something?"

"What? Uh, no. Well, yeah. I think I get how you came up with that answer, but does it work for other numbers?" *Crap.*

"Uh, let's switch the numbers around to nine and six and it has to equal…"

"Sixty–nine?"

Joel smiled wickedly, cocking an eyebrow. "You read my mind."

Is he flirting or am I just super horny today? Chad wondered as he picked up the pencil and slightly lifted his legs to help hide the growing trouser snake inside his shorts.

"Okay, so nine minus six equals three so three ex equals sixty–nine and sixty–nine divided by three equals… twenty–three. Twenty–three," Joel said, frowning. "I think I like the original equals number better."

"Me too, but now I'm scared because I think I might just be understanding how you did that."

"You like sixty–nine?"

"I don't know. I'm a virgin."

"I meant the number."

"I'm a dumb blond teenage boy so, you know, everything is about sex."

"I'm also a teenage boy and it can be about both sex and the real thing or completely unrelated to sex and still be about sex because I'm also a teenage boy."

"Do guys talk like this?"

"What do you mean?"

"I mean I don't really have guy friends outside cheerleading, and they don't really pay too much attention to me outside that capacity."

"I don't know. I don't usually talk this way to my guy friends. I just, I don't know, feel comfortable with you. Can't explain it."

Chad's heart started racing.

"I feel the same. I mean, I can talk to Courtney about anything. She's a lesbian so I guess that's like having a guy friend."

Joel laughed a little harder than he intended. "I don't think it's the same thing, but I get it."

Looking around the living room of Joel's apartment, he noticed a Nintendo game station begging for attention. "Well, since we've pretty much become experts in algebraic equations, wanna play Mario?"

"Oh thank God! I thought you actually wanted to study!" Joel said, closing his textbook and standing up, giving Chad a fairly good idea of what Joel was hiding beneath his shorts. "Want something to drink?"

Forcing himself to look away from Joel's crotch, Chad's voice cracked as he responded with, "Yes."

After walking over to the fridge and opening it, Joel sounded disappointed as he told Chad, "Our options appear to be limited to orange juice, tap water, or Coors Light."

"Uh, water's fine," Chad told him.

"Good choice, considering the orange juice is probably a month past it's prime and Coors Light is like drinking watered down piss but my dad loves the stuff."

Over the next couple hours, they played a video game, and Chad had to hide his erection by sitting in a very uncomfortable position until Joel said he needed to grab a pillow to rest his hands on and offered to get one for Chad too, which he gladly accepted. Crisis averted. They decided to call it a night when Joel's dad got home. Chad could tell where he got his looks and figured that's what Joel would look like in twenty or so years. After the introductions, they said their goodbyes and wished each other non–algebra dreams. Tomorrow was the quiz. Tomorrow would tell whether they got it. Tomorrow would tell a great many other things as well.

<   <   <   >   >   >

September 6, 2002

Dear Princess Diarrhea,

I used to jerk off for Jesus.

I know this sounds odd, and trust me, I don't fully understand it myself, but there it is. Somewhere along the line I got this notion that jerking off was wrong. But it feels so good! I guess I started dedicating my orgasms to God because orgasms are good and God is good, so this totally makes sense to me. Ugh. I don't know why I feel guilty when I masturbate. I've never even been to church. Sure, Meghan has convinced me to come to her youth group a few times and practically forced me into her prayer circle during the mid–morning break, but still, I'm not religious nor am I particularly fond of religion. Oh, the guilt!

Now I find myself jerking off for Joel.

Jesus Fucking Christ. I just had to jerk off again. Every time I think of Joel my dick springs into a full salute. Have you ever had to hide a boner? In Algebra? When you sit in the front of the class and the teacher has a full frontal view of your crotch? That shit is the worst. I couldn't tell you how many public places I've pulled out my penis for self–gratification since first meeting Joel three days ago, but Sweet Lawd Jeezus (I was channeling my friend Courtney there) it's gotta be about at least a dozen!

Stupid penis.

Don't get me wrong, I love my penis. I just wish it didn't have such control over my brain that requires a quick tug–and–release so often in order to come back to reality. Goddammit Joel! What pull do you have on me? Fuck. I must be gay.

< < <   > > >

Later

"Hey there, Joel!" Chad bellowed out from the top of the stairwell in the 300 wing of Ravenwood High, waving his hands wildly to get Joel's attention as he looked all around him to find out where the call came from.

"Chad!" he called back as their eyes met, a smile spreading across his face revealing well-defined teeth that reminded Chad of denture commercials.

Running down the stairs to catch up with his friend, Chad thought to himself how jealous Nikki had been since they started hanging out. Not that she said anything, but her body language and attitude reflected her reluctance to share her boyfriend with other people. Her bitter tongue didn't help matters.

Chad was unprepared when Joel reached over and hugged him, saying, "Hey, I was going to go to Portland to hang out with some friends. You should come."

Did I hear him right? Chad thought, wondering if his inadequate ears were failing him over the loud rumble of people screaming out their "Have a great weekend!"s and "Later dude!"s and "I'm starving!"s—it was the same ordeal every Friday afternoon when school let out—or if he indeed heard what Joel said. "Uh, what?" He decided he needed clarification.

"Come with me. I'm going to Portland. Now," Joel said, almost demanding at this point.

"Now?"

"Yes. I am getting in my car and driving there."

"Uh, you sure you want me to tag along?"

"Absolutely."

"Really?"

"Did I stutter?"

"No, your speech is impeccable. Mine took seven years of therapy."

"No shit."

"Yes shit."

"Sorry, Chad. I, uh, didn't realize."

"You didn't offend."

"Still, it wasn't very thoughtful."

"But offering to take me to Portland to meet up with some of your friends sure is." Chad couldn't hide the goofy grin his face forced out against his will.

"Yeah?"

Joel's smile made Chad melt. Joel's muscles rippled as he adjusted the shoulder strap of his backpack, making Chad stiff. "Okay, what the hell. Why not?"

"Awesome!" Joel said, wrapping his arm around Chad's shoulder and making Chad uncomfortable in his genital region.

A few girls giggled past them. Joel obliged with his smile. The giggling girls galloped away.

"So, you're from Portland? Which part?" Chad asked as they walked towards the student parking lot.

"Uh, NoPo. St. Johns. Kinda ghetto but the people are great. Super homey. I'm not going there today. Meeting my buddies downtown then possibly Powell's afterwards."

"No possibly Powell's, definitely Powell's. I love books."

"Me too!"

The warm air baked their skin as they opened the door to exit the building. The clouds also seemed to be frightened of the sun, as they'd only scatter here and there in the sky, usually in the early morning or late evening. Their hiatus made Chad miss them. These blue clouds and giant fiery orb of death were not his cup of tea.

"Crap. My car," Chad said, stopping in his tracks as he spotted the shit mobile. "Fuck it. I'll just leave it here."

"You sure?" Joel asked. "I can follow you to your house if you want to drop it off."

"Nah, let's go."

And off to Portland they went.

Driving down the old highway after it stopped being Main Street that led to Chancellor that led to the freeway that would take them to another freeway that would take them close to their destination, Joel decided to take the opportunity to get to know Chad a little more, and vice versa. "So, you've lived in Ravenwood your whole life?"

"What? Oh, yeah. Mom bought a house here right before I was born when she moved from Seattle."

"Huh. What made her move down here?"

"I don't know. A job maybe. Never asked."

"You're a horrible son."

"I know."

"So, a single mom buys a house on her own? That must've been some job."

"She's a secretary at the middle school."

"Really?"

"Yeah." Chad suddenly questioned the reality of their living situation and tried to figure out why he never wondered about it before.

"Well, no offense, but your town is a bit sleepy for me. Where are the gangs? The nightly pops of gunfire?"

Chad laughed. "It's not that sleepy. This town is haunted."

"Haunted? Seriously?" Joel looked beyond skeptical.

"My street especially."

"Where do you live?"

"Song's End."

Joel's eyes lit up. "Like the folktale?"

"There's a folktale?" Now Chad played the skeptic.

"Yeah, my grandfather used to tell it to us kids during pow wows every year. Something about a vampire that wiped out the entire Oh–ah–ha... uh, something tribe."

"Oaxaciian tribe. Yeah, I know that story. Didn't realize it got outside of the locals, though."

"I thought he was always pulling our leg, like it was about obeying your elders or everyone will die!"

"Yeah, it's probably true. We've got a bit of a supernatural phenomena over here."

"Shut the front door."

"I'm serious."

"Serious?"

"Completely. From what I've witnessed, I can't account for the rumors of our mostly peaceful vampire population, but as for scary ghosts that haunt their living relatives with twisted nursery rhymes until they use some witchcraft to bring them back from the dead, I can without a doubt tell you it's true."

"You're fucking with me."

Not yet. Dammit, Chad! "You remember that girl we saw at the diner Tuesday?"

"The drunk Asian?"

"No, her blondish friend."

"Oh, the rescuer." Joel swerved to avoid hitting a dead possum. He failed. Squish.

"Yeah, her twin sister is the ghost–turned–flesh who was with them. She's also Courtney's sometimes girlfriend."

"No shit! You're not just pulling my leg because I've heard your town's sordid past story are you?"

"I would never. She doesn't know that I know this. I accidentally overheard—which in and of itself is kind of amazing considering how horrific my hearing is but that's an unneeded tangent—them talking right before they got back together sophomore year."

"Huh. Wow. I don't know if I believe you, but now it's making me wonder about the other stories my grandfather used to tell me. Thanks for making me wish he was still alive so I could ask him."

"Oh, crap, sorry."

"Don't be." Joel smiled as they approached Chancellor, meaning only about twenty minutes to Downtown Portland. Assuming the bridge isn't lifted, that is. "Seriously, knowing that story just might have merit makes me happy."

"How'd he hear about it, I wonder?"

"Well, contrary to the story, my grandfather said that not all of the tribe got wiped out by Song's End's vampirical bloodlust rage–a–thon. Apparently about a dozen or so girls were married off to neighboring tribes in an effort to keep their lines going. I don't think any of them survived the winter after. Sad, really. An entire native nation gone and only stories to tell of their existence."

"Yeah, stories and, oh yeah! My house that sits upon their mass burial grounds!"

"There's that, too, I guess."

"I'm just glad it wasn't smallpox. I have enough white guilt."

Joel turned his head toward Chad, looking into his sparkling blue eyes twinkling from the sun's reflection, his short blond hair soaking up the rays, glowing. His smile faded into the abyss when he realized he had to ask, "So, how long have you and Nikki been together?"

"Valentine's Day 2000, so... two–and–a–half years?" Chad said, scrunching up his face as he tried to do the math.

"Wow, that must be a high school record."

"Yeah, it's kind of a big deal."

"I don't know. I've never had a girlfriend."

"Shut up!" Chad yelled, eyes wide and straightening up in his seat, staring at Joel as he drove south on Interstate 5. "Now who's fucking with whom?"

"Impressive English skills, Walker. And no girlfriend because I'm gay."

"Well, that explains the no girlfriend thing."

"Yeah."

"We cool?"

"Uh, yeah! So, boyfriend?"

The mischievous smile over Chad's lightly freckled face caused Joel to chuckle. His dimple caused another reaction.

"Not right now, but yes, I've had a few."

"Cool."

"Really?"

"Yeah."

"Huh. That was not the reaction I expected from a small town boy."

"Why?"

"Because even when I lived in Portland and told people I'm gay they didn't believe me. Said I didn't fit the stereotype in their head."

"You don't. But from my experience, people rarely do."

"You have experience in matters relating to the LGBT community?"

"And the Q. Let's see, my best friend is a lesbian, I live next to a lesbian couple and their five kids, next to them are the Hollinses who have a gay daughter and a gay son, I know of at least three of our teachers who are gay, we have an annual gay rodeo, two gay bars I've never been to because of my underage status and I'm a good boy who would never dream of getting a fake I.D., First Congregational United Church of Christ Ravenwood is super gay friendly and is also where the Gays for Jesus members meet, and our mayor is trans. I don't even know if she's post–op. Maybe she's, uh, I think the technical term is chick with a dick?"

Silence.

"Is our small town too gay for the gays?"

"I guess I need to get out more. I had no idea. Wow."

More silence.

"Wait, we aren't going to meet up with one of your exes are we, because that sounds desperate and awkward?"

"No. Besides, the last guy broke my heart. Bad."

"I'd ask, but don't want to make you hurt." Chad meant it.

Joel smiled at his consideration. "Bastard only used me because his girlfriend wouldn't put out. As soon as she started giving him what he wanted, he told me I was just a piece of ass to him. I have serious trust issues with straight boys. I'm not sure why I find myself even friends with you." *Really?*

"Well, maybe because I'm different."

"Different how?"

"I have a confession."

Joel's heart started racing.

"Confess."

Joel's tension noticeable.

"Nikki is going to kill me for telling you this, but she has a *huge* crush on you."

Joel's tension released. Those were not the words he was hoping for.

"No surprise there. Most girls do," he replied nonchalantly.

"Modest much?"

"It's true! I swear, it's like I have this aura about me that women just fall for. Especially older women. Like in their forties. I'm jailbait for crying out loud! And gay! This has nothing to do with modesty, it's just the truth." Joel paused for a second before adding, "Okay, so I am a little immodest about it. Just wish it worked on the guys I like."

It's working on me. "Don't try so hard. The right guy will find you. Trust me."

"You think?" *Because I think I found him.*

"As long as you're honest with yourself." *Hypocrite.*

"Thanks," Joel said with a side smile afterwards as he took the exit. "My friends said they'd meet me at Pioneer Courthouse Square, so keep an eye out for pretty much any open parking spot between here and there."

"That's quite a few blocks."

"Welcome to Portland."

"Just park in a garage."

"And pay those exorbitant fees? Never! I'd rather be raped in the ass with a chainsaw."

"Wow. I won't bring up parking garages again."

Three blocks from the square, a red minivan prepared to pull out, the driver of which could barely see over the steering wheel.

"There!" Chad yelled, grabbing Joel's leg and pointing, nearly causing Joel to have a heart attack. "It's so close to the promise land!"

They waited somewhat patiently with the turn signal clicking and blinking to indicate they'd be taking the spot while the minivan went forward and backward over and over again, barely inching its way out of the spot it once occupied. Joel sped up and reversed into the space so quickly, Chad didn't even have a chance to comprehend his mad parallel parking skills because someone banged on the passenger side window and shouted, "Get your ass out here, fucker!" and nearly made him piss his pants.

Welcome to Portland.

"That's Matthew. He's also my cousin but he's like my best friend," Joel told a frightened ghost–white Chad.

"Seems like a great guy? I hope I packed another pair of shorts," Chad said in a cry voice, which made Joel look horrified, which made Chad say, "Kidding!"

After Joel got out and hugged his friend slash cousin, Matthew asked, "Who's the new guy? Don't tell me you've already got another boyfriend?"

"No, just a friend. Chad."

"I don't know, Cuz. He's pretty cute!" Matthew teased. "Erik and Robb are probably at the Starbucks getting their Frappuccinos because they think it makes them grownups. I like my coffee like I like my women… hot and strong and with a spoon in them."

"Eddie Izzard! Love him!" Chad said gleefully.

"I love you, Chad!" Matthew said, putting his arm around his shoulder. "You'd better snatch him up. I don't like most of your boyfriends."

"He's got a girlfriend," Joel told him quietly, sounding more pathetic than Chad had ever heard him before.

"What is it with you and straight guys? Jesus, Joel. Work on your gaydar!" Matthew joked as they walked.

It's working. Maybe it has a glitch? Joel thought, following behind Matthew and Chad, staring at Chad's calves and tracing the lines up to his ass as it bounced inside baggy shorts.

"You're hot," Chad told Matthew.

"Uh, you sure this guy's straight?" Matthew asked, scrunching his face into a quite exaggerated confused expression as he craned his neck backwards.

"I mean your arm around my neck is making me all sweaty. I don't know if you Indians are like hot–blooded or something, but…"

Matthew removed his arm from around Chad's shoulder, stuck his index finger out, pointed it towards Chad's chest, and stabbed him repeatedly as he said, "Native. American. Asshole."

The color dropped out of Chad's face, puddling into the pit of his stomach he suddenly wanted to purge.

"Just fucking with you, Chad!" and he laughed until they met up with Robb and Erik and he told them all about the incident while they sipped their Frappuccinos.

"Hold my books. Gotta pee," Chad announced as his eyes saw the men's room sign at Powell's City of Books, eyes wide as if this was a sudden realization.

Joel grabbed the pile from Chad's hands and waited outside the restrooms.

Quickly running up to the nearest urinal instead of finding a stall as he normally would do, undoing his button and zipper while approaching, he prayed he'd make it in time. He did. Barely.

"Jeezus, I hate when I have to pee so bad I feel like I'm going to explode." Realizing he said that out loud instead of in his head like he meant to, he looked around to make sure nobody else was in the bathroom.

"I know that feel, bro!" came a call from the stall.

"Shit."

The urine flowed in a seemingly never–ending stream.

Joel stood outside the restroom.

The door opened.

Not Chad.

A few minutes later, Joel decided to sit on the ground, leaning against one of the bookcases that lined the Purple Room's restroom waiting area. The heat from their late afternoon romp around downtown caught up with him. That and the fact that they decided to walk to Powell's rather than drive over because they parked practically halfway between it and Pioneer Courthouse Square. He set the books beside him and waited. Part of him wished he had a white stage beard he could put on for when Chad came back out.

Alas, there was no beard around.

The door opened.

Chad walked out to find Joel slumped against the wall pretending to be asleep. "Sorry about that."

"What? Oh. I thought I was going to have to find you. Thought maybe you got stuck or something."

"Ha ha."

"What'd you do, drain the Niagra?"

"Something like that. Now I'm thirsty."

"Assuming you were peeing that whole time, you probably need to replenish half your bodily fluids."

"Only part of the time. I had to let go of my fear of public restrooms and just go. That's pretty important."

"You have a fear?"

"Usually a shy bladder. After having to pee so badly and holding it in for so long, I lost so much energy from the release that I couldn't even move for like an hour. I collapsed on the floor and just lay there hoping I'd have enough strength to get up and zip. My fear is tenfold now."

"I knew I should've walked in to check on you."

Chad blushed.

Joel handed Chad his stack of books from on top of his own, not-so-subtly touching his fingers as he took them and said, "If you're thirsty, they've got coffee here, or we can probably get something at a market on the way back to the car."

"We should probably just buy our books and leave before I spend any more of my mother's hard earned cash I stole from her purse this morning."

"Agreed. Hold my books. Gotta pee."

Overlooking the lights of Portland, Chad watched as Joel's eyes gazed upon the city below. After Powell's and buying Snapples at a sketchy convenience store lined with heavily barred windows punctuated by a few bullet holes, Joel said they should take a drive up to a spot off the Terwilliger curves by the V.A. hospital.

The view paid off.

"Do your parents know? I mean, that you're gay?" Chad asked, hoping the question wasn't too daring this early in their friendship.

"Yeah. I told them a couple years ago. My dad said, 'Yay! A two–spirit!' and my mom said, 'Since we're having a coming out party, I want a divorce. I'm moving to New York to be a writer.' which kind of put a damper on the rest of the day. That was a crappy Christmas."

Chad decided silence was better than words. Sometimes words screw things up.

"You can say it sucks. It does. But they both seem happier now and actually get along better than they did when they were married, so there's that."

"That's something."

"It is."

Joel looked forward, avoiding eye contact. Chad ignored the view to stare at Joel's face, which suddenly started saddening, even in the dim light filtering through the car windows.

"You're thinking something bad."

"I'm thinking I shouldn't have come here."

"Why?"

"James and I used to come here."

Joel's eyes started welling.

"The douchebag?"

"The douchebag."

Silence.

Chad didn't know what he could offer to make the situation better. After a few seconds, he got up the nerve to put his hand on Joel's thigh. "Why'd we come here? I mean the view's great, but..."

"Closure. I've always loved this view. My grandfather died at the Veteran's Affairs center back there, and this is pretty close to the view from his room. I was hoping to bring back the good memories, but my brain only wants to bring up the bad."

The knot in Chad's throat strangled him, tightening its grip with every passing second. He had to do something to make the pain stop. He knew what he had to do. He hesitated at first, but deep down he knew that he wanted to. The little voice in his head kept chanting, *Go on. Do it.* over and over. Leaning in, he pulled Joel's face towards his and kissed him

Joel returned it.

When it was over, Joel still looked sad.

Crap, I made things worse.

"I really loved him," Joel said as tears started falling down his cheeks, landing quite ungracefully on his shirt and lap.

Right words be damned, Chad thought as he said, "I've never been in love."

"But Nikki?"

"Don't get me wrong. I mean, I love Nikki a lot, and we are like really really really really good friends, but something's missing."

"Something, like…?"

"Something like I think I might be gay."

The silence that followed was deafening.

"I take that back. I know that I am gay."

"Okay. Sorry. I don't have any gay friends that have come out to me so I am not sure how this is supposed to work," Joel said, using the palm of his hand to dry his face.

"It's okay. I'm freaking out a bit. I can't believe this just happened," Chad said as his own eyes began watering his cheeks like a goddamned irrigation system.

They hugged.

They let go.

"I feel it's important to tell you that I have reservations," Chad said to Joel as he now avoided looking into his eyes, wiping his face and staring ahead over the anonymous city lights of Portland, suddenly aware of the lack of stars in the night sky from all the light pollution.

"Reservations? You mean like a hotel?" Joel asked with a nervous chuckle that almost made him choke on his own spit.

"Humph… uh… no? I mean about my feelings. About you. Us."

"So there's an us?" Joel asked before realizing how pretentious and demeaning and horrible those words sounded as they spewed forth from his mouth. "I mean, I really like you. A lot. I mean alottalottalottalottalottalot. But…"

"No buts. Well, yes butts. I mean, I have a feeling I would like that sorta thing based on personal time."

"But what are your reservations?"

"I'm not ready…"

"I won't pressure you into anything you're not ready for."

"…to tell Nikki that I'm gay."

Silence.

"I know."

Joel looked down at the steering wheel and contemplated the situation; understanding the predicament Chad was in, and that tiny little flurry of pitter–patter heart rhythm that happens when your crush just might actually crush on you back. Then Chad's hand made its way to Joel's thigh again, gently rubbing just above the knee. The sensation, even through a baggy pair of blue jeans that he decided to wear on what was arguably the hottest day of the year, was full and wonderful and exciting and Joel hoped that he could control his penis's desire to become erect.

He couldn't.

Chad noticed.

The hand traveled up Joel's thigh.

"I thought… you said… you had reservations?" Joel asked with a dry, cracked voice.

Chad lifted Joel's head, turning it towards his.

Eye contact.

Pause.

"I have reservations, but I know what I want. Who I want."

Their lips met again.

Hungry.

Fervent.

Carnal.

All those pent–up emotions and years of self–denial and worrying about doing the right thing and saying the right words and living up to impossible standards that were built on lies and trying not to disappoint those he loved rollercoastered through his head until they melted away into the dark abyss of blissful joy and unabashed lust.

Chad's hand slowly made it's way to Joel's crotch, causing him to twitch and break from their kiss. "Chad, I…"

"I know you want me."

"I do, but…"

"I want you. Since the day I first saw you in school and had to go jerk off in the boy's bathroom which made me late to my next class and still have an awkward boner until I got home for another tug and write my feelings down in my diary and yes I have a diary and yes that is when I knew without a doubt that I am gay and had absolutely no idea if you were too but hoped and prayed and yes I actually prayed to Jesus silently in a prayer circle that you were gay too and maybe just maybe I'd have a chance at becoming your boyfriend."

"Um, wow, uh, okay so that was a lot to take in. I was just going to say I have to pee again."

"Sorry. I had to get that off my chest."

"And now that it's off?"

Chad smiled his ridiculously perfectly straight white-toothed smile that makes everyone go all goo–goo; his eyes lighter and brighter than ever, like the bricks that were piled on him finally fell off from lack of cement keeping them in place. "I feel like I can fly."

"I can pee later," Joel said quickly before grabbing Chad's face and pulling it in towards his for another passionate kiss that lasted so long the fogged car windows cliché happened.

September 7, 2002

Princess Diarrhea,

Yeah, I totally had sex.

The next morning, all Chad wanted to do was be with Joel. However, all that morning wanted was to take up his time with other planned things.

"I need you to mow the lawn before cheerleading practice!" Ms. Walker called from downstairs. "It's your punishment for not telling me where you were after school yesterday."

"Are you kidding me?" Chad cried, racing down the steps in his practice clothes, squeakers crying as if he was being starved to death.

Ms. Walker glared at her son with all seriousness and said, "Does this face look like it's kidding?"

"Nope. Get right on that."

He fed the cat and mowed the lawn.

After putting the mower away in the garage that was created from a space that originally housed a den but the previous owners thought a garage would more useful than living space, Nikki walked up behind him, wrapping her arms around his waist.

"Jesus! You scared me," he told her, heat concentrating on where her fleshy arms pressed against his sweaty body.

"I love watching you mow the lawn," she said, a wicked smile over her round face.

"You were watching me mow?" Chad asked, reluctantly maneuvering his way to face her.

She kissed him.

It felt wrong.

"Yes."

"Are you stalking me, Miss Boloski?"

"Always."

Another kiss.

Fuck. What am I going to do with her?

"Chadwick Allen Walker!" someone yelled from the street. It was Courtney. "We runnin' late, faggot. Let's go. Where's your car?"

"Uh, still at the school? Why'd you call me faggot?"

"Fool? It's me!" Courtney said much louder than a regular person, open hands pointing towards her sizable chest. "Now tell me why yo' car's at the school?"

"Uh, because Joel and I went to Portland and didn't think we needed to take two cars?"

"You went to Portland with Joel?" Nikki asked, releasing her arms. The hurt in her eyes was beyond obvious.

"Yes?"

"Whatevuh. That means we be runnin'. Come. Now." Courtney wasn't joking.

"I'm not running. I'll see you after practice," Nikki said quietly, looking as limp as a deflated birthday balloon.

Another kiss, this one merely a formality.

Nikki walked home slowly.

Chad watched for a moment, not knowing what he could or should do or how he was going to do what he had to do, especially after the events that unfolded the previous night. "Shit."

"Shit what?"

"I have to shit," Chad lied.

"Then shit."

"I will shit."

"Shit already."

"I'm going to shit."

"Shit now before I fuckin' punch you in the gut, bitch!" Courtney's face held no humor.

Chad walked into the downstairs bathroom, pretended to poop, flushing for good measure. Twice. Even washed his hands in case Courtney might be outside monitoring his activities. "Leaving now. Bye, Mom."

"See you in a few," she said, drinking her coffee and reading yesterday's newspaper.

After cheerleading practice ended and most of the other cheerleaders had left, including his ex–girlfriend Jennifer and Sheree who usually stayed to help Courtney clean up but said they had some very important shopping to get done and invited Courtney to go with them but Chad said he needed to talk so she declined. Their coach lounged in her office and said she'd be there for a few hours to go over scheduling conflicts. She probably stayed to avoid dealing with her deadbeat husband and the kids she resented having with him due to societal pressure to fit in like a regular person.

"This better be good, asshole. You makin' me miss a shoppin' trip with my bitches," Courtney told Chad, arms folded tightly across her chest, making her cleavage threaten to release the nipples held within her sports bra.

"Courtney, I need to tell you something important, but you have to promise not to tell Nikki."

"You know damn well that gone be hard for me!"

"Yeah, well, it's hard for me to tell you what I have to tell you, too."

"I can only promise for so long."

"Fair enough. I just need some time to figure this out."

"Figure what out?"

"Courtney, I'm like ninety–nine point nine percent sure I'm gay."

"About time." Her arms dropped and attitude thawed.

"You knew?" His reaction both confused and elated.

"Since third grade."

"Thanks."

"Any time."

Courtney uncharacteristically grabbed Chad and gave him a bear hug, squeezing him so hard he felt like he was going to burst. Sure, she was his best friend and they practically told each other everything, but showing their feelings towards one another was a rarity, especially since starting high school.

"And Courtney?"

"Yes, sweetie?"

"I'm not a virgin anymore." His voice constrained, much like the rest of him.

"You're not just talking about the Poe song are you?"

"Nope."

She let go.

"No shit! Gay and cherry poppin' all at the same time? Boy, you move fast! Oh Lawd Geezus, please tell me you didn't find some dirty old man off the Internet?"

"Not the Internet. Joel."

"Holy fuck!"

"Yep, there were holes involved."

"Joel's gay?"

"Big time."

"For once, I did not see that comin'."

"I did and it was amazing."

"Pervert."

Chad smiled.

"So, how do you feel now?" Courtney asked, her tone smooth as margarine.

"Well, I thought my ass would feel a lot more sore than it does, but I'm worried I may have been a bit rough with Joel's. You know, because of my lack of experience in these matters."

"I meant about not bein' no virgin no mo', but I won't stop the juicy details from flowin'."

"Oh, uh, that? Hard to explain. I mean it was great, but I thought I'd feel different. I don't."

"Yep. Ain't that the truth."

"Maybe it's the guilt afterwards."

"You know your mom'll be okay with you so why ya feelin' all guilty and shit?"

"Nikki."

"Crap, there's that. Fuck, boy. You got yo' self in a predicament."

"Damn straight."

"Don't damn them cuz they ain't like us."

"That's not what I meant."

"I know. But tell me one thing."

"What?"

"Please tell me you didn't lose your virginity in a car?"

Silence.

"You lost your virginity in the backseat of a car? Jesus, Chad! You are such a cliché!" Courtney said louder than a normal person would have said such a thing. For Courtney, it was perfectly logical.

Chad wiggled, fidgety, and prayed their coach didn't hear as her voice bounced off the walls of the gym, echoing her sentiments. "Well, not just the backseat. Also the front seat. And the hood of the car. And..."

"Really?!" Courtney shouted, throwing her hands up in the air and barely missing her fabulous Afro. "How many times did you do it?"

A wicked guilty smile spread across his face revealing his perfectly straight and brighter than bright white teeth. "Wouldn't you like to know."

"I would, otherwise I wouldn't've asked, fucker."

<   <   <   >   >   >

"You should come over," Joel said on the other end of the phone, soft and seductively.

Talking as quietly as he could so his mother wouldn't overhear, but not wanting to leave the kitchen (even though Squeakers was begging for second dinner) for fear she'd pick up the other line to listen in on their conversation, Chad said back, "I want to. Bad. But I am babysitting my cousins so my aunt and uncle can go out with my mom and apparently her date."

"Damn. My dad apparently has a date, too. I've got the apartment to myself tonight." Joel's voice contained a mixed bag of mischief and sadness.

"That figures. This day has been shit. The universe is conspiring against me. I can't help but wonder if it's because we had sex." Chad was serious.

"We did have lots of sex."

"I know."

"Lots of hot man–on–man sex."

Joel's seductive tongue made Chad uncomfortable given the setting.

"You're giving me an erection in front of my mom. Please stop," Chad said in barely a whisper as he adjusted the front of his jeans.

"Sorry." Joel's voice sounded anything but apologetic.

"This sucks. I want to be with you. All the time."

"Me too."

"Is this infatuation? Like, am I going to go all Glenn Close on you?"

"Glenn Close?"

"You know, *Fatal Attraction*?"

"Never saw it."

"There's a bunny."

"Oh, how cute."

"She cooks it."

"Oh, how gross."

"Because she was completely obsessed with a guy."

"So she cooked his bunny?"

"Yep."

"Straight people."

"Yep."

"I promise never to cook your cat."

"Thanks? He wouldn't take too kindly to your attempt. He's kind of an asshole," Chad said as he stared at his cat.

Squeakers walked away, giving up his futile attempt at convincing his human he needed to be fed again, leaving behind a mess of orange fur on his pant leg.

"Mmm… asshole."

"Stop."

"That's not what you said last night."

"Please. For the love of Baby Jesus."

"Well, for the Baby Jesus."

"Get off, Chad! We need to leave now!" Ms. Walker yelled, the door already open, hands motioning. "We have to get to my brother's in ten minutes."

"Oh gawd, did your mom just tell you to get off?" Joel asked, chuckling.

"The phone," Chad clarified, the bulge in his pants obvious now. "I'll talk to you tomorrow. We should study."

"Yeah, study. Human Anatomy?"

"Obviously that's what I meant by study."

"Tomorrow then."

"Tomorrow."

"Chad!" Ms. Walker yelled. "Now!"

"Tomorrow."

"Can't wait."

< < <   > > >

September 8, 2002

Dear Princess Diarrhea,

I'm not sure when I first found out that I'm a sassy black woman trapped inside a blond blue−eyed white boy, but if I had to guess, it'd be in the third grade. That's when I first met Courtney. She's black. I feel that is important because she was like the only black person I knew at that time in my life. I'm also pretty sure her family is the only black family in Ravenwood. I mean, we have all these white families here, most of whom have been here since the town was founded. I don't think we ever had a mission to convert Indians or anything awful like that in our past because all the Indians were already dead, but they just gathered here. And then the Spaniards worked their way in claiming inheritance rights, then the Chinese to dig ditches and build railroads, Russians moved from

Alaska to our more temperate climate, and in the early seventies, my Mom said we had an influx of Vietnamese because of the war.

Still, only one black family.

Maybe that is why I grasped onto Courtney's ethnicity; so I could be in her shadow and try to make myself stand out, too. She doesn't stand out because she's black, she stands out because she's Courtney. She could be invisible and still stand out.

Now I find myself struggling with a new identity.

No longer am I content to stay in Courtney's shadow and simply let life happen. I want to take control. I want to live it. I want to be honest and free. I want to make sure nobody gets hurt. But no matter what choices I make, even if those choices are 100% without a doubt the best thing for all involved, someone will suffer the consequences.

Sometimes I wish I was as carefree about my decisions as Courtney pretends to be. She says what's on her mind no matter what. And those times she regrets what she says, she keeps to herself or just tells me or Nikki or both of us.

Fuck. Nikki just got here. With Courtney. Unannounced. I'll write later.

Chad saved his diary file and quickly closed out as Squeakers walked out of, and Nikki and Courtney walked into, the guest room slash office. Well, guest room is a generous word. The closet had a blow up mattress for sleepovers just in case.

It'd never been used, probably because Squeakers peed on it. Twice. He hated guests.

"Hey, were you lookin' at porn? That why you shut down yo' computer when we be walkin' up here?" Courtney asked, inquisitive and displaying her devious smile covered in glossy red lipstick.

"Uh, no?" Chad said back, a nervous giggle escaping.

"Shut up! You were! Why'd you close it?" Nikki asked, punching him.

"I was writing."

"You write?" Nikki asked, somewhat shocked, holding her punch this time.

"Diary. I was writing in my diary. My password protected diary."

"Mm hmm. That where you keep all yo' dirty little secrets you been hidin'?" Courtney's arms were in their usual crossed position when she felt the need to be defensive.

"Yes."

"I want to read," Nikki asked, her curiosity taking over as she clenched her fists, readying them for action if the next words out of Chad's mouth didn't match her expected response.

"No."

"Why?"

"It's personal. Private."

Another punch.

"Asshole."

"Sweet Lawd Geezus, Nik? Why you be like that?" Chad asked, rubbing the pain away, seeing a bruise already starting to form on one of the welts.

"I'd let you read my diary. If I had one, that is," Nikki offered, knowing it was a lie.

"You shouldn't."

"I read Anne Frank's diary." The look of superiority over Nikki's face was humorous.

"Gurrrl! That bitch is dead," Chad and Courtney said together.

"Sometimes you two scare me."

"Seriously, a diary is really more for the person writing it than the world to see. It's cathartic."

"Damn, boy! You learnin' some real big words in Mrs. O'Hurley's class!" Courtney said.

Chad's face bowed in shame as he sunk into the chair. *Fuck, now Nikki knows.*

"What? You've got Mrs. O'Hurley for English this year?" The hurt in her eyes almost too painful to watch.

"Yes?"

"Fucker."

"Sorry."

"I hate you."

"You should."

"Why?"

"I may have let slip to Joel the other night that you have a crush on him?"

"You WHAT?! How could you?" Nikki's eyes bulged from their sockets, heat radiating off her face like a space heater. The redness quite terrifying.

"I'm sorry, Nik! It was a total slip!" he lied, hoping she'd buy it, giving him more time to contemplate how he was going to dump her.

"You whore!" she screamed, pummeling his arm to the point he started crying from the pain.

"That's my line from *The Money Pit*, remember? I'm Walter, you're Anna!" Chad cried.

The pummeling worsened.

Oh my gawd, what have I done? Chad thought, failing to shield himself against the onslaught, knowing that he had probably just waved on another world war. He could hear the A–bomb drop, a mushroom cloud forming over Nikki's head.

"Nik! Nikki! NIKITA!!!" Courtney yelled, trying to pry her off of him without ruining her manicure. "I need those arms to hold me during cheer! Stop!"

"Fucking cheer!" Nikki responded, relenting her attack. "And fuck my dad for naming me after a boy."

"Girlfriend. You gotta work on yo' anger management issues," Courtney said as she continued holding back Nikki's arms.

Chad reeled in agony.

"Whatever," Nikki said, brushing her hair back after Courtney gave them back to her, and seemingly seamlessly transitioning into a giggling school girl with, "So what did he say?" Her smile decidedly creepy.

Hugging the recent injuries the feisty Russian presented him with, Chad nervously told her, "I… I… I can't tell you."

Nikki's nails dug into the palms of her hands, drawing blood. "Why not?"

"I promised?"

"Goddammit, Chad! What good is having a boyfriend if he's going to lie to me?"

Courtney, who was oddly quiet during most of this conversation slash fight, said, "Girl's gotta point."

"Really? Now you're taking her side?"

"Ain't no side, cracka!" Courtney said, pulling her head back but her hair seemed to stay in place, shrinking her face. "You just shouldn't be keepin' no secrets. 'Bout nothin'."

He knew what she meant as he looked into her wide eyes, but now wasn't the time. Would it ever be? "We all have our secrets."

"Hey, you think Nikita was the boy yo' daddy mighta been screwin' when you were born?" Courtney asked Nikki, sensing Chad's hesitation and knowing it would draw her attention away.

For now.

"Really, Court? That's in poor taste, even for you." Nikki looked genuinely hurt.

"Sorry, Nik. Just curious."

"I'm sorry for being a raging bitch. Being a girl sucks on a monthly basis."

"Being a boy is no better."

"Bitch, you best be shuttin' your trap right now 'fore I slap you with the back my hand," Courtney said, shaking her head and flattening her bitch–slap hand.

"Bitch, please. I know you both on the same cycle," Chad said, shaking his head and wagging his index finger in the air. "We known each other too long."

"True dat," Courtney said, loosening up.

"Word," Nikki said.

"Oh, honey. Noooooooooo," Chad and Courtney said in unison.

"Why?" Nikki asked.

"You really shouldn't try. You white," Courtney said.

"What the hell? And Chad's not?" Nikki asked, throwing her hands into the air.

"Only on the outside!" Chad and Courtney declared, high fiving each other afterwards.

"Oh my gawd. This is hell. Crap! No no no no no!" Nikki yelled. "I left my purse downstairs on the floor!"

She ran down the stairs towards the front door where she left it.

"This isn't going to end well," Chad said.

"If we wasn't upstairs, I'd say you should run," Courtney said.

"Squeakers, really? Why? Amanda, you have anything to clean up cat pee?" Nikki could be heard crying pathetically as her voice traveled up the stairs and into the office for Chad and Courtney's ears to swallow.

"Let me guess, you left your purse on the floor again and Squeakers pissed on it?" Ms. Walker could be heard asking.

"Worse. In it."

"Lysol's under the kitchen sink."

Chad shook his head. "When will she ever learn?"

"When you gonna break the news that you gay?" Courtney asked in an unusually quiet voice.

Chad looked like he shrunk two sizes in the chair. "As soon as I'm healed?"

"Gurrrl, you ain't gonna be healed 'til you fess up and be true."

Courtney had a point.

"I know. I just... I... think I need her to calm down before I break up with her."

"Chad, you know nothin' 'bout girls."

"That's the problem."

< < <   > > >

September 8, 2002

Princess Diarrhea,

Now that Nikki and Courtney are gone, I have further dilemmas. Nikki seems really fragile lately. I don't think it's just her period. I mean, it could be, but I think something else is going on. Do you think she suspects something is up with me? No. She can't. Can she? Ugh. I don't know. Am I being paranoid?

I should have told her this morning. Just got it over with. But my arms are sore from the punches! She's seriously got a hardcore blow. Crap, now all I can think about is getting a blowjob. From Joel. Go away, erection! The mind is stronger than the penis! Joel. He'll be over soon. Then I can get my blowjob. Oh my gawd, why can't I think of anything other than sex? What is wrong with me?

DING DONG!

Ms. Walker opened the front door before Chad had a chance to run down the stairs. "Oh, hi! You must be the infamous Joel."

"Uh, yes? Infamous?" He was nervous. *Does she know?*

"Joel! Yes, Mom, this is my friend Joel," Chad said loudly as he ran down the stairs. "I hope you like lasagna. My mom makes it every Sunday. Every. Sunday."

"Love lasagna! It's vegetarian, right?" Joel asked, serious expression on his face.

"Chad! You didn't tell me he doesn't eat meat!" Ms. Walker said sharply.

"I'm kidding!" Joel said, laughing. "I eat meat. Serious. Chad knows I eat meat."

Chad's eyes bulged. "It's true!" he squealed. "Come on up to my room, Joel."

"Okay."

"Dinner will be ready in half an hour. I'll come get you two when it's done," Ms. Walker called as the boys went up to Chad's room to quote–unquote study.

"Thanks, Mom!" Chad said as he slammed the door to his room, pushed Joel against the wall, and kissed him like he hadn't seen him in months.

"I missed you," Chad said in between kisses.

"I missed you," Joel said before the next one.

As Jennifer and Nikki can attest to (with the exception of the Valentine's Dance in the year 2000 when Nikki lunged herself onto an unsuspecting Chad like a puma going in for the kill right after Jennifer broke up with him), Chad only ever kissed or made out to reenactments from scenes in movies. But with Joel, it was unscripted. Raw.

Time got away from them as they made out. Their make-out session turned into shirtless time, and shirtless time turned into Joel performing fellatio on Chad.

"Dinner's ready!" Ms. Walker said as she opened Chad's bedroom door, quickly closing it before saying, "Sorry! I knew I should've made appetizers!"

Thirty seconds later, with Chad completely humiliated and Joel horrified at what just happened, the door opened again and half a dozen small squares landed on them.

"Condoms. Thanks Mom," Chad said, even though the door was now closed and she was back downstairs probably drinking herself to oblivion. "Fuck."

"Really? I don't think I can get it up right now, and you're looking limp," Joel said.

"No, I mean the situation."

"Yeah, there's that."

"I mean, obviously she's okay with me being gay, but this is not how I wanted to tell her."

"You mean you never dreamed of having your parents walk in on you getting a blowjob from another guy and shouting, 'Surprise! I'm gay!'?" Joel laughed. "I'm shocked."

"This is important. It shouldn't be a joke."

"I find humor in any situation. It's a coping mechanism."

"I wish I did. I'm going to throw up now."

"Seriously?"

"Figuratively. Maybe literally." The condoms fell off his chest and onto the bed as he stood up. Walking over to where his shirt was unceremoniously tossed onto the hardwood floor, he continued, "I need to talk to my mom now. Please walk with me. I'm scared."

Joel smiled, took Chad's hand, and was about to walk out of the room when Chad said, "Put your shirt back on."

The smile became mischievous.

"You sure? Because she'd be all sorts of distracted with this going on while you tell her what you need to." Joel's hand air-rubbing his chest made it all the more ridiculous.

"Shirt. Please. Or the distraction will be from my penis," Chad begged.

Joel pouted, put his shirt back on as requested, took Chad's hand again, and they walked side-by-side down the stairs to have the big coming out talk so many kids freak out about. At least this one would be filled with Americanized Italian food.

"Chad, relax," Ms. Walker said, putting the lasagna dish in the middle of the dining room table, salad and waters already set, her glass of chardonnay filled to the brim and showing signs this wasn't its first time that evening as multiple lipstick stains graced most of the rim.

Chad hid his face, refusing to look at his mother as he said, "You caught me with my pants down."

"I didn't see anything if that's what you're worried about. Joel's head did a pretty good job covering it up," she said, failing miserably at containing a laugh.

"Seriously, Mom. This is embarrassing and awkward and important."

"So you're gay? Who cares? You're still you," she said, the laugh that wanted out had disappeared, replaced with a Josh Groban song she abhored.

Joel squeezed Chad's hand, smiling before saying, "I'm sorry."

"About giving my son a blowjob? Puhleaze!"

She took a swig of wine.

Chad sunk into a chair.

Joel choked on his spit, or so Chad thought, praying it wasn't a stray pube caught in his throat.

"Joel, this is what I live with every day," Chad said, avoiding eye contact with everyone at the table now.

"Awesome," Joel said. "My dad and I talk about sex all the time, so it's no big deal. Apparently he's banging this one chick right now who is super kinky. Says he really likes her."

Chad pretended to vomit and Ms. Walker blushed.

"Sorry. My filter was never installed," Joel confessed.

"Filters detract from the truth. You're better off without one," Ms. Walker advised, giving him a wink.

"Thanks. Can we eat now? I'm starving. Never got to finish my appetizer!" Joel said with a chuckle.

"Joel! Really? That was not appropriate," Chad said, unable to keep his no–eye–contact order in place.

Ms. Walker laughed, told Joel to plate up, and the three of them chatted about more than Chad felt comfortable with. His mother looked like she was enjoying every minute of it. Every minute until the elephant everyone tried to avoid walked in and sat down between them. "When were you planning on telling Nikki?"

Chad sighed. "Tomorrow. I have to."

"Okay. Before school or after?"

"Jesus, Mom? I don't know. Tomorrow!" Chad cried, throwing his fork onto the plate.

It clinged so loud, Squeakers hid under the couch out of fear for his life. He found a dust bunny. They played.

"Calm down, sassy pants!" Ms. Walker cried, throwing her fork onto the plate.

"I'm just going to pretend I'm not here," Joel said, pushing his seat back.

"Have some more wine, Mother."

"Chadwick!"

"Sorry. I'm really emotional lately." Chad slumped back down, letting the tension fall apart.

"Your time of the month?" his mother asked, knowing his mood cycle all too well.

"Probably."

"You have a cycle?" Joel asked. "Wait, is there something I don't know, because I'm pretty sure I explored your areas fairly thoroughly and didn't see anything out of the ordinary down there?"

"I think it's a monthly surge of testosterone or something. It used to be like every three months, but this last year it's been every month. It's also tied to Nikki and Courtney, and apparently Jennifer and Sheree, too. We must hang out too much together or something," Chad told Joel.

His mother already knew this.

"Cheerleaders and their plus one," Chad added. *Hmmm... I wonder why Kayla doesn't seem to be in on this conspiracy to ruin everyone's life?*

"And it makes you emotional?" Joel asked.

"Angry," Chad said, then whispered into Joel's ear, "And horny."

"Well, that explains a lot," Joel whispered back, hoping Chad could hear it at such close range to his hearing aid. Chad smiled, indicating he did. "Well, Ms. Walker, that was a fantastic meal. I'm stuffed."

"Dessert?" she asked cheerfully.

"Yes please," he said despite his previous announcement.

"Maybe Chad could oblige," she said.

"Mom!" Chad yelled, throwing his hands into the air.

"I meant to get the damn pie out of the fridge, pervert!"

Dessert was Ms. Walker's chance to drill Joel. Apparently chocolate was his weakness, and he gave out answers to her queries like candy from grandma.

"How long have you known that you're gay? Or are you bi? Where's your scale?" she started in.

"Since I was seven, definitely not bi, I'm all the way over on the fully homosexual side of the scale."

"I'm bisexual but straight leaning. Even had a three–way relationship for a few years. That's how… never mind."

"Cool."

"Your parents know? When'd you tell them?"

"Yes, told them a couple years ago. They got divorced right after."

"Because you're gay?"

"Because my mother already planned on divorcing my dad and always has to make everything about her, so when I came out she said she was leaving us and moving to New York."

"Bitch!"

"Amanda, that's my mother!"

"Sorry! I was just…"

"Kidding! She's a bitch. Still love her to death, though."

"And your dad?"

"He loves the fact that he's got a two-spirit offspring."

"A two-spirit?"

"A gay son."

"Okay."

"It's an Indian thing."

"Okay."

Chad just sat there, eating his pie, not knowing whether to stop the Sixty-Four Questions Game or let it unfold to completion. The pie tasted too delicious to ruin with words. He opted to be an audience member. Until…

"And you're free of STDs?"

"Mom!" Chad yelled, wide-eyed, spitting out the bite he'd just forked into his mouth, missing his plate as it landed on the table.

"Yep, got tested again last week. Just in case."

"Just in case what?" Chad and Ms. Walker asked in unison.

"Uh, the douchebag," Joel said quietly.

"Oh, the douchebag," Chad said.

"Who's the douchebag?" Ms. Walker inquired.

"His ex. He's got a past history of only dating straight guys. No idea why he'd even want me," Chad said.

"Uh, because you've got a girlfriend and have pretended to be straight for years?" Ms. Walker blurted out. "Sorry, I blame the wine."

"You've thought I was gay for years?" Chad asked.

"I've known you're gay for years. Beth and I talked about it after Brendon came out. He was nine, you know."

"Mrs. Hollins knows? Oh gawd."

"She knows a lot more than you think."

"What do you mean?'

"I mean I think I've had too much chardonnay and enough questions for the night. Whew! I'm all in." She got up, walked over to the couch, and plopped herself down, taking her wine with her, of course.

After looking at the clock, Joel told Chad that he should probably get going. It was almost nine o'clock on a school night.

Chad begged him to stay the night.

Joel half-assed his protest.

Chad used his ASPCA face.

Joel said he'd call his dad.

"Yeah. Chad's. Sure, I'll give her the phone," Joel said into the receiver after calling his father. He held it against the palm of his hand as he told Chad, "He wants to talk to your mom. Says he wants to make sure it's okay with her."

"Okay."

"Ms. Walker?"

"So we're formal again?"

"My dad wants to talk to you. I'm spending the night. Tell him it's okay."

She motioned her hand in such a way that he wasn't sure if she was indicating to hand her the phone or telling him to go away.

"Give her the phone," Chad told Joel, sensing his befuddlement.

He did.

"Heeeeyyyyyyy!" Ms. Walker said into the cordless.

"Oh gawd, she's just doomed you from ever being able to come over ever again. Ever," Chad said, covering his face with his hand.

"Yeah, it's fine. Uh huh," she said before looking at Chad and Joel and telling them, "It's fine. Go upstairs now. I'll take care of the dishes," then continued into the receiver, "Yeah, I'm totally cool with it." She continued talking while the boys went up to Chad's room.

"Should I be concerned that your mom is still talking to my dad?" Joel asked, stopping at the top of the stairs.

"I don't know. She's pretty drunk," Chad told him.

"I'm going to pee."

"I'll join you."

"Shy bladder. Like you."

"I'll be waiting in my room then. Just gotta use the computer really quick."

"Diary entry?"

"Diary entry."

Joel smiled, then walked into the upstairs bathroom and closed the door.

Chad went into the office and closed the door.

September 8, 2002

Dear Princess Diarrhea,

So, I came out to my mom today. I guess it's official now. No choice but to tell Nikki tomorrow.

The next morning, Chad woke to find Joel in his bed, in his arms holding him. He smelled of sweat and Old Spice. Perfect. Then the alarm went off and ruined everything. Bastard.

"What?!" Joel snorted.

Chad slammed his hand down on the alarm clock to turn Celine Dion's shrill voice off. "Morning, Joel."

Joel smiled, realizing where he was and what he was doing. "Morning, Chad," he said quietly, unsure if Chad could hear him. Unsure to what extent his hearing loss really was. He wiggled a bit then said a little louder, "Oh, I'm naked!"

"Me, too. I sleep naked."

"Okay, so do I. I've just… I've never… done this before."

"Slept over?"

"Stayed the night with anyone."

Chad brushed his hands through Joel's thick black hair, unprepared for the sensation from his fingertips that traveled to his core. "Now you have."

"Oh crap! What if your mom walks in on us again?" Joel said, eyes wide.

"That will never happen again. Her little boy's all grown up and having sex."

"You sure?" His eyes looked up from Chad's chest, making him somehow even more adorable.

"I know my mother." Chad's slight grin to one side made his cheek dimple.

Rubbing his hand over Chad's torso, breath tingling the tiny and nearly invisible hairs, Joel said, "Um, so, I guess I could run home real quick before school to shower and change."

"Stay here," Chad commanded. "I'll use the downstairs bathroom."

"Okay."

Kiss.

Eye contact.

Smiles.

Another kiss.

"I hate to do this, but we really should get ready for school," Chad told Joel as he pulled his arm away from under Joel's head, suddenly worried he hadn't seen his cat since yesterday afternoon.

"You're right," Joel said, putting on his boxers. "I can use the downstairs bathroom if..."

"No! I mean, it's small and gross. Please, use mine."

"Okay," Joel said, reaching over and kissing him again. A wicked grin formed. "We could use it together."

"We'll be late for school."

"We could ditch school."

"I can't. My mom works for the district. She'd find out." Chad put on yesterday's underwear.

"Damn."

"Damn."

Joel gave Chad another kiss, opened the bedroom door, nearly tripped over Squeakers sleeping on the other side, apologized to the cat, and went into the upstairs bathroom to shower.

"Squeakers!" Chad said, picking up his old cat and plopping him on the bed.

He walked down the stairs, fed his cat, then went into the downstairs bathroom with a super tiny shower stall he had to duck into and crouch the entire time. The showerhead barely went to his chest. It was probably made for midgets.

DING DONG!

DING DONG DING DONG DING DONG DING DONG DING DONG!!!!!

The doorbell continued to ring over and over, the DING DONGs nearly overlapping each other, or so it sounded as if they were.

Chad screamed from the downstairs bathroom while trying desperately to rinse out the shampoo stinging his eyes, "Just a minute!"

The doorbell continued to ring.

Joel walked out of the shower in the upstairs bathroom in only a towel, suddenly realizing he hadn't brought a change of clothes with him because he wasn't planning on spending the night. The doorbell's incessant ringing and lack of sleep due to other nighttime activities made him decide to answer it. It had to be important. He opened the door to find Nikki, crying.

"Oh! This is all sorts of confusing, but thanks for the peep show, Joel. Where's Chad?" Tears streamed down her face by the bucketful.

The downstairs bathroom door opened and Chad was in horror as he saw the scene playing out in front of him: his boyfriend in only a towel, water dripping from his hair all over his tan muscular body like a horribly cliché—albeit still damn sexy—porno; his girlfriend at the door crying. *Shit. Well, now or never!* "Nikki, we need to…"

Nikki cut him off with, "My dad had a heart attack last night. I just got off the phone with ChiChi. He says it was bad." She wrapped her arms around Chad tightly. "I hate him being so far away where I can't be with him."

Holding Nikki as her tears wet his T-shirt even more than his barely toweled off body was already accomplishing perfectly well on its own, Chad looked at Joel and mouthed, "I can't right now. I'm sorry."

Joel mouthed back, "I know." He bowed his head, closed his eyes, and tried to hold back his own tears.

"Who's here?" Ms. Walker asked, peeking her disheveled head up from the couch where she'd apparently spent the night.

< < <   > > >

Monday morning. Almost every student in the halls of Ravenwood High walked zombie–like with matching expressions; a mass of lifeless bodies aimlessly wandering around. It didn't take long before Chad found out about a big party the night before at Stacey Hill's, who lived in an uptown estate in Ashley Heights on a hill called, no shit, Stacey Hill. The zombies were merely hung over. The bitch never invited him. Not that he would go, but still, there were sentiments to be taken into consideration. Chad seriously thought about telling Courtney to kick her off the cheerleading team, but when he saw her wearing dark sunglasses and a very un–Courtney–like sour expression, he knew she was there last night.

"Whiskey and me ain't friends no mo'," she said as she stumbled towards her locker in six-inch stilletos.

"Alcohol is the Devil's juice!" Meghan scolded as she followed her older sister.

"Shut the fuck up you dick–faced whore!" Courtney said, the intensity of her words present, but their volume decidedly not so much.

"My dad had a heart attack and almost died!" Nikki cried so loud it made Courtney cringe, which is saying something, considering.

Courtney slowly walked back up to Nikki, pushing her little sister aside with the full weight of her body, put her finger to Nikki's lips, and said, "Shhhhh. You're bein' too loud."

Kayla ran up to Courtney and said, "Baby! I knew I shouldn't have let you drink so much. Come on, I'll help you to class, okay?"

Courtney singing *Ebony and Ivory* while Kayla practically carried her to first period was both entertaining and disturbing at the same time.

"So they're back together again?" Nikki said as she watched them leave before leaning into Chad's shoulder for another sob session.

This would be number four since she came to his house. Four.

There's a shoulder to cry on, but by this point his shirt was completely moist from a seemingly never–ending supply of teenage girl tears that it bordered on the ridiculous. The humidity made him perspire, adding to the mess. Chad was unprepared for the clinginess Nikki insisted on heaving upon him. Before Joel, he found this sort of thing cute. After Joel, he found it awkward and annoying. Nikki never behaved like much of a girl, but toss some tragedy into her life and suddenly she becomes one! Praise Jesus! It's a miracle!

Finally picking herself back up mentally after being dissed once again by her sister, Meghan plastered on a smile and said, "See you at prayer circle, Chad!" before skipping away.

Chad thought, *Crap. Well, praying did kind of work, so...*

"Hey, Chad. Thanks again for letting me raid your closet," Joel told him, a melancholy look over his normally cheerful face; nothing like the one he wore when they woke up that morning that felt so natural and right.

"You look great in my clothes," Chad managed through Nikki the Cling–On's hair. Her hug stifling. His hug forced.

They both wanted to say more, but both knew the timing was crap.

"Well, until Algebra," Joel said, his voice unable to hide his hurt.

"Algebra," Chad said, almost broken watching Joel disappear.

Psychology was torture.

"Today we will be learning about how to deal with grief," the teacher began, causing Nikki to go into hysterics.

Prayer circle was hell.

"Jesus, I pray for my sister Courtney as she deals with her anger most likely stemming from her confused lesbianism, and I also pray for a speedy recovery for Nikki's father, even if he is a sexual deviant who will burn in the fiery depths of hell," Meghan prayed as she held hands with about a dozen kids, including Chad, her judgment uncharacteristically imposed and completely unlike her. Her words punctuated with animosity that stung him like bees.

Algebra was conflicting.

"Who can tell me about SIN?" the teacher asked while writing SIN on the whiteboard in blue dry erase marker, causing Chad to glance over at Joel who was glancing over at him in the front row of the class, not even realizing their feet were touching and hands dangerously close to revealing the nature of their newly founded yet distinctly secret relationship.

By the time school was over, all Chad wanted to do was crawl into a hole and die. All Nikki wanted to do was smother him with her feelings. All Courtney wanted was to go to Starbucks for a Grande Caramel Macchiato.

Guess who didn't get what they wanted?

Chad fixed out of the corner of his eye Joel walk into the boy's restroom. "I gotta pee. Be right back!" he said, handing Nikki off to Courtney who had no time to prepare for the emotional basket case she'd suddenly inherited. Grabbing Joel from behind while at the urinal, Chad nibbled his ear, caressed his neck and torso, and whispered, "I am so sorry."

Turning around, Joel pressed his lips against Chad's, clutching the short blond hair on the back of his head as he whispered back, "This is only temporary."

Another kiss.

"Shit, that's hot!" Courtney shouted.

She was back.

"Oh gawd," Joel said, quickly putting his penis away into the shorts he borrowed from Chad that morning.

"Courtney! Men's room!" Chad screamed.

"Bitch, please. Quit mackin' on yer boyfriend. Girlfriend is a wreck and I ain't in no condition to deal with that shit right now."

"Wait, she knows?" Joel asked.

Chad smiled a toothless grin.

Courtney shook her head, bobbing her Afro back and forth, defying the laws of gravity. Her hair was really that amazing.

"I love you, Court, but you can seriously be a selfish bitch sometimes," Chad told her.

"Chad," Courtney said, tears threatening to leave her eyes and destroy her perfect mascara. Even in a hung–over state, she'd managed to flawlessly do her makeup.

The way her mood shifted, he knew their cycles were in–sync. He also knew that he was missing something important. Something he should know. But what?

"It's been twelve years. Today."

"Twelve years? Oh my gawd, your dad! Courtney, I'm so sorry!" Chad said, hugging her as she allowed herself a brief moment of vulnerability.

"What happened?" Joel asked.

"Gunshot wound to the head for bein' a nigga walkin' his dog too late at night in a white neighborhood," Courtney told him.

Her vulnerable moment had passed.

Chad let go.

"Oh, Jesus, I... I... I'm sorry."

"My mom's the sorry one. Went and downgraded right after he died to some low–life neighbor who makes me call him Daddy so we'd be all secure an' shit. Bastard's just an asshole who drinks too much and smell's like onions even after a goddamned shower. Sneaky little white devil couldn't wait to take advantage of my momma and the life insurance policy."

"They catch the guy?"

"Nope."

"Why not?"

"Did you not hear the part about me sayin' he was a nigger? Did. I. Fucking. Stutter?"

"That can't be... wait. Never mind. That shit happened all the time when I lived in St. Johns."

"You from NoPo? Chad why you not tell me yo' man's from the ghetto? You go take Nikki home. Joel and I are goin' to bond. You like coffee?" Courtney spewed, grabbing Joel and whisking him away.

When Chad exited the boy's room, he spotted Nikki in the middle of the floor. She was a blubbering whale of a mess. For a brief second he thought about trying to sneak out of the school and leave her there so he wouldn't have to deal with her hormones, but then his stupid conscience got in the way. Thankfully when he picked her up off the ground, she said all she wanted to do was go home and crawl into bed. Chad prayed that when he walked through the Boloskis's front door, he wouldn't be raped through the nostrils by the putrid smell of Leftover Stew.

So much for the power of prayer.

< < <　　> > >

September 9, 2002

Dear Princess Diarrhea,

Erections and jeans have got to be the worst combination ever. I mean, worse than orange juice after brushing your teeth. Worse than wearing pink and red together when it's not Valentine's Day. Worse than seeing Cher's son's horrified expression between her legs during her "If I Could Turn Back Time" music video in which you can see that if he could he most certainly would turn back time and refuse to be in the video and watch his mother in a V–shaped ribbon barely covering her goods for a bunch of navy guys. Gawd, what kind of mother would do that? Who am I kidding, my mother would do that.

Anyway, I am having a problem dealing with my dick every time I think of Joel. I mean, I realize that I am a rather healthy seventeen–year–old male and my penis pretty much has more power over my actions than my brain does, but c'mon, does it have to react while trying to figure out algebraic formulations?

Solve for J.

I'll solve for J… with my dick up his ass!

The Nikki situation isn't making this any easier. I know I need to tell her that I am gay and that I am being unfair to both her and myself, but how exactly do you tell your girlfriend of two—and—a—half years that you are breaking up with her right after she tells you her father might be dying? I don't have the balls to do it. Well, she doesn't have balls and that is part of the problem so perhaps I could approach it from that angle? Oh! The struggle!

<   <   <   >   >   >

"Chad! Joel's on the phone!" his mother called from the kitchen.

He saved his diary, closed the file, and ran down the stairs to find his mother chatting away with his boyfriend. She handed the cordless over as soon as she saw him. "Hey, sexy."

"Hey, sexy."

"I am so incredibly sorry about everything today."

"Why? What could you have done?"

"I don't know. I'm sorry."

"Stop apologizing."

"I'm sorry. I will."

"So, and you know that I am being a totally understanding boyfriend because I can't believe I'm about to ask this, but how is Nikki?"

"Joel, we don't have to talk about Nikki."

"I feel bad for her, Chad. I have to come to terms that she is one of your closest friends that you've taken to another level for the last few years. You need to do the same. I want to know if there's anything I can do for her?"

"Really?"

"Really."

"Jesus, what did you and Courtney talk about at Starbucks after school today that is making you be so not jealous?"

Chad pictured Joel's smile on the other end of the line in his head.

"I wouldn't say I'm not jealous."

"No?"

"No. And it's private."

"Please. Nothing Courtney says is private."

"She said us brown people need to stick together, especially brown people with extra labels attached to them."

"That sounds like Courtney."

"She also said that if I broke your heart she'd cut off my dick and shove it down my throat."

"That sounds like Courtney."

"She also said she's happy for you."

"I know."

"And one more thing."

"What's that?"

"She said that our timing is shittier than a Honey Bucket at Fort Vancouver on the Fourth of July!"

They laughed heartily over that one. So much so that Chad thought he might piss his shorts. It was the most Courtney thing of all. Neither of them could shake the image of a portable restroom overflowing with fecal matter for what seemed like days. But then their laughter faded. It was time to be serious again.

"This isn't just a crush, is it?" Joel asked, so quiet and small that Chad had to extrapolate the words he heard and jumble them together with ones he thought he heard to form what he hoped he actually said.

"What do you mean?" Chad asked, figuring that'd be the safest response in case he misheard and let people in on just how much of a hearing loss he really had.

"I mean, this isn't just some infatuation because I'm the new guy, is it?" There was so much pain and uncertainty in his voice, even with the flatness of a telephone line between them.

Chad's throat tightened. "No. Of course not."

Silence.

"Okay. I gotta go. Dad wants to go out for some father–son bonding time at the bowling alley."

"That sounds like fun."

"I wish you were coming with me."

"One day. Soon."

Silence.

"I love you."

Chad froze. "I'll see you tomorrow." *Asshole.*

"Bye."

"Bye."

CLICK

Slamming the phone onto the base, Chad said out loud as he walked out of the kitchen, "Jesus, Chad. What the hell is wrong with you?"

"Uh oh. Why is Chad talking to himself in the third person?" Ms. Walker asked from the sofa, placing her wine glass onto the coffee table in case the answer was so shocking that she'd do the unthinkable and drop it, letting all those fermented grapes that gave their lives for her personal imbibement be destroyed so unceremoniously.

"Because Chad is an asshole."

"Why is Chad an asshole?"

"Because Joel told Chad he loved him and Chad couldn't say it back."

"You can't force the words. You have to mean them."

Her words were oddly comforting.

"I mean, we've only known each other for a few days. It's too soon to know that I love him, isn't it?" Chad asked, sitting on the sofa next to his mom, his voice full of uncertainty.

"Okay, so I know that I am probably the worst person to be giving relationship advice given my past…"

"By past you mean three–ways with married couples and one night stands when it's Fleet Week?" Chad interrupted, hoping to shut this talk down before it had a chance to fully develop, but feeling like an asshole even more now.

"Precisely. But I know one thing, and that is when it comes to love, you just know."

"Really?"

"Yeah."

He fell into her arms and she held him, hugging him tightly against her chest. These moments were few and far between since Chad started middle school, but she cherished them more now that they were so rare.

"I know Nikki is going through some crap right now, and this is probably an incredibly confusing time for you as well, but what does your heart tell you?" she said quietly, but enunciating every word so her son could hear them clearly.

Chad took a moment to gather his words. "It tells me that I feel complete when Joel and I are together. Like, that when we're apart I feel broken and lost, but when I think of him I'm suddenly whole again. And then I think of his damn sexy ears and all I want to do is nibble on them and perform umax on those lobes."

"Lust and a Star Trek reference? That's my boy." She smiled and rustled his hair.

"Mom?"

"Yes?"

"This isn't just lust, is it? I mean, if it was, I wouldn't feel so emotionally distraught over just the thought of losing him, would I?"

"Only you would know. But what I can tell you is that lust is part of the territory of love. It just comes and goes as it pleases."

"Mom?"

"Yes?"

"Do you think other kids are lucky enough to have parents like you who don't judge and allow their kids to talk to them about anything and everything, even if society deems those conversations as bordering on the unhealthy side of natural parent slash child relations?"

"I hope so." Ms. Walker kissed the top of her son's head, and offered, "We should go bowling for some more mother–son bonding time."

"Joel and his dad are going bowling for some father–son bonding time."

"Fancy that."

"Yeah, fancy that."

"We're still totally crashing their party of two though, aren't we?"

"Absolutely."

Stale and fresh cigarette smoke stabbed Chad's eyes as they walked into the bowling alley, instantly making them bloodshot. Of course, the person who reeked of stale cigarette smoke while chain-smoking just inside the front doors could have partially contributed to the assault.

At least they didn't play country music.

While his mother paid, Chad looked for Joel, trying to be inconspicuous but trending towards the amateur stalker vibe. The place seemed inordinately busy for a Monday night. Chad was not well pleased with this, as it made searching for his boyfriend difficult. And then he spotted him, still wearing his clothes, holding a pair of blue balls and judging them for both size and comfort in his grip. Dirty thoughts raced through his mind, along with an impossible tightening of his scrotum indicating that he was bordering on the verge of needing release despite a multitude of orgasmic sessions in recent days, as he stared at Joel holding his balls.

"Shoes," his mother said, shoving a pair of size-eleven-rented-quite-used-standard-issue bowling shoes into his face. The smell beyond atrocious; somewhere between sour foot fungus and Lysol.

"Oh my gawd!" Chad cried as he vomited in his mouth. The swallow that followed far worse than he expected, but at least he could safely bet his manhood was quite inattentive, saving him from any motherly embarrassment about public boners. "That shit is nasty!"

"They sprayed it. I watched," she said, handing off the pair. "Now, let's go find Joel and have a little Monday night fun! Who knew that Mondays are two-for-one?"

"Awesome. That explains the crowd. And they're over there," Chad told her, pointing towards the direction he'd spotted Joel. "There he is, clutching a pair of blue balls."

"You did not just say that?"

"I so did just say that."

"Race to see who gets to say it to his face!" his mother squealed, cheating with a head start.

Chad stayed put, remaining the ever—embarrassed teenage son forced to endure his mother's shenanigans. He strolled over at a miserly pace. The rosy complexion his face had taken barely visible in the low light. However, for as much as he knew what to expect from his mother, he was completely caught off guard by Joel's father.

"So this is the boy who's been fucking my son!" he said quite loudly, reminiscent of Courtney.

All Chad could do was recoil in horror as his jaw dropped to the floor, landing amidst used napkins, cigarette butts, and what may have at one time or another been nacho cheese sauce.

All Joel could do was laugh.

"Okay, so Chad, this the unfiltered version of my dad you didn't meet last week. I apologize for his crudeness, but at least you know where I get it from now," Joel told him, helping to lift Chad's lower lip.

"He knows?" Chad said, Joel's fingers still on his chin, conflicted between his emotional and bodily reactions to the situation.

"He knows," Joel said, taking a look around to make sure nobody they knew was close by before giving him a quick kiss on the lips.

Chad pulled away, not quite comfortable with the PDA Joel thrust on him, but at the same time wanting it more than he could allow. "Uh, hi?"

Joel's dad laughed. "Sorry about that, I just wanted to make a memorable first impression. Or second impression would be more appropriate. How about first impression since you and Joel started making sweet sweet love to each other?"

"Trust me, you did." *Sweet Lawd Geezus, this is going to be a nightmare.*

"Joel! Your blue balls are gone!" Joel's dad said, eyes wide.

"Please. Dad. Shut up." His embarrassment radiated off of him as he picked them back up again to judge for ease of use, fingering, and rollability.

"So what do I call you? Joel's dad?" Chad asked, realizing that even though they had been introduced the week before, they never actually exchanged names.

"Jeff." His hand went out for a shake.

"Hi, Jeff." Chad shook said hand.

Perhaps bowling isn't going to be a bust after all, Chad thought, suddenly at ease with the whole situation and even for a short moment considering returning Joel's public display of affection, especially as he watched Joel bowl the first frame and got to really see what his ears looked like from behind. *Gawd, he's got amazing ears. So lickable. So beautifully large and attention–grabbing. And his ass. His delicious, bubble ass that screams to be in baseball pants for the world to ogle. So buoyant. Squishable.*

"Your up!" Chad's mom yelled, causing him to make sure she was talking about bowling and not his current penile state.

"Oh, yeah, balls. I need a ball." He got up out of the awkward swinging seat, found a lovely pink sixteen–pound ball that his fingers fit nicely into and started running up to the line from the table.

Strike.

Chad knew it before it even hit the pins, turning around and walking away from the lane like a scene from a cheesy blow–up–all–the–things movie. It was like watching the whole thing in slow motion for Joel, Jeff, and Amanda… or so Chad imagined as a smug smile formed on his face as he walked back to his seat, not even bothering to look back to make sure his suspicion was correct.

"I guess now is as good a time as any to mention that Chad thinks he's pretty badass when it comes to bowling," Amanda said before looking Chad square in the eye and telling him, "Get your ass back up. You only got nine."

The smug look turned sour as he spotted the single pin staring at him from the far side of the lane, mocking him. The center pin laughed as if to say, "Fuck you!" while flipping him off with its whole being.

"There are no words for the amount of disappointment I have in this lane. Obviously there is a flaw in its construction. That should have been an easy strike," Chad said quietly, mostly to himself but audible for those around him as he got up, waited for the pink ball to load back into queue, then tossed it down the lane without a care as to if it connected with the pin flipping him off at the end of the road or not.

Nine.

"Well, that's better than me. I got three. I suck," Joel said, trying to cheer Chad up, not sure how to take this news about bowling badassery.

"You do suck. Very well I might add," Chad said, trying to get a rise out of Joel but realizing the current public setting with parental units adjoining might not be the best timing for said comment. His regret showed by the sudden change of color in his face.

Jeff laughed. Amanda laughed. Joel hid his face. Chad apologized.

"Ah, the joys of having gay teenage boys," Jeff said, wiping the tears from his eyes as he got up to bowl his turn.

< < < > > >

September 10, 2002

Princess Diarrhea,

Have I told you about Joel's sexy ears? I don't know what it is about ears that I find to be the sexiest part of a person, but I love ears. It's like the first thing I notice about someone. I have an ear fetish. I can admit that. To my diary, anyway. Fuck. His ears are amazing. They're so big and gorgeous and curvaceous and delectable. Oh, the nibble!

I never thought about my reason for loving ears so much, but I just realized it might be because mine suck so much. Having hearing loss on the verge of being a disability has its disadvantages (especially since I refuse to learn sign language because then when my hearing goes completely nobody will be able to tell me no and I will just always get my way) so when I see big ears I'm immediately drawn to them. Like they're somehow better than mine. Like they work or something. Mine suck at being ears without the aid of electronic devices that give me horrible headaches and difficulty sleeping because the faint buzzing/hissing/SCREAMING sound that I hear all day from the amplifier haunts me in my dreams, making me clench and grind my teeth all night long.

Ah, but Joel's ears… [drool] Yes, I typed drool. In brackets. Fuck off. My diary, I can do what I want. Besides, big ears are like handles; you can grab those motherfuckers while getting a blowjob. Goddammit! Why do I have to make everything about sex? What is wrong with me? Now I won't be able to think of Joel's ears without them being handles during a blowjob. Stupid brain. Stupid penis. Being a teenage boy is not all it's cracked up to be.

< < <   > > >

"Writing in your diary early today, are we?" Ms. Walker asked as she walked past the office while Chad hurriedly saved the file.

"Yeah, I've had a lot I need to get off my chest lately. Ever since, well, you know."

"The startling revelation of your homosexuality?" Her sarcastic tone somehow underlined with unconditional love.

"Something like that." Chad smiled and followed his mom downstairs. "Nikki's dad chose the worst time to have a frickin' heart attack."

"Life happens like that," Ms. Walker said, heading straight for the coffee maker to pour a cup. "You want one?"

"Thanks," he said, grabbing the first mug his mother filled. "I mean, I had something important to tell Nikki and she cut me off with her father's health issues. Mercury must be in retrograde or something."

"What the hell does that mean?"

"I have no idea. Heard a kid in school say it. Pretty sure he was stoned out of his gourd."

"You would know."

"Because I've seen you stoned?"

"You have?"

"Like a month ago with Mrs. Hollins! Seriously, Mom, you weren't that candid."

"Shit. We'll be more careful next time." She took a sip of her coffee laced with just a hint of half–and–half. "I mean, if there is a next time."

Chad put his black coffee down on the counter, the handle still entwined in his fingers. "Please, there will always be a next time with you and Beth.

"Oh, so now she's Beth? Marijuana does seem to downgrade titles," she said, chuckling before her next drink. *Now's a good time to tell him, right? No. Later. Not before school.*

"I don't think I have ever called her Beth. I don't know why I even said that, Amanda," Chad said, pretending with a disproportionate amount of effort to be an adult and not laugh while sipping hot coffee.

Deciding to brush off the lecture about only referring to her as Mom or Mother, she instead asked, "So last night was fun, wasn't it?"

"Yeah, it was. Joel's dad is, um, interesting?" Chad told her, shaking his head up and down.

"That's for sure. I mean, as far as first impressions go, that one should rank towards the top of any list," Ms. Walker said with a devious smile. "Soooooo... what else did you think about him?"

"He seems nice. Technically it wasn't the first time we met, but it was the first time since Joel and I started having the sex."

"You met before? I must have been laughing too hard to have heard that part."

"Yeah, at their apartment when I was over studying for an Algebra test."

One of her eyebrows cocked. "Were you really studying?"

"For about five minutes. Then we played video games."

"Is that what the kids are calling 'the sex' these days?" she asked, her voice tinged with mocking over adding 'the' to 'sex'.

"No, we actually played video games. Mario Kart in particular. This was pre."

"Pre what?"

"Pre loss–of–virginity."

"We're bordering on that unhealthy parent slash child conversation, aren't we?"

"Psychology be damned. Crap, Psychology. I've got a paper due this morning," Chad said, deflated as he looked at the clock. "And apparently only fifteen minutes to bust one out."

"You can do it!" his mother shouted enthusiastically with a thumbs up before refilling her coffee cup.

Chad ran back upstairs to the office and quickly typed out some bullshit paper about the importance of honesty in a relationship and tried desperately to leave out the irony of the current circumstances controlling his life. The printer jammed when he tried to print. The cat meowed horrendously because there was apparently a hole in his dry food dish where kibble had once been, but now only bare porcelain remained. Giving the dish a shake with one hand, paper in the other, he called out a goodbye to his mother, ran towards the front door, and tripped over a corner of the living room rug.

"Are you fucking kidding me?" he said to himself as he got up, checking for scrapes on his elbows and a possible bloody nose.

Scrapes?

Yes.

Bloody nose?

No.

He had just sat down in his car when he realized that not only did he leave his paper on the floor after tripping, but his backpack was still upstairs in his bedroom. "Perhaps the universe is trying to tell you something, Chad."

Operation School Equipment Retrieval: Complete.

He picked up Nikki who was still a blubbering mess, listened to her sob stories about how unfair life is, and tried desperately not to snap at her and tell her, "Get over it! Life sucks! Move on!" It took every fiber of his being to hold in his anger and frustration and honesty and truth from vomiting all over her. His impatience made the trip slightly shorter. Speed limits were apparently only a suggestion that morning. As they walked towards the front doors of the school, drizzle dampening more than just his clothes, Nikki started crying again into his shoulder. Chad almost lost it, but then he spotted Joel, and all that frustration melted away like ice cream on a hot summer day.

"I love his ears," Chad said out loud without even realizing the words were not internal.

Wiping the snot from her upper lip, Nikki asked, "Whose ears?"

"What?" *Fuck! FUCK FUCK FUCK FUCK FUCK!!!!!*

She glared at him with a look he was all too familiar with that basically said, "I know you heard me, asshole!"

"Uh, Joel's?" The questioning tone had returned.

"I don't know. It's like the least sexy thing about him. I mean, they're a bit large for my taste, but if they are any indication as to other parts of his anatomy, I guess that'd be a small price to pay."

"Whore."

Nikki smiled for the first time since what seemed like months, but alas, merely a day, as she said, "We should totally make out now."

"We should totally get to class," Chad said quickly, the thought of making out suddenly repulsive despite the fact that they've kissed a thousand times before. "Besides, Joel's watching."

"Let him watch," she said, grabbing the back of Chad's head and pulling him towards her mouth.

As Nikki violently kissed him, her eyes closed, raping his mouth with her tongue, Chad's eyes remained on Joel who watched helplessly as the situation unfolded. He looked on the verge of tears. So was Chad. Joel walked away at a brisk pace. Chad wanted to follow. Nikki finally stopped. Chad felt sick like he was going to throw up. Nikki looked at him with a beaming smile that used to make him happy, but now made him feel like life was threatening to vacate his body. She took his hand and they walked to their first period class as if everything was okay.

By the time third period rolled around, Chad waited, looking constantly for Joel to enter the room and brighten his shitty day and make everything better because he was in it. The bell rang. No Joel. Shitty day just took another dump on him.

Maybe he's running late.

He never showed up to Algebra.

Maybe he'll be at lunch.

As he waited, watching Nikki and Courtney eat and laugh and look around and gossip, even being joined by Sheree and Kayla and Jennifer who rarely ate lunch with them anymore at the COOL table, Chad decided that Nikki had enough company of the Team Estrogen variety to distract her, so he walked out into the student parking lot to see if Joel's BMW was still there. It wasn't.

Rain began pouring down.

"I don't care if my mom does find out," he said as he got into his car and drove to Joel's apartment.

To make matters worse, "Only Lonely" by Hootie and the Blowfish played on the radio. It was a fucking shit parade on a rainy day.

Drenched from the downpour, Chad stood at Joel's door and waited for him to open it after he knocked. "Hey," he said. "Can I come in?"

"I guess."

The sheer amount of hurt and frustration and confusion and depression in those two words made Chad break a little.

Chad walked in. "I'm sorry. I'm sorry about this morning and I'm sorry for soaking your carpet right now."

"I'll grab a towel."

"Thanks."

Joel went into the hallway, grabbed a towel from the linen closet, and handed it to Chad who attempted to dry himself off. The rain saturated through.

"I'm sorry that I thought I could be an understanding boyfriend who could deal with you not being ready to come out," Joel said, stopping Chad from responding with his hand. "I really thought after Courtney and I talked I could do it, but seeing you two this morning was worse than being used like a toy. It hurts. A lot." Joel fell to the ground, crying.

"Oh my gawd, Joel, I'm so sorry!" Chad said, falling to the ground to hold him. "I didn't want to, but she wouldn't take no for an answer. I seriously thought I might vomit in her mouth. We made out all the time and it never felt so awful. I felt sick and guilty and at one point wanted to punch her in the face. I don't like having those feelings."

Joel cried into Chad's arms. This was nothing like when Nikki would do it. For Joel, he had compassion. For Nikki, it had turned to contempt.

"I'm sorry I'm having a bad time keeping my end of the bargain. I don't know if I can do this again," Joel told him quietly, hoping he heard by the mere inch-and-a-half proximity of his mouth to Chad's hearing aid.

"I can't make you."

"Part of me wants you to make me."

"Which part?"

"The part that wants you to take off your wet clothes, throw them into the dryer, get on my bed, spread your ass cheeks."

"I won't protest."

"But the other part wants you to leave and never come back because it hurts too much to see you with someone else that I'd rather lose you than go through that ever again."

Chad's throat tightened. He gulped air. "It won't happen again. Promise. I'm breaking up with her next time I see her. I'd call, but that would be an asshole maneuver, and this is kind of important."

Joel smiled. "So, option one?"

"Only if you can help me get these clothes off."

Where the hell is Chad? Nikki wondered, growing angrier every second that passed. *Bastard wasn't at lunch and now he's leaving me stranded at school to what, walk home by myself? Maybe I should just go over to Courtney's. Lunch was fun with all the girls hanging out. Who needs boys? Who am I kidding? I need boys! I need a boy to rip off all my clothes and make violent love to me right here right now! I need to feel alive! I need Chad to...* "Is that a bare spot in the grass?" she asked out loud as she was pacing. "Heidi the Horse must have been grazing here during lunch today."

Heidi the Horse was not her real name, but none of the kids actually knew her last name because that's just what everyone had called her since kindergarten. Sure, she was a bit on the strange side; sitting under a tree and eating grass instead of a normal lunch, neighing her responses when asked questions by mocking classmates, galloping in the hallway between classes, all of which didn't help her situation or the given nickname. Beneath all that, for those who really got to know her, discovered a very pure and sweet natured soul who found comfort and tranquility in imitating a horse. Sadly, too few would ever take the time to get to know her before she died an untimely death.

"Goddammit, I'm going to kill that little prick!" she screamed into the air, embarrassment creeping in as she stood alone in front of the school by the student parking lot.

"Gurrrll! You need to calm yo' tits," Courtney said as she walked up behind her while holding Kayla's hand.

"C'mon, Nik! Let's go get pedis!" Kayla said, quite bubbly.

It creeped Nikki out how similar her and Sheree looked, even though she knew they were identical twins. Still, she never questioned when she suddenly showed up in Ravenwood two years ago after Easter if she'd really been in juvenile detention like Sheree told her, or why she didn't move with the rest of the family, and more important, why they never mentioned her. Then again, her own family was up to its eyes in secrets, so perhaps the less she knew the better.

"Are you contemplatin' in there or did you just not hear us?" Courtney asked, nudging her shoulder.

"Sorry. Yes! Pedi time!" Nikki said, plastering a fake smile over her angry face that soon would be replaced with a real smile over a happy face as she realized just how much she really needed some pampering and girl time with her best friend, even if it involved her best friend's sometimes girlfriend.

"Oh my gawd, Courtney. Have you discovered the joys of rimming?" Chad asked her with a deadpan expression.

After leaving Joel's house, he had to tell someone about the experience, and that someone had to be Courtney, so he went to her house to tell her in person because important stuff should not be done over the phone.

"The fuck you talkin' about? Ass lickin'?" The disgust was obvious in her overly exaggerated facial expression.

"Oh. My. Gawd. Yes."

"Boy, you Kray Kray. Cunt licking I am down with, but my tongue ain't nevuh goin' to the poophole in The Great Divide Canyon."

"Jesus, Courtney. It is absolutely amazing. I mean, I thought blowjobs were amazing. Okay, so I still think blowjobs are amazing, but holy fucking Christ, that boy's tongue is talented beyond belief!"

"Chadwick, if you are seriously getting' off by havin' another boy lick yo' pasty white ass, it is high time you tell Nikki."

"That I think rim jobs are amazing?"

"That you gay, sweetie! Quit beatin' around the bush! Trim that shit up and tell her."

Chad suddenly felt small and insecure and like he was back in middle school and the kids were making fun of him for being a bastard and a freak and a toe–head. And for wearing hearing aids. And for acting like a black girl. And for being a cheerleader.

"I know. I just don't know how."

"Gurrrrrl, you best be figurin' it out. She my best friend! They only so much time I can hold out 'fore let it slip that her boyfriend a fag."

Chad shrugged his shoulders, scrunching his face. "I thought I was your best friend?"

"Bitch, you both is. But you know my mouth. Sometimes I just spout out stuff at the worst time."

"I know it is important that I tell her. I just need some time to figure out how."

"What you need is to grow a pair and tell her you like suckin' dick."

"I can't just say that!" His eyes wide as he stared at Courtney, readjusting himself as they sat on her bed. He suddenly wondered if her and Kayla ever had sex in it and realized there were just some things he didn't want to know as his eyes caught sight of a torn pair of pink panties in her wastebasket.

"Well, she sure as hell ain't going to be rimming your shitty ass, and judgin' by that shit–eatin' grin on yo' face when you be tellin' me 'bout it, you gonna miss that shit."

"Oh gawd. You're right. Hug now."

They hugged.

While holding each other, Courtney said, "You know, for the longest time I really hoped you and Nik would get together, even though I knew without a doubt that you're gay as all get out. Then as soon as you did at that Valentine's Dance freshman year mere seconds after Jennifer dumped you, my damn lesbian brain suddenly clicked and I realized I was in love with Nikki. There was no way she'd ever love me that way. She's not gay. But you? I knew. I've always known." Her ghetto vibe sometimes took a vacation when she talked serious, which Chad knew to be her natural voice.

"Why didn't you tell me?"

"You gotta figure it out for yourself. You'd had enough of people telling you what and who you are. When it comes to your true self, it has to be from your own realization. You have to be honest with yourself and make peace with it. Then and only then can you open yourself up to happiness."

"I meant about being in love with Nikki."

"Oh. Well. Ditto for me, too. Besides, Nikki already knows about me and I've already promised her it won't taint our friendship. Trust me. She'll be fine. You might not survive her wrath, but she'll be fine."

"Thanks for the enthusiastic pep talk, Court."

"Anytime, MoFo."

"You need a girlfriend."

"Bitch, please. I ain't got time for that. Besides, my on–again–off–again thing with Kayla is prolly back on again."

"It's not like either of you ever date anyone else. Why bother breaking up if you are just going to keep getting back together?"

"Keepin' it fresh, yo'!"

"I don't get it."

"Girl's a witch."

"I know she can be mean sometimes, but…"

"No, like actually a witch. Spells and shit."

"Well, okay then. Thought Sheree or Jennifer would have filled me in on that little detail." Chad glared. "Or you."

"We all got our secrets."

"Shit. You've got me there."

Courtney's glossy red lips spread into a wide grin. "You know, she was in such a pissy mood at you for ditchin' her at school, you might want to take advantage of that anger and do somethin' to make her break up with you!"

"I can't do that. We've been friends for too long. I don't think I can destroy that friendship because I no longer want to be her boyfriend because, well, she's not Joel."

"Well, honey. There ain't no guarantee that tellin' her you gay will keep that friendship either. At least in the short–term. 'Sides, she loves the gays!"

Chad smiled, knowing all too well how much Nikki loved her dad and her dad's partner and Courtney and even to a very tiny extent Kayla. "Okay. Well. I'm going to do it. I'm going to tell Nikki right now."

"You go, gurrrl!" Courtney said, giving him a playful shove.

"I will, gurrrl!" Chad said, giving her a playful shove back.

"Seriously, Chad. Get the fuck out. Kayla's comin' over for sexy time and I don't want her knowin' I had a boy in my bed!"

"Really, Court?" Chad said, not wanting the details of lesbian romance rituals even though he just verbally vomited his own. "I mean, awesome!"

RING!

"Hey sexy thang? Why ain't you over here yet?" Courtney asked into the receiver. Her big smile faded into sadness. "Uh huh. No. I get it. I mean, we ain't never had no family meeting, but I know they happen. Love you too, babe."

Courtney's eyes were on the verge of tears.

"No Kayla for sexy time?"

"Says her parents have some important news."

"If her dad says he's gay, the gay world will explode. He's a total DILF."

"That's fo' sho'!"

Chad gave her a hug. She said she'd be all right and told him to go tell Nikki the news before he chickened out. He said he had to stop by his house first to check in and change and not smell like humped asshole as he tells his girlfriend that he's breaking up with her because he's gay. Courtney agreed that would be the best course of action.

Walking through the front door of his house, he did not expect the scene laid out before him. His mother, of course, was present, but so was the entire Hollins family.

"Okay, what's going on?" Chad asked, his hand glued to the doorknob.

"Family meeting," his mother explained.

"Yeah, I knew the Hollinses had a family meeting, but why are they holding it at our house?" Confusion was an understatement.

Smiling an uncomfortable smile, Ms. Walker calmly said, "You might want to sit down. We've got some news to tell you."

Suddenly defensive, Chad crossed his arms as his face burned. "If it's about Kayla being a witch, I know."

"Wait, what?" Ms. Walker asked, shocked.

"Cool. Now I don't need to come clean about that news!" Kayla said, to which Sheree laughed.

"Hey, I'm a witch, too!" Brendon Hollins, the boy, said.

"Yes, we know that you are a gay little boy–witch," Sheree said mockingly before asking, "Wait, Mom? Dad? Am I your only straight kid?"

"Uh, Chad. Why don't you sit down please?" Mr. Hollins asked, flashing the smile that could melt the iciest snow beast.

Kicking the door closed, Chad obliged, probably because he really liked Mr. Hollins. Probably because the man had always been so nice to him. Probably because he never made him feel like a nobody. Probably because he always made him feel welcome in their home. Probably because of all of the above and then some.

His mom sat on the edge of the sofa, building up the courage to tell everyone the news she'd gathered them all to hear. Just when they thought she was going to talk, her mouth poised for verbal action, she'd recoil like a Slinky.

The tension building.

The room suffocating.

The time seemed to have stopped counting, or simply gave up.

"Oh for God's sake, just tell them!" Mrs. Hollins said, throwing her hands up into the air.

Mr. Hollins looked Chad square in the eyes and told him, "I'm your dad."

"Holy shit!" Sheree yelled wildly. "So I guess I'm not the only straight kid after all!"

Chad just sat there, taking it all in. Suddenly all those times with Mr. Hollins over the last three years started making sense as to why he was so willing to help when he had three kids of his own. The time he fixed his bicycle right after moving to town. The time he comforted him after being bullied at school sophomore year. The times he took him out driving so he could get his license.

"Are you okay?" his mother asked, almost too afraid to get up off the sofa.

"Yeah. I am. I mean, I think part of me always wondered and the other part of me always hoped," he said, smiling.

"Yay! I have a brother!" Brendon squealed. "I hope you don't mind that I'm gay."

"I hope you don't mind that I'm gay!" Chad said before realizing the words had come out of his mouth.

"Well, okay, so that's out now, too," Ms. Walker said, walking into the kitchen. "Beth, want some wine?"

"Amanda, when have I ever turned down wine?" Mrs. Hollins asked, her flashy copper hair that came from a cheap generic box of hair dye catching the lamplight.

"True. Black Butte, Frank?"

"Yep," Mr. Hollins replied.

Kayla looked relieved.

Brendon looked ecstatic.

Sheree looked deflated.

"What's wrong, Sheree?" Mr. Hollins asked before his wife had the chance to.

"I'm your only straight kid," she said.

"And that's a problem?" he wondered, not certain as to why her heterosexuality would be an issue.

"No, I just... I'm confused. I mean, I've known Chad since we moved here and never once did either of you ever ever EVER EVER EVER let on that he's my half-brother. Even when he dated Jennifer! Even when Mom and I were talking about why I wanted him to date Jennifer because I thought slash knew he's gay and she said both her and your mom thought you were gay and I thought, great! He wouldn't violate her with his penis! But then you've been with Nikki for, like, two-and-a-half years and always make out still and I thought, well, we all must be wrong."

"Wait, you thought I was gay when I was with Jennifer and you didn't say anything because I was... safe?" Chad asked. "Mom, I might need a beer as well."

Surprisingly, she handed him one when she came back into the living room before passing out the other beer to Mr. Hollins and a glass of merlot to Mrs. Hollins.

"Okay, this is turning out to be the most awkward family meeting ever," Chad said, unsure if he should take a drink of the adult beverage in his hand that his mother personally put there, especially in front of the man who, up until two minutes ago, was just his neighbor, but now also his biological father, and surrounded by all these kids he'd known for years who now were his siblings.

"Cheers to awkward family meetings!" Mrs. Hollins said, raising her glass.

"Wait!" Kayla said. "We don't have anything to toast with yet." She flicked her fingers and three glasses appeared, one for Brendon of cream soda, one for Sheree of Coke, and one for herself of ginger ale with a twist of lime. Nobody batted an eye except for Chad who stared at her in disbelief. "This is what we were drinking at home before we came over, I just teleported them here," she told him before adding, "Okay, now we can!"

Her perky smile unnerved him.

"Cheers?" Chad said quietly to everyone else's loud ones before taking a hesitant sip of the thick dark beer he knew Mr. Hollins—correction, his dad—loved so much.

The bitterness was overpowering.

"So, does your girlfriend know you're gay?" Mr. Hollins asked, putting his arm around Chad's shoulder and making him feel all sorts of uncomfortable for all the dirty thoughts he'd ever had about wanting to fuck him because he was so incredibly good looking.

"Uh. Crap. Hey, Sheree, Kayla. Nikki doesn't know," Chad told them.

"Know what, that her boyfriend is gay?" Kayla teased. "Deep down she knows."

"You can read her mind?" he asked.

"If I wanted to." Kayla raised an eyebrow to indicate that she was willing to if he asked.

"You'll have to teach me that," Brendon said. "That way I can find out if a boy I like is gay or not instead of trying to use my horrific gaydar. I think it's broken. Maybe we can fix it or something?"

"You've got to tell her. Soon. Because I have got to tell Jennifer and more than likely Dad will want to throw you a coming out party because he loves those things," Sheree said. Mr. Hollins, Mrs. Hollins, and Brendon all nodded in the affirmative. "Like now. Before cheer practice Thursday at the very least since that is when we do the most gossiping. Does Courtney know?"

"Courtney knows so much more than anyone should," Chad told her.

"What? Why didn't she tell me?" both Sheree and Kayla said at the same time, which for identical twins seemed completely normal for some reason or another.

"I asked her not to. I'm still scared to come out, but apparently not around you guys," he told them with a cheesy smile. "Seriously, it's just another label I really don't think I'm prepared for."

"Label?" Brendon asked.

His innocence quite endearing.

"Chad the Deaf Dumb Blond Male Cheerleader," Chad said to clarify.

"Ah, now I get it. So what if you add Gay to that? Ooh! Do you have a boyfriend?" Brendon squealed, folding his hands between his knees and smiling so big it spread across his suddenly–noticeably–thinning–face puberty was busy providing him.

Chad remained silent.

Ms. Walker started laughing and said, "Yes, which is why he needs to grow a pair and tell Nikki the truth!" She must have started early on the wine because her current glass was only half empty, and he knew his mother's tolerance level. "Sorry, Chad."

"Oh my gawd, who is it?" Sheree asked.

"Is it someone we know?" Kayla asked.

"Joel," Chad told them quietly, finding himself unable to lie since this meeting was all about honesty.

"Oh, how sweet," Kayla said, smiling a goofy grin.

"Oh, how awful," Sheree said, face green, frowning her disappointment. "He's so hot."

"He's hot? Do you have a picture?" Brendon asked, wide–eyed and waiting with anticipation for what he hoped was an affirmative.

"Calm your hormones, Bren," Mrs. Hollins told him.

"No. No picture," Chad said, suddenly saddened.

"Damn," Brendon said, sinking into the chair.

"Trust me, Bren. It's for the best. He's only like the hottest guy at school. And ears for miles. Drool. And he's new, so, you know, that takes it up a couple notches," Sheree told her little brother.

"Yeah, if I wasn't a lesbian I'd totally bang him," Kayla told her little brother.

"Thanks," Brendon told his older sisters, sinking into the rug.

"He's actually so much more than I deserve," Chad said to nobody and everybody.

Mr. Hollins put his hand on Chad's shoulder to get his attention, then looked him in the eye that Chad instantly recognized as his own and told him, "Never tell yourself that. It's not true."

Chad smiled. "With all due respect, you don't really know me."

The words stung.

Chad immediately regretted their exit from his mouth, but there was no going back now. "I'm sorry, I…" he started, but Mr. Hollins interrupted.

"No, I'm sorry. I'm sorry I wasn't there for you growing up. Amanda, I mean your mom, she thought it would be best to raise you without me in your life because I'm married and have kids of my own and she didn't want to have to worry about what the neighbors think and I can't blame her. Beth and I were in a relationship with your mom for over a year, and I know this is probably a bit of a major over share as Sheree would say, but when she found out she was pregnant, we were thrilled to know that another child would be joining our lives. But reality is, society just doesn't want to accept the fact that there is room for love in multiple forms. It doesn't have to be limiting. I don't blame your mom for wanting to start over. I can't. So Beth and I scrapped together the money we had in savings and from an inheritance my uncle left me who, side note, also gay, so yeah, it apparently runs in the family or we just have a high acceptance policy that God decided to put as many gays as possible into, to buy this house for her because we loved her and wanted her to feel safe. If I really wanted to have a role in your life, I probably could have insisted on her staying with us in Seattle, but that wouldn't have been fair to her. So blame me for not being around, not your mom."

Mrs. Hollins's wedding ring barely tapped her wine glass, breaking the silence that followed Mr. Hollins's speech. She quickly sat up straight as if that would help.

"Blame me," Ms. Walker said. "I panicked."

"I don't blame any of you," Chad said. "I've had an amazing childhood. My mom knows way more about me than any parent should know about her child and vice versa and I love our relationship. The only thing that saddens me is that I didn't get to share all that with you."

Mr. Hollins pulled Chad in for a hug. "I love you, Chad."

"So, do I call you Mr. Hollins still, or can I call you Dad?" he asked, squeezing tighter than he wanted, but his body had an unconscious need to hold onto the moment for as long as it could.

"I'd love it if you call me Dad," Mr. Hollins said.

"You can call me whatever you want," Mrs. Hollins said, going in for a hug from the other side.

His mom was right behind him, holding all three of them. Brendon joined in, followed by Sheree, then Kayla, who couldn't help but feel relieved this moment was finally over after keeping it secret for so long, said, "Just when I thought our family couldn't get any more complicated."

Everyone laughed.

Chad's sense of self suddenly exploded and imploded all at once. This morning, he was an only child. This evening, he was one of four. And now he had a dad and stepmom to add to the equation.

Life is funny like that.

< < <   > > >

September 10, 2002

Dear Princess Diarrhea,

Okay, so the weirdest and most wonderful thing happened tonight and no it isn't just about sex, even though I discovered the joys of getting a rimjob, which is pretty damn amazing. No, I found out who my father is.

And even better, it's someone I know and love already! Mr. Hollins! My dad!

Dad.

That seems so crazy to see the word "DAD" on a screen, but I love it! Holy shit! I now have two sisters and a little brother, and the funniest part is that three of the four of us are gay. Dad must have rainbow sperm! Oh my gawd, I just wrote that. I should delete it. Fuck. No. It's too awesome to delete. Must stay. Okay. I'm keeping that here for posterity's sake. I'm so psyched that if it wasn't almost midnight I'd call Joel right now and tell him the news. No, it can wait until tomorrow. I still can't believe I just blurted out that I'm gay during this whole family meeting thing.

I must be coming to terms with it.

< < <   > > >

< < <   > > >

September 11, 2002

Dear Princess Diarrhea,

I don't know how long I can hide my love affair with Joel. I want to share it with the world, but at the same time I want to greedily keep it all to myself. Is that why telling Nikki is so hard? It can't be. Courtney knows. Mom knows. Joel's dad knows. Hell, my whole other family knows! Before long, word will get out.

Small school.

Small town.

People talk.

Of course, all anyone is talking about today is the one–year anniversary since 9/11.

I wonder if after the "affair" part is over if it will change the dynamic of our relationship? Actually, I think that's what scares me the most. Fuck. Why is it I gotta fall in love with the hot new guy, find out he loves me, then be a pussy about telling both him and Nikki how I feel? Ah, the mysterious inner workings of Chad Walker at their finest. Next Oprah. Shit. If I don't do something, anything, I risk losing everything. Of course, the same holds true if I do do something. Jesus Fucking Christ, why does life have to be so difficult?

Wednesday was only a half–day in honor of the attacks on 9/11 the previous year. The students only cared about: Yay! Half–day! Because of that, all the classes were squished into much shorter sessions. On top of that, Nikki had apparently decided it was time to give Chad the silent treatment and wouldn't talk to him. He didn't push it either, knowing that he'd rather tell her the news when it was just the two of them and not during school hours which may or may not but definitely leaning towards the may side of the scale cause World War III to break out and this time the Russians would win and nobody would be left in the aftermath.

Math.

Algebra.

Joel sat quietly and barely said a word before class, and after he said he had to get to his next class because the schedule was all messed up and lunch wasn't until after fourth period instead of the usual after third period and he hates when things are different and he has no control over things which made Chad wonder if he'd done something wrong.

His worry was even more present when lunch finally came and Nikki decided to sit in between Jennifer and Sheree, leaving him to sit with Kayla and Courtney who couldn't stop talking and ogling and touching each other, staring into each other's eyes like cows for what seemed like hours. That, and as Chad pulled apart the skin off his fried chicken and shoved it into his mouth with a disgusted look on his face he usually reserved for doughnuts because he was both forcing himself to eat it and internally reveling in the fact that it was delicious deep fried chicken skin swishing around in his mouth that during his midlife crisis would come back to bite him in the stomach by way of a dad–bod belly, he coveted the peanut butter and jelly sandwich in Courtney's hands as it kept losing pieces of itself to her mouth.

Fifth period.

Sixth period.

Twelve–fifteen.

Done.

Because of the half–day, Courtney convinced the cheer coach to cancel cheerleading practice in honor of all the people who lost their lives the previous year, not that it would have taken much to convince her or that anyone could deny Courtney what she wanted. Chad was just thankful he still had a little bit of time to plan how to tell Nikki that it's not her, it's him. When he spotted her as he headed towards the student parking lot, the hot humid air against the dark gray sky instantly caused him to perspire, and caused his nerves to kick into overdrive.

"We need to talk," he told her, peeling his shirt off his chest and flicking it to wick some of the moisture from his body.

"Yeah? It can wait. My sister's coming over to plan Dad's homecoming next week. ChiChi says he's out of the hospital and wants to visit!" she said, giggling with a huge grin framing her clenched teeth, her shirt hugging all the various curves her body had to offer from her extraordinarily large breasts to her quite sizeable hips. For a short fat high school girl, she didn't care what people thought of her attire, something Chad found endearing about her back when things were new.

"Oh, wow. That's great. I get it. Want me to drop you off? Maybe we could talk in the car?" he asked, instantly regretting the decision as soon as the words escaped his lips as the image of Nikki's ferocious rhinoceros face came to mind because he tells her he's gay and she isn't very happy about that revelation so she punches him so hard teeth go flying everywhere and he loses control of both his bowels and the car and they crash into a ditch built by a bunch of underpaid Chinese immigrant laborers at the turn of the last century where his father will have to identify the bodies.

"Sorry, no can do, Nat's picking me up. There she is! Gotta go! See you tomorrow!" she said as she walked at a brisk pace towards her sister's car.

Natasha waved at him. Natasha's two kids waved at him. Chad waved back out of courtesy and forced out a grin so he wouldn't appear to be an asshole, which, honestly, he felt like.

"I take it you still haven't told her yet, have you?" Joel asked, causing Chad to jump practically a foot off the ground.

"She hasn't given me a chance. Like you, she's been blowing me off all day," Chad said, suddenly regretting the words as they reminded him of sexual activity.

"Sorry. I'm having a really shitty time with us. Like, when we're together, I just let all the shit I'm worried about hide in a corner, but as soon as we're apart, it comes back. With friends."

"I get it."

"Do you?" His harshness cut like paper; unassuming at first but noticeably more painful as time passes... or salt and vinegar find their way in. "Why can't you just tell her?"

"Tell her what? 'Hey, Nik! Guess what? I'm a fag!' I don't think so," Chad shot back.

He didn't like fighting, but didn't like being attacked either. Unfortunately, he was horrible at both offense and defense.

"Fine, then I'll tell her for you," Joel said, turning away sharply.

"No. No you won't. I will tell her when I'm ready."

"You'll never be ready."

"You really think this is easy for me?"

"Who said it was going to be easy?"

"You!" Chad shouted, knowing it was a lie and that it would weaken his defense more than help it at this particular crossfire once the word escaped his lips, but it was too late for take-backsies.

Joel's face looked like a mop head twisting in the bucket wringer as he said, "I did not! Come to your senses, Chad. Face the facts and move on with your life."

"I can't."

"Why? Why is this so fucking difficult for you?"

"Maybe if you were in my shoes, you'd see what's so difficult," Chad told him, failing to look Joel in the eyes, trying desperately to remain as calm as possible on the outside even though his insides were being torn to shreds.

"And maybe if you were in mine, you'd understand what I'm going through right now, too." Joel took a deep breath and looked up at the swirls of grays above him, eyes beginning to water.

"Joel, I do."

Joel almost said something, but Chad cut him off. "Listen, I had some really life–changing news yesterday and all I wanted to do was call you and tell you and share the joy, but it was late and I didn't want to wake you and make you a Mr. Cranky Pants, so I thought I'd be able to tell you today but it's like you keep making excuses not to see me."

"I'm sorry." Joel's voice had softened like butter left out on the kitchen counter.

"I'm sorry." Chad's voice genuinely apologetic.

"News?"

"I found out who my dad is."

Silence.

"Holy crap!" Joel said loudly before adding, "Is it good or bad?"

"Good?" Chad didn't know why he said it like a question, but there was no going back in time like Huey Lewis and the News's catchy 1985 hit.

"Good as in, 'I know who my dad is!' or good as in, 'Yay he's not a child molester but he doesn't get out of prison until I'm thirty!'?"

"Good as in it's Mr. Hollins. Sheree and Kayla's dad."

"Fuck me."

"Maybe later."

"No, that's huge. Isn't he, like, your idol?"

"I don't know about idol, but as far as fathers go, he's pretty amazing. Even if he has spent my entire life never telling me."

"That's great. Really." Joel's excitement faded as fast as it came. He was back to sad, depressed Joel who may or may not at any minute get angry again, which made Chad sad and want to make him feel glad again.

The parking lot had emptied faster than usual, making the asphalt sea spread. Chad had to yank his shirt again, wipe his neck, forehead, and upper lip. If there was one thing Chad hated most, it was feeling moist.

"We could hang out at my place if you want?" Chad offered.

"I don't know," Joel said, shuffling his feet, his face not hiding the conflict inside.

"Or we can go to Starbucks. Or the park. Just talk. In public. No sex attached. Get to know each other better. You know, build this," Chad said, trying to smile as Legos danced in his head, but scared the answer would be no.

"No."

Joel's response crushed him.

"No?"

"I mean, not now. I don't know. I need us to be us, you know? It can't be us and… her."

"But…"

"No buts. I can't hide my feelings for you. I love you, and I know that we've only known each other for a week, but I know that, and a little piece of me dies every time I see you with her and know that she doesn't know about us. I know my past is playing a role in this, but I can't help it. I've been hurt too many times by guys just using me." He looked small and helpless despite his actual size, moist eyes about to break their invisible dam.

Chad looked away, unable to cope with seeing the pain he caused and continue causing. "I promise I will tell her. Just timing is shitty every time I get the nerve."

"More excuses," Joel said, instantly regretting, but letting the words speak for themselves rather than amend with a less intense option.

"Joel…"

"You know what, Chad? I really need some time to myself, okay?" Joel's dam broke.

"Okay." Chad's hands fell.

As Joel walked past him, he squeezed Chad's hand resting at his side and whispered something he couldn't understand because of his stupid hearing aids and their inability to pick up on the sounds he most wanted to hear while letting the sound of a car alarm going off a mile away echo incessantly. Chad squeezed back anyway right before Joel let go, went to his car, and drove off. Instead of leaving, Chad laid down in the grass and let himself become one with the humidity, allowing all the uncomfortable feelings to permeate. Ten minutes later, Mrs. O'Hurley, his English teacher that Nikki was supposed to have but he was lucky enough to get, walked over, and sat in the grass next to him.

"This is not the most comfortable thing you could be doing with your life right now, Chad. Sitting on moist grass on a moist day just soaking in the moistness," Mrs. O'Hurley informed her student.

"Do you have to say the word 'moist'?" Chad asked, still lying down.

"Moist is a wonderful word that conjures up so many vivid emotions and responses because it can be both descriptive and provocative and is usually both at the same time." She had a way with words. Best. English. Teacher. Ever.

"Still, it's gross."

"Still, it doesn't explain why you're allowing yourself to bask in all the moist glory it has to offer on this fine afternoon you should be spending with friends, or in a less–than–ideal world which we sadly live in, doing your homework." Yep. Teacher.

"I don't want to go home, and all of my friends have plans that don't involve me." His bluntness couldn't even penetrate margarine.

"That is sad. I'm going to Ravenwood Tavern for a few drink with other teachers," she told him bluntly. Unlike most of the teachers at school, she didn't care that her students understood that she had a life outside the classroom. It made her more human. Relatable. And Ravenwood Tavern was what the locals called Ravenwood Bar & Grill since that was what it was called before the new owners took it over and made it the best goddamned place to eat pizza on the entire planet. "I would invite you along, but that would be awkward."

"Thanks," Chad smiled, knowing her offer was genuine and his response would be the same.

"I mean, first it would be taking a student to a bar and drinking and then the other teachers will start talking and then the whole school board would get involved and there would be this huge scandal and my husband would divorce me and my kids would never speak to me again and that would just be awful."

Chad laughed. "I'll save you from that scenario, Mrs. O'Hurley."

"Tammy. School's out. And you should be my T.A. next semester if your schedule allows it. Don't tell anyone because I will deny it, but you're my favorite student."

The sentiment touched Chad more than he ever thought something a teacher told him could. His inability to control the tears that started flowing instantly caused Mrs. O'Hurley to startle.

"Was it something I said?" she asked, straightening up, eyes wide.

"Yes," Chad managed. "But in a good way, I promise!"

"Thank goodness!"

"Sorry. I am an emotional wreck right now. I've got a lot of stuff going on and it is all a little overwhelming that you actually care."

"Of course I care, that's why I want you to be my teacher assistant. You would be with me during my prep period, so basically we'd sit around and chat or grade papers and tests or really we would probably end up just do nothing. It forces you to take a break from your day and decompress," Mrs. O'Hurley told him, only reinforcing his preconceived notions about why everyone loved her so much.

"Thank you. I will think about it."

"Do more than think about it. I'm putting your name into the office first thing tomorrow morning. I know we still have over four months until next semester, but us teachers have to plan ahead of time!"

"You mean you don't just wait until the last minute and pull a lesson out of a magic box and say, 'Tada! Let's bore them to tears with Shakespeare's *Julius Caesar* for the next two weeks!'?" Chad said jokingly.

"Why do you think we are going to the tavern? We are planning next week." Mrs. O'Hurley looked serious.

"Really? I thought you had all your planning done by the time school starts?" Chad looked shocked.

"There is a basic outline we adhere to based on both district and state standards, but when it comes to the actual lessons, not so much."

"Wow. Okay. Cool. Maybe I could be a teacher then."

"Reason number two for being my T.A. is because you would be an awesome teacher."

"Do you really think so?" he asked, no longer concerned about the moistness overtaking his body.

"I do. Now I have to go figure out how we are going to torture you kids. I am glad we had this conversation, Chad."

"Likewise, Mrs. O'Hurley. Sorry, I just can't call you Tammy yet."

She smiled, got up, waved a goodbye, and then walked towards the faculty parking lot adjacent to the student's, disappearing around a corner.

Chad decided it had been far too long since he had been to Ravenwood Park, so he spent the next hour playing on the playground like a kid, helping push the kids on the swings who'd decided to do the same after school despite the humidity and threat of rain, making the Merry-go-round go around at near breakneck speeds much to the delight of the children hanging on for dear life, and showing them all just how you are supposed to play hopscotch. As he watched a little boy chase a couple girls, he remembered the time he chased Jennifer Hoang and Brenda Greely while playing tag and he tripped over his shoelace and lost his front tooth when he fell flat on his face on the walkway. Watching a little boy and little girl swing and dare each other to go higher and higher, he remembered when Courtney and he would try to outswing the other, laughing the whole time even though he was terrified to death he'd fall and break his neck.

It felt good to laugh and be surrounded by laughter. But then the reality of his situation set in as he sat on the bench watching the joyous giggles of children filter through the thick air, bringing him back to the choices he had to make in his life due to biological urges he could not control.

Suddenly the laughing children sounded like fingernails on a chalkboard.

<   <   <   >   >   >

September 11, 2002

Dear Princess Diarrhea,

I need to take Courtney's advice and be honest with myself. I need to tell Joel I am in love with him because I am. I need to tell Nikki that I'm gay and still love her just not in the way she thinks and that I hope we can stay friends because I really want to stay friends and that I understand if she can't. Oh, gawd, I can't imagine my life without Nikki, but I also can't imagine it without Joel more. No. I have to do it. No more time to think about it, just pick up that goddamn phone and call her and tell her that you need to talk and you don't care that it is infringing on her dad's homecoming party because, dammit, this is important.

<   <   <   >   >   >

RING!

"Hey, come over."

"You have the worst timing, Joel," Chad said into the receiver already in his hand, ready to dial Nikki's number.

"It's important. Can you come over? Now?"

Chad let a moment pass to think about it. "Okay, I'm on my way."

Chad hopped into his car that decided not to give him shit this time and drove downtown to Joel's apartment. The whole while the wheels were whirling in his head trying to figure out why, after saying he needed some time alone, two hours later he wanted to be with him. Two hours wasn't nearly enough time to sulk and think about the problems at hand, unless decisions were already made and actions needed to be taken.

"So, we need to talk," Joel told Chad when he opened his front door to let him in.

"Oh, gawd, what? Are you breaking up with me?" Chad's cry face beginning to surface.

"What? Crap, what do you know?"

"What do I know? Huh? Oh fuck. You're cheating on me, aren't you? I knew you were too damn sexy to be monogamous."

"Jesus Christ, you are paranoid! No, that's not it."

"Okay. Whew. I can breathe again. I mean, we just finally got to an honest place in our relationship where I finally feel comfortable telling Nikki I'm gay and I know that I haven't told you how much that means and today has been hell and tomorrow everything will be different and…"

"Sit down."

"Shit, why?"

"Just sit. I've got some possibly relationship damaging news to tell you."

Chad sat in the closest chair.

"Crap. I knew I fucked this up. Crap. Goddamnmotherfuckingcocksuckingsonofabitch! What the hell is wrong with me?"

"I think my dad is dating your mom."

Chad became stoic. "It's worse than I thought."

"I found a pair of her underwear in the laundry." Joel looked like he was going to vomit.

"How do you know it's hers?" Chad clenched his teeth, wincing his eyes, preparing himself for the answer.

"Because she grabbed it out of my hand."

"Oh my gawd. This is bad."

"You think? If they get married…"

"…we'll be brother–fuckers! And to think I was going to rim your ass like you rimmed mine yesterday!"

Joel's attitude shifted. "Well, chances are pretty slim."

"Yeah, practically zero to none," Chad said, contorting his face to show the absurdity of the preposterous suggestion of their parents marrying each other.

"Totally." Joel so close they were practically touching.

"Where are they now?" Chad asked, pinky finger intertwining with Joel's.

"Ravenwood Bar & Grill."

Their hot breath greeted each other.

"That's a pretty happening place this afternoon."

Chad put his hand on the small of Joel's back.

"Yeah."

Joel let slip a little sigh of ecstasy as Chad let his fingers slip downward.

"Rimjob?" Chad asked

"Yes please."

September 11, 2002

Princess Diarrhea,

I used to love eating peanut butter and jelly sandwiches. On white bread. Yes, that spongy stuff that is probably more chemicals than food. I'd eat them daily. Sometimes two or three times a day during summer. I miss peanut butter and jelly. But I know I have to move on. Nostalgia is one thing, but clinging to the past because it is comfortable and familiar and easy is another.

Nikki is my peanut butter and jelly now. I know that she will always have a huge impact on my life, I just need to let her go. It's not fair to her what I've been doing. But like that peanut butter and jelly sandwich of yesteryear, it's time to say goodbye because circumstances dictate that change is necessary and difficult.

First thing in the morning I am telling her the truth and breaking up with her. Fuck you, nostalgia. I am going to go make myself a peanut butter and jelly sandwich now.

<   <   <   >   >   >

"I've decided to trust you," Joel confessed the next morning as he caught up with Chad at his locker.

"Good, because she already left her house this morning before I could tell her, and as fun as it would be to break up with her in Psychology and let loose the full array of emotional artillery that is Nikki Boloski, my instincts are telling me to steer clear of such insanity. Yes, I know it's another fucking excuse and I am a fucking asshole for making you put up with my fucking utter avoidance of the task at hand, but before the day is over, she will know."

"Okay," Joel smiled.

"Why are you being so understanding today?" Chad asked.

"Because you rimmed me yesterday. That's love. It means you want all of me, including the shittiest parts," Joel told him, their closeness both exhilarating and frightening given the location and proximity to prying eyes, and his words surprisingly deep.

"I never thought about it like that. I just wanted to return the favor because I wanted to give you the same pleasure you've given me," Chad said, resisting the urge to grab Joel's hand.

Joel smiled.

The world was almost okay.

"Also,"—[gulp]—"I didn't see my mom this morning or last night. Did she stay at your apartment?"

"I don't think so. Dad's door was closed this morning. Crap. Maybe?"

"Figures."

The world threatened to fall apart again.

Courtney walked up to them and said, "Hey there, bitch. Why you not tell me my girlfriend's yo' sistah now?"

With Courtney hiding their hands with her proximity, Chad linked his fingers with Joel's before saying, "Because you've been ignoring me, bitch."

"Cool off yo' sassy pants! I ain't been ignorin' you!" she said, pushing her face back but her hair remained in place.

"Yes. You have. Ever since you and Kayla got back together, it's been nothing but Dyke Fest 2002."

"Okay, so we have been spendin' mo' time together lately, and that's on me, but you know better than keepin' secrets from me."

"I just didn't have the time."

"Like with that little convo you still gotta have with Nik?"

"Yeah. I've got a plan. I want it to be perfect. I want it to happen so we're both at peace with it."

"You gotta fuckin' unrealistic goal is what you got." She was right and she knew it.

Joel let his hand fall out of Chad's.

The bell rang.

They all went their separate ways.

Chad walked into his first period class, sat down in his usual seat, and dreaded the moment Nikki would walk through the door and sit down next to him. But she didn't. She ignored him as she made her way to the back of the class and sat down next to Lily and they giggled. Chad's nervousness gave rise to anger.

Is she seriously avoiding me? What the hell? Shit, does she know something's up and is avoiding the impending conversation? Shit. Shit shit shit shit shit.

Their eyes met; his fire, hers ice. She gave a hint of a smile before turning back to Lily to discuss whatever they had decided was so funny. He gave no hint whatsoever that he was being avoided.

When the teacher started lecturing, Chad could barely understand what he said through the plethora of voices circumnavigating his head. Most of the voices tried convincing him that this was a good thing, as it would make telling her easier since she was physically already pulling away. The dissenting voices, however, convinced him that she was plotting her revenge for keeping something a secret from her. One particular voice had him certain that Mrs. Boloski's next Leftover Stew would feature whatever remained of his body after the wrath of Nikki finished him off.

The bell rang.

Class was over.

Chad learned nothing.

Nikki and Lily were still laughing as they walked toward the door, with Nikki telling Chad, "See you at lunch, okay?" leaving before waiting for a response.

"Lunch," Chad said, unable to get up out of his seat for a moment.

When he finally managed, he strolled zombie–like to his second period class, dropped his backpack to the floor, and waited for the torture to continue. He was not disappointed.

The bell rang.

Fuck. Prayer Circle. Maybe I could skip?

No sooner had the words flitted through his brain, when Meghan appeared in the doorway gleefully exclaiming, "Prayer Circle! Isn't Jesus the best? Let's go, Chad!"

Thankfully everyone's prayers they shared with the group were positive and not all hateful like Monday's session. Still, Chad felt guilty about even belonging to the group despite not having any long–held religious convictions.

The bell rang.

Algebra.

Joel.

Chad smiled as he ran to third period, growing two sizes when he saw Joel already seated in the front row. As he sat down, he leaned in to give Joel a kiss before realizing what he was doing. Joel quickly put his head down to check his shoelaces in an effort to avoid contact. Their heads collided rather than their lips.

Awkward.

"Sorry," Joel said, rubbing the top of his.

"I'm sorry I lost my balance and hit your head," Chad enunciated loudly so the whole class could hear.

"Dude! I thought you two were going to kiss!" a stoner kid in the back row shouted before being joined by laughter from others just like him.

"Shut up, Jack!" Kevin, the varsity football team's quarterback said, punching him in the arm. "They'd make a cute couple!"

The laughter stopped.

Chad smiled at Kevin who smiled back. When not playing football, Kevin was on the cheerleading squad with Chad, so they'd known each other for years. Chad felt somewhat comforted knowing that at least most of the football team had his back in case things with Nikki got terse. Scratch that. *When* things with Nikki get terse.

The bell rang

Letters and numbers danced on the white board in a flurry of blue blur.

The bell rang.

After Algebra.

"So, maybe I could come to cheer practice after school and watch if you want?" Joel said, his smile the exact opposite of forced.

"I'd like that. Nikki probably won't be there because she's still practically giving me the silent treatment since finding out her dad's coming home to visit," Chad told him.

"So I get to ogle your goodies all by myself?" Joel asked with devilish intent.

"Ogle away," Chad told him.

They walked to the cafeteria like Siamese twins conjoined at the shoulder. As they entered, Joel said he forgot his lunch in his locker, to which Chad told him to leave it. After all, it was Cheese Zombie day.

"What the hell are Cheese Zombies?" he asked, praying it wasn't cheese that had been bitten by a zombie and now a rotting version of its former self, something he wouldn't put past the School Lunch Board's approval committee.

"Seriously?" Chad asked. "Everyone knows what Cheese Zombies are! They are only the most delicious thing you could ever put in your mouth!" He blushed before adding quietly, "Okay, so second best after your dick."

Joel blushed now. "I must try this Cheese Zombie then."

And he did. And he loved it. And he swore to always make sure he ate them whenever it was that time of the month to devour their gloriously cheesy, buttery, bready deliciousness dipped in overly processed metallic tasting tomato–like soup.

"How is it I've never had this before!" Joel proclaimed, not even caring that he was sitting next to Chad who was sitting next to Nikki who was sitting next to Courtney who was sitting next to Kayla who was sitting next to Sheree who was sitting next to Jennifer who sat next to him on the other side of the circle.

"Isn't it amazing?" Jennifer said, continuing to get closer and closer to Joel as she prepared to offer herself for him to try as well, ever the stereotypically flirtatious Vietnamese girl.

Sheree caught sight of her friend's intentions and grabbed her thigh and shook her head no.

"Why?" she whispered into Sheree's ear.

"I'll tell you later," Sheree whispered back.

Jennifer glared.

Without warning, Nikki got up from the table ten minutes before lunch was officially over and said, "Gotta run! See you all at cheer practice, okay?"

"Um, okay?" Chad said, holding up his hands, watching as she skipped out of the cafeteria, leaving her tray and trash at the table. Lily joined her at the entrance. They giggled and skipped together out of sight. "What the hell is going on with her?"

"Beats me. Bitch actin' crazy as fuck today," Courtney said, licking her fingers of any lingering butter. Kayla stopped her on the last finger and put it into her mouth instead, licking it like a cherry lollipop.

"Ugh, get a room you two!" Sheree grumbled, averting her eyes to avoid seeing her twin sister and her very good friend being coquettish with one another. Even after two years of on again off again dating, she still couldn't understand why Courtney would be with her, especially after what Kayla was responsible for. Then again, she herself forgave her, so perhaps Courtney did, too. Obviously.

"Seriously, it's like watching my sisters make out with each other!" Chad said, pretending to be grossed out but still on a Cheese Zombie high.

"Well, one of us is…" Kayla started to say, but stopped herself when she realized that at least one person at the table was not privy to the recent news of Chad being hers and Sheree's little brother, and continued with, "…like your sister. I mean, you and Courtney are soul sisters after all!"

"True dat," Courtney said, kissing Kayla, getting a jeer from a kid, who got flipped off by her as they embraced without even looking in his direction.

When it was over, Kayla told him, "You're just jealous that you've never even kissed someone and that you'll die a virgin."

"Is that a threat?" the kid shot back, huffing up like a chicken hawk.

Kayla's eyes quickly changed from their typical teal to a raging red as she asked back in a low crackling growl, "Do you want it to be?"

The kid shut up, turned around, grabbed his tray, and left the cafeteria.

"I love my witch," Courtney said with a marshmallow face.

"I love my bitch," Kayla said with an equally marshmallow face.

"I hate it when you let your fury side out," Sheree said with a sallow face.

"I thought Chad was kidding when he said you were a witch! That's awesome!" Joel said, eyes wide with excitement.

"Oh, really? So we're having a coming out now?" Kayla asked deviously.

"NO!" Chad shouted loudly, almost standing in his chair.

Just kidding, little brother, Kayla's voice said in his head.

So you can *read my mind?* Chad thought back.

I can read thoughts and send them.

Fuck me.

Don't worry. I only use my powers for good now. Well, mostly.

The bell rang.

"Yay! English!" Chad said with delight that he was saved by the bell.

"Isn't Mrs. O'Hurley the best?" Sheree and Kayla said at the same time.

"Yes. I'm going to be her T.A. next semester. She asked me," he told the group.

"Lucky bastard," Jennifer told him. "I'd kill to be her T.A. next semester."

"I'd kill for a little T and A with my sweet thang right now!" Courtney shouted, laughing as if it was the funniest thing she'd ever said. Kayla apparently agreed. They left together and weren't heard from again until cheerleading practice started after school.

Fake smiling through gritted teeth during cheer practice, Chad stared at both Nikki and Joel sitting merely feet apart, and asked Courtney, "What the hell am I going to do?"

With the same fake cheer smile, Courtney said back, "The sooner you tell her the better. Bitch holds a grudge. Lift me."

Lifting her up and holding her butt in his hands to steady, he said, "Damn, your ass is so firm. Joel's ass is so firm. Shit! No penis! Stop!"

"Drop me like a hot potato, hornball," Courtney said, cool as a cucumber.

Chad willingly did as she commanded. Courtney faced Chad to hide his physical reaction.

"Maybe you need to wear one of those penile torture devices or somethin' so your dick don't get all pokey."

Eyes closed, Chad started quietly saying a bunch of random things to make him stop thinking about sex. "Gramma, algebra, fuck, no, not algebra, puppies, soup, cat poop, lots of dead crack babies, mom, ladybugs, whew! I think the coast is clear." He looked down to confirm.

"Seriously, MoFo. You need to tell Nikki you gay for Joel."

"Okay. I will. Right now." Chad started walking towards the bleachers.

"What?! No, I don't mean like right this second!" Courtney whisper–screeched through clenched teeth.

Chad ignored her. As he walked in Nikki's direction, he realized there was only one way to let her know that he was the reason, not her.

"Hey, sexy," Nikki said, smiling and about to get up to greet him despite mostly ignoring him for the last two days.

Chad ignored her, walked up to Joel, grabbed the back of his head, and started kissing him. Nikki stared. Courtney and the rest of the cheerleading team stared. Joel stared with shock at what was happening. When he pulled away, Nikki ran off crying, Jennifer punched Sheree in the arm and yelled that she knew it, and Courtney rolled her disapproving yet approving eyes and walked off towards where Nikki went.

"Of all the ways to tell your girlfriend you're gay," Joel said, a shocked smile unable to leave his face.

"I know I'm an asshole. I just didn't want to tell her, I just wanted to kiss you," Chad told him, the same shocked smile on his face as he held Joel's hands in his.

From the floor, the full realization of what just transpired finally hit Jennifer as she suddenly figured out that Joel was probably also gay. "Are you fucking kidding me? Why can't I fall in love with a straight boy?"

Sheree tried to console her, but Jennifer instead went into hysterics.

Chad decided now was as good a time as any to tell Sheree, "Maybe you should let your brother console her."

"Brendon?" Jennifer asked through her ugly cry face that scared the bejeezus out of everyone.

"Me."

Jennifer looked at Sheree and Chad and repeated three times before slapping her forehead with, "How did I not put this together? I'm supposed to be smarter than you all. I'm Asian!"

Chad refused to let go of Joel's hand as they walked down the bleachers to the floor where the rest of the team either congratulated them or payed up wagers. Or both. Apparently questions revolving around his sexuality had been floating around for years.

Just outside the gym, Courtney and Nikki were having a heart–to–heart after finding out about Chad and Joel. Back against the wall, head in her knees, Nikki's tears seemed never ending. Courtney rubbed her back like a toddler after getting a boo–boo. After a few minutes, Nikki stopped crying and put her head back to rest on the brick.

"I love you, Court."

"I love you too, Nik."

"I'm not a lesbian, Court."

"I know, Nik."

There was a brief pause of silence between them as the words filtered through, settling as if dandelion seeds in a gentle breeze.

"Don't you think it's weird dating a girl who has an identical twin sister you're really good friends with?" Nikki asked, shattering the stillness, avoiding the scene that caused her current state.

"Uh, no. They are so totally different. Now, it is weird that I'm datin' a witch who's responsible for killin' a bunch of my friends, but that was so 2000."

"No shit!"

"Shit, girl! She told me everything, something about a split soul after she died. Can't blame her for bein' so pissed."

"Kayla's a witch?! She died?"

"Nikki, do I need to slap you over the head with a blunt wooden object, 'cuz bitch, I will?"

"Okay, I am done freaking out. Kayla is a witch. I can live with that. I mean, we do live in a supposedly haunted town and I live on a supposedly haunted street and we supposedly have a largely unnoticed vampire population and one of your brother's friends is supposedly a werewolf and I am none of the above. But she died? When?"

"When she was four. Hit by a truck in front of her house."

"And she, uh, undied?"

"Yeah, she hijacked Sheree. Remember freshman year when she actin' all crazy and eatin' so much chocolate and matchin' her denims and shit?"

"Kind of."

"Kayla was trying to get out."

"Yeah, I think the less I know the better."

"Nik, since we havin' this whole Show–and–Tell convo, I got somethin' else to come clean about."

"If it's about you masturbating to images of me in that red dress again, I don't need to know."

"What?! Oh gawd, girlfriend, you did look amazingly fuckable in that thing! No, it's about Chad."

"Can we not talk about my gay and quite recent ex–boyfriend anymore? Crap, you knew he's gay, didn't you?"

"Seriously, Nik, I've known he gay since grade three and didn't want nobody violatin' you with their dick 'til you really ready for the deed, so I kept my cunt lickin' lips shut 'til he was ready to be honest with himself."

"Bitch!"

"Don't be hatin'! I was only tryin' to look out fo' my besties. No, this is deeper shit than that. Ever notice how similar Chad and Sheree and Kayla look?"

"Well, yeah."

"Kayla let me in on a secret. He's their half–brother."

"What?! Does he know?"

"Since Tuesday he does. They all went to his house and had this big family meetin' and BOOM! drop the bomb that Mr. Hollins his daddy. Gotta worry sometimes about them Hollinses. Lovely people, but still, they like their secrets."

"That's just so…"

"Fucked up. You can say it. His mama and Mrs. Hollins are like best friends. Apparently that three–way Chad's always jokin' she was in was with them."

"Lucky whore. He's a total DILF." Nikki slumped.

Courtney stayed by her side. They sat, saying nothing for what seemed like an eternity until Nikki broke the silence.

"Why am I not mad? Pissed, yes, especially that he couldn't tell me but had to fucking kiss Joel right next to me in front of the entire cheerleading squad. And Joel? Really? The hottest guy in school? Really? Why couldn't Chad fall for an uggo?"

"Uh, 'cuz he's totally adorable? And they fell for each other. Fast," Courtney said, widening her eyes so wide the whites looked like they were about to fall right out of her chocolate face. "Like really really really fast."

"You mean… like they've… done it?"

"Boy on a fast track to do anything and everything with Joel! Sorry, girl, but I can't keep those secrets in no mo'! He been confidin' in me all week and I hate keepin' secrets! You know how much I hate secrets! Fuck secrets!" Courtney screamed, crying, proclaiming her hatred of secrets while concealing her own lone secret she swore she'd never tell another living soul as long as she lived.

Chad walked out to find Nikki and Courtney on the floor, the tracks of their tears still evident. "Nikki, I…"

Nikki got up and said, "You know what, Chad? I can't. Not right now. Maybe not ever. Sorry, Court, I need to go." She stormed off, leaving Courtney on the floor looking like a hot mess.

"Don't hate me faggot, but I let loose an array of yo' dirty little clandestine activities," Courtney cried as her mascara ran down her face like black lightning.

"I don't hate you, kitty puncher. She was bound to find out sooner or later," he said, starting to cry over the loss as he fell by her side.

Joel walked out of the gym to find his boyfriend and his boyfriend's best friend sitting in a puddle of emotional goo. "Is this a bad time?"

"Never," Chad said, smiling through the tears, still holding Courtney as she held him as well.

She pushed Chad away and said, "I need to tell Kayla Nikki prolly gonna need me tonight."

"She'll understand," Chad assured.

"Yeah, we should probably go have a talk with our parents about their illicit activities, Chad," Joel said, giving him a look that begged for an answer as to why complications beget complications.

"Why? I thought both yo' parents knew 'bout you two?" Courtney asked, cry face over and mascara mysteriously vanished from sight with one fell swoop of her hands.

"Oh, they know about us. But apparently we still need to have a talk about them. Joel caught them in a compromising position," Chad told her.

"Oh, fuck. You didn't walk in on them makin' whoopee, did you?" Courtney asked, the horror spewing off her face stemming from the time she caught her mom and the white devil pretending to be her daddy the one and only Mother's Day she tried to surprise her with breakfast in bed.

"Oh gawd no! Shit no! Sweet Baby Jesus, why?" Joel asked with an equally horror–filled expression. "Only found her underwear which she promptly grabbed out of my hands and then I went to my room and closed my door and rocked myself back and forth and tried to erase the image of Chad's mom and my dad having [insert faux-vomit sound here] straight sex, which is probably worse than actually witnessing the act, right?"

"Whatever. I got bigger shit to deal with. Tomorrow's game at Chancellor's gonna suck ass 'cuz nonezuss got our shit together. Wiggers kissin' Indians, white girls unable to deal with nothin', Asians crushin' on the gays. Shiiiit. I didn't work this hard to build this team to get thrown down by no Chancellor cunts," Courtney said as she stormed back into the gym and proceeded to scream about bringing it the next day or she'd take their trophies and rape them all up the ass with them. She really knew how to motivate her team. Cheerful. Pleasant. Still, she wasn't wrong.

Chad and Joel went back into the gym hand–in–hand to witness the rest of the team huddling and promising to bring their best the next night as they gathered their bags. Jennifer told Chad he needed to be in on their motivational group hug moment. He relented and joined his fellow cheerleaders.

"I said you'd make a cute couple," Kevin the quarterback said to Joel who almost jumped out of his skin. He put his hand on Joel's shoulder and said forcefully, "You break his heart, and you deal with me."

"I don't plan on breaking anything," Joel assured nervously.

Kevin smiled, then ran up to the cheer team still reeking of sweat and grass from football practice and said, "I hate that I have to play football tomorrow! I'd rather be cheering with ya'll!"

Joel caught a hint of Kevin's redneck heritage and thought that it was rather sweet that he was protective of Chad rather than being the stereotypical bully figure in his life. Then he watched as Kevin picked up Nathan, another cheerleader, and kissed him passionately before putting him back down. Chad walked over to Joel who appeared to be in absolute and utter shock.

"Did I forget to mention that our quarterback plays for our team?" Chad said with a half–smile.

"But he's such a…"

"Farm boy? Yeah, he is. Parents own a dairy on the outskirts of town, and are the co–presidents of our local PFLAG."

"That's so completely outside my comprehension level right now that I might just spontaneously combust."

"And Nathan, his boyfriend? Class president."

"No shit. I seriously moved to the gayest place in the world."

"Yeah, well, you also moved to the place with the highest rate of unsolved deaths and disappearances in the state, so don't throw a parade just yet."

"Eek! Speaking of parades, we need to march on over to have a chat with our parents about stuff."

Chad deflated like a three–day–old helium balloon. "Yeah, stuff."

The energy that radiated from the team just moments ago faded into oblivion. Everyone started gathering their things and exiting the building at one door or another. When Joel picked up his backpack again, he noticed that the floor where his hands touched had a slight indentation, like someone dropped a bowling ball. Hard.

"That's where Kylie hit," Chad said quietly.

"Oh my gawd! She all right?" Joel asked.

"No."

"She's?"

"Yes."

A moment of silence passed as the emptying gym let its unadulterated self be exposed.

"We don't have to do this tonight, Chad. A lot has happened today. We don't need to add parental drama to the mix," Joel told him.

Chad grabbed Joel's hand. "No. We have to do this. Shit, we're on a streak of revelations. Why break that?"

Joel squeezed. "C'mon. Let's go."

"Your place or mine?"

"Let's try yours first. It's closer."

"Sounds like a plan."

They opened the door to Chad's house, greeted with the smells of fry bread, salmon, and huckleberry pie.

"Those are a few of my dad's favorite things," Joel told him.

"My mom hates huckleberries," Chad told him.

"This is bad."

"Very bad."

Chad's mom and Joel's dad peeked their heads out from the kitchen when the door closed. They both rushed over to greet them with a bombardment of questions.

"How was cheer practice?" Ms. Walker asked.

"How was school?" Mr. Talzan, Joel's dad, asked.

"What did you learn today?" Ms. Walker asked.

"Anything exciting happen?" Mr. Talzan asked.

"How's Nikki?" Ms. Walker asked, mostly to make her son feel uncomfortable.

"How's your sex life?" Mr. Talzan asked, mostly to make his son feel uncomfortable.

"Stop!" Chad shouted, dropping Joel's hand. "Mom, practice was great, learned I am braver than I thought, and Nikki's a bit distraught over having a gay ex–boyfriend."

"And Dad, school was just that, Chad came out to like everyone during cheer practice and I learned that this town is queer heaven, and I'm keeping my sex life to myself. Well, myself and Chad." He smiled at Chad after the last remark, winking.

"Awesome!" Ms. Walker said, gleefully. "We've got some news, too!"

"If it's about you two hooking up, we know. Joel told me right after," Chad told them.

"Yeah, sorry, but one cannot keep such things a secret for too long around here," Joel said, grabbing Chad's hand again, mostly for security.

"I mean, it was just a one–time thing, right?" Chad asked.

"Yeah, I mean, you really hit it off Monday night bowling and decided to bang each other and now that it's done you realize what a mistake it is, right?" Joel asked, squeezing Chad's hand hard, bracing himself for the answer.

Ms. Walker and Mr. Talzan looked at each other before she told them they better sit down. Chad and Joel froze in place. He asked them to please sit down. Chad and Joel were still frozen in place. They both said that they were going to wait until they all could sit down before revealing the news. Chad and Joel remained frozen.

"Fine," Ms. Walker said, throwing her hands up in defeat.

"We've been dating for about two months," Mr. Talzan confessed.

Chad just stared in disbelief.

Joel said, "But we've only been in Ravenwood for two months?"

"Yep." Mr. Talzan's response may have been short, but Joel knew the meaning behind it, and he knew that.

"So Amanda's the girl you moved here for?" Joel asked, his face like pistachio pudding. "I need to sit."

"I warned you," Ms. Walker said.

"Me too," Chad said, walking to the sofa, afraid to let go of Joel's hand.

"Uh, yes?" Mr. Talzan told them.

The news was still frighteningly fresh for Joel to deal with. They moved from his childhood home into an apartment thirty miles away in another town, hell, another state, and all for a girl? What kind of father does that?

"Why?" Joel demanded.

"Uh, have you seen her? I mean, I know she's not your type, but still, you've got eyes?" Mr. Talzan said, the sarcasm floweth over.

"Not even you are that shallow," Joel said, suddenly questioning whether his father just might be.

Ms. Walker laughed. "We met on an online dating site."

Mr. Talzan smiled.

"You realize how pathetic that sounds?" Chad told them.

Ms. Walker responded with, "Hey, I was skeptical at first as well, but as soon as we started talking…"

"…we realized right away that we had a connection and couldn't wait to meet each other," Mr. Talzan finished.

They smiled at each other. Then they started touching each other. Chad and Joel, despite the fact that they were holding hands, were quite disgusted at the fact that their parents were doing the same.

"So you really did move us here for a girl?" Joel said, angry and hurt.

"Calm down, son," Mr. Talzan said. "After talking with Amanda, I decided that even if it didn't work out between us, I was moving here with you because I want you to be safe. Trust me, this decision didn't come lightly. I only wanted you to be able to live openly without judgment, and Amanda assured me that Ravenwood was the place to do that."

Joel let the words sink in. "So, you moved here because of… me?"

"Yes."

"And you wanted me to feel safe as an openly gay kid?"

"Yes."

"Oh my gawd, Dad! I love you!" Joel said, getting up to give his father a hug. "And that is the cheesiest thing you could have ever done! This is the twenty–first century, you know."

"I know," Mr. Talzan said, still holding his son. "Still, North Portland doesn't have the greatest reputation."

"That'll change," Joel told him, certain that time will be on his side.

"I hope so," Mr. Talzan said, knowing that minds are tough to modify.

After they were done, and the syrupy sappiness subsided, Ms. Walker decided it was an appropriate time to ask, "So Nikki knows you're gay? How'd she take the news?"

"Well…" Chad started, hesitating on how exactly he could tell his mother that she pretty much raised an asshole.

Joel came to the rescue to confirm his assholeness with, "He walked up the bleachers and kissed me while I was sitting next to her. In front of the whole cheerleading team."

Mr. Talzan laughed, holding his hand up for a high–five which Chad politely, though admittedly had reservations about, high–fived him right back. Ms. Walker gasped in shock, though admittedly she may have overstated her astonishment.

"I'm sorry. I'm a jerk." Chad bowed his head in shame.

"Why are you apologizing to me?" Ms. Walker asked. "You should be apologizing to Nikki."

"I know. Chad's an asshole."

"Joel, it's time you learn that when Chad's angry with himself, he starts talking in the third person," she informed him.

"Good to know," Joel said, then a thought couldn't shake his mind and he had to ask Chad, "Why'd you never talk in the third person when we argued about Nikki?"

"I don't know. Maybe because it felt like we were supposed to argue with each other without me stepping outside myself. Huh, I'll have to ask my Psychology teacher tomorrow morning and oh my gawd I will also have to face Nikki in that class and shit that is going to suck major ass." Chad's whole body slumped at this realization.

"Joel tells me you like sucking ass," Mr. Talzan said before busting up again. He laughed a lot. A lot.

Chad let go of Joel's hand and punched him in the arm, "You told him?"

"Yes?" Joel said, rubbing his shoulder, smiling through gritted teeth.

Ms. Walker looked like she was going to throw up but quickly gathered herself together after swallowing a glass of wine in one large gulp and announced, "Let's eat!"

<   <   <   >   >   >

September 12, 2002

Hey there Princess Diarrhea,

So, today was, how shall I put it? Interesting? It was Cheese Zombie day for lunch, and you know I am a whore for those. What else? Oh yeah! I came out! In the most awful and wonderful way, I basically showed Nikki that we are over and Joel that we are together. Fuck. Poor Nikki. I just kissed him in front of the whole team. The whole fucking cheerleading squad watched as I kissed my boyfriend.

Boyfriend.

This week has been such a rollercoaster, and it's not even over yet. Joel and I also found out that my mom and his dad have been dating basically since they moved to town two months ago. Online dating website? Seriously? What kind of desperate does one need to be to go online to find love? Ugh. Maybe things get harder when you are older. I don't know. I want to be happy for my mom, but also selfishly don't want anyone to take her away from me, even if it is Joel's dad who basically looks like what Joel will in twenty years, so yeah, he's hot and all and nice and obviously really cares about Joel despite the bluntness and crudeness his comments about shit can be.

<   <   <   >   >   >

"You think my dad's hot?" Joel asked, folding his arms as he stood behind Chad.

"This is my diary. It's private. I can say what I want. Go away," Chad told him, covering the words with his hands playfully.

"I didn't mean to pry, just want you to come to bed." His words may have sounded innocent, but his intentions were anything but. Or, er, butt?

Chad smiled, knowing what he meant. "I'll be there in a minute. Just need to finish this entry, okay?"

"I can wait."

"In my room. Please. I'm not sure I'm ready to share all of my inner thoughts with you just yet. Someday, yes. But not right now."

Joel pretended to be hurt, but completely understood. After all, he wasn't ready to share everything about himself either. "I won't pry into the inner workings of your brain, but one day you will have to tell me why you call your diary Princess Diarrhea."

"Promise."

"Don't be long."

Chad smiled. Joel walked out of the office and into Chad's bedroom and shut the door. Door shut meant that Joel was getting naked. Joel getting naked meant that they might be having sexy time. Sexy time meant that Chad had to finish his entry before sexy time turned to sleepy time.

< < <   > > >

Sorry. I got interrupted. Not that you can tell time gaps or anything.

Anyway, tomorrow I need to figure out if there is any way I can turn back time and just be friends with Nikki like we used to be before she found me hurt and vulnerable at the Valentine's Day Dance back in 2000. The three of us—Courtney, Nikki, and I—were a trio, a triangle, a Triforce straight outta Zelda! Okay, my geek is showing. I am going to miss that. The trio, not Zelda. (Fuck, now I want to play Zelda. Curse you, tangent!) But I guess that is the price I just might have to pay in order to be myself. That is probably the price I will pay because I didn't take her aside and have a conversation with her. At the park. Privately. Shit. No. No time to be sad! Fuck. I need my sadness.

I really hope she is going to be okay.

< < <   > > >

Chad walked into his room after closing his diary file to discover Squeakers cock–blocking his boyfriend. "Really, Squeaks? What the hell?"

The feline ignored him, opting to nest on top of a sheet over Joel's crotch. He seemed quite settled and content, much to the dismay of Chad.

"Um, it appears I have a pussy in my lap. That's never happened before," Joel said, not really sure if he should attempt moving the cat or leave him be. "I thought you said he hates everyone who isn't, well, you?"

"He does. Or did. Apparently he likes you now. Figures." Chad pouted. "You're naked under there too, aren't you?"

"Uh, yes?" There was a slight uncomfortable tinge in his voice, not unlike when a clown rounds the corner unexpectedly.

Chad glared at Squeakers. "I hate you."

The cat continued to ignore him.

Chad closed the door, turned off the light, took off his clothes, set his hearing aids on the nightstand, and crawled into bed next to Joel. He relented to the fact that sexy time was apparently off the table, and opted for cuddle time as he reached his arm over Joel's chest and nuzzled his head beneath Joel's neck.

"I've never had a cat before. He's not going to attack my dick while I sleep, is he?" Joel asked, genuinely terrified of the scenario playing in his head of his penis being ripped to shreds and becoming a useless squid–like apendage.

"What?" Chad asked, unsure if he heard him right.

"Cat. Crotch attack." Joel pointed to his man–region to accentuate the point.

Chad chuckled. "No. I don't think so."

"I hope he doesn't. I'm rather fond of my penis and would like it to remain attached."

"You wouldn't want a detachable penis?"

Joel looked at Chad with a serious expression on his face as he told him, "Thanks, asshole. Now I'm going to have that song stuck in my head all night and won't be able to sleep. Fucker."

"Oh my gawd! You know that song?" Chad asked loudly, lifting himself off Joel's chest.

"Yes, I know that song. I recorded it, on a cassette no less, back when KNRK played it and would listen to it over and over and drive my mother crazy. Until she destroyed the tape in the microwave after a heated battle over appropriate music for eight–year–old boys," Joel said, hint of a tear in his right eye beginning to well.

"I'm sorry. My mom bought me the CD," Chad said, regretting the comment as it bordered on gloating.

"Goddammit."

"What?"

"My penis."

"What about it?"

"It's growing."

Chad started his hands down Joel's chest towards his pubic area and said, "I could probably nudge Squeaks off without causing too much damage."

"Okay." Joel's smile may have been invisible in the dark, but Chad knew he wore one by the sound of his voice.

Chad's hand continued traveling.

Then squeaky bed coils crept into his room, obviously emanating from his mother's bedroom, causing Joel to immediately say, "And I can't do this anymore."

"Neither can I." Chad slid his hand back up and resumed the position he was in before rousing the detachable penis subject. "Besides, I'm going to need my beauty rest for tomorrow. Got a big game against Chancellor and us cheer professionals need to be in top form to outshine those bitches."

"Thanks for keepin' it real, yo'," Joel said.

"Goddammit."

"What?"

"My penis now."

"You've got to be kidding?"

"No. I love it when you talk black to me."

"Our parents are having... [gulp]... intercourse. In your mother's bed."

"So let's drown out the noise by making some of our own."

"I don't know if having a Bed Squeakathon to see who can make the most noise while fucking is the best way to compete with family." Squeakers jumped off the bed, out of Joel's crotch right after he spoke. "But we can try!"

< < <   > > >

Running his fingers through Joel's mane later that night, Chad said, "Your dad has super straight hair, but yours is a bit wavy."

"Yeah, my mom has naturally wavy hair. She straightens it." Joel moved his head slightly so Chad could rub another area. "She probably has some white ancestry, but she'll never admit that."

"Why?" Chad asked, unable to figure out why the feeling of Joel's hair in his hands felt so comforting, the sensation of which struck him to his core.

Sitting up, Joel showed no signs of sarcasm as he said, "Uh, because the white man took our country, our way of life, and our religion, and left us with gambling, fireworks, and alcoholism."

Chad didn't know what to say. Everything Joel said was true, but still. The words seemed harsh. And he was as white as they come; blond, blue eyed, pale by comparison to other white people.

"I'm fucking with you. She won't admit it because she's a nationally recognized author known for being one–hundred percent Tillamook Indian and there's only like fifty of us left. There'd be a scandal."

"Still. All true." White guilt filtered through his response.

"Still. We negotiated the gambling and fireworks. The whiskey intolerance kind of comes with the territory of being Indian apparently." Joel seemed saddened by this.

"That sucks." Chad's hand caressed Joel's arm downward.

"Yeah," Joel said, seeing where Chad's hand was heading.

"Good thing we don't drink whiskey," Chad said, his hand reaching Joel's upper thigh.

"Yet."

"I have a feeling I'd prefer beer," Chad told him, the bitterly smooth taste suddenly present on his tongue from the one he had recently.

"Really?"

"Yeah, my dad likes beer. Gawd, it's weird saying that. I mean, growing up without a dad and suddenly being told I have one and he's my neighbor and now I have sisters and a brother and a stepmom? Crazy." Chad shook his head. His hand rubbed Joel's thigh.

"Yeah, that is crazy." Joel's smile faded. "Speaking of…"

"Crazy? Courtney says she might be okay now. I don't know. I told her in the worst way possible."

Chad let his hand rest. Joel noticed.

"That was an asshole maneuver. Still, I'm not complaining," Joel said with a wink and side smile that made his tan cheek dimple.

"Should I talk to her?" Chad asked, uncertainty in his voice.

"Let her come to you," Joel told him. "You had to deal with this situation your way, so let her process and deal on her own time."

Shaking his head yes, Chad said, "You're right."

"Of course I am. I'm also…" Joel looked towards his crotch.

"Oh! You are!"

Chad woke up an hour before the alarm and couldn't get back to sleep, so he decided to slip on a pair of underwear and take a shower, leaving Joel to slumber alone in his bed. After the shower, and clad only in his boxer briefs, he went downstairs into the kitchen to start the coffee. To his surprise, the light was on and the coffee already made. He poured a cup, took a drink, then nearly spilled it all over himself as Mr. Talzan, sitting at the breakfast bar, said, "Good morning, Chad."

"Holy shit, you shouldn't scare people when they're drinking coffee in their underwear," Chad said, putting the mug down on the counter to steady himself before picking it back up again.

"Sorry about that," Mr. Talzan said quietly, taking a sip of his coffee.

"What?" Chad asked.

"I said sorry," Mr. Talzan said loudly.

"Oh. Thanks. My hearing aids are still in my room," Chad told him, debating on getting them and some clothes to wear so he wasn't practically naked and vulnerable in front of his boyfriend's father.

"Well now don't I look like an asshole," Mr. Talzan told him loudly again to compensate.

"You don't have to yell."

"I don't know how deaf you are."

"Usually if you enunciate your words I can pick up on most of them."

"So it isn't near complete?"

"No, only about fifty percent." Chad decided to walk over to the counter opposite Joel's dad, coffee cup in hand, and slouched over, using the lower cabinets and his mug to hide behind.

"I see. Total loss or certain pitches?" Mr. Talzan asked, knowing that his dad had lost his ability to hear middle and high frequency, but could hear low pitches perfectly.

"Really high and really low I can hear, but it's that middle ground that, like, ninety-percent of all sounds are comprised of that my ears suck at being ears," Chad informed him, taking a long swig of black coffee. He noticed that Mr. Talzan took his with a hint of cream and saw that the sugar jar was open as well, a teaspoon resting beside it.

Mr. Talzan shook his head.

Squeakers meowed his way down the stairs.

"Like that I can hear just fine!" Chad said, smiling.

Joel followed the feline in his boxers, rubbing the sleep out of his eyes. "Your cat was begging to be let out." He yawned, opened his eyes to find Chad also in his underwear and his dad in the clothes he wore the day before drinking coffee together. "Morning, Dad!" He swooped in next to Chad, kissing him on the cheek. "Morning, sunshine!"

Squeakers continued meowing incessantly, his howls like Audrey II begging Seymour for food. The noise only stopped when a thick *PLOP!* thudded onto a plate and shoved into the cat's face. When Chad stood back up, he found his mother had also entered the kitchen wearing only a bra and panties. Matching bra and panties to be exact, which Chad had rarely seen.

"Am I the only one who had the decency to get dressed before parading around?" Mr. Talzan asked, throwing his hands up into the air.

"Apparently, sweetie," Ms. Walker said, leaning over to give him a kiss.

"Okay then!" Chad said, then drank the last of his coffee before adding, "I'm going to go change and head to school. Courtney wants to go over a few routines before tonight's game."

"Uh, I am going to head home and shower and I'll see you at school," Joel said, following Chad up the stairs and into his room to put yesterday's attire on.

"You know you can always borrow mine if you want," Chad said at the doorway as he let Joel enter first, slamming the door behind him, grabbing Joel's head and torso to pull him back and suck on his earlobe.

"Oh gawd," Joel cried. "No. I miss my clothes when they aren't on me."

"I get it," Chad said, spinning Joel around to face him so they could kiss.

"Thanks for the offer, though," Joel said, kissing him again before getting dressed.

Chad put in his hearing aids, threw on his practice shorts and shirt from the day before, tossed his cheer gear into a duffle bag, grabbed his backpack, and said, "I'll see you in a bit."

Another kiss.

Joel smiled. "I love you."

Chad smiled. "I know." *Goddammit, you asshole! Why you gotta be all Han Solo? Just say it back!*

But he didn't. He walked out of the room, said goodbye to his mom and Joel's dad who were practically making out on the breakfast bar, left the house, and drove to school where he found Courtney and a handful of other cheerleaders stretching. He waved, dropped his backpack, and jumped out of his skin when he heard, "Thanks for cutting me off, asshole!" It was Sheree.

"What?" Chad asked.

"You drive worse than Jennifer, and that's saying something," Sheree told him, arms folded.

"Why, because she's Asian?" Chad asked.

"Uh, yeah!" Sheree said.

"Stereotype much? I mean, completely true, but a bit racist, don't you think?" Chad asked.

"Trust me, she's the first to tell you that it's the only thing she's not good at. Said she gets too distracted by shiny things."

"Yeah, that's true."

"Anyway, I almost ran into you!"

"Sorry. I, uh, kinda left in a hurry."

"Yeah? Well, Joel's car was still in front of your house. So your mom lets him sleep over? Like, in your room?" she asked, both out of curiosity and to get juicy details about her fascination with watching two guys have sex with each other, but that fascination quickly diminished when one of the two people in the scenario was her brother, which made her turn green. "Never mind, you don't have to tell me."

"Yes, my mom lets my boyfriend sleep over and have sex with me in my bed," he said, knowing the answer would make her cringe more now that they were siblings. Chad was going to love having an older sister to torture. He was not going to love having two older sisters, however.

"All right, bitches!" Courtney shouted as a little over half the team had gathered in the gym. "Let's get started with Sky's Cheer!"

After leaving the boy's locker room when practice was over, Chad ran into Joel waiting for him. "Fancy running into you here."

Joel didn't smile.

Shit, I really fucked up this morning by not saying 'I love you' back. What the hell is wrong with you, Chad? "Listen, I..."

"We should find an alternate route for you to get to first period," Joel told him.

"Why?"

"Uh, because?"

"You're being ridiculous." Chad kissed him on the cheek.

"Yeah, so, we should avoid the main hall at all costs. Maybe both of us until the administration can take it down," Joel said, nervously twitchy like a meth addict awaiting his next fix.

"Take what down?"

"Something bad."

"Oh my gawd, Joel. Why so cryptic?"

"Please."

"Whatever it is, I'm sure you're just overreacting."

"I'm not."

"Well now you've got me curious and I have to see this thing you want me to avoid," Chad told him, grabbing his hand, dragging him to the main hall where he stopped and stared at the large banner about Homecoming.

It had the Homecoming King and Queen options to vote on. Chad's name was crossed out in sloppy red paint under the King header (something he wasn't even aware he was being considered for), and repainted under Queen. A few kids laughed. A few argued that it was a cruel joke. Nikki just glared at Chad with fiery eyes that burned through his very soul and pierced it with the hot coals of Nikki's pain as she held the paintbrush dripping onto the floor.

Chad started laughing.

Joel looked confused.

Nikki ran off, crying, dropping the brush and leaving a splatter of blood red over the mismatched vinyl tiled floor in desperate need of being waxed again in nearly the same spot where a murder-suicide occured at the end of their frehsman year.

"What about this is funny, Chad?" Joel asked, fuming.

"It just is!" Chad managed between fits. "I mean, c'mon. That's so middle school!"

Courtney walked up to them, saw the banner and the crossed out name and the added one under her own, pulled out a fat Sharpie from her bag, and scribbled in another option for King. "You gotta have an equal number, yo!" she said, capping the marker with a loud *POP!* like a gunshot.

"No," Joel said to her.

"Yes," she said right back.

"You should've just put Chad's name back into the King column."

"Hey, you two may just gotta chance at bein' the first gay Homecomin' King and Queen!" Courtney laughed a hearty laugh that made her Afro laugh along with her. She squeezed their heads together and kissed them both. "You're welcome!" She started walking away, then stopped, turned her face over her shoulders and yelled, "Sonofabitch! Chad, now you my competition! This. Means. War." A brief smile escaped her hard expression before she walked off.

Joel just stared, seeing his name stand out amongst the other options, not just because it was in bold black, but because it was twice the size of the other names on the list. "Sometimes Courtney is more than I can handle."

"You'll get used to her. At least you don't have to face Nikki in a couple minutes and try to figure out how you are going to apologize to her," Chad said, letting his laughter subside.

"Seriously? She pulls a stunt like this and you're planning on apologizing to her?!" Joel shouted, dropping Chad's hand.

"Yes?"

"She's trying to humiliate you. Probably on par with how you humiliated her yesterday when you kissed me to let her know that you're into boys not girls. I say you are even."

"I say you are wrong."

Joel shook, his anger visible. "You need to stop chickening out and stand up for yourself."

"I did. Yesterday. When I kissed you, remember?"

"I mean, look at that!" Joel pointed to the banner. "That's discrimination!"

"That's a joke." Chad grinned.

"That's wrong!" Joel's face was red.

"I can't take it seriously," Chad said.

"I can't date a fucking queen," Joel said, storming off.

Chad watched as he disappeared around the corner.

"What... the hell?" Chad asked the universe, shaking his head, deciding it would have to wait until Algebra when he saw Joel again to figure out what that was all about. He grudgingly walked to first period, going over every possible way the situation could go when he entered the classroom to find Nikki who was probably busy plotting his slow and painful death using blunt metal objects not meant for such activities as torture and maiming. When he got there, Lily looked like she was having a quiet yet stern talk with Nikki. The only word he could make out was 'ruined' from their conversation.

All during Psychology, Chad wondered what Lily thought had been ruined, and why Nikki started crying and apologizing to her. After class, he got his answer when Nikki rushed past the crowd to get out the door, and Lily stayed behind.

"It was supposed to be a surprise," Lily told him, readjusting her books.

"What was?" he asked, shoving his textbook into his backpack.

She sighed. "That you were nominated for Homecoming King. Nikki and I have been working on the poster for the last couple days."

"Oh." *Shit, so that's why she's been spending so much time avoiding me lately?*

Silence... for a brief moment.

"Well, I'm sorry about what she did to it. It's mean. We can fix it. Maybe." She looked visibly hurt.

"Don't worry about it. Courtney already took it upon herself to add another name to the King section to even out the numbers."

"Bitch!" Lily shouted, their Psychology teacher's ears perking up at the swear.

Chad got up. "Leave it be. The rest of the banner looks amazing. So what if the last couple names are a bit wonky!"

"Thanks. I really am sorry."

"It's my fault for not being honest with her earlier."

"So it's true? About Joel?"

"If by true you mean that he's gay and we're, uh, a couple? Then yes."

"Damn."

"Now I'm the sorry one."

She laughed. "I need to get to class. See ya."

"Me too," Chad said, then ran as fast as he could to make it to his second period class before the tardy bell rang. He arrived just in time.

All during second period, he wondered if there might be any way he could possibly get out of Prayer Circle, but knew that Meghan would probably be at his classroom door before he'd have a chance to escape. Surprisingly she wasn't, which made him curious. Instead he found her walking out of the girl's bathroom, taking a swig from her water bottle, and sporting what looked like a rather painful black eye.

"Meghan!" Chad asked, rushing up to her, biting his tongue from saying the Lord's name in vain yet again in front of her. "What happened?"

She forced out a smile that Chad noticed was not at all natural and said, "Oh, I ran into a doorjamb. Again!" She even managed to force a laugh out as well.

Chad pulled her in for a side hug. "You've got to watch where you're going, silly."

"Yeah, I should not walk around my house without my glasses on. I cannot see anything." She pushed the rims up the bridge of her nose before asking, "Is it true? That, uh, that you, uh… like boys?"

Shit, she looks so hurt and sounds so disappointed at the thought. Just tell her. Be honest. "Yes."

Meghan's fake smile faded as a multitude of emotions rushed over her, but it surprisingly transformed into a real smile by the end. "Well, Chad, Jesus loves you just the way you are!"

Chad smiled back. "Thanks, Meghan."

Meghan's prayers that day were focused on the importance of honesty. Chad could tell that she was struggling, and wondered if it had anything to do with the bruise over her left eye. *Lisa "Left Eye" Lopes. The "L" in TLC. 1990s hip hop at its finest. Don't go chasing waterfalls, please stick to the rivers and the lakes that you're… Ah, curse you sudden but inevitable tangent!* "Amen."

As Chad walked to Algebra, he ran into Joel on his way as well and stopped him. "Why are you so mad at me?"

"It's me, okay." Joel looked like he was trying to hide his hurt, but made no effort to dissuade or deflect with fakeness.

"Okay, so let's talk about it." Chad debated over taking Joel's hand, unsure if he could handle the rejection if he refused the gesture.

"Right now?" Joel asked, letting his fingers slip into Chad's.

"Yes. It's important to be honest about shit." Chad curled his fingers around Joel's, their foreheads making contact.

Kevin walked by, grinning from ear to ear when he saw them, dressed sharply in a suit like the football players always did on game day, both away and home. Today he wore gray with a hot pink tie. "I knew it about ya'll! You're so stinkin' cute together!" he said before he disappeared into the crowd toward their Algebra class.

"How about after class. We can grab lunch and then I will, uh, be honest about shit." Joel smiled, used their noses like a teeter–totter pivot, and kissed Chad. "Okay?"

"Sounds good. Although skipping Algebra sounds better, but Kevin saw us and as much as he loves the fact that we are, you know, a thing, he'll be the first to rat us out that he saw us right before class," Chad told him.

"Bastard," Joel said.

"Hey, I'm a bastard! Kevin's just a goody–two–shoe cowboy!" Chad said.

"It is kind of adorable that he's a gay quarterback cheerleader hick," Joel said, wondering both if he missed a label or if he should even bother putting labels on him considering his anger towards Chad's refusal to be angry about the Queen situation they needed to clear the air about.

"You should see him naked. That milk does his body good," Chad joked, holding Joel's hand as they started walking to class. The halls were clearing quickly, meaning that they'd probably end up barely making it before the tardy bell rang.

"Really? You've seen him naked?" Joel asked, crushed.

"I've seen all the cheer guys naked and half the girls, including my recently revealed sister. Oh fuck, I might throw up now," Chad told him as the image of naked Sheree from junior year's Regional Cheer Competition popped into his mind, her nipples refusing to leave his mind's sight.

"And yet you still didn't know you were gay?" Joel asked, trying to mentally picture Kevin without clothes on, but his stupid brain kept leaving jeans and cowboy boots on.

"Nope. Not till I saw you!" Chad told him, smiling one of his signature goofy toothy smiles.

Their feet entered the door just as the bell rang.

"Don't bother opening your books today because we are having a quiz over the last chapter. Hopefully you've been keeping up on your homework," the Algebra teacher said, much to the dismay of nearly every student in class.

Her words were so monotonous, Chad could only guess what she said based off his classmates' communal reaction.

"Balls," Joel said.

Chad cringed.

Balls is Nikki's preferred expression when things are wrong. Balls should not come out of Joel's mouth. While Chad told himself they'd need to clear the air about certain words, he could not shake the image of shoving his balls into Joel's mouth. Well, couldn't shake it until the foreign equations on the quiz in front of him laughed at his stupidity. The mocking continued throughout the entire test.

"That wasn't so bad," Joel said after class.

Chad was pale. "What test were you taking? I think the only thing I got right was the extra credit question."

"C'mon. Food will cheer you up. Hey! Aren't you supposed to bring the cheer?!" Joel asked, clapping and laughing after.

"I feel sick."

"I'll make it better," Joel told him, holding out his hand. "Then I'll probably make it worse because we still need to talk."

Chad took Joel's hand. "Yes we do," he said, getting up from the desk.

"TACOS!" Kevin shouted with cupped hands, strutting out of the classroom and towards the cafeteria.

Chad perked up.

"I take it you like tacos?" Joel asked as they walked hand–in–hand down the hall.

"Who doesn't like tacos?" Chad asked, suddenly cheerful.

"My mom."

"She's weird."

"You have no idea."

They rounded the corner and were greeted by a cool gust in the covered breezeway between buildings.

"I don't. I've never met her."

"Because she lives in New York."

"Yes, your mother, the famous author who can't let her public witness her shoving a taco into her overeducated pretentious mouth."

"Hey! That's my mom!" Joel said, feigning offense.

"Sorry. I looked her up on the Internet. Some book critic really doesn't like her."

"Because she turned him down for a date once."

"Asshole!" Chad said, then quickly added for clarification, "The critic, not your mom."

"He's not wrong. She's very worried about her career. She viewed me being gay as an inconvenience toward her mainstream success, hence divorcing my dad and the move across the country." Joel looked down as the pavement gave way to an open door and changed to mismatched vinyl tiles in varying shades of greens and whites.

"I'm sorry," Chad told him, squeezing Joel's hand and kissing his cheek.

As they approached the cafeteria doors, Courtney was already at the COOL table eating a taco, and next to her sat Nikki, eating her feelings. Just when Joel was going to suggest they avoid making eye contact, Nikki spotted them, ran up to Chad, hugged him, and apologized.

"This week has been hell for me, and I shouldn't be taking it out on you," she said, smothering him with wet sobs. Again.

Using his free hand not holding Joel's, Chad patted her back and said, "I'm sorry for being an asshole. I should have told you, not played it up like another big Hollywood production." He rubbed the scar on Nikki's right arm as if he was in autopilot mode, a crooked smile covering up the sadness that lay beneath.

"That gunshot wound hurt like hell," Nikki said while Chad's fingers brushed the scar she got at a Fourth of July party they weren't supposed to be at, avoiding eye contact like the plague, or worse, she might catch the gay, or worse still, cry. Again. "But this?" She gulped loud enough to cause the residents of a senior living facility a mile away to wake from their late-morning nap. "This hurts more. And the stupid thing is that I should've seen it coming years ago."

Joel stood there, awkwardly, holding his boyfriend's hand as his boyfriend's ex-girlfriend hugged said boyfriend again. He would have let go, but Chad's grip had tightened to the point that he thought he'd lose feeling any minute.

Nikki released. "And I'm sorry for this morning. I was angry and Lily and I spent so much time on that banner and now it's ruined and she hates me and all I want to do is eat until I vomit then eat some more."

"Well, at least you have goals. Shitty ones at best, but goals nonetheless." Chad smiled.

Nikki's eyes bulged as she punched his arm, surprisingly lighter than usual. "Asshole!"

"We're getting in line," Chad told them, leading Joel.

As they stood, waiting for the chance to load their plates up with overly processed beef food product piled into genetically modified deep fried corn tortilla shells then topped with metallic tasting iceberg lettuce and shredded government cheese and what apparently the School Lunch Board considered hot sauce, Joel leaned into Chad's ear and whispered clearly, "Our talk can wait."

Chad leaned into Joel's ear and whispered back, "I don't know if it can," before being unable to control the urge to lick his ear.

"Freak!" Joel said, wiping his lobe.

"The freak who…" Chad said, about to say 'loves you' but both chickened out and spotted the principal walking in their direction. "Fuck."

"The freak who fuck?" Joel asked. "That doesn't make sense. Fucks, yes, but fuck?"

"Fuck, as in the principal is walking towards me. Made eye contact and is in a beeline headed my way."

"Shiiiiiiiiiiiit," Joel mouthed, bug eyed with his face opposite the school's top authority figure.

"Mr. Walker, it has been brought to my attention that you are a queen," the principal said before twisting his tongue, twirling his eyes, and amending with, "I–I–I mean that your name has been mistakenly added to the Homecoming Queen court instead of the King's court."

"Uh, yes?"

Joel tried to let go of Chad's hand, but yet again, Chad squeezed so hard it made letting go impossible. So tight, tingling numbness crept up his arm from his fingertips like a burglar robbing his nerves.

"I'm going to have the janitors remove the banner immediately, and reaffix your name as a contender for Homecoming King. I apologize for this intolerance. Trust me, the person responsible for it will be disciplined," he said, putting a hand on Chad's shoulder.

Students started walking around them in line. Joel looked saddened at their stagnation.

"It's okay, Mr. Paulsen. There is no need to take the banner down. Besides, Joel here has been added to the King nominations!" Chad said, holding up their interlocked hands. "And wouldn't it be fabulous if we were King and Queen?!" He'd never used any stereotypical gay inflections before, but found the opportunity presented itself too well not to.

"Uh, er, um. Well…?" Mr. Paulsen attempted.

"Besides, Nikki Boloski already apologized about the whole incident. I kind of deserved it," Chad told him, stretching his lower jaw in an unnatural way afterwards.

"Don't ever tell yourself you deserve to be treated like that. You deserve to be treated with respect and dignity, and what that poster displays is neither," Mr. Paulsen said sternly. "And Ms. Boloski will be dealt with accordingly."

"Please don't suspend or expel her. She has a lot of family drama going on right now and I just broke up with her because, well…"

"You're gay?"

"Yes?"

"The way you won't let go of… of… I'm sorry, what is your name again?" Mr. Paulsen asked.

"Joel. Talzan. Joel Talzan, sir. I'm new." Joel looked nervous, giving his answers military style.

"That's right. You transferred from Portland. Your dad works for the railroad, right?"

"Yeah," Joel said, surprised he knew the details, despite not remembering his name.

"Anyway, I can't let something like this go unpunished. We have a zero tolerance policy when it comes to discrimination, and if I let one incident go, it will have a domino effect."

"I understand," Nikki said behind him, shocking them all since they didn't see her coming. "When do you want to meet with me?"

"Well, and don't let this get around, but the fact that you came to me to ask that means it'll be a pretty minor offense. Are you done eating lunch?" he asked, his tone soft and comforting, despite his intentions on doling out punishment.

Nikki tried her damnedest to keep her eyes on the principal, but they kept darting towards the ground. "Yes."

"Then let's go get this over with, okay?" Mr. Paulsen said in barely a whisper.

"Okay."

Mr. Paulsen gave a quick smile to Chad and Joel, then they watched as he and Nikki walked out of the cafeteria towards his office.

"Wow," Joel said. "I can't say I've ever been Team Nikki, but that takes balls."

"Sweet Lawd Geezus, Joel! Do you have to say balls? That's Nikki's word!" Chad said.

"Sorry! I say balls too! She doesn't have ownership of balls!"

"Fine. It's me who has a problem and I need to get over it."

"And lunch is half over and we still haven't gotten our tacos yet."

"Eek! I hope they have bibs or I'm gonna need a shitload of napkins so I don't stain me uniform!"

"Why do you have to wear that all day?" Joel asked, grabbing two trays from the stack, handing one to Chad.

"Spirit. Supposed to get the school pumped up for the game. This will pretty much be my Friday and sometimes Saturday life, so, yeah, hope you weren't planning on weekend dating because I'll be out of commission until November," Chad said to Joel before looking at one of the lunch ladies and asking, "Can I have a bib?"

"Anything for you, sweetie!" she said cheerfully before walking out of sight for a few seconds to grab one. "Here you are. We gonna win tonight?"

Chad grabbed the bib and put it on as he said, "Of course we are!"

She smiled, knowing all too well they didn't have a chance in hell, plopping two extra tacos onto his tray, making Joel all sorts of jealous.

"Are you kidding me? Why do you get extra tacos?" Joel asked, scrunching up his face.

"Cheer perks. Like this," Chad told him before kissing him on the lips.

"You finally figured out you're gay, sweetie?" the lunch lady asked.

"Okay, did everyone know before me?" Chad asked to nobody in particular.

She smiled, plopped two extra tacos onto Joel's tray, and said, "Growing boys need to eat more meat!"

Chad whispered into Joel's ears as he was getting ready to pay for his lunch, "I'll eat your meat," making him all sorts of uncomfortable.

"Chad, really? Inappropriate." Joel put his wallet back into his pocket, grabbed his tray, and watched as Chad got waved through. "Another perk?"

"Prepaid lunch ticket," Chad informed him as they walked toward Courtney, Sheree, Kayla, and Jennifer who looked like they were all finished eating and were now busy chatting away about the day's gossip. "It's probably a free lunch ticket considering my mother's pay, but she's never said anything and I've never asked, so I just keep telling myself she prepays for it every month and pretend like everything is hunky dory."

"Wow. Thanks for making me feel like an ass for asking," Joel said, looking at his tray instead of forward.

"Sorry!" Chad cried. "That's not what I meant by adding the rest! I was just thinking out loud and…"

"I'm kidding!" Joel said, flashing a smile that radiated brightly over his tan face.

When they put their trays onto the table and sat down, Kayla, in all seriousness, asked, "If you want me to dispose of Nikki discreetly, Chad, I will do it."

Sheree shoved her sister lightly, "You've got to stop joking about killing people again, or they will start talking again!"

Joel couldn't shake the fact that the word 'again' was brought up twice. "Again?"

Kayla looked around to make sure nobody was listening in on their conversation. "Okay, so, I'll tell you everything tomorrow when you guys come over for dinner."

"We're coming over for dinner?" Chad and Joel asked at the same time.

"Oh yeah, Mom and Dad told me to ask you both to come over for dinner Saturday night, so there, now you know," Sheree said nonchalantly before taking another bite of her half-eaten taco.

"What if we have other plans? And no, Kayla, please for the love of God don't do anything to Nikki!" Chad said, wondering if he was ever going to get to eat.

"You don't. Stop being a whiny little bitch," Kayla said, causing Courtney to go into uproarious laughter, which Jennifer immediately followed suit.

Chad looked at Joel.

Joel looked at Chad.

"Fine. We'll be there," Chad said grudgingly.

"Awesome!" Sheree said. "I think Mom's making Fettuccine Alfredo!"

"My favorite!" Joel squealed.

With only minutes to spare, Chad and Joel finally got a chance to eat their lunch. Chad thanked Baby Jesus he asked for a bib, as half his second taco splattered his chest when he took a bite. Joel was not as fortunate since he did not ask for a bib, and thusly unprepared for the explosive powers folded into that once crispy shell.

"Shit. Really?" Joel asked the universe, staring at his chest covered in taco–seasoned grease.

After kissing his forehead, Chad said, "If you want to go to the boy's locker room, I've got an extra shirt in there you can wear."

"Thanks. I'm going to have to take you up on that offer. This shit is the worst," Joel told him, pulling the bottom up as the grease started sticking to his skin beneath.

Looking at the clock and seeing they only had a minute to spare before lunch officially ended, Chad said, "C'mon. We gotta hurry."

They got up, said they'd see everyone later, and walked towards the trash to throw away their garbage. Halfway to the disposal area and tray table, Courtney shouted, "Don't do nothin' I wouldn't do!"

Chad shouted back, "Trust me, we won't!"

He winked. Courtney smiled and, oddly, laughed silently or simply opened her mouth wide. Chad wasn't certain what kind of expression was going on over her face. After dumping their load, they made their way to the boy's locker room where Joel immediately took his shirt off, went up to a sink, and tried to clean the grease off his chest.

"Jesus, Joel. Why do you have to be so goddamned sexy?" Chad asked, turning away so he wouldn't get a boner.

Sensing Chad's discomfort, Joel slowed down the motion of lathering soap over his pecs and upper abs. "What do you mean?" he asked in a soft, seductive voice.

"I mean that!" Chad said loudly, unsuccessful at his attempt to not get an erection and beginning to show through the black pants of his cheerleading outfit.

"Oh, this?" Joel asked, using his middle finger to caress his right nipple under a thousand tiny bubbles.

"Yes!"

"I'm sorry. How important is fourth period?" Joel asked, grabbing Chad's hands, putting them onto his soapy chest.

"Important?" Chad said, telling himself to resist the urge to rub his hands all over Joel's upper body and then some.

"Well I've got P.E., so I'm here," Joel told him, stepping back and rinsing off.

"Tease," Chad said, trying to figure out what to do about his penis.

Joel smiled, grabbed Chad's dick, started rubbing, and said, "You bet I am. But alas, kids are starting to pile in, so..." He let go. "Grandma, clawing cats, monkfish, dead crack babies, Nikki," forcefully whispering the last word.

"You are so going to have to make that up to me tonight!" Chad told him, surprised that it went down so quickly.

Joel kissed Chad. "I will."

The rest of the day went by in a blur as all Chad could focus on was trying to perform the cheer routines during the game while trying not to think about what he was going to do with Joel afterwards. He was grateful there weren't any other surprise quizzes being doled out, as his adolescent brain was still recovering from the horrific train wreck during Algebra.

"When's the game?" Joel asked, meeting up with Chad a few minutes after class at his locker.

"It's at five o'clock, so we're heading over on the bus pretty soon," Chad told him, throwing his Algebra book into the locker as if it offended him, which, in all honesty at this point in his life, it really did with its pretentious little solve–for–imaginary–numbers shit.

A pouty frown formed on Joel's face. "Damn. Thought we could go together."

"Let's see if I can turn that frown upside down."

They kissed.

It worked.

"Sorry. Gotta go with the team. Well, teams plural. Cheer and football." Chad felt the need to clarify.

Nikki walked up to the two of them and said, "Hey, so, apparently I have detention all next week," making Joel jump and shout, "Jesus!" to which she responded with, "Alas, not Jesus. Just me."

Chad smiled. Nikki really seemed to be back to her old self. The Nikki he grew up with. The Nikki he was friends with well before they added making out to their routines. The Nikki he remembered. The Nikki he no longer despised. "Well, that's better than expected, right?"

She smiled. "Yeah. Thought for sure I'd get suspended at the very least. Good thing I have no social life."

Joel felt guilty for reasons he couldn't quite understand. "I'm sorry for how things went down yesterday."

"Don't be. I'm sorry for making a huge scene this morning," Nikki said, quieter than her usually spunky self.

They all stood there in awkward silence for eternity. Okay, twelve seconds.

"I've got to catch the bus before Courtney chews my ass out for making us late," Chad said, teetering on whether to kiss Joel before leaving.

"Have fun. Hope we win," Nikki said, turning away.

Chad quickly kissed Joel on the lips once her eyes were averted.

"See you there!" Joel shouted as Chad ran off. "Nikki!" She turned back around. "I'll take you to the game if you wanna go."

"Really?" Nikki asked, unsure if she should accept the offer, knowing the hurt she must have caused even if genuine anger spurred her reaction.

Joel hesitated, wondering why he extended the invitation to his boyfriend's ex–girlfriend who, just this morning, he wanted expelled for discrimination. However, her apology sounded heartfelt and genuine and honest and her reaction this morning was, in a sick and twisted way, justified by her emotional state despite the hateful undertones overflowing through her undertaking such rash actions without thinking them through thoroughly. "Yeah."

"Well, and please don't take this the wrong way, but won't this be awkward?" Nikki asked, pulling her shirt over a section of bare skin on her portly belly she suddenly realized was exposed.

"Yes, it will be extraordinarily awkward," Joel told her, trying to hide the fact he saw her fleshy stomach and said nothing. "Still, I know how long you've been friends, and I would hate to be the one responsible for taking that away from you as well."

Nikki smiled, the hurt in her eyes still evident as she fully realized that any chance of her and Chad reconciling was truly out of the question. "Thanks."

"Hug?" Joel offered, extending his arms, wincing.

"We're not there yet." Her demeanor calm and calculated.

"Understandable." Joel retracted his outstretched arms and pocketed his hands.

Silence.

"Ready?" Joel asked, tilting his head in the direction of the student parking lot.

"Yeah. Can we stop at Starbucks first? I've got a craving for a Grande Caramel Frappuccino that won't go away," Nikki said, almost disgusted with herself for asking.

"My favorite!" Joel shouted with glee, flashing a bright smile that reminded Nikki why she thought he was the hottest thing she'd ever laid her eyes on that first day of school in the cafeteria.

"Thanks!" Nikki said before adding, "My treat, okay?"

"I can pay for my own," Joel said.

"Call it payment for gas money. I insist," Nikki told him, wondering if she should add, 'And for being a bitch this morning.' but decided against bringing up the quite recent past.

"Okay." Joel shrugged.

As they walked towards the student parking lot, Nikki let herself fall behind and couldn't help but stare at Joel's behind which, even in baggy basketball shorts, looked spectacularly bubblicious. *Goddammit, Chad. Why Joel? Not that I'm his type, but still.* When she spotted his BMW, she continued her thought with, *And the bastard drives a Beamer. Shit, I'm now the jealous ex–girlfriend. Is this how Jennifer feels? Poor girl.*

"Eek, it got a bit chilly this afternoon," Joel said as he unlocked the car door for Nikki, shivering as an unexpected breeze glided through. "Hopefully I won't regret wearing shorts."

Nikki got in, put on her seatbelt, and waited for the awkwardness to subside. It didn't. Even after Starbucks. Even after getting to the Chancellor High School stadium. Even after the game started and they watched their flawless cheerleaders somehow make the Chancellor cheerleaders look like shitty Chinese knock–off versions of the real things. Even when the game was tied at halftime, surprising Ravenwood High School kids with joy and Chancellor High School kids with confusion. Even when Joel turned to her and said, "Shit. My ex is here." Especially then.

"Your ex?" Nikki asked, wondering if she heard right. "I thought you're from Portland? Why would he be here? It is a he, right?"

"Yes it's a he, and yes I went to Roosevelt High School and so did he and I have no idea why he's at this game." Joel covered his face in hopes the guy he really really really wanted to avoid wouldn't see him.

"Shit. He's walking towards us. Want me to make a scene?" Nikki asked, not really sure what kind of scene she could make, but knowing that it wouldn't take much to bring out the raging rhinoceros she usually kept locked up inside its zoo cage.

"Uh, thanks but no. Crap." Joel let his hand slide down and casually glanced in the direction the boy was coming from.

Nikki scrunched her face and said, "No offense, but he looks like a pompous ass."

"He is a pompous ass who only used me for sex then dumped me once his girlfriend agreed to start sleeping with him," Joel told her, immediately regretting the revelation.

"Asshole!" she shouted, standing up just as Joel's ex walked up to them, punching him in the face, causing his nose to start bleeding profusely.

"What the fuck!" the boy shouted, holding his nose as blood poured out like a running faucet.

Surrounding students gawked at the scene.

"Oh my gawd, Nikki, why?" Joel asked, trying desperately not to laugh.

Nikki didn't respond, just stood in place with her hands folded across her chest, giving the bleeding boy her bitch-face.

A kid next to them offered his mostly unused napkins to sop up the mess, to which the boy accepted, shoving one far up into his nostril as he held his head back, letting it drain into his throat. Still staring up, tears welling from both the pain and the embarrassment, the boy said, "I was coming over to apologize, Joel."

"Shit, James. Really? Why? Suddenly find your soul?" Joel said defensively, the pain and anger evident.

"Ouch. That hurt," James said, eyes trying to look down over the bulging napkins coming out of his nose, quickly being painted red.

"So did telling me that I was nothing but a piece of flesh for your personal gratification." Joel couldn't stand up, his anger and frustration and confusion getting the better of him as he sat there, visibly shaking and wishing Chad would comfort him.

"I'm sorry. It wasn't true. I just thought it'd be easier than breaking up with you. I was wrong."

James's words seemed sincere, but Joel had a hard time accepting them at face value. After all, this was the guy who not only broke his heart, but broke his spirit as well.

"Why are you really here?" Joel asked, still refusing to look at James.

James knelt down to say to Joel at eye level, even if the ridiculous contraption adhered to his face made him look like a menstrual pad, "My boyfriend plays for Chancellor."

"Your boyfriend?!" Joel shouted, spit flying onto James's face.

"Yes, my boyfriend!" James shouted back, one of the blood-tinged napkins falling into Joel's lap before he spread his legs and let it fall onto the bleachers.

"What the hell? You told me you're straight?" Joel asked, his tone quieter, his anger not.

Picking up the napkin and shoving it back into his nostril that wasn't quite finished releasing his body's entire reserve of blood, James told him, "I thought I was. I was wrong."

"You hurt me. A lot," Joel said, looking down to avoid James's eternity pool eyes.

"I know. I'm sorry," James said, hoping Joel would look at him, just once.

"I don't know if I can accept your apology yet. Maybe not ever." Joel held himself.

"I understand." James stood up.

Nikki didn't know if she should sit down or continue giving the boy she gave a bloody nose to her bitch–face. She opted for the latter. Courtney taught her well.

"I don't think you do. You called me a clingy queer drama queen in front of all our friends after telling me that I was nothing to you." Relentless tears escaped his eyes, ripping down his cheeks like river rapids.

Chad overheard. "So this is the asshole?" he asked, looking at the bloody mess that was James, arms folded and bitch–face firmly planted. He and Nikki could be twins.

"Yes," Nikki told him while Joel said, "James, this is my boyfriend Chad."

James offered his hand out, remnants of still–fresh blood encrusted into his fingertips, nails, and palms. Chad refused to take it. James put it back.

"Why are you here?" Chad interrogated, redness overtaking his face involuntarily.

"Quandre," James said quietly. "He's one of Chancellor's linebackers."

"And apparently his boyfriend," Joel said, still shaking and not from the cold that had crept up despite the sun still above the horizon for at least another hour in what was supposedly still summer.

Chad loosened up. "I thought you said he was straight?"

"I thought he was," Joel said, extending his fingers and making a fist over and over at an attempt to calm himself down. It wasn't working.

Noticing Joel's pain, Chad squeezed his way past Nikki and sat down next to him, wrapping his arm around his shoulders.

"I just wanted to come over and say I'm sorry for being a dick. I'm going to go back to my seat now. It was good to see you again, Joel. Again, sorry," James said, taking one last look at the boy he broke before walking back to his seat on the other side and far away from the fat girl with the fist of fury.

Joel's tears kept flowing, though not as full as they were moments ago. "Goddammit."

"I'm sorry. How'd he get a bloody nose?" Chad asked.

"I gave it to him," Nikki said, still glaring at James as he walked back to his seat.

"Why?" he inquired.

"Because he deserved it for what he did to Joel." Her bitch–face a permanent fixture now.

"So you defended your ex–boyfriend's… boyfriend?" Chad asked, face crumpled in the most unsexy manner imaginable.

Nikki softened like sponge cake. "I guess I did. That's weird, isn't it?"

Chad laughed. "A little odd, yes."

"I can't seem to shake this anger," Joel told them.

Chad kissed him on the mouth, but immediately felt that the connection with Joel wasn't present. Dismissing it as nothing more than Joel's current emotional state, he asked, "Is that why you got so upset about Nikki's shenanigans this morning?"

"Yes." Joel's answer curt.

"I think I understand," Chad told him.

"You don't." Joel's tone snappish.

Chad realized that he did all the holding and Joel was just there, sitting, not touching back. "Help me understand, then."

Joel looked up into Chad's eyes and told him, "Right before prom junior year, he tackled me with a couple buddies of his, tied me up, put a fucking crown on my head, lipstick all over my mouth, and taped a sign on my chest that said Roosevelt Prom Queen, and left me in front of the school, wrapped around a column for everyone to laugh at." His shaking only worsened as he told them.

Chad's anger grew. "I'm going to go finish off that little shit!"

Nikki grabbed his arm while Joel grabbed his legs.

"Please, don't!" Joel said.

"Let go of me!" Chad shouted, fuming with more rage than he thought could ever come from him.

"He said he was sorry! I have to make peace with it now!" Joel said, still holding onto Chad's legs as he tried to work his way out of the grip.

Other people started paying attention. A couple middle-aged men made their way towards them.

"I already punched him!" Nikki yelled, her hands slowly sliding further down his arm as she tried to keep her grip.

"You did! Not me! I should be the one to punch him, Nik! I can fight my own battles!" Chad screamed, spit flying everywhere.

"It's not your battle!" Joel said, the tears he'd been crying finally giving up their endless flow. "It's mine, and it's done."

"It can't be. Not that easily." Chad began giving up his fight.

Letting go of his arm, Nikki said, "I'm sorry. You weren't here and Joel looked scared and hurt so I punched him in the face for him."

"My hero," Chad said sarcastically.

"She was my hero," Joel said, finally able to let go of Chad's legs when he noticed he stopped struggling to break free.

The men stopped and waited.

The game was about to start back up.

"I need to get back down there. Thanks for being here, Nik," Chad said, hugging her before asking, "Wait, why are you here? Together?"

Joel fidgeted. "I asked her to come with me? We had a nice chat over frappes. We're good."

Chad let go.

"Oh my gawd, guys! Does this make me your fag hag?" Nikki asked, squealing with delight as she faux jumped up and down, but still causing the bleachers to sway with her despite her feet never taking air.

The men took this as a sign their interference was not needed, and they walked away with their hotdogs.

"Shit, I think it does," Joel responded.

"Yay!" She hugged Chad again, told him to get back down before Courtney ripped him a new asshole, and sat down next to Joel to give him a side hug. "I promise not to be such a raging bitch next time one of your ex–boyfriends walks up to you."

"Thanks," Joel said, giving her a side smile.

"Unless you want me to," she said.

"Thanks," he repeated.

< < <   > > >

September 13, 2002

Princess Diarrhea,

Do you ever have days where life takes so many twists and turns that you have to keep pinching yourself to make sure you're awake and not dreaming? Jesus. Sorry. Sometimes I take for granted that you aren't a real live person I am venting to. Shit. Sometimes I wish you were.

Anyway, this morning started out with awkwardness by way of being named a Princess in the Queen's court and in the running for Homecoming Queen, which I thought was hilarious, Joel thought was offensive, and Courtney being Courtney made it the best situation ever. Instead of revealing everything that happened, what with fights and makeups and strange new alliances, the day ended better than expected. I had no idea, based off what transpired before school, that all my people would be at peace with one another by the time our game against Chancellor—WHICH WE WON!—was over. It should feel weird that Nikki and Joel are cool with each other now, but it doesn't. I don't know how to explain it, but it feels right. Natural. Like, we had to swim through all the shit to get to this place right here and now, even though the shit was neck deep and filled with unprocessed corn.

I've got a feeling it will be smooth sailing from here on out. Hopefully life doesn't insist on throwing me any more curve balls for a while. Huh, I wanted to add another cliché to utilize the rule of three, but can't think of one more right now. Oh well.

< < <   > > >

Chad closed out his diary file and headed downstairs to find his mother crying, the phone in her hand. Nothing good could come out of this. Still, he had to know.

"What's wrong, Mom?" he asked, slowing his pace on the last few steps.

She wiped her face, some of which was now on her hand. "You might want to call Joel."

"Why? What happened?" Chad sounded genuinely worried.

And alarmed.

"Call him," she pleaded.

"He's supposed to be on his way here. Mom, you're scaring me. Tell me," he said, gathering up the courage to take those last few steps to flat ground.

Ms. Walker looked like she was trying to talk, but words failed to come out. Chad walked over to give her a hug, still unaware of what was making her so upset. As they hugged, the phone rang, making them both jump. Chad grabbed it out of her hand.

"Hey, Joel. What's going on? My mom can't stop crying," he said into the handset.

"It's my dad." Joel's voice sounded like he had just finished crying. Again. Chad was well aware of that sound after what happened at the game.

"Oh my gawd, is he okay?" Chad asked, hoping for an affirmative but bracing himself for the worst.

"He's fine. His job, however… he… we're probably going to have to move to Wenatchee if he wants to keep it," Joel told him.

"Wait, you just moved here and now you might have to move again?" he asked.

"Yes."

"I don't understand. Why?"

"Low man on the totem pole." *Oh my gawd, I really just said that as an American Indian?*

"I don't accept that. No." Chad kept shaking his head.

Joel chuckled nervously. "I don't think he has a choice. He can't afford not to work. Not with all the benefits he gets. Not with the amount of time he's already put in."

Chad tried not to cry. He failed.

"Stop. This isn't a for sure thing. My dad just wanted your mom to know," Joel said.

"It's going to happen. The universe has been conspiring against me since the day I was born," Chad said, unable to stop the tears from rolling down his face which his mother kept trying to wipe but he kept shooing her away because her hands were smothered in makeup and her own tears.

"It's not." Joel's voice held confidence.

"It is. And tell your dad that was an asshole maneuver telling my mom over the phone," he said, staring at his mother who gave a half–smile and a look that said, "My Hero!".

"Chad says you're an asshole, Dad! There. Done. He's crying now. Again. Jesus, I've never seen him cry so much. Shit," Joel said. "Anything else?"

"Yes. Come over," Chad demanded.

Joel hesitated. "I don't know. My dad is a complete mess right now. He hasn't been this way since Mom left."

For a second, Chad felt guilty. For a second. "Tell him to pussy up and get his ass over here, too."

"Pussy up? Don't you mean grow some balls?" Joel asked.

"Balls are weak and sensitive. Pussies take a pounding and can keep on going. Pussy," Chad said before adding in a softer tone, "I think. I mean, I don't know firsthand, but I figure if they can push out baby humans and women can still smile at them after, and balls make us guys crumble into piles of goo with a tiny little punch, they've got to be stronger."

"Logical deduction. Pussy up, Dad! We're leaving!" Joel said. "See you in a few minutes."

"I'll be waiting," Chad said, clicking the phone off.

Ms. Walker stood in the kitchen considering drinking herself into a stupor. Instead she did the unthinkable and poured her boxed wine down the drain. Chad didn't know whether to stop her or let her continue with her mission. Once the box had emptied, he decided it was safe to intervene.

"Why'd you do that?" Chad asked, putting his hand on her shoulder.

"I don't need it. At least for a while," she told him, trying to put on a smile but failing miserably.

Squeakers indicated his own disappointment by biting Chad's ankle.

"Goddammit, Squeaks! What the hell?" he cried, grabbing the bite site.

His "MERRORAAHROOOOWW!" that followed could only mean one thing: suppertime was hours ago.

Hours to a cat is a lifetime.

Normally Squeakers just squeaked, hence his name. But deprive the feline of food and his attitude changes completely, along with his voice. The same holds true when the litter box needed to be cleaned out.

Wincing from the throbbing pain emanating from the connection between his lower leg and foot, Chad reached into the cupboard, grabbed a can of Friskies, and dropped it in a dish, letting some splatter onto the floor around it. "There you go, asshole." He couldn't help but notice the cat's kibble dish was practically full, save for a quarter–sized bare spot in the center.

"Don't yell at the cat for wanting something he doesn't have," his mother told him when Chad tossed the can into the sink, deciding he'd put it in the recycling later.

He never did.

"He's only doing it because he knows I'll give in," Chad said, folding his arms across his chest, hating himself for being such a pushover.

"That doesn't mean you have to give in," she said, inching her way closer along the counter.

"Yes it does. I don't know how much time I've got left with him," he said, still pouting.

"Are we talking about the cat, or Joel now?" she asked.

"Yes," he said.

She paused. "So you let Joel push you around?"

"No, not like that, I just, I don't know, can't stop letting him, shit, I'm not sure what the right thing is, making his needs more important than mine?" Chad told her.

"Because you love him?" she asked, shoulders now touching.

Yes! I love him! I LOVE HIM!!! "I don't know, maybe."

"And he knows that, right?"

"No. Maybe. Shit. What's the point now? He's moving to Wenatchee and I'll never see him again so why bother continuing this stupid affair? I knew telling Nikki would ruin everything." Chad's logic failed as his emotions were allowed to filter into the equation and add letters and numbers and make it all confusing like Algebra.

His mother was used to the dramatic flair her son had when things didn't quite go his way, but nonetheless, didn't patronize him for expressing his emotions. "You don't know he's moving."

"Yes I do. I pissed off The Powers That Be somewhere along the line and they pay me back by making my life a poop parade." His arms still across his chest, lips still in a pout formation.

Ms. Walker used every fiber of her being to resist laughing at his last statement that she risked losing an eye or two from holding it in. She lost her battle.

"Bwahahahahaha!"

"What's so funny?" Chad asked.

"Poop… parade!" she sputtered between laughs.

"Shut up," he said.

Her laughter continued until she thought she'd pass out. Chad kept pouting, despite wanting desperately to laugh with her. However, his anger at the situation life continued throwing at him didn't let him.

The doorbell rang. The cat ran away to hide. Chad answered the door to find a blubbering wet mess formerly known as Jeff Talzan next to Joel holding him up with one hand, a duffle bag in the other.

"Hey, so, I think he may have had a bit too much to drink tonight before I got home, and we all know how well us Indians handle firewater," Joel said as he carried his father to the sofa before letting him collapse into the cushions.

"Great, and my mom just dumped the last of her wine down the sink to keep herself from doing the same," Chad said, giving his mom the stink eye.

All Mr. Talzan could say, with saliva dribbling out of his mouth and tears racing out of his eyeballs, was, "I'm sorry!" over and over to the point that Ms. Walker threatened to slap him if he didn't stop. He didn't.

SLAP!

He grabbed his cheek.

"That's for telling me you might have to leave in a few days!" Ms. Walker said loudly.

SLAP!

"And that's for telling me over the phone!"

He grabbed his other cheek.

Chad and Joel stared.

"I'm sorry, Amanda, I couldn't drive but I had to tell you," he said, still consoling his burning face.

"Oh, Jeff! I'm sorry!" she said, kissing him copiously despite the wet mess he'd made of himself, straddling him to the point her skirt slid above the panty line.

Turning to Joel, Chad said, "This is our cue to go to my room now before we are scarred for life."

"Agreed," Joel said, grabbing Chad's hand and leading the way.

When they got to his room, Chad found he just wanted to be around Joel, near him. No activity. No making out. No sex. Just close to him. All the thoughts he had about making him pay for giving him a boner before fourth period were so far away that he'd forgotten about them.

Joel, on the other hand, was frisky.

"So, what shall we do now?" he asked playfully, rubbing Chad's thighs while they sat on his bed.

"Honestly, I just want to be here with you. But at the same time, if you're moving, what's the point?" Chad asked, trying not to let his emotions get the better of him.

Joel stopped rubbing and let his hands rest around Chad's knees. "The point is we still aren't done. Even if I have to move, it doesn't mean we are done."

"Yes it does," Chad said coldly.

"Why?" Joel asked, starting to tremble from the very real possibility their relationship might be on the dissolving end of the spectrum.

Chad started crying as he said, "Because you'll move and find someone better and break up with me over the phone or through an email and then I'll be a complete hormonal mess like I am right now only worse because you won't be with me to keep it all together and sorry I'm being a clingy queer drama queen right now and dammit I should not have said that but too late now since Chad is a complete and utter asshole who only thinks of himself."

While Joel tried to comprehend everything Chad said, and also how he was able to say it all in one breath, his trembling stopped, replaced with the realization that he just might be right. "The same goes for you, Chad. Once I leave, Kevin might dump Nathan for a chance to be with you. I've seen the way he looks at you."

"Kevin? I don't think so," Chad laughed through muffled tears. "He is so not my type."

"Not your type!" Joel shouted, throwing his hands up in the air. "The guy is a frickin' stud!"

"He's not you," Chad said quietly. "You are my type. Only you. I can't imagine anyone else filling that void."

Joel's leg started twitching a bit as he said, "I get it. I mean, I've been with other guys, but there was an emptiness I can't explain with them. I don't have that with you. I think it's because I love you."

There were those words again. The words Chad couldn't say. The words he so desperately wanted to say back because he felt it with everything that made him who he was, but wouldn't allow himself to say them out loud for fear he'd only get hurt in the process. But isn't that the risk you have to take, especially when you know you've found your one true love?

"Don't say that," Chad said, cutting off his emotions with the surgical knife of logic.

"That I love you?" Joel asked. "Because I do. I love you, Chad Walker."

"Stop." Chad's voice ice.

"No." Joel's voice fire.

"Please. I've had enough hurt in my life." Chad's voice melting.

"I'm not going to let you end us because you're afraid. Let go of whatever fear you have." Joel's fire dying down.

"I can't promise you'll like what you see when I let go of my guard." Chad's ice water.

"Trust me when I say that I want to know you. All of you." Joel reached over Chad's ears, pulling his head towards his own, careful not to press any of the sensitive buttons or switches on the hearing aids.

Chad's water fell into a puddle as the tears started, letting himself be held by Joel as he let it all out. No words, just pure emotion.

Joel didn't protest.

<   <   <   >   >   >

September 14, 2002

Dear Princess Diarrhea,

Joel might be moving in a few days. I fucking hate every fucking deity that ever fucking existed in the entire fucking history of this goddamned fucking universe.

<   <   <   >   >   >

"You don't mean that," Joel said, looking over Chad's shoulder.

"Yes I do," Chad said, debating over whether to keep writing or leave it.

Joel's hands rested on Chad's shoulder.

Chad saved the file and closed it.

"So, when are you going to tell me the story of Princess Diarrhea?" Joel asked, rubbing Chad's shoulders.

"It's dumb." Chad stared at the blank monitor.

"It's intriguing." Joel continued rubbing.

"It's more intriguing than knowing the story," Chad said, closing his eyes and letting his body sway with the massage.

Joel kissed the top of Chad's messy bedhead. "Somehow I doubt that."

"Fine," Chad said, turning around to face Joel. "So I was at the store buying a Matchbox Twenty CD a while ago, and this little girl over in the video section started screaming. I mean full on squeals of unadulterated joy. And when she finally regained the ability to act like a regular person again, she shouted loudly, 'Look, Mama! The Princess Diarrhea! I want it!' and her doting mother didn't even bother correcting her. Apparently that's just what they called *The Princess Diaries* in their house or something."

"That's hilarious," Joel said with a snicker afterwards.

"It is. So when I started keeping a diary, the name stuck out. The End," Chad told him.

Joel knelt down. "So, this diary thing is a fairly new part of your life?"

Chad watched as Joel's hands crept closer to his crotch. "Yes."

"And do you tell it everything?" Joel asked.

"More than I should," Chad said as Joel's hands started tugging at the waistband of the gym shorts he wore.

"Breakfast is ready!" Ms. Walker shouted from the bottom of the stairs.

"Damn," Joel said, snapping Chad's waistband as he let go, standing up.

Chad remained seated, the bulge quite obvious beneath his shorts. "I'll be down in a minute. You should go. Now."

Joel smiled. "If you insist." He pulled down his shorts, grabbed his ass cheeks, and jiggled them before walking away, pulling the shorts back up as he did.

"Ass," Chad said, thinking of every possible horrible thing he could to make his erection collapse.

Breakfast was bacon, eggs, and hominy. Lunch was tuna fish sandwiches and spinach salad. Both meals made Chad realize that he could picture family meals together forever with his mom and boyfriend and boyfriend's dad. Dinner, however, was reserved for his own father and other family, something he still couldn't picture building an entirely different relationship with.

"It's not too late to back out," Chad told Joel as they changed into less casual clothes in Chad's room.

"I wouldn't miss this for the world," Joel said, kissing Chad before adding, "I mean, you get to find out a little more about your dad and brother and sisters and stepmom. Cherish this opportunity."

Chad smiled, straightening out his collar down as Joel popped his polo shirt collar up like a preppy frat–boy. "You're right. I'm just really really really really really nervous."

"It'll be okay. I'll be right next to you the entire time," Joel reassured him.

"Thanks," Chad said. "Shall we?"

"Ready."

They walked down the stairs, said goodbye to their parents who were busy making dinner for two in the orange kitchen, unable to keep their hands off each other which made Chad hope to Sweet Lawd Geezus that they weren't going to have sex in the kitchen after they left the house, and continued walking a couple houses down to the Hollins residence where a knock at the door had barely been tapped out before it opened.

"Come in, Chad!" Brendon squealed, smiling brightly as he noticed Joel had his polo shirt collar turned upward like he did while his dogs, Rex and Deschutes, wiggled and twirled to greet them as well. "Hi, Joel!"

"Hey, Brendon," Chad said, smiling. "Yes, hi, guys," he told the Boxer–Boston Terrier–Pit Bull mutts as they showed him their bones. It should have been enough to calm him down, but his nervousness gained a few extra notches as he stepped foot inside the house he'd been in countless times before as a friend, but now he was suddenly family.

"Hi, kid I don't know," Joel said, following behind Chad, unsure if the dogs were going to eat him or not. Fortunately they only sniffed his legs and ran off.

"Hello guy I set my best friend up with despite knowing you were gay," Sheree said as her and Kayla walked towards them from the dining area that was already set with place settings.

"Hello guy I almost killed freshman year at that basketball game," Kayla said with an eerie smile Chad never quite thought he'd get used to.

Chad's eyes widened with fear.

"Ooh, maybe you shouldn't come on so strong, Kayla," Brendon said, cocking an eyebrow as he let Rex and Deschutes outside from the dining room's French doors.

"Sorry. I can't help but go straight for the shock value," Kayla said, shrugging. Her apology sounded anything but. "But to be honest, I wasn't entirely myself that day."

Brendon and Sheree laughed. Apparently having a psychopath killer for a sister was just a matter of fact for the Hollins family. His family. Mr. and Mrs. Hollins stepped out of the kitchen for a minute to greet them, told them dinner would be ready in about fifteen minutes, and asked if anyone wanted something to drink. Everyone declined the offer.

"Okay, so, here it is," Kayla started as the parents went back to the kitchen to finish. "I've been banned from bringing up my sordid past during dinner, so I'll go ahead and give you the Reader's Digest Condensed Version."

"Um, okay?" Chad said apprehensively as he sat down in the living room that was practically the same as his own. "Do you have to?"

"Yes." Kayla was dead serious.

"Can't wait," Joel said, waiting with salacious fervor as he grabbed Chad's hand and made Brendon make puppy dog eyes and a goofy smile and hope that someday soon he'd have moments like that with a boyfriend all his own.

They listened without interruption.

"Well, here goes. So back in 1999 after the family moved here, my restless spirit got a little, well, restless. When we lived at the old house in West Seattle, I didn't mind just hanging out and pretending to be part of a family that ignored me. But here, in this house, there was a power I didn't quite understand until I was singing to myself and realized that Sheree and Brendon could hear me, which made me realize I still had my witch powers even as a ghost. Then I used a spell to take over Sheree and made her evil for a while when my bad half stayed behind while my good half went to heaven with her dead boyfriend. After bargaining for a second chance not only for me but to save my sister, I was able to return from the dead, but, you know, there's always a price to pay and this time it was being pregnant. So, back up a few decades now, when our great–great–great–grandma Jessica lived and died here, and despite the house having been cleansed by our aunts and grandma…" Kayla paused. "…her spirit never quite left either. Hence, one of the twin babies I had right before sophomore year that… died." She looked at Sheree and added while squeezing her hand, "The other I gave to our uncles to raise. And after that, I've been able to be a normal, happy, gay teenage girl ever since!"

"Wow. I thought you got knocked up somewhere between juvie and boarding school?" Chad said, taking it all in.

"No juvie. No boarding school. Just death." Her voice not as scary as Chad once thought.

"And all the people who died?" Joel asked, wondering why she left those parts out except for the baby.

Kayla paused, took in a deep breath, and said, "I... I... I regret every single one of them. Even the ones that deserved it." She looked at Sheree who barely smiled back. "But the thing I regret the most is that I was forced to live with their souls trapped inside mine until the day I died."

"Died? Again? I don't get it," Chad said. "Can you explain it to me like I'm blond because I am."

"Oh my gawd, Chad! I say that to her all the time!" Sheree bounced off her seat.

Noticing that Kayla was struggling and on the verge of tears, Brendon intervened. "She swallowed the souls of the people she killed in order to regain human form. Basically she was like a dozen people in one body, but none of them knew they were trapped inside her. I made sure of that." He squeezed her free hand. She smiled her thanks. "So then she died during childbirth and they all went their merry way to the afterlife as her body spit them out. Don't worry, obviously she was resuscitated or she wouldn't be here! Basically, she swallowed before she spit," he said, clueless about his innuendos, or at least pretending as much.

"And speaking of swallowing," Mr. Hollins said seductively, making Sheree cringe since she knew he was making a sexual reference while pretending it wasn't. "Dinner's ready."

Sheree had made certain to get to the table first to claim her usual seat that she always sat in because she was a stickler for routines. The one time Brendon sat in her seat a year of hell followed. She'd be damned if that ever happened again. After holding her chair, she directed Chad and Joel where to sit.

"This smells amazing!" Joel said as he stared at the large platter of Fettuccine Alfredo dotted with giant pink prawns and a sprinkling of fresh parsley.

"Thanks! It's about the only thing I can't screw up from scratch!" Mrs. Hollins said with a smile before taking a large swig of red wine practically poured to the brim of her glass. Was. It was now half empty.

"I made the bread and broccoli, and Brendon made dessert," Mr. Hollins said, taking a sip of the regular sized serving of red wine in his glass during the rare occasion he preferred it over his usual beer.

"Ooooh, what's for dessert?" Joel asked, his enthusiasm far more than Chad could ever conjure up despite him being a cheerleader.

Obviously he's not nervous at all. Why are you, Chad? Chad asked himself, trying to fake a smile or feign interest, but his anxiety stressed him out to no end.

"It's like the most decadent chocolate creation ever!" Brendon said excitedly before leaning across the table to whisper to Joel, "Hopefully it doesn't taste like shit."

"Brendon!" Mrs. Hollins yelled. "Watch your language!"

"What? I'm twelve! I'm not the uncoordinated slob child you once knew anymore. I'm now a fabulously fashionable young fag!" His forced gayness obvious to even the most uneducated person.

Sheree rolled her eyes. Mr. Hollins giggled. Kayla side hugged him. Chad wondered how his baby brother was dealing with his sexuality better than he ever could dream of. Joel waited with anticipation at Mrs. Hollins's response.

"Fine," she said.

"Yay! Fuck fuck fuck fuck fuck!" he said loudly. "Huh, I thought it'd feel better to cuss openly. It doesn't." He looked genuinely disappointed.

"All right, shall we eat now?" Mr. Hollins asked, not waiting for a response as he piled on a large helping of the noodle dish smothered in a sauce of heavy cream and butter and Parmesan cheese.

Mrs. Hollins plated up next, passing it down to Chad and all the way back around to Sheree who put the remaining contents onto her plate, spying who took most of the prawns and glaring at Brendon for being the culprit. She reached over with her fork to grab a couple off his plate. Brendon took it all in stride.

"This is seriously one of the best things I've ever put in my mouth, Mrs. Hollins," Joel said before adding, "And that bread is so good. Garlic?"

"Yep," Mr. Hollins affirmed after swallowing a rather large bite he'd just shoved into his mouth.

Chad sat there, quietly, as the Hollins family and his boyfriend chatted away during dinner. It wasn't that he didn't want to engage in the conversations, he just didn't know his place with this particular dynamic.

Mr. Hollins forced him in with, "Chad, stop being quiet. You're freaking me out."

"Sorry, I, uh, I don't really know how to do this," Chad said back.

"Eat? Talk? What?" Mr. Hollins asked. Even with a questionable look on his face, he was incredibly handsome.

"Yes?" he said.

"Pretend we are in the cafeteria where you are a Chatty Cathy," Sheree told him.

"But there are parental units," Chad said through clenched teeth, nodding his head to the left where Mr. and Mrs. Hollins sat. "And you know what I say during my Chatty Cathiness."

"Chad, what the hell are you talking about?" Mrs. Hollins asked, slamming her wine glass onto the table, shocking everyone that it didn't shatter. "I've known your mother for a very long time, and I know that you two are way more alike than you'd ever admit, and I know what she says when we are at work where there is a possibility of middle school kids overhearing her and trust me, she doesn't give a flying fuck."

"Fine. You asked for it. Mrs. Hollins, your Alfredo is second only to Joel's dick as far as things I've absolutely loved putting in my mouth," Chad told her, shoving another forkful into his oral portal.

Mr. Hollins spat out his food as he busted up into uproarious laughter, splattering the table in creamy white sprays. Mrs. Hollins gasped with faux shock, incredibly thankful she did not take a drink of her red wine before he answered. Sheree and Kayla both looked disgusted for different reasons. Brendon merely asked, "Why would you put Joel's penis in your mouth?"

Mr. Hollins told him, "One day, hopefully many many MANY years from now, you will understand."

Brendon shrugged, dipped his garlic bread in the sauce leftover on his plate, said, "Okay," and nibbled the coated edge before his eyes widened as realization smacked him in the face like a bitch slap. "Oh my gawd, that's what a blowjob is, isn't it?"

"That tasty, huh?" Joel joked, twirling the last bite onto his fork.

"You bet." Chad had already finished eating.

Chad finally felt he knew his place in this dynamic. He simply had to be himself.

<   <   <   >   >   >

Sunday morning, Chad and Joel were woken up with a quick series of knocks on the bedroom door, an "I'm not looking! Phone's for you!" from his mother as she tossed the cordless at them, surprisingly landing next to Chad's hand, the unmistakable voice of Courtney blaring through the receiver. Chad put one of his hearing aids into his ear—overkill to say the least—turned it on, and put the phone up to it to find she wasn't waiting for anyone to listen. That's so Courtney.

"Wait, Court, slow down. What?" Chad said, confusion all over his face while the covers slid off his bare chest as he sat up.

Joel's eyes directed towards the top of Chad's ass crack, and he playfully started rubbing his fingers gently over it. Chad didn't protest, either because he didn't notice, didn't care, or because he didn't understand a single thing coming out of Courtney's mouth.

"Bitch! You best be shuttin' yo' trap fo' a second. Da fuck you talkin' 'bout?" Chad said, his inner sassy black woman coming out.

"I. Said. We. Need. To. Talk. A. Bout. Home. Com. Ing. Bitch," Courtney said slowly but loudly.

"I'm not competing with you!" Chad told her.

"Fool?! I'm talkin' wardrobe! Let's go shoppin'! Now! Shit! Stores ain't open yet cuz it's Sunday! At eleven!" Courtney's enthusiasm far too much for the early hour.

"Okay?" Chad said, looking at Joel who was still looking at Chad's ass, making his fingers disappear.

"I'll call Nikki and Sheree and Kayla and Jennifer and we can all go together! Won't that be fun?" Courtney said.

"Okay?!" Chad said, eyes widening as he suddenly noticied where Joel's fingers were.

"Shiiiiiiiiiiiit! Two those yo' exes and two yo' sisters," Courtney said, stating the obvious.

"And you my soul sistah!" Chad said back.

"Ha HA! Damn right! Meet at the mall or you pickin' me up?" Courtney asked, although she really didn't expect him to pick option one.

" 'Course I'm pickin' you up, gurrrl!" Chad said, trying not to let what Joel was doing distract him, but it was increasingly difficult not to.

"And Nik?" she asked.

"Duh!" he said, eyes rolling back in ecstasy as a couple extra digits entered.

"Now what'm I gonna do for the next four hours?" Courtney asked, mostly to herself.

"I don't give a shit," Chad said, clicking off the phone and tossing it aside. "Fuck me."

"As you wish."

< < < > > >

September 15, 2002

Dear Princess Diarrhea,

I can't believe I'm about to say this, but my penis is worn out. Joel has been extra horny since finding out he might have to move away to Wenatchee, and my dick has been paying the price. Holy shit. I mean, I'm a healthy seventeen–year–old boy and all, and I've masturbated, uh, I think my record is like eight times in a day? But sex is a whole other matter! Sex is a workout. Scratch that, sex is work. Fun work, yes, but not something I want to do all the time. Did I really just admit that? I guess being a porn star is out of the question then, right?

On top of the sexual escapades of Joel and Chad, I have to go shopping with my friends for Homecoming. Honestly I think Courtney is just making an excuse to not be out of the loop in anyone's life since all those lives seem to involve me in one way or another. Promise, no ego about that. Who knows, maybe a shopping excursion is just what we need?

Joel walked out of the bathroom, a towel around his waist. He closed the office door behind him and let the towel fall to the floor as Chad turned around. "Oh no, my towel fell off," he said like a horrible actor might say the lines he read only moments before, revealing a semi–hard–on.

"You can't be serious?" Chad asked, his body letting out a universal sigh.

Joel noticed Chad's body language and lied. "Not really. Just wanted to surprise you." He picked the towel back up and wrapped it around his waist again.

Despite knowing he was not telling the truth, Chad let him believe he wasn't aware when he said, "Whew! Because this," he pointed towards his penis, "is out of commission for a while."

"Yeah, mine too," Joel lied again, smiling.

Chad smiled back, saved and closed his diary file, and said, "I should take a shower and get ready to go."

"Yeah, I should get dressed." The disappointment in his voice undeniable.

Chad looked out the window. "Ugh, it's raining."

Joel let the towel slip off again and made his penis swirl in a circle like a helicopter as he danced and sang, "It's rainin' men! Hallelujah, it's rainin' men!"

Laughing, Chad got up off the chair, kissed Joel, and said, "You're adorable, you know that, right?"

"I've been told," he said, shrugging. "But when it comes from you, I know you mean it." He kissed Chad back.

Tell him! Now! Tell him 'I LOVE YOU!' Do it! Chad yelled inside his head.

He didn't.

Joel drove silently with Chad next to him in the passenger seat. The ride to the mall was full of Nikki exclaiming about how excited she was about her dad and ChiChi coming to town in a few days, and Courtney exclaiming abut how she was going to obliterate the competition by being the most fabulous Homecoming Queen ever. She was used to winning and getting her way. Of course, her massive extracurricular schedule, volunteer work, and ultra social life she led made her a shoe in for most school related awards or contests, and despite her outward bitchiness, Courtney deserved to be Homecoming Queen. However, even with this being her fourth nomination, chances of her winning were slim. Chances of another blond, blue–eyed Aryan princess winning again were a safe bet. Still, she wasn't one to let history dictate her future.

"Maybe I should straighten my hair?" Courtney said, patting her Afro.

Her glossy red lipstick reminded Chad of fresh cherries as he looked at her over his shoulders before he said, "Gurrrl! No you di'n't! Ain't no way you makin' yo' hair straight. Mm mmm. No ma'am. Not gonna happen on my watch!"

"Ha! I just teasin'!" Courtney told him before she broke out into Dionne Warwick's "That's What Friends Are For" (not the shitty Rod Stewart version from a few years earlier.) She sang the entire song. Even after arriving at the Ravenwood Factory Outlet slash Shopping Mall. Even after they got out of the car. Even as they walked in the pouring rain to the first of many stores they'd end up going to. Even as she was almost finished with her acapella cover, and her girlfriend, Kayla walked up and wrapped her arms around her. Once she was done, she kissed Kayla on the mouth. "Okay, bitches. We gotta mission."

"I don't. I'm just here for the food," Brendon piped up, peeking out from behind Sheree and Jennifer.

"Tagalong?" Chad asked, smiling at his half–brother.

"Nope. I asked if he wanted to come with us and Mom and Dad were excited about having the house to themselves which makes me think they're probably having sex right now and that makes me want to vomit and the only thing that can cure me of that is spending an obscene amount of their hard earned cash on clothes I don't really need," Sheree said, displaying the full range of emotions her words expressed.

"Awesome! He's with us," Chad said, pulling Brendon towards Joel and himself.

"Yay! Bonding time!" Brendon squealed.

Courtney looked around to figure out what shop they should check out first, and Chad let out a sigh of relief when it was a women's clothing store that would obvously have absolutely nothing for the boys. "We goin' here, girls."

"We goin' elsewhere," Chad told them.

"What kinda fool you take me for?" Courtney asked, sticking out her lips, raising an eyebrow, her face almost disappearing inside her fabulous 'fro. "What the point of havin' a gay best friend who ain't gonna shop with you?"

"I'm not that gay," Chad, Joel, and Brendon said in unison.

"Fine. But no purchases 'til we all have our say. Browsin' time only, got it?"

Her tone sounded more demanding than usual. The hurt in her eyes only visible for a second that let Chad in on the fact that she didn't really want to shop, but actually wanted to spend time with him outside of yelling cheers. Great, now he had guilt. Chad half–smiled as the girls all went to some trendy overpriced dress store.

"Dammit, Chad, why do you gotta be such an asshole?" Chad said aloud without realizing the words were actually coming out of his mouth until it was too late.

"Why does Chad talk to himself in the third person?" Brendon asked inquisitively, tilting his head slightly to the right like one of his dogs.

Chad's head slumped. "Because I know that Courtney wanted to hang out, and I really don't want to sit there in that store and say over and over, 'Oh my gawd, yes! That's the one!' while she says that it is shit and tries on yet another dress that is basically a carbon copy of all the others."

"I don't want to do that either," Joel said, grabbing Chad's hand. "I just want to spend time with you."

Chad smiled.

Brendon looked like he was about to lose his shit.

"Why are you guys so stinkin' adorable?" Brendon asked, not really expecting an answer.

Poor kid, Chad thought, looking at the little brother he never thought he'd have. *Poor me. How much longer will I have this?* His smile faded.

Joel put his arm around Brendon and asked, "So, since you seem to be the most fashionable queer guy we know, where should we look for fancy clothes to wear to a school dance? Or should we just be about as unoriginal as every straight guy and go straight for the tux rental shop?"

Brendon didn't mind the hand around his shoulder, but couldn't keep up appearances any longer. "Honestly, I have no idea. It's exhausting being this, er, on all the time. I can't fight the fact that I'm a slob who can barely dress himself, no matter how much I try to alter my wardrobe."

"So you're not a fancy gay?" Chad asked, noticing that his outfit looked far more coordinated than anything he owned or would probably ever own.

"No," Brendon told them. "Honestly, my dad helped pick out my clothes today."

"Dad has good taste," Chad said.

"I keep forgetting you're my brother! That's so weird still," Brendon said.

"Yeah, I know how that feels. I don't know if it'll ever go away," Chad told Brendon, squeezing Joel's hand, which garnered a few looks from an elderly couple that at first he thought was judgment, but then he saw them both reach for each other's hand and lean in closer to one another as they continued to walk away hand–in–hand.

Joel rolled his eyes. "Crap, and here I was thinking that I'd finally know someone with a sense of style who could tell me that wearing basketball shorts every single day is a fashion faux pas I need to eradicate from my life. Thanks for ruining that for me, dickwad."

Chad gasped and Brendon laughed.

"I really like you, Joel! You tell it like it is… like Courtney! Isn't she amazing? I hope to be her someday. Well, not actually her because I like being a boy, but, you know, someone who doesn't take anything from anyone and just let's herself be herself." Brendon had the biggest smile over his face before it turned to disgust. "Yeah, I hate pretending to be something I'm not. Like fabulous. Ugh."

"Don't be. You shouldn't change yourself for anyone. Be you," Joel told him, rustling his perfectly coifed hair.

Brendon didn't mind one bit, and even added to the mess by taking both his hands and brushing through until it looked almost as out of place as when he wakes up in the morning. "Thanks. Still, being me has gotten me nowhere in the dating department."

Chad stared at what could be a miniature version of the boy's father—their father—with a little baby fat that'd go away in the next year or so, and wondered why no boy had snatched him up yet. Then the fact the boy was only twelve entered into the equation, and the further fact that Ravenwood's a small town that, yes, had a disproportionate amount of homosexuals as compared to other small towns, it was still small and thus diminished the pool of acceptable slash available candidates. It was then that he realized just how lucky his chance meeting with Joel that created an instant friendship that quickly turned into a romantic relationship really was. He kissed Joel on the lips. "I love you."

Brendon melted like ice cream on a hot summer day.

Joel kissed Chad back. "I love you, too."

Suddenly Chad realized what he'd done. He'd said it. The words. The three little words he'd wanted to say since the moment he laid eyes on the dark and mysterious stranger in Algebra class two short weeks ago. "Holy shit, I really said that, didn't I?"

"Yes." Joel was all smiles.

< < < > > >

September 15, 2002

Dear Princess Diarrhea,

I did it. I finally told Joel that I love him. It wasn't romantic or forced or planned, it just happened. In a mall. Well, technically an outlet shopping center's covered corridor that we call the mall because that seems better than That Place Where Big Chains Sell Their Slightly Broken And / Or Discontinued Items At Deep Discounts. I can't believe I said it. Still. Shit. I'm waiting to wake up and find out that I was still chickenshit and actually said something along the lines of, "I love pancakes."

No, it was real.

Now I'm going to figure out if the power of prayer really works, because Joel can't move away or I will fall apart. I wonder if Meghan will think it weird to ask Jesus to work His mojo so I can keep my boyfriend from having to move to Wenatchee?

Oh, and we also got our coordinated costumes for the dance. I swear to Baby Jesus, Courtney couldn't have picked a more mundane theme for the dance this year. "America: United We Stand." I mean, I get how awful last year was. But still, she usually comes up with more original themes for the dances. Did I forget to mention that she is also head of the dance committee on top of the bazillion other clubs she belongs to? She's like an extracurricular extraordinaire. No, she IS The

Extracurricular Extraordinaire. Yeah, so everything's all red, white and blue and screams patriotism. I'm just thankful what Joel and I are allowed to wear aren't as flaming as the outfits the girls all chose. I mean, I'm proud to be an American and all, but there is no way in hell you'd catch me wearing formalwear that makes me look like our flag. That's ridiculous. Like Joel maybe moving. Shit, he might not even be here this Saturday! If after praying for him to stay during prayer circle tomorrow doesn't keep him in my life, I'm never speaking to God again. Ever. Fuck him/her/whatever.

Addendum: I don't mean that.

Post Addendum: At least, I don't think I do.

<   <   <   >   >   >

When Chad walked into his bedroom after finishing his diary entry, he saddend at the sight of not finding Joel lying on his bed, waiting for him with a smile. Everything else was optional. Mr. Talzan had decided they should go back to their apartment for the night because he needed to work early in the morning, and they were out of clean clothes, and Joel wasn't getting his homework done with the distractions. Ms. Walker begged and pleaded for them to stay. She knew that her pleas were unreasonable and bordering on sadistic, but didn't care. She didn't want them to go, either of them. And she also wanted to tell Mr. Talzan something, but couldn't conjure up the courage to do so until after he left because that is how courage works. It was something important one simply doesn't say over the phone like telling your romantic partner you might be moving across the state. Only assholes do that.

So instead of finding Joel on his bed, he found Squeakers lying on the pillow Joel used every time he slept over. Even the cat seemed to be asking where the black haired boy was.

Deciding to take a chance that his soulful feline might have the answers he needed to give his life direction, Chad rested on his stomach and stared at Squeakers, looking into his eyes.

"You know what you have to do, my young padiwan. Now go, Grasshopper. Be with him."

Chad, being strange and not all there half the time, and currently in a very fragile place with the real possibility of

Joel leaving his life forever (or at least in the teenage sense), really thought that Squeakers spoke, and asked back, "Can you really talk?"

With this, Squeakers said, "No dumbass. I'm just your conscience, not your cat. You really are crazy aren't you?"

"It's been suggested," Chad answered his self.

Chad sighed. For a moment, he really hoped that something, anything, would give him insight on what to do if the Talzans moved. He'd lose his love. His mother would lose her love. Then they'd be loveless together, mother and son, and he knew how horribly cliché their lives would be after that and he'd be *that* gay son who never moved out of his mother's house and lived with her, alone, until the day he died. Okay, so maybe his imagination might be bordering on the dramatic lately.

He turned over onto his back, head on his pillow. Squeakers crept closer and started licking Chad's hair, bathing one section at a time as he'd done since the day they found him scared and starving as a kitten thirteen years ago on the side of a road and brought him home and fed him and loved him and gave him a name.

"What am I going to do?" Chad asked out loud, noticing a couple cracks in the ceiling and lightly petting his feline companion as said companion continued grooming his boy.

< < <   > > >

Chad found Joel at his locker the next morning. Well, actually, Chad waited by Joel's locker the next morning like a stalker. Locker stalker. "Hey, sexy."

"Hey sexy," Joel said back, his dimpled grin making Chad crumble like three–day–old cake left out on the counter, uncovered.

They kissed.

Joel undid his locker combination, put a book in from his bag and grabbed the books he'd need for the first part of the day as Chad rubbed his hands all over him. "What's gotten into you, Chad?" he asked, zipping his backpack.

"I really missed you last night. I think I've gotten spoiled having you home all the time," Chad told him, still rubbing, forehead on Joel's shoulder.

"Your home," Joel said before realizing how dickish that sounded and adding, "But I totally agree. I missed you last night. And this morning."

Chad smiled and wondered if he meant for sex or simply being together. Then he realized he didn't care what the answer was, because Joel missed him as well. And with that, Chad started crying.

"Don't cry, Chad," Joel said quietly, hoping he'd hear him, putting his hand on the back of Chad's head.

"Sorry," Chad said through sniffles. "I really don't want you to go."

Rubbing his fingers through Chad's hair on the back of his head, deflecting the glares and curious eyes passing them, Joel said, "I don't either. Stop crying."

"Okay," Chad said, despite the fact that he didn't stop, had no intentions of stopping, or care that he might be causing a scene.

"Or not," Joel said.

"Okay." Chad didn't even know why his emotions were getting the better of him all of a sudden. He decided his hormones were all out of whack, even though his time of the month had passed. Yesterday.

Just then, Nikki walked up with Courtney who was holding hands with Kayla who was standing next to Sheree and Jennifer. All five focused on the two boys, one of whom looked broken.

"The fuck?" Courtney asked in a way only she could do.

"I'm having a moment, girls. Leave me alone," Chad said, face still deeply inside Joel's chest.

"You need to kiss him, Joel," Jennifer told him, arms folded across her chest. "I know when he kissed me, it always made everything better. Even though they were fake kisses."

"Same here," Nikki said. "Big Hollywood reenactments most of the time, but still."

Feeling the mounting pressure, Joel waited for the rest of the gang to pressure him further, but they didn't. Deciding to take their advice, he lifted Chad's chin, and kissed him like he'd never kissed him before, full of want and tenderness and lust and passion and love.

When they were done, Chad looked up and smiled. "Thanks, I needed that."

Nikki turned to Jennifer and said, "He never kissed me like that."

"I think I came in my pants," Jennifer said, before adding, "Shit, is that why I keep falling for gay guys?"

They all laughed, but quickly scattered away as the bell rang signaling first period would be starting in five minutes. Only Nikki and Joel stayed behind with Chad.

"I'll see you in Algebra, Joel," Chad said, giving him another peck on the mouth.

"Until then," Joel said, letting his fingers linger in Chad's hand as long as they could while he walked away.

Giving each other a smile, Chad and Nikki walked to class. It took every fiber of her being not to hold his hand, mostly out of habit. Chad suddenly found himself having the same problem. Both of them were thankful they could still be friends… or at least pretend to be. Neither of them knew how long they could keep up appearances without having a real discussion.

By the time the mid–morning break rolled around, Chad found Meghan in the usual spot with a couple others, and gave her a big hug before saying, "I need a huge favor this morning."

"Anything for you, Chad," Meghan said, her open smile revealing the braces and rubber bands helping to straighten her out.

"Joel might have to move away and I want to pray that he doesn't," Chad told her.

She seemed a little confused, somewhat hurt, and also a hint of mischief in her voice as she asked, "You want me to ask Jesus if your gay boyfriend can stay in town so you can keep being homosexual lovers?"

Chad winced as he caught wind of a little Courtney in her tone, something he wasn't prepared for. "Yes?"

Meghan shrugged. "Okay. You want to take the lead on that with the circle? Somehow it would feel awkward if I make that request. I mean, I will totally reiterate it at the end, but as far as bringing it up, I am not sure. It would be weird."

"Yes?" Chad said, suddenly nervous.

Meghan put her hand on his shoulder and said, "Just breath. And just talk to Jesus like a friend, because He is."

"Thanks, Meg." He side–hugged her, making her cringe a little as his hand caught hold of her upper arm, but Chad didn't notice. "You're the best."

And he prayed.

And they prayed.

And she prayed.

And when all their praying was over, Chad felt a warm comfort come over him he wasn't expecting. It felt like a blanket wrapping him up at night, and a calm voice telling him everything was going to be all right.

"You feel that?" Meghan asked, seeing the look she'd recognize anywhere since she had experienced it so many times herself. "That is the power of God's love embracing you, Chad."

"Really?" Chad asked, also noticing that the sun was peeking through the morning clouds and bathing him in its rays through the nearly floor to ceiling hall windows that connected the 200 wing to the 400 wing.

"Yep. That is pretty amazing, huh?" she asked, radiating her own sunshine.

"It is," Chad said, as he spotted Joel walking up to him. "Hey, sexy."

Meghan turned around to find Joel, and knew that any more bonding time or witnessing about her Lord and Savior were probably over for the time being. "Hi, Joel," she said with a forced smile.

"Hi person I don't know," he said to Meghan before turning to Chad, kissing him, and saying back, "Hey, sexy."

"Sorry, Joel, this is Courtney's sister, Meghan," Chad said, hand gesturing towards the person next to him.

"Of course! I should have known," Joel said.

"Why, because I am black?" Meghan said, arms folded across her baggy overalls.

"That was going to be my biggest guess, but your attitude also just gave you away," Joel said, flashing her a smile that cut through her like margarine.

"Sorry about that," Meghan said, letting her arms fall to her side, and her bitch–face diminish into a grin. "As much as I love my sister, sometimes it is difficult living in her shadow."

"It's okay. What'd you pray about today? World peace? Child hunger? Nuclear disarmament?" Joel asked, feigning curiosity for pleasantry's sake.

"You," Meghan told him. "We prayed for you."

"And my eternal soul?" Joel asked, trying not to laugh.

Chad said, "No, we prayed that you won't have to move. That somehow your dad will be able to keep his job here so we can be together."

Not knowing how to take that news, and also getting nervous as the clock ticked down towards the tardy bell, Joel could only respond with, "Really?"

"Yeah." Chad smiled at him, taking his hand. "Really."

Looking at her watch, Meghan's eyes bulged out and hit her glasses as she said while running off, "See you later! Going be late for class! Eeeeeeeeeeeeekk!"

Joel and Chad started walking towards their Algebra class, the halls nearly empty, the tardy bell threatening to ring any second.

"She's adorable," Joel said.

"Yeah. I don't know where the attitude she was flaunting just now came from, because she's usually sweet and innocent and everything pure about this Earth. Basically the complete opposite of Courtney." Chad held onto Joel's hand tighter than he intended to, but feared letting it go... or having it torn away from him by outside forces beyond his control.

The tardy bell rang.

They didn't care.

Walking into class, still hand–in–hand, the teacher said, "Take your seats, delinquents." The smug smile on her face as she wrote Ts on the attendance sheet was quickly replaced with enthusiastic glee over the day's topic of Dimension Theorem for Vector Spaces. More than a few heads slumped at the mentioning of this. Chad and Joel giggled, along with Kevin who whoop–hollered when she wrote b_j on the whiteboard, which also caused a few "Ew!"s to be uttered.

Kevin turned to one of the girls who seemed to be the most disgusted and said, "Shut up, Angie. Dicks are delicious."

"Gawd, Kevin! Gross!" she shouted, causing the teacher to momentarily lose her train of thought as she continued putting up the rest of the equation they'd be using as part of the theorem.

Chad turned to Joel and whispered, "Now I'm going to have that stuck in my head all day."

"Me, too," Joel whispered into Chad's ear with cupped hands to help facilitate the message. He gave it a quick lick, causing Chad to tremble.

When the lecture finally ended, Chad and Joel ran to the closest boy's bathroom, went into the handicap stall, and took turns giving each other blowjobs. Both the "Dicks are delicious" statement and the *bj* they stared at all during class made them both incredibly horny. Being a teenage boy is the worst. Getting caught, however, was not on their minds.

"I will need to report this," Charlie, the creepy rent–a–cop security guard who's always checking out the hot girls on campus said as they exited the stall together, leaning against the wall.

"What? No! You can't!" Joel protested.

Chad remained calm for reasons Joel could not understand. Didn't he know that this could mean expulsion?

"You're not going to report this, Charlie," Chad told him confidently as he washed his hands, splashing some of the water onto his face in case there were remnants of his and Joel's tryst from moments before left behind, but somehow he doubted that.

"I could lose my job if I don't," Charlie said, his chicken hawk aura filling the bathroom air as his chest puffed out to assert his manliness.

"Please, don't. It won't happen again, I..." Joel started to say, but Chad interrupted.

"You won't report it because I won't tell them that you have a thing for my sister, Sheree." Chad folded his arms across his chest, knowing this bargaining chip had to work in his favor. He just hoped the bet paid off.

"I, uh, what? Uh... your sister?" he said, stumbling over his words like a drunk on flat pavement.

"Yeah, Sheree is my sister. She'd confirm all the times she's caught you staring at her ass. And tits."

Chad knew that Charlie would be putty in his hands. Joel on the other hand was worried sick and looked green like he was going to throw up. Chad kissed him, tongue and all, in front of Charlie just to make him squirm. It did. He left without saying a word.

"Whew! That was close!" Chad said, letting his arrogant appearance go.

"Close? He probably stood there the entire time we were sucking each other off! Pervert!" Joel said before washing up himself.

"Pervert, yes Charlie is. Though you know it'd go down different if it was Courtney and Kayla he'd caught instead of us," Chad said, grabbing Joel's hand after he dried it off.

"True. I mean, if he's gotta thing for Sheree, her lesbian twin sister has got to be a middle aged straight guy's fantasy." Joel smiled, then kissed Chad for like the hundredth time that day.

They walked towards the cafeteria through empty halls.

"What's for lunch?" Joel asked as they walked through the breezeway, a sideways drizzle pushing its way onto them.

"Hotdogs," Chad told him.

Silence.

"I might need a Round Two after lunch," they said in unison as they looked at each other before bursting into laughter that they both had the same thought.

<   <   <   >   >   >

After school, Joel decided to hell with going home to check in with his dad, and opted to follow Chad to his house. They had stayed about an hour after classes ended to go over the week's cheerleading practice schedule with Courtney, but mostly it was just an opportunity for Courtney to spend time with Chad, as she really didn't need anyone's help planning stuff because she was a multitalented multitasking superhuman who could plan an entire fundraiser while taking a shit. Actually, she did that once. Maybe eight times. What else is one going to think about while evacuating their bowels?

Chad knew his mother would be home by the time he got there unless she was planning a girl's night with Mrs. Hollins, so when they arrived to find that Joel's dad's car in the driveway, they braced themselves for the worst. Chad was too choked up to say anything. So was Joel.

They hesitantly entered the house to find a sober celebration taking place.

"I'm staying here!" Mr. Talzan said excitedly.

"What?!" Joel said, letting go of Chad's hand and walking towards his dad.

Mr. Talzan shook his head. "One of the guys has family in Wenatchee, and a couple others offered to move, so we're staying put!"

Joel hugged his dad. "That's awesome!" He turned to Chad and said, "You didn't even have to work any of your bathroom magic!"

Mrs. Walker looked at Chad who looked at her and said, "Don't ask," to which she shrugged off as the best option.

Father and son let go before Mr. Talzan said, "But there is other news."

"Good or bad?" Chad asked, wondering if he should sit down before letting the news filter its way into his ears.

"Good?" Mr. Talzan said.

Then, before either of the teenagers could brace themselves for what was about to happen, it did. Like a bomb. A big, ferocious, atomic bomb landing in the middle of the living room and exploding, ripping everything to shreds.

"You're getting married?!" Chad and Joel yelled at the same time after, respectively, his mother and his father told them the news.

"Next month!" Ms. Walker squealed, revealing the engagement ring gracing her finger, but unable to keep her hand still so it instead looked as if she had spirit fingers with bling.

"I'm moving in this weekend," Mr. Talzan said.

"And I'm moving in too?" Joel asked, hoping this wasn't the part where his father says he's SOL and has to find his own place.

This was a confusing time for all.

"Uh, yeah. Here. With me." Mr. Talzan was all smiles.

"But, um, and please don't take this the wrong way, but I don't know if I'm ready to move in with you, Chad." Joel looked serious. And sick.

"Agreed. Wait, what?" Chad was further confused by this revelation upon revelation being sprung upon him in biblical proportions.

"The office will obviously have to be converted into a bedroom for you, Joel," soon–to–be–Mrs. Talzan said.

"Huh? You already know that we're together, so why can't he just move into my room with me?" Chad asked to everyone, especially his boyfriend.

"Have you seen my closet? I've got too many clothes to make that work." Joel's logic was hard to argue with.

"True." Chad shook his head in the affirmative.

A look of utter disgust swept over Joel's face with the realization of it all. "We're going to be the only gay couple slash stepbrothers at school. The gossip that will ensue."

"Let them gossip," Chad said, kissing Joel on the mouth in front of their parents and not giving one iota of a care that they were present.

< < <   > > >

September 16, 2002

Dear Princess Diarrhea,

Joel has to move… in with me! I mean, downside is that our parents are getting married, which will technically make us stepbrothers, which will create a whole portion of society that will further condemn us for our sins against humanity as we continue our relationship as brother–fuckers, but who cares! They're not moving out of town!

Yay!

So now the only problem is that apparently Joel wants his own space and that makes me sad. Then again, his space will be at the expense of my extra room. I mean, it isn't really my extra room, but shared residential property that I am practically the sole user of, but still,

I'm a greedy little bastard who, yes, now has a father, but still a bastard nonetheless, and I don't know if I'm ready to share my space with someone else, especially since I want that someone else to share my bed instead.

Sweet Lawd Geezus, I'm adding siblings like candy at Grandma's house! Shit, only this next sibling I'm fucking. That is going to take some time to get used to. Joel and I are going to need to have words. Not just about our living arrangements, but also about Nikki. Something has been bothering me, and I think I know what it is.

Nikki and I need closure in order to fully move on.

<   <   <   >   >   >

Chad walked into his bedroom to find Joel in his bed, naked, and his cat Squeakers bathing his head. He couldn't help but smile. Yesterday, this was all he wanted. Then the smile faded. "We need to talk."

"If it's about the room, I'll consider not having my own. But you have to realize how big of a step that is for me to not have my own space to get away when I need to," Joel said, still unsure what to make of Chad's cat licking his hair. "And what's up with this?"

A couple short chuckles escaped Chad's mouth before he said, "He was probably abandoned before he was weaned."

Joel thought about that for a second. "So he likes to suck on things?"

"Yeah."

"That's so gay."

"Yeah." Chad stood there in the doorway before realizing he probably should close the door before his mother or Joel's dad walked by to witness the nakedness of Joel, even if it was covered by the sheets, and to some extent, the bedspread. "That's not what we need to talk about," he said, closing the door behind him.

"Oh. If it's about Round Three, I'm out," Joel informed him, somehow making an ugly face that made Chad love him even more.

"No. It's about Nikki." Chad walked over to the other side of the bed, taking off his shirt and tossing it onto the floor.

"Oh, shit. Are you straight again?" Joel asked jokingly, but part of him suddenly questioning as it seemed to spring upon him out of nowhere.

"No." Chad's shorts fell to the ground.

"Bi?" Joel looked a little nervous, but figured if that was the case, he still had a shot. Even though he knew there was nothing to worry about, the uncertainty in the air made him question everything.

"A world of no." Chad's underwear landed next to his shorts.

"Then what is it?" Joel asked, not wanting to move his head too much so the cat could continue to cleanse his cranium because it felt so damned amazing.

Chad slipped under the covers, leaving his bedside lamp on. "I need you to trust me."

"I trust you," Joel said quickly. He meant it.

A slight side–smile dimpled Chad's cheek. "Nikki and I need a proper breakup."

Joel just stared at him blankly.

Squeakers just kept licking.

Chad wondered when he should ask if he heard him okay.

"I don't understand," Joel said.

"It's difficult to explain," Chad said.

"Try me."

"Okay."

Chad tried to explain.

Joel tried to understand.

In the end, Joel agreed that there was no harm in what Chad suggested.

The next morning, Chad knew what he had to do. The only problem was that he would have to wait until after school was over to do it. He debated over letting Nikki in on the scheme, but by lunch, he knew he had to tell her. She agreed.

Ravenwood Park.

After school.

FADE IN

EXTERIOR RAVENWOOD PARK – DAY

SCENE: A light drizzle of rain at a playground where CHAD and NIKKI are talking next to a swing set.

(very cheesy acting must take place during this scene in order to fully appreciate the content)

                    CHAD
        Well, Nikki. It is time for us to depart.

                    NIKKI
        Oh Chadwick, must you go?

                    CHAD
            (erratic head movements)
        Yes, my darling. I must.

                    NIKKI
            (arms around CHAD's shoulders)
        Please, stay with me.

CHAD

I have to go, get on with my life.
(turns head in opposite direction,
stage right)

NIKKI

But you have a life with me, Chad!

CHAD

(facing NIKKI again)
No, darling, it won't work. We must go our
separate ways.

NIKKI

Is there another?

CHAD

Yes.

NIKKI

(angry eyes. yell)
Who is she?!

CHAD

No she. He. Joel.

NIKKI
(desperate. shock)
Joel? So you are leaving me because he
has a penis?

CHAD
(head facing ground)
Yes.

NIKKI
(excited)
I could get a penis!

(cue audience laughter)

CHAD
(head still facing ground)
No.

NIKKI
Why not? Don't you want me to have a
penis?

CHAD
Darling, with your complexion? No. You
mustn't.

                    NIKKI

But...

                    CHAD
        (looking into NIKKI's eyes. channel
        William Shatner acting style)
Make it easy on yourself, just forget
about me.

                    NIKKI

But I can't. The thought is too painful.
        (put back of hand on forehead)

                    CHAD

Believe me, it pains me too.
        (hand in a fist over heart)

                    NIKKI
        (longing in eyes)
Oh, Chad!

                    CHAD
        (longing in eyes)
Oh, Nikki!

(CHAD and NIKKI kiss madly, passionately. lots of ferocious head movements. tongues swiveling in each other's mouths. pull away quickly to make a very loud SMACK! sound. walk away from each other in opposite directions. drizzle turns to downpour)

END SCENE

FADE OUT

The crowd cheered and clapped. By the crowd, Joel, Courtney, Kayla, Sheree, and Jennifer who had all begged to be present during their production of *Chad and Nikki's Big Hollywood Break Up*. Nikki turned back to Chad and they hugged, faced their adoring audience, and took a bow.

"Thanks, Chad. You were right. We didn't have any proper closure. And now, albeit in a quite odd manner of going about doing so, we do," Nikki said, a bittersweet smile forming afterwards.

"This was important, and cathartic," Chad said before hugging her again. "Thanks for indulging my weirdness."

"Our weirdness. I needed this just as much as you did," Nikki said, reluctantly letting go of the hug so Joel could take her place.

Joel pulled them both in for a group hug, making Nikki the Oreo filling between their two cookies. "Was that scripted, or did you just adlib the whole thing?"

Nikki laughed. "We pulled that entire stunt out of our asses!"

"Impressive," Joel said, shaking his head up and down.

Leaving the boys, Nikki walked over to the girls who all congratulated her on her performance, giving her kudos and accolades and even a supportive, "That was better than anything I could ever pull off, girlfriend!" from Courtney, which was saying something considering her aspiring acting career she was only partly serious about pursuing.

Joel asked Chad quietly, "Why don't we ever have big Hollywood screen kiss moments like that?"

"Because with you, it's real." Chad kissed him. "I don't have to pretend."

The rain had soaked them all through to the bone. Figuratively. Some would say literally, but if one was literally soaked to the bone with water they'd probably be dead and bloated and floating in a pool or lake or ocean somewhere and that would be awful. It was time to leave. The girls all decided to hang out at Sheree and Kayla's house at Courtney's insistence because she didn't want to be around her stepdad for some reason or another that probably had to do with him being The White Devil. The boys decided to go to Chad's house to dry up. They followed each other in a chain since they were all practically going the same way. Chad's mom's car was not in the driveway. They'd have the house to themselves.

After Chad opened the front door, Squeakers ran over to greet him and shower him with his usual squeaks and squawks, but suddenly stopped in his place when he saw the rainwater gliding down his boy. A look of utter disgust and disappointment was about the cat as he turned around and walked away.

Joel walked in after the feline fiasco, stripped all his clothes off with the door still open for all the desperate housewives to catch a glimpse, leaving them in a pile next to his shoes, and ran up the stairs saying, "I'll get towels!"

Chad told himself, *I don't think I will ever stop loving that ass.* He closed the door, tried to untie his shoes, got the laces in a knot on one, and fell over as he tried to undo it. He instead kicked the shoes off, along with his clothes, and met Joel at the top of the stairs as he handed him a towel. They proceeded to dry each other off before ransacking Chad's closet and dresser drawers for dry duds.

Ms. Walker walked in a few minutes later, pushing the wet pile of clothes and shoes with great force in order to open the door so she could enter the house. She shook her dripping wet head and said, "Teenagers."

< < <   > > >

September 17, 2002

Hey Princess Diarrhea,

Nikki and I finally had a proper break up, so, yeah, that's finally done and over with. She seems to be okay now. I hope so. I know I feel better now.

I'm worried about Meghan. The last couple days she's been a little, well, not herself. Actually she's acting like Courtney when she gets defensive and wants to deflect. I don't know if I'm overthinking it. Maybe I am. Everyone has bad days, why wouldn't Meghan?

Huh. Maybe I'll pray for her.

< < <   > > >

"I wish you were already moved in," Chad told Joel the next morning before classes started, holding his hand and making it nearly impossible for Joel to empty his backpack and refill it with the morning's demands.

Joel smiled back. It was half–assed as his concentration focused on not dropping his bag in his effort to only carry what he needed for the first three periods of the day with only one available hand, realizing he'd make a terrible amputee. "Yeah. Soon."

Chad let out a loud sigh. "Listen. I'm going to move the computer out of the room so it will be all yours."

Joel slammed his locker shut. "You don't have to do that just yet," he said, pulling his backpack over his arms, taking Chad's hand again after it was in place.

"I do. For you. So you can, you know, get away. I know how important that is." Chad looked him in the eye. "And because I love you."

The words made Joel's heart flop around like a mudskipper.

Meghan passed by, smiling a phony smile and trying desperately to hide an even larger black eye than the one that had just started healing. She ran off before Chad could ask.

Courtney strolled up to them, ever in the company of her lesbian lover (for the time being, anyway.) "What up, bitches?"

"I'm worried about Meghan. Seriously? Another black eye?" Chad asked her, genuinely concerned there might be more to her story than running into stuff sans glasses.

"What?" Courtney asked, scrunching her face up. Her Afro remained in place as usual. "Girl clumsy as fuck. That's what momma says, anyway."

Joel looked uneasy. "Are you sure?" He shifted a little more, clutching Chad's hands as if his life depended on their entanglement. "Your stepdad doesn't… beat her, does he?"

"Fool! That white devil loves that cunt!" Courtney spouted, spittle flying everywhere.

Chad wiped his face. "That is true. I've seen the way he looks at her when she's not watching. He adores her."

"Whatever. 'Sides, Darryl an' I ain't got no bruises. If he be beatin' her, why ain't he beatin' us?" Courtney said, trying to think if there ever was a time she or her little brother had been hit before getting angry and shouting, "Why you makin' me defend that asshole?! I hate the muthafucka!"

Now Chad played the part of the nervous one. It was true; Courtney hated that man with every fiber of her molecular structure. She hated him even before he married her mom. She hated him when he'd insist on sitting with them at church (when they still went to church.) He hated him because he wasn't her dad, and she loved her dad because he was kind and caring and generous and loving and everything the white shadow who took his place in her mother's bed was not.

"You should talk to her," Kayla said before Chad could conjure up the courage to do so himself. She gave a quick look to let Chad know that she'd read his mind… and his hesitation.

"You think?" Courtney said without a hint of defensiveness she normally had up at all times. Kayla had that power. Not mind control or anything wicked like that. Love. Love is a powerful thing.

Kayla smiled at her girlfriend. "Yeah, I do. She's becoming a woman. Well, last week she did."

"Oh hell no! I thought she'd already had her period? Damn, girl's a late bloomer. Shit, I was ten!" Courtney said louder than a regular person would about beginning menstruation in a public school surrounded by teachers and students alike with ears wide open.

"Wait, how do you know she started her period last week? Is that some kind of special witchy magical power?" Joel asked, both loving the supernatural aspect of his new home, and scared shitless about what might be thrown at him next.

Kayla laughed, sounding eerily like her twin. "No, she asked me for a pad."

"With wings?" Chad asked, excitedly.

"Yes," Kayla told him.

"Airplane stickers!"

By the time prayer circle rolled around, Meghan was chatting wildly about how she tripped over the rug in her bedroom and hit the bedroom doorknob on the way down and how it probably looked a million times worse than it felt and her whole demeanor was a complete one-eighty from where it was just over an hour-and-a-half ago when she wouldn't even say a word. The rest of the circle laughed and said they'd pray for agility and coordination and she thanked them, took a quick drink from her water bottle, grabbed hands on either side of her, and started the session.

Chad felt it was awkward and all for show, something he was quite familiar with. After it was over, he tried to talk to Meghan but she said she had to go and ran off towards her third period class. He just stood there as the circle dissipated, scattering bowling pins during a spare in which he was the lone survivor.

Joel walked up to Chad and asked, "Hey, what's up? Did you get to the bottom of her latest injury?"

"No," Chad said curtly. "Wouldn't even talk to me."

Taking Chad's hand, Joel said, "Maybe she's embarrassed."

"That's not it. Told everyone she tripped. Maybe she did. Still, I don't know why she's being so… I don't know. It's just not like her," Chad said, unable to fully understand why holding Joel's hands seemed to make anything tolerable.

They started walking towards third period, bracing themselves for whatever their Algebra teacher planned on throwing at them that day. Like a chimpanzee and her feces; only her feces were in the form of blue and red and black dry erase markers and foreign words, not actual poop. That'd be gross. Ew.

"Well, maybe she is suddenly uncomfortable with you because she just started her period. Girls are weird like that,"

Joel offered as they closed in on their intended, though dreaded, destination.

"Maybe. Or it could be because I'm gay and she is trying to reconcile her faith with my sexuality and how they can be compatible," Chad said, hurt by the possibility that their friendship could be destroyed over something he couldn't keep inside any longer or actually control.

Joel squeezed Chad's hand. "I love you."

"I love you, Joel."

Chad was thankful that at least Joel was there to make Algebra somewhat tolerable, even if he felt completely clueless as to what was going on. Then halfway through the class he could barely hear what the teacher lectured about and fiddled with the hearing aid in his right ear and cursed it. Dead battery. The spares were in the freezer at home. He took it out, tossed it into a small pocket in his backpack, and massaged his ear to make it feel like a normal ear again, turning his left ear towards the front of the class to amplify the words he still couldn't understand, including the problems the teacher was solving and randomly asking for help with on the whiteboard. He hated that he could barely see Joel out of the corner of his eye. At least their feet touched. Through shoes and socks, but touching nonetheless.

"Fucking batteries," Chad said after class, shoving his textbook into his bag, crushing his English assignment that had somehow gotten loose. "Fucking papers. Fucking every fucking thing." He started crying uncontrollably.

"It's just a battery. Do you think the office might have a spare?" Joel asked, rubbing Chad's back.

"It's not just a battery. I've got a really bad feeling about Meghan and my wild imagination won't let it go," Chad told him, taking the paper out and using the edge of the desk to straighten it as he ran it over multiple times.

Joel shushed him, hugged him, told him, "We'll find out what's really going on. Promise," and wiped the tears from his eyes.

"Okay." Chad looked up to find Joel's reassuring smile.

As they walked out, the teacher snuck another glance at the two boys and let a happy grin attach itself to her normally stoic mouth as she erased the equations away. She wasn't a fan of Chad's foul mouth, but was a fan of how much he cared for his friends.

Instead of being able to enjoy lunch, they found themselves at the receiving end of Courtney barking orders about all the stuff they needed to perfect during cheerleading practice after school. Good thing it was limp pizza day and nobody had an appetite to stomach steam–infused doughy mess that remained, except for Joel and Kayla, who spent the entire time picking off the remnants of everyone's trays, even Nikki's. Normally Nikki never left anything, not because she was fat and liked food, but because she was raised to eat everything on her plate, and to only plate up what she could eat. Something made her stomach churn with worry that morning, and Chad was too busy worrying about Meghan to notice, and Courtney was too busy worrying about the Homecoming game to notice, and nobody else at the table knew what to look for when she didn't act like herself.

The rest of the day was frustrating as hell for Chad as he continued to rely on only one ear, making his focusing skills work in overdrive, thusly forcing a major headache to plant itself in his brain not unlike the ones he'd get from just wearing the damned things. By the time practice rolled around, he was tempted to toss his other hearing aid into his bag, but Courtney insisted he keep it in so he wouldn't miss a cue and drop her on the gym floor and crack her head open and cause the emergency room doctors to shave off her hair she loved so much and make her go into a deep depression no amount of chocolate could bring her out of and then she'd have to kill him. Slowly. With a blunt wooden object so it splintered. She always had a flair for the dramatic, just like Chad. No wonder they became fast friends that fateful day in the third grade when he was crying at recess because one of the boys called him a fag and said he should just be a girl if he was only going to play jump rope with the girls and she rushed over to the boy and punched him in the face and told Chad that if anyone ever made fun of him again to tell her and she'd put a stop to it. Anyone who did so after that paid the price with blood.

With Courtney running them like horses, Chad had to get some water. He walked out of the gym to find Meghan slumped in a bench just outside the door. "I need a drink,"

Chad said, grabbing Meghan's water bottle she clutched just as much as the cross around her neck.

"Chad, no!" Meghan cried.

Too late.

The liquid hit Chad's lips.

He immediately spit it out.

"Vodka?! What the hell, Meghan?" he asked, the image of this innocent little girl suddenly shattered like glass.

"Sorry." She'd shrunk to half her size, making the bruised eye somehow bigger.

"I don't understand? How long have you been doing this?" he asked, not wanting to hand the bottle back.

Lump in her throat.

Heart about to explode.

Sweat gliding down her forehead.

Guilt.

"Years." Blank.

"Why?" Chad wrapped his arms around her.

"Carl. Mom." Her voice small and emotionless.

"Your stepdad and mother?" he asked to confirm.

"Yes." Still no expression.

Chad felt nervous for asking, but knew he had no choice but to let this progress. He had to know. "What about them. Do they hurt you in some way?"

"Yes." Her voice no longer emotionless.

"Do I need to find a teacher or the counselor?" he asked, trying to figure out if he could safely dispose of the bottle so she wouldn't get in trouble for bringing alcohol on school property.

"No." Her hands firmly hidden between her knees.

"What do you need?" he asked, suddenly not wanting to touch her for fear the bruises he could see were just the manhole covering a sewer full of shit.

"A friend." So quiet.

"I'm here," Chad whispered.

"I know," she said. "I am scared."

"Meghan, you're like my little sister. You can trust me."

"I want to, but…"

She looked so small, her shaking visible, tears threatening release from their lidded prison.

"I know what it's like to keep a secret and fear what people will think if they found out. But I also know how incredibly powerful letting that secret out can be. When I decided to come out, granted it was probably the most chickenshit and bravest thing I've ever done, I did it because I had to let it go. Holding onto stuff, keeping it inside, especially secrets that are harmful, will eat you alive until there is nothing left of you but an empty shell. If I am not the right person to tell, then please, Meg, find someone you can trust. I don't want anything bad to happen to you, and I'm afraid that using alcohol as a coping mechanism will only exasperate the problem."

Chad let his words sink in, allowing time for Meghan to comprehend their meaning and make a choice. He hoped some of the big words weren't too much for her, but also knew that she was a very smart girl. Avoiding eye contact, Meghan stared at the ground until she was ready to talk.

"My mom beats me every time Carl molests or rapes me."

The words were like hornet stings to his ears.

"Oh my gawd," Chad said, pulling Meghan in to hug her, not knowing if that was causing more harm than good. "I'm so sorry. I–I–I had no idea."

She cried.

"I was only nine, goddammit! Nine! He stole something from me, made me feel ashamed, made me feel worthless. And then my own mother, knowing what he did to me, made me want to die when she blamed me for his actions. Said I was trying to steal him away from her. Called me a whore. Beat me like a whore. Then let him keep doing it. For years."

"So you started drinking…"

"…to numb the pain."

Silence as Chad let Meghan just be held.

"Courtney?" Chad whispered, selfishly hoping that Meghan was the only tragedy.

"Not that I know. And she does not know. Should I tell her? She kind of hates me?" So much pain.

"She doesn't hate you," Chad assured her. "She just thinks you hide behind religion."

"I do not hide behind it. My relationship with Jesus is what gets me through the torment. If anything, it has made me stronger. But sometimes it is not enough, so vodka or tequila or rum or gin or whatever else I can get my hands on fills the void."

He rubbed her shoulder lightly, praying he wasn't adding to her pain. "She needs to know."

"She will kill him." Her tears relentless.

"Does that matter?" Chad asked, starting to cry with her.

"Yes." She lifted her fogged glasses to wipe her face.

"Then I won't kill the mother fucker, I'll just kick his and Momma's sorry asses out on the streets. Or better yet, call the cops and let them do it while we watch," Courtney said, walking up to her sister and grabbing her for a hug.

"Courtney!" Meghan said, "How long?"

"I heard it all. Why didn't you tell me?" Courtney asked, still holding her little sister.

"I was scared. He never?" Her lips as close to Courtney's ears as the Afro allowed.

"No," Courtney whispered back, gently kissing her sister on the cheek.

They pulled apart, hands on each other's elbows.

"Thank Jesus."

"I'm sorry I wasn't there to protect you, sister," Courtney said, looking into Meghan's eyes and seeing how much pain they held inside.

"It is not your job," Meghan told her, failing to make the smile she tried to let out.

"I'm your big sister," Courtney said, guilt ransacking her conscience. "It's the most important job I have."

Another hug.

"Chad?" Courtney said.

"Yes?" he replied.

"Can you take us down to the police station?" she asked.

"Now?" he and Meghan replied.

"Yes now. There ain't no way I'm going home if those monsters are there." Courtney's anger and disappointment was mounting.

"But they will split us up! Put us in foster care!" Meghan cried. "Please, there has got to be another way?"

"Let those fuckers try to split us up! We ain't goin' into no foster system. Bull shit. You stayin' with me. You an' Darryl." Courtney wouldn't let her sister go, and somehow even managed a reassuring smile despite wanting to do murderous things to the people charged with protecting them.

"I'm going to grab our bags and tell the gang we're taking off, okay?" Chad said, getting a nod from Courtney.

The drive to the police station was silent, save for a few sniffles he caught in the rearview mirror.

Chad said he'd go in with them. Courtney said no, thanked him, and told him to go home. He pleaded to stay. She begged him to go so Meghan could tell the people who needed to be told everything without fear, and while that hurt Chad a little, he understood. After all, there were definitely things he told his diary he would never reveal to a living soul. Sometimes you need to know when to back off, and this was one of those times.

He decided to drive to Joel's apartment instead. The drive was awkward.

"Sorry for showing up unannounced," Chad said as Joel opened the door.

"That's okay. You don't need an invitation," Joel said, moving aside to let Chad in.

Chad found himself unable to avert his eyes off Joel's bare chest glistening in a light sheen of sweat, or the fact that Joel wore loose–fitting running shorts that made his testicles sizzle with the hot burning coals of desire, but decided he had to tell him what just happened, and not about Meghan. "I have to get something off my chest."

"Your shirt? Mine's already off. It'd only be fair." Joel playfully tugged Chad's top to signal he'd help remove the item of clothing in question.

"Maybe later. Or never. Gawd." Chad looked like he was going to throw up.

"What is it?" Joel asked, letting go of the shirt.

"So, I was driving down Main Street and this super hot guy was running," Chad said, not knowing if it was too early in their relationship to be telling stories about having attractions to other guys, but since this was the only other time this happened, he felt it important to share despite the consequences.

"Oh, really? Tell me more." Joel's eyes widened with anticipation.

"Yeah, so I'm staring at his perfect body. I mean, it was almost as sexy as yours." Chad felt himself start to choke up and do that thing where you start telling a story and decide halfway through that you'd made a mistake and try to stop, but like an accident during rush hour, it only causes a multi-car pile-up that forces you to move forward.

"That nice?" Joel's hands beneath Chad's shirt, rubbing his stomach.

Chad involuntarily started gasping for breath when Joel's fingers started playing with his nipples. It took a second to recover. "Yes, that nice. Anyway, so I am driving much slower than I normally would so I could savor the moment, and then I realize who it is."

"Oh, you know Hot Running Man?" Joel asked, fingers still firmly in place, teasing with light pinches.

Chad's head slumped. "It was my dad. He even waved at me."

"Well, he is a total DILF, so at least there's that." Another pinch.

Chad lightly smacked the top of Joel's head and shouted, "Joel! That's my dad you're talking about!"

"Fine," Joel said, letting Chad's shirt drop back down. "So I suppose a good ass fucking is out of the question?" turning around to display said ass after sliding down his shorts.

A mischievous smile formed on Chad's face. "I didn't say that."

Chad welcomed the distraction.

< < <   > > >

September 18, 2002

Dear Princess Diarrhea,

I had reason to worry about Meghan. Apparently her stepdad really is the devil Courtney has been claiming he is. Fucker's been abusing her and raping her and JESUS!!! I WANT TO KILL THE BASTARD!!!!!!!!!! What is wrong with people that they think it is okay to destroy someone else's life for their own selfish reasons? What goes on in their head that they tell themselves that what they are doing is okay? Do they even have a conscience? And what kind of mother beats her own child after her husband rapes her little girl? I don't think I ever want to know the answers to any of these questions, I just hope that Meghan isn't going to be broken for the rest of her life because she deserves so much better than what has been going on for the last five years of her childhood that was robbed from her far too soon. I'm not normally a death penalty kind of guy, but for something like this, I hope the fucker gets it. He won't. I know how chickenshit our judicial system is lately. I wonder if the rumors about child rapists being the lowest of the low in prison are true? A big part of me hopes so, that way, even without a death penalty option, it still might happen. I don't even care if that makes me a bad person for wishing ill on another human being, because anyone who does that to a child is not human. They're monsters.

Thursday morning started with a bang. Or a thunderclap. In all the confusion, Chad couldn't be sure what the loud noise was that woke him well before his alarm clock, but when the lightning flashed through his bedroom window, he was fairly certain a thunderstorm was taking place and not a drive-by shooting or domestic dispute. The heavy raindrops that followed confirmed this.

"Son of a bitch!" he heard his mother swear from her bedroom, the door to which was closed and down the hall on the opposite side of the house, and his door was closed and he wasn't wearing his hearing aids because he was supposed to be sleeping, so he figured the neighbors probably heard that lovely outburst as well and got all sorts of embarrassing shades of red in the dark over their assumed reactions.

Chad put on a pair of underwear and watched from his bay window as the street began to flood towards the cemetery that capped it. Living on a dead end street where, literally, the end of the street held the dead, was just a part of his life he'd always been used to. Dead people never scared him much, something he never questioned, but suddenly realized as he stared at the cemetery gates guarding the gravestones behind it, he may have inherited from his father who was the head medical examiner for the City of Ravenwood. The last one committed suicide a couple years back.

The lightning strikes continued getting closer until Chad could swear one was right over their house, but a few minutes later they were making their way north. The thunder started getting muffled from the distance until it disappeared behind the thick forest that surrounded the town. When the shower trickled to a drizzle, Chad went downstairs to start a pot of coffee. There was no way he was going to be able to get back to sleep, so he decided to embrace the day. After taking a piss, of course.

The kitchen light was already on and Chad found his mother spilling coffee grounds everywhere in her attempt to make the brown water of life. She looked frightening. Her hair out of place and sticking up so unnaturally, that he knew he would never have long hair himself because that's what he would look like waking up and that was something he never ever ever EVER wanted to happen. A few years later he grew it out anyway—apparently forgetting this moment—with disastrous results.

"Jesus, Chad. When Jeff and Joel move in, you can't just walk around in your underwear anymore," she said, still trying to get the grounds from her hands and into the coffee maker.

"Jesus, Amanda. When Jeff and Joel move in, you can't walk around with that hair anymore," he said, taking over coffee making duties from his mother.

She put her hand on her head and said, "That bad?"

"Worse," he told her, filling the carafe from the tap.

"Ugh. I'm going to put my sheets in the wash," she said, still holding her hair down as she walked away.

"Why? Did you wet the bed?" Chad asked, laughing as he poured the carafe into the holding tank.

She glared straight into his soul as he turned the coffeemaker on. "Yes. A little."

"Oh my gawd, Mom! I was just joking! Sorry!" he said, trying his hardest not to laugh and cry at the same time.

Ms. Walker rolled her eyes, went upstairs to her room, grabbed the sheets off her bed, brought them back down, started the washing machine, and poured herself a cup of coffee in hopes it would make everything better. It didn't. As soon as it hit her lips, a wave of nausea crashed into her and she quickly ran to the downstairs bathroom just in time to for the wave to go back out in the form of vomit.

She came back to the kitchen, pale and green, sat on a barstool, and dropped her forehead onto the counter. "Oh, Jesus, what is happening to me?"

"Maybe you should call in sick," Chad suggested.

She agreed, grabbed the phone, called the district office, put the phone back on the wall charging unit, then crawled onto the living room sofa.

Thinking about what he could do to take care of his mom, he suddenly remembered that Nikki's dad would be arriving later that day. As he walked towards the living room, the phone rang right next to his ear, causing him to spill a little coffee onto the floor and his toes.

"Really?" Chad said into the cordless after he picked it up, dancing around the spillage.

"Yes, really." Nikki. He turned the volume up as high as it could go since she sounded a million miles away.

"Hey, what is it? That storm wake you up too?" he asked, grabbing a towel and wiping the mess.

"That and I got a call from ChiChi," she said.

He could hear the unmistakable sound of crying in the background even without the aid of electronic amplification devices, not just from one person, and knew that what she was about to say was bad. Very bad.

"Dad... Dad...." She paused. "Dad had another heart attack at the airport right before they were supposed to board their flight."

Chad gulped. "Is he okay?"

"I'll find out more later. ChiChi was hard to understand, but I think he said he'd call after the doctors check him out? Anyway, I'm not going to school today," she said, her voice the calm in the midst of a storm.

"Okay. My mom's sick so I'm tempted to stay home and take care of her," he said.

"No you're not! You're going to school, I can take care of myself," she shouted immediately after he told Nikki.

"Or I am going to school. Do you need anything?" Chad asked, not really sure what he could offer in the ex–boyfriend capacity of their relationship still on the mending side of friendship.

"I've got a paper due in Mr. Slutz's class and he's an asshole about late work, even if you are dying," she told him.

"I'll pick it up on my way to school in a couple hours. Anything else?"

"A hug."

"I'll give you one of those when I get there to take your paper for the asshole."

"Thanks."

The rain had apparently put a damper on everyone's spirits, not just their clothes. Oddly, this wasn't the first time it had rained in a while, since it had been raining off and on for the last couple weeks, but it was the first real storm, which always signaled the official end of summer and the beginning of what autumn had in store for the season. Every downtrodden face Chad encountered dripped with the drizzle that refused to die. The football coach chatted wildly about the field not drying enough before tomorrow's Homecoming game to a teacher he could never remember the name of. A couple princesses in the Queen's Court decried the fact that Saturday's parade had a ninety percent chance of showers in the forecast and their hair was going to pay the ultimate price by way of frizz. Chad laughed.

"You're on that float too, asshole!" Angie shouted as she continued to walk away, fretting over the rain.

"Fuck me," Chad said just as Joel walked up behind him.

"Here in the halls?" Joel asked, reaching around to hug Chad from behind, kissing his neck.

"I forgot that I have to be in the parade. On the Homecoming Queen Float. I don't even know if we can call it a float. I think it's Kevin's dad's flatbed trailer, which means it's probably also going to be covered in cow manure. Joy." Chad was not well pleased.

"I was unaware there's a parade. Does this mean I have to be in this parade? I hate parades. There won't be clowns, will there?" Joel asked, remembering the time his parents thought it'd be fun to take him to watch the St. John's Parade just down the street from where they lived and a couple clowns threatened to steal him away and he peed his pants and has been terrified of them ever since. Or so his memory told him. In actuality, the clowns tried to give him a sticker but he started screaming bloody murder and his parents were the ones who stole him away while he peed his pants, crying. Memories are funny things like that.

"Yes?" Chad told him.

"I'm not going," Joel told him.

"Not even if I beg you to walk by me while I sit in a princess chair on a dairy farm trailer?" Chad asked, conjuring up his most adorable face he could muster.

Joel tapped his toes, shook his head with his eyes rolled up, and said, "Only if you promise to protect me from the insane clown posse."

"Promise," Chad said, kissing Joel.

"This isn't, like, a big deal, is it?" Joel asked, suddenly nervous.

"Uh, it's like a huge community event. It's Homecoming!" Chad said, as if the name itself spelled out the obvious.

"I guess I never paid much attention to what that actually means," Joel confessed.

"It means, 'Welcome back everyone who ever went to Ravenwood High School!' Hotels fill up months in advance for this thing. Tonight's the official start. Don't worry, I'm not going to it, even if it is at Ravenwood Bar & Grill and after yesterday's School Lunch Board approved pizza–like–food–product I'm in the mood for real pizza and they have the best," Chad said, realizing he may have said too much. He squeezed Joel's hand reassuringly.

Joel smiled at the gesture. "Thanks. My cousin's coming over to help me pack."

"Matthew?" Chad asked, eyes wide, mouth pushed about as far down and out as possible, lips puckered, and looking completely and utterly goofy.

"Yes, Matthew," Joel said.

"I'm coming over after cheer practice to help, too!" Chad told him, kissing him on the lips as the bell rang.

"Okay. I'd like that. Besides, we can make out in front of him and make him all sorts of uncomfortable. It'll be awesome," Joel said, a wicked smile on his face.

Chad talked quickly and excitedly. "Why? He was all pushing for us to get together and a few hours later we were getting to know each other in the biblical sense. Or is it because he's gay and doesn't have a boyfriend? That's it, isn't it?"

Joel laughed heartily. "No. Trust me, he's not gay. He's been with like twenty–eight girls that I know of. He's the epitome of a man–whore. Even had sex with some girl he claimed was so ugly he'd never tell me who it was, then to make himself feel better, had sex with his girlfriend's best friend an hour later while they were all at the same party. Boy's all sorts of confused. Only thinks with his dick. Still, he's my cousin and I love him. He's kinda like my Courtney!"

"Wow! That dramatic?" Chad asked, remembering the time Courtney was discussing her theater class and spouting her Satan monologue before saying how ridiculous the whole thing about pretending to be a tree was in the same breath. Just for argument's sake, Courtney stood with her arms at her side and stared blankly, getting accolades from the teacher for her perfect example of a strawberry tree. Courtney was not amused.

"Yeah," Joel said, letting the word pour out of his mouth like thick molasses.

They kissed each other one last time before Advanced Algebra would bring them together again, briskly walking separately to their first period classes before the tardy bell rang. After first period, Chad dropped off Nikki's paper for Mr. Slutz who wasn't even in the class, so he left it on his desk, prominently displayed front and center. Then he scribbled on a Post–it note:

After second period, Chad noticed that Meghan didn't show up to prayer circle and started to worry, especially since he didn't even think about not seeing Courtney that morning at his locker to give him shit like she usually did or in the class he knew she had with Nikki when he dropped the paper off and left the note he immediately regretted writing. He decided to lead the group that day, praying for victims of sex abuse, taking everything he had to not drop the F–bomb a dozen times, or mention anyone's name. Not that protecting the innocent would matter. This was a small town. Word would travel fast once the news agencies got ahold of the story. Everyone loves a scandal… except those involved.

When they finished praying, Chad opened his eyes to find Joel waiting for him. The group all said their usual casual "So long!"s and "Ciao!"s and even a "Toodle–oo!" as they parted. Chad walked up to Joel, who wrapped his arms around him as they kissed.

Taking Joel's hand as they walked towards class, Chad said, "I'm really worried about Meghan."

"Why? Where is she? I didn't see her," Joel said.

"Shit got real yesterday after school. Have you seen Courtney?" Chad asked, hoping they had run into each other in the halls or something.

"Nope. What shit?" Joel asked.

"Shit. Bad shit. Like the worst shit possible," Chad said.

"You're not going to tell me what the shit is, are you?" Joel asked.

"Not until I talk to Courtney or Meghan first. Sorry, it's just, personal and not mine to tell," Chad told him, hoping he'd understand his need for being cryptic.

A little hurt, but trusting Chad, Joel said, "Okay."

"Okay?"

"Okay."

Kevin walked up behind them. "You ready to bring it tomorrow, Chad?"

"Oh, it's already been broughten!" Chad teased back, bobbing his head from side to side while quoting a teen movie that made fun of teen movies, even if secretly *Bring it On* was his favorite movie of all time that he could watch over and over and over again. Okay, so it wasn't that big of a secret, nor a stretch for a cheerleader to love a movie about cheerleaders, especially one that starred both Brad Pitt's child slash lover from the movie adaption of *Interview with the Vampire*, and Faith from *Buffy the Vampire Slayer* in leading roles. Both Chad and Courtney also loved how much the movie got wrong, but who cares! Kirsten Dunst and Eliza Dushku and Jesse Bradford and Gabrielle Union!

Once they reached Algebra class, smiles faded.

Angie glared at him when they walked through the door, apparently still upset about being laughed at earlier that morning. Kevin whispered something into her ear that made her cringe. They'd been like that for as long as Chad could remember, and yet still remained friends. It gave him hope for him and Nikki.

The bell rang and the teacher wasted no time to get into lecturing about math. "We're going to go off the book and go over some real world applications of Algebra. Now, who can..."

Lunch couldn't come soon enough for Chad. Listening to the teacher argue with Angie that Algebra would be a part of her life and Angie arguing that she would never allow it to be was fun for the first two minutes. But the remaining half–hour before the teacher shut down the argument by telling her that she will assuredly be living her life in the real world after graduation, so she better start preparing herself for it unless she wanted to live the dream of burger flipping.

Angie finally shut up after that. When he and Joel made it to the cafeteria, he winked at Creepy Security Guard Rent–A–Cop Charlie, making him squirm, before spotting Courtney shoving a cheeseburger into her mouth.

"Whew! She's here," Chad said.

"Who?" Joel asked before spotting Courtney. "Ah."

After grabbing their lunch, they sat down at the COOL table surrounded by all the cool kids. Well, really the outcast table that over the years became the cool table filled with the most unlikely cast of characters. They only called it the cool table because someone years ago had carved the word COOL in the middle with a razor blade. No matter where the table ended up, they found it and sat there.

"Courtney, how's Meghan? I haven't seen her today?" Chad asked quietly.

"Girl be hangin' with Grams today. Told her to take a day off and burn whatever needs be burned," Courtney said, her sandwich nearly gone.

"So she's doing okay?" Chad asked.

"She's broken, but she'll fix herself up soon. Girl's a survivor," Courtney told him, beaming with pride. "And thanks for yesterday."

She side–hugged him.

He smiled.

Jennifer asked, "What the hell is going on here?"

Without missing a beat, Courtney told the table loudly and pretty much everyone else in the cafeteria, "The white devil has been raping my baby sister since she was nine–years–old and the woman who gave birth to us has been beatin' her ever since because of it and now they sittin' in a muthafuckin' jail cell awaitin' trial. They asses goin' to prison."

Joel grabbed Chad's hand and squeezed, letting him know he understood why he didn't want to tell him what happened to Meghan. Sheree cringed at the news, both Kayla and Jennifer consoling her as it hit close to home, even though it had been over three years since her attack.

"How are you handling all this?" Chad asked, knowing it had to be affecting her as well, but also knowing her well enough to know that she could handle just about anything.

Courtney broke down in tears. "Carl killed my daddy!"

"What?" Chad asked, not sure if he heard right despite fresh batteries in his hearing aids.

"That fuckin' white devil thought the police were at the house to arrest him for a murder he thought he got away with and started confessin' right there to the cops that he'd killed him. Momma had to be pried off. Worst, Darryl was home and saw the whole thing. I shoulda warned him to go to Brendon's or Wayne and Kwirk's or anywhere but home. He lucky I wasn't there or he'd be dead!" she cried, Kayla turning to hold her girlfriend as she let herself be vulnerable.

"I... I..." Chad started, but couldn't find the words to finish. He hugged her from the other side.

In true Courtney fashion, the moment was over almost as soon as it began. "So, best thing to come out of this is Grams is movin' in! That's why they burnin' shit, to make room. She's also gettin' Meghan a new bed because that old one has too many nightmares in it. I told her we switchin' rooms 'cuz she got the better one, but Grams said I had to take the master because she'd already claimed it and Darryl be the only one who ain't switchin' which is good 'cuz his room smells like twelve–year–old boy, and lawd knows what he does when that door's closed!"

"I was gonna help Joel pack up since he's moving in this weekend, but I can help you if you want?" Chad said, suddenly realizing the group wasn't aware of their ever-evolving situation.

"Damn, you move quick!" Courtney said, holding her hand up for a high–five that Joel nervously accepted.

"What? You're mom is letting your boyfriend move in with you?" Sheree asked, wearing confusion like last year's Versace. "I'm telling Dad."

"Yes?" Chad said.

"It's worse than you think. Our parents are getting married," Joel informed the group.

Jaws dropped.

Chad chuckled before saying, "My Love Affair with Joel will now be revised to say My Love Affair with My Stepbrother! Yay!"

Nobody laughed.

"That was a joke, guys. Come on," Chad said with sad eyes as his burger got cold, crinkle cut fries getting limper with each passing second.

Sheree was the first to pipe up. "Well, Dad used to date his sister, so you're not the first brother–fucker in the Hollins family."

"I must hear this story," Joel told her, deadpan.

"I'm sure you will if you ever come over for Christmas. They love to tell it," Sheree told him.

Jennifer was still in shock. Courtney and Kayla were making out. Sheree finished her lunch, sucking down the last of the remaining bubbles from her carton of chocolate milk before crushing it in her hands and dropping it onto her tray. Chad and Joel finally got to eat theirs.

Jennifer just stared blankly.

Sheree shoved her.

It didn't break her trance.

"Chad!" Matthew shouted, extending his arms for a hug when Chad arrived at the Talzan's apartment. He squeezed tighter than Chad expected.

"Hi," Chad managed with limited breath, praying he didn't pop like a pimple.

"Joel tells me you two are shacking up? That's great! I knew you weren't straight. Ugh, I could kiss you for making him so frickin' happy!" Matthew said then did just that and kissed him on the mouth. "That's not a gay kiss, that's a happy kiss. There's a difference." He wiped his lips with his forearm.

"Okay?" Chad said, eyes full of worry.

"I told you that he's like Courtney!" Joel said, laughing as he snatched Chad out of Matthew's hands and gave him a real kiss. With his tongue.

After a minute of Chad and Joel making out, Matthew decided enough was enough. "So, is you're S&M bondage gear going to Goodwill or you taking it all with you?"

"Asshole!" Joel said, punching Matthew's arm.

"You didn't answer the question," Matthew said.

"You're serious?" Chad asked, gulping. He'd stumbled upon some bondage porn accidentally while researching bandages after a cheer injury and unwittingly made a typo. Not all of it looked horrible. Most of it terrified the shit out of him. Yes, he kept looking.

"No! He's being a dickwad!" Joel assured, glaring at his cousin who was busy laughing.

"I don't know. I think it'd be hot if you tied me up and spanked me," Chad said, winking.

"What?" Joel asked, mouth open and eyes searching for a hint of sarcasm.

"I'm joking!" Chad lied. Part of him was curious, even if it would be just a one–time thing and he hated it and never wanted to do it again.

"Damn. Because that'd be hot." Joel looked genuinely disappointed. He wasn't.

"Oh my gawd, you two! Go fuck and get it over with so we can get some actual work done!" Matthew said, putting a stack of books into a box.

"You wish!" Joel shouted. "Then you could find the video camera and record us have this amazing gay sex and upload it onto the Internet and make gobs of money until someone shuts the site down because we're both minors!"

Matthew held an expressionless face as he looked Joel square in the eyes. "You've ruined my get rich quick scheme, fucker."

"Sorry to disappoint," Joel said, preparing another box with packing tape.

For the next couple minutes, actual packing took place. Teenage boys being teenage boys, after those couple minutes were up, bite–sized microwavable pizza imposters were being consumed alongside violent combat involving squirrels and frying pans from the video game console they played.

"So, you're mom must be pretty fucking hot for Uncle Jeff to want to marry her," Matthew said, killing something on screen that resembled a gargoyle straight out of *Ghost Busters*.

"Really?" Chad said, a pizza roll dropping from his mouth and into his lap.

"Yeah, she is. Chad's dad's totally hot, too. I'd fuck him," Joel added nonchalantly.

"Really? Goddammit, Matthew. You're a bad influence on my boyfriend," Chad told him, tossing the snack from his crotch towards Matthew's face. Miraculously he caught it in his mouth, smiled, winked, and chewed.

The banter continued for the next hour and a half until Chad said he should probably get going to check on his sick mother, suddenly feeling guilty he opted to hang out with Joel and Matthew instead of taking care of the woman who'd taken care of him for his entire life. Joel kissed him, he said his goodbyes, and drove towards home wishing Joel had already moved in and feeling guilty about being so selfish until after he got home and found no sign of his mother except for a note that read:

He was pissed. Apparently so was Squeakers, who proceeded to vomit on his shoes after he read the note.

< < <   > > >

September 19, 2002

Hey Princess Diarrhea,

The Homecoming game is tomorrow, which means we will have to give our all. Not the football players, us cheerleaders. Everyone knows we are the real stars of the game. I mean, yeah, so our quarterback is a gay dairy farmer who's dating the class president and one of our linebackers is a straight girl who used to win child beauty pageants until her parents yanked her out after JonBenét was murdered, but still, the real focus is on how well we pump up the crowd.

Yay.

I don't know why, but I'm not feeling it. I want to, but I don't. Maybe there is just so much stuff happening all at once and I am so torn about being happy while my friends lives are falling apart that I can't focus on what I have to do. Like homework. Math homework. Fucking Algebra. Part of me was rooting for Angie this morning when she had a full–on quarrel with Mrs. Falls. I hate the fact that Mrs. Falls teaches math because I really like her, but I really don't like math. Math hard. Why am I wasting my energy talking about math in my diary when there are more pressing matters at hand? Shit, like my English assignment I need to start. At least I like English.

< < < > > >

Chad saved his diary then started his English homework he'd had all week to do and hadn't started yet because he was too busy dealing with life and all the stuff she insisted on throwing at him. Typical excuse.

After finally sitting down to read the short story "A Very Old Man with Enormous Wings" by Gabriel García Márquez, he knew he not only wanted to read more about this magical realism thing he'd only heard about, and especially more by this author, but also found himself completely consumed by the need to break it down into a simple argument about how people use people and throw them away when they are done. He finished the essay in less time than it took him to read the story.

He went downstairs, put Matchbox Twenty's *Mad Season* CD into the player, grabbed a Coke out of the fridge, and sat down to unwind while listening to mostly depressing songs about life.

The phone rang.

"What do you want?" Chad asked into the cordless phone that was thankfully not on the charging unit but right next to him on a side table.

"My parents went out with your mom and Joel's dad and I'm done with my homework and now I'm bored," Sheree's pathetic voice said into the receiver.

"I'm busy not doing anything," Chad said.

"I'm… are you listening to Matchbox Twenty?" Sheree asked.

"Yes. "Angry" is on."

"Me too!" Sheree squealed.

"Awesome."

"It is awesome! I listen to that album when I'm depressed and want to make myself feel better by listening to someone else's shitty life," Sheree told him, all bubbles.

"Stop fucking with me. I do too," Chad confessed, straightening up.

"You know, we have way too much in common. I have no idea why I never put two and two together and figured out we're related," Sheree said, taking a drink of Coke straight from the can after as she connected all the dots in her head. "You should come over so we can play a game. Kayla and Brendon are dying for some sibling time."

Chad looked at the clock. 8:07 pm. "Yeah, I'll be right over. Need me to bring anything?"

"Nope. Oh wait, Kayla says to bring your Coke because she doesn't want you to leave it out and let it go to waste because that will make her sad," Sheree told him.

"She needs to stop spying on me," Chad told her.

Nondescript mumbling could be heard on the other end.

"Kayla said she sensed the Coke can's presence and had a disturbing vision of it being left for dead," Sheree said. "I don't get it either. Just bring the can."

"Got it." Chad clicked off the phone, tossed it onto the chair he was sitting in, turned off the stereo, and left the house. Two doors down, Chad didn't know whether to knock or just walk right in, as his immediate family status was still relatively new. He opted for the latter, half expecting the dogs to bark him out. They didn't, instead remaining by Brendon's side pretending to sleep. The half-opened-one-eyed glare each of them gave clued him in.

"Don't worry, Kayla," Chad said as he opened the door. "Coke is right here with me."

They played Clue. Brendon won. Kayla accused him of cheating. Chad and Sheree couldn't stop making lists of their common interests. It was everything they hoped it would be, until Chad started freaking out about the possibility he might be a witch.

"Not gonna happen," Kayla assured.

"Yeah, witches are from Mom's side, and you've only got Dad's baby batter in you," Brendon said with a straight face.

"Oh thank God, and ew," Chad said, shaking his head. "So is your mom a witch?"

"Nope. Her and Sheree got skipped," Kayla told him. "Which is sad, really, because I can't ever have kids again and Brendon's gay so…"

"I am so going to have kids!" Brendon shouted as he stood up, the rope in his lap landing on the game board. "Oh, there that is."

"Anyway, the chances of continuing our side of the line are fairly slim. At least we have a few cousins left who might be able to," Kayla finished, glaring at Brendon for interrupting her.

"It might not be such a bad thing for the line to die out. There's a lot of evil in it," Sheree said coldly, looking her sister square in the eyes but thinking mainly of her closest cousin, Kelly, who, albeit, was not a witch in the technical sense, but still carried the recessive gene. They had a falling out the previous year over something stupid. They would never reconcile.

"True," Kayla agreed. "But that evil has been extinguished."

"I'm regretting bringing up the subject," Chad said, feeling small and out of place again.

"Don't be. You'd find out one way or another about all our family's dirty little secrets!" Brendon told him, squeezing his hand and smiling a big goofy smile that both reminded him of his own and a lot of their father's.

"Wait, you can't have kids?" Chad asked Kayla as his brain finally processed everything.

Kayla looked on the verge of crying from the pain. Sheree rubbed her thigh before taking her hand.

"The twins I had right before sophomore year almost killed me. Okay, so it did kill me for a few minutes. The first one managed to destroy my uterus. No amount of magic can heal it." Kayla held in her tears.

"I'm sorry. I didn't mean to upset you," Chad said, uncertain if he should hug her or not. He wanted to, badly. He felt awful for bringing up the subject, but also had a nagging curiosity and burning desire to make sure he wasn't a witch himself. Yes, selfish reasons. He hugged her anyways, despite his reservations. "I'm sorry."

"Thanks, but I have to deal with it. I'm just glad Courtney knows because every time we'd get close I'd push her away so she wouldn't find out about my past or that I'm a witch. That's why we kept breaking up. I'd feel comfortable enough to tell her everything and then freak out that she'd go all apeshit and never want to talk to me again. But a couple weeks ago I just told her. Everything. Came clean about what my split evil half did, about being a witch, about being in love with her more than I could ever explain in words, and she just smiled," Kayla said before getting a mischievous grin on her face. "Then we had crazy hot lesbian sex for hours before going to Stacey Hill's party and getting shitfaced."

Chad and Brendon both looked like they were going to throw up.

"You really could have left that last part out!" Brendon yelled, crying from the pain of scratching his eyes out to erase the image.

"I don't think I will ever have a boner again, bitch," Chad told her, staring at his penis beneath his shorts and silently telling it goodbye.

"When are Joel and Jeff moving in," Sheree asked, both relishing in her timing and a little piece of her dying on the inside when she said the name Jeff out loud, as that was the name of her one and only true love who died three years ago before being reborn as her nephew two years ago.

"This weekend. Probably Sunday, what with Homecoming," Chad told her.

"Is he moving into your room?" Brendon asked with salacious inquisitiveness, eyes widening with anticipation for the answer.

"No. Said he wants his own room so he can get away," Chad said, sadness filling his voice. "Which means I have to give up my second room. That sucks."

"You're such a selfish asshole!" Sheree told him. "I mean, the guy just moved here a couple months ago, and now his dad is marrying your mom and they have to move again, and you guys just started going out a few weeks ago. Give him some space!"

The words hurt, but Chad knew she was right. This was all happening so quickly. He decided that since Joel had been in at least two serious relationships he knew of that both ended badly, perhaps he should be a little more understanding. "I guess."

He looked at the clock. 10:49 pm.

"Brendon! Get to bed, now!" Kayla screamed.

"You're not my real mom! You can't tell me what to do!" Brendon shouted back, quickly regretting it as he ran up the stairs, Kayla chasing him.

"Well, goodnight, Chad. See you in school tomorrow," Sheree said, looking down at the Clue game board and deciding to leave it until the morning.

"Night, Sheree. And thanks," Chad told her, giving her a hug.

"Any time," Sheree said, hugging him back. "See you in the morning all decked out in your cheerleading best!"

Chad gave her a double thumbs up, then started walking back towards his house. A quick glance at Nikki's house across the street let him know that the Boloski family was still awake. Part of him wanted to check on them, but the other part didn't want his nostrils to be victimized by the possibility of Leftover Stew simmering on the stove. He was about to turn around when he caught sight of Nikki sitting in her front lawn.

She waved.

Fuck.

He waved back, then walked over and sat next to her. The grass was wet, quickly soaking through. "Hey."

"Hey," she said back stoically.

"I left your paper for Mr. Slutz, and maybe even a note that called him out for being an asshole without saying as much," he told her without looking at her.

"Thanks. Dad's stable. He won't be able to make it here until Christmas it looks like though, and that's assuming his heart can take it." Nikki cold as ice. Frozen. Something he'd gotten used to when she didn't want to let herself feel anything.

"I'm sorry." Chad lay down to face the stars in the sky, wispy clouds dancing about.

Nikki followed suit, not even caring her back began quickly dampening from the massive downpours earlier that day. "I miss this."

"Me too," Chad told her.

He took her hand and held it, not romantically, but as a friend showing another friend that they were in solidarity. They looked at each other. Nikki let her blank face melt slightly into a grin. Chad smiled back, but only briefly. He suddenly realized she may not know about Courtney and Meghan. But should he bother bringing it up?

"Talked to Courtney today. I can't believe all that shit. That's messed up," Nikki said.

Whew!

"It is, isn't it?" Chad asked, relieved and freaked out that his thoughts once again inspired the next conversation, another reason he thought he might be a witch. Turned out it was just peculiar circumstance. Again. Weird.

"I can't imagine what poor Meghan has been going through, and then to find out the bastard killed their dad so he could take his place in the family? That's rough. That's crazy. That's straight out of a Lifetime made for TV movie or *All My Children*." Nikki rolled her head back and forth on the sodden lawn. "I only hope Meghan is half as strong as Courtney."

"Me too," Chad told her.

The front door opened and a pleasantly plump and pinned Mrs. Boloski shouted, "Nikita! You need to stop laying in grass with homoshekshual boyfriend and go to bed! Shkool tomorrow!"

Both Nikki and Chad started laughing at her mother's outburst.

"Goodnight, Nik," Chad said as he gave her a hug on the wet lawn before getting up.

"Goodnight, homoshekshual," Nikki teased, mimicking her mother.

His mother still wasn't home when he got there. He went to bed, letting the cat lick his hair until he fell asleep.

< < <   > > >

September 20, 2002

Dear Princess Diarrhea,

Today is the day we vote for Homecoming King and Queen. I already know I'm voting for Joel to be King because he's already a king in my book. Great, now I have an image of Joel as King Kandy stuck in my head. What the hell? Oh well. I'd totally go to Candyland and get trapped in King Kandy's castle to become his companion and be forced to lick his lollipop all day. Jesus, Chad! What kind of sick fuck are you? Shit. Would it be awful to vote myself as Queen because I selfishly really do want to have Joel all to myself?

Chad found Joel at his locker licking on a lollipop, giving him an instant boner he had to hide from his classmates. "Hey, sexy."

Joel removed the lollipop from his mouth, shoved it into Chad's, and said back, "Hey, sexy."

"Mmm. I love it when we share," Chad told him, holding his bag in front of his crotch and bending into a familiar pose.

Joel chuckled. "You're hiding something from me, aren't you?"

"Yes, my hard on," Chad told him, giving the sucker back to Joel to suck on for a while.

"Our schedule is all out of whack because of the assembly," Joel said. "I hate assemblies."

"But you have your speech so you can make an impassioned plea for the school's vote, right?" Chad asked.

"What?!" Joel shouted, letting the sucker fall to the mismatched vinyl tiles, dying an untimely death.

"Your speech? For Homecoming King? Please tell me you've got something planned out for the assembly?" Chad asked rapid-fire.

Joel's face looked pale and clammy and with a ninety percent chance of vomit in its near future. "Nobody told me about that. I fucking hate talking in front of large crowds. I might pee my pants. I never wanted this. I'm going to kill Courtney."

"The fuck you is," Courtney said as she walked up to them.

"Nobody said I had to have a speech," Joel told her.

"Fool? It's Homecomin'! Everyone knows the courts have to campaign! That only the last part!" Courtney's words cut through Joel like a million razor sharp teeth during a piranha attack.

"I can't. My throat will tighten and words will sound like pig squeals and then everyone will make fun of me as the pig-squealing-faggot," Joel said. "No. I won't say anything."

A wicked thought entered Chad's brain. "I've got a plan. Promise you won't kill me."

"I'm going to regret this, aren't I?" Joel asked, squinting his eyes.

"Probably." Chad smiled.

The day went by so quickly that by the time sixth period rolled around, everyone seemed overly excited about the assembly to follow. Mrs. O'Hurley, however, had made sure that the fear of God would be on everyone's mind as she informed everyone at the start of class that she'd be randomly selecting students to read their essay. The silence that followed was every teacher's wet dream. When Mrs. O'Hurley announced that only three students would be chosen, a universal sigh of relief discharged.

Chad did the math. *Three out of twenty–eight is just over a one in nine chance I will get picked. Son of a bitch! I just did math in my head!*

The first student Mrs. O'Hurley picked was a shy girl with a rather unfortunate case of acne covering every part of her body the eyes could see and then some. She focused her essay on the crabs and what metaphor that could be. The teacher nodded along, thanked her, then asked Angie to the front of the classroom where she proceeded to explain the story without anything original, to which Mrs. O'Hurley asked if she'd ever written an essay before because what she did was basically paraphrase the story. Disappointed, she didn't even bother letting Angie finish. She may have been a favorite teacher by most, but she was not easy by any means. In fact, the exact opposite held true.

Two down.

The moment of dread for the remaining students as the teacher's eyes scanned the room lasted a lifetime.

"Chad."

Chad? There's another Chad? Chad asked himself before the blood rushed out of his face when he realized he was the Chad in question. "Uh, are you sure?"

"Yes. Read your essay," Mrs. O'Hurley demanded.

"Okay," Chad said, picking up the paper and walking to the front of the class. *Hold your shit together, Chad!* "You want me to read the whole thing?"

"Yes," Mrs. O'Hurley said.

Chad let out a nervous breath.

"A Very Old Man with Enormous Wings: Captivity of an Angel by Chad Walker. Throughout history, there are examples of people enslaving others for their own selfish prosperity; the Egyptians and Israelites, Americans and Africans, Romans and whoever they wanted, etc. Gabriel García Márquez's children's story "A Very Old Man with Enormous Wings" is certainly a fine illustration of how even the people you would least expect, when given the opportunity of fame and fortune, would indulge in such an inhumane (yet uniquely human) practice like slavery. With the theme of how we treat each other and its direct correlation to self-worth, Márquez has created a beautifully heart-wrenching masterpiece.

"Can holding another captive ever be justified? What if you were faced with the choice of locking someone up for fear of them taking away your only child? Pelayo and Elisenda after encountering "a very old man, lying face down in the mud" of their courtyard, consult their neighbor who "knew everything about life and death." She informs them that they have an angel on their hands and that he was probably there to take their sick child. The neighbor, however, does not hold angels in high regard, but rather "the fugitive survivors of a celestial conspiracy." This is our first clue that even amongst the wise, some believe that others are indeed inferior. Fear leads Pelayo to lock him up in the chicken coop with plans of sending him on his way in the morning with a raft and some food and water, but once word got out that there was a real–life angel in town, the locals flocked to the chicken coop to catch a glimpse, and "Elisenda… then got the idea of fencing in the yard and charging five cents admission to see the angel." It is humbling how fear dissolves so quickly at the chance of making a lot of money. By comparing the couple's luck with the change from dreary weather to something more accommodating to crowds for an outdoor spectacle, we are almost led to believe that this enslavement and profiteering of a celestial being is possibly a gift from God for them having endured the plagues of rain, crabs, and sickness. The same could be said for the American tobacco and cotton plantation owners and their African slaves, many of whom used the Bible to justify their use of other human beings, particularly a few verses in Ephesians that basically say that slaves should be happy and go about their business doing whatever pleases their masters for it is God's will. It is difficult to argue against using people for the sake of profit when we still see it in our society, many times by willing participants.

"Much like reality television, the newness and unchanging nature of the angel fades, and with it the audience. Instead of the initial flood of people begging to be healed by this slave they've paid to see, he is abused with stones and "an iron for branding steers." This is also the first sign the angel shows that he does care about what happens to him, and leaves the people who've come to see this attraction with a sense that perhaps something isn't right about his circumstances. Of course, this only leads them to some other new and exciting and cheaper form of entertainment, a "tarantula the size of a ram and with the head of a sad maiden," showing us that our morals can easily be subdued for pleasure, even at the expense of another living creature.

"After the crowds have gone and their courtyard is "as empty as during the time it had rained for three days and crabs walked through the bedrooms," this leaves our family with more than enough money to live comfortably, but again with the dilemma of having an angel they no longer want but are too afraid to dispose themselves of. The angel is also in a predicament that he cannot care for himself, and as such, is reliant on the rare generosity of his captors. This is not unlike how some slaves in the American South found themselves after slavery was abolished; without the necessary skills to create a better life for themselves so they stayed with their former masters. It is only when his captors no longer treat him as property, but as a living, breathing creature not unlike them, that the angel's transformation begins. When his feathers do finally start to grow back, he carefully hides them, as if he is secretly planning his escape "for he was quite careful that no one should notice them." The angel's eventual departure isn't met with resistance, but with "a sigh of relief" on the part of Elisenda as she watches him fly away. With the angel no longer providing an income, it could be said that he had become a burden they felt compelled to hold onto, probably for fear he would steal away with their child had they freed him. However, it could also be an allegory that simply treating people with kindness can lift their spirits and carry them on their way."

Half the class started clapping. The other half looked pissed.

"And that is how you write an essay," Mrs. O'Hurley said, joining in with the clapping half. "Thank you, Chad."

With only a few minutes left before the class would be let out, Mrs. O'Hurley decided to let them go early to get good seats for the assembly. She asked them to go quietly. They went cheering.

"Chad, hold up," Mrs. O'Hurley said, holding the stack of papers.

He stayed behind as his classmates piled out of the room.

"What is it?" Chad asked, nervously waiting with anticipation.

"Thank you for that essay. It showed a level of maturity most colleges don't even see," she told him.

"Uh, thanks?" Chad replied.

"That must have taken you hours. How'd you find the time?" she asked.

"Uh, well, I think I spent like twenty minutes on it and wrote it right after reading the story. Last night. I apologize, but I am a horrible procrastinator," Chad informed his teacher, awaiting the look of disappointment in her eyes that she'd shown towards Angie.

"Don't apologize," Mrs. O'Hurley said, giving him a slight smile, the light reflecting off her oversized glasses and silvering hair.

"Okay." Chad smiled back.

"Also, thanks for not cussing in the essay. Though I must admit, I heard you say the word fuck at least a dozen times in my head while you read it," she told him.

Chad's jaw dropped.

"Sorry to shatter your image of me. I shouldn't have said that," she said.

"It's okay. It only makes me like you even more," Chad said, giving her a hug to which she reluctantly accepted.

"We shouldn't hug," Mrs. O'Hurley said, her teacher mode switched back on.

"I'm gay. You won't be sued for sex abuse." Chad's logic was hard to argue with.

When the hug ended, Mrs. O'Hurley told him, "I'm still counting on you to be my T.A. next semester. Don't let me down."

"I won't."

Chad headed towards the auditorium to find Joel and Courtney. He had to make sure his plans for Joel went off without a hitch. He just hoped it didn't backfire.

Joel was a nervous wreck.

Courtney tried to console him, telling him everything would be okay.

The senior class president, Nathan, told everyone, "Good luck!" before he headed to the podium to start the Homecoming Assembly. "It's Homecoming!" he said loudly into the microphone, stating the obvious but still making the audience cheer and holler. "Today we will hear from our Homecoming Court, so everyone make sure you have your ballots out so you can take notes on who you want to be your Homecoming King and Queen!" More cheers. More hollering. Ballots waved in the air from almost everyone like a purple paper storm. "How many Ravenwood alumni do we have today?" he asked, and about fifty people shouted back. "Awesome! So glad to have you back. You're all going to the game tonight, right?" They all shouted yes. "Excellent! Well, let's get this started! As always, lady's first, so let's have our Princesses in the Queen's court come out!"

Chad's heart sunk into his stomach as he realized he'd be the ass–end of the Princess Train. At least Courtney would be right next to him as the six Princesses made their way onto the stage to thundering applause. Loud chatter about there being a boy in the Queen's Court could be overheard from some of the former students. He smiled, waved, then walked off stage when it was time for the real show to start.

Angie was first. Her speech was as shallow as her outward appearance. Her claps were louder than Chad expected.

Stacey Hill was next. Her speech was about how she threw that bitchin' party. Her claps were in–sync with name chanting.

The next two were so boring and pretentious, that Chad wondered how their names even got put onto the roster. Courtney told him they must have given the nomination committee blowjobs because they both were freshman before she plastered on one of her giant smiles and walked out to the podium and didn't say a word for a full minute because the cheers simply would not die down. She played it up like an actress winning an Oscar; putting her hands to her heart, pretending to wipe away joyful tears. The works. "I just want to say I love you all! Just being nominated is an honor in and of itself! But seriously, yo. I'm startin' to feel like Susan Lucci with my nominations, so just give me the damn title already, 'kay?"

The crowd went wild.

Chad was next. "Oh shit," he said quietly.

"Just do what Courtney told you to do," Joel told him, squeezing his hand.

"Kiss me first. I need some oral courage," Chad said.

"I'll give you oral," Joel told him.

"Really?" Chad asked, about to add some more words, but Joel's mouth firmly planted itself on his before he could let any out.

"Now get out there, Princess!" Joel said, giving him a playful shove.

Chad made his way towards the podium and thanked Baby Jesus that the stage lights blacked out the faces in the crowd. His bladder insisted it needed to be emptied. His lunch insisted on coming back up. He told them both to go to hell. "First of all, I'd like to thank my ex–girlfriend Nikki Boloski for being so pissed at me after finding out that not only I am gay but already had a boyfriend that she crossed my name off the King Court and added it to the Queen's Court, but also the amazing support from my friends and family since coming out." A few cheers sprang out in the crowd, and a very loud one that obviously came from Kevin. Nikki even stood up and took a bow, or so he assumed it was her in the blackness. "I'm asking you for your vote, not just because I'm your typical blond blue–eyed choice, but because deep down, you all know you want a gay Homecoming King and Queen!" The audience laughed and clapped and Chad walked off the stage.

Nathan made his way back to the podium. "Let's hear it one more time for our Princesses!" Another round of applause that was mediocre at best. "Now, onto our Princes in the King's Court! Gentlemen!" he said, before stepping back to join the six guys, including Joel who looked nervous and sweaty. The crowd cheered, clapped, and when it started to die down, Nathan went back to the microphone as the Princes all went backstage again. "Now, as your class president you all love, I am your obvious choice for Homecoming King," he said, allowing some of his flair to shine through. The audience loved it. "As a cheerleader who is dating the quarterback, I think I pretty much have this in the sack, but then again, Kevin didn't even make the list, so perhaps I shouldn't get too cocky!" Only a few students started laughing until the pun hit the rest of them. "Vote for Nathan because he's smart, funny, sexy as all get out, the second best cheerleader after Courtney Jones, and you really like him!" He struck a Nixon pose with his hands, making the crowd laugh and cheer and clap loudly.

The next guy was a generic brand of vanilla pudding, followed by three more generic versions of the same speech that basically boiled down to a chalky aftertaste like you'd expect from a sugar–free variety. Joel started freaking out when he realized he would be next. Courtney told him he had this. Chad just stared at his sexy boyfriend. It was Joel's turn. Chad gave him a big kiss on the mouth before he went out.

The audience almost lost their minds when Joel walked out on stage. Catcalls, whoops, hollers, laughs, cheers, and of course, claps from sore hands followed. He just stood there with a smile, his boxers, and nothing else on his front to hide his nakedness. After about thirty seconds of standing there and giving the crowd a chance to look him over, he turned around to show a sign hanging from his neck onto his back that said: VOTE FOR JOEL BECAUSE, DAMN! For the first time that afternoon, a majority of the students stood up and cheered. Joel turned back around, waved, and walked backstage.

"That's cheating," Nathan told him sarcastically. "You'll probably get their vote because of your sex appeal alone."

"I just didn't want to say anything," Joel admitted, searching for Chad and Courtney.

"I'm just jealous I didn't think of that approach," Nathan told him, giving him a wink before heading back to the podium to end out the assembly. "Let's have another round of applause for our Princes!" Claps. Cheers. "I present to you one more time, our Homecoming Court!"

"Shit!" Joel cried. "I have to go back out there?"

"Just for a second," Chad told him.

They took their places, with Chad and Joel on either end of the stage. Chad suddenly felt a surge of jealousy as he realized most of those cheers and catcalls were for Joel. After glancing over at Joel, he saw that Joel was staring at him with the biggest smile on his face, letting him know he only had eyes for him. Leaving his place in the Princess Court, Chad rushed over to Joel and kissed him in front of the entire school.

"Dang, guys!" Nathan said at the podium, fanning himself off. "Don't forget to put your ballots in the boxes before you leave today! Tomorrow night we will have a new King and Queen!"

"Okay, where are my pants?" Joel asked after the assembly concluded, causing those in the audience closest to him to laugh and one to shout back, "You don't need them!"

Kevin walked up the steps on the side of the stage, walked right up to Chad and Joel and said, "That was awesome. Both of you. But really, Chad, the first part of your speech made me cry a little." He hugged him.

"Thanks?" Chad said, Kevin's arms still tightly around him. Today he wore a pinstriped black suit with a purple paisley tie. The wool suit made Chad's chin itch. He smelled like sweet cream, sweat, and the unmistakable scent of decomposing grass that was obviously cow manure yet he found oddly pleasing.

"Seriously. I'm so glad you're finally honest with yourself. I've been wondering for years when you were going to come out," Kevin told him, still hugging.

"Really? Did everyone know except me?" Chad asked, trying his damnedest not to rub his chin on Kevin's shoulder to alleviate the itch.

"Probably," Kevin said.

"Ugh. Even my dad said he's known for years," Chad said, letting go so Kevin would know hug time was over.

"So it's true?" Kevin asked. "Mr. Hollins is your dad?"

"Yes?" Chad said, scratching his chin.

"He's a DILF," Nathan chimed in, grabbing Kevin's hand.

"Total DILF," Kevin agreed, squeezing Nathan's hand.

"Guys, c'mon. That's my dad," Chad said, feigning disgust.

"Uh, duh! He's the D in the Dad I'd Like to Fuck!" Kevin said loud enough for a teacher and assistant principal to overhear. "Sorry!" he shouted to them, a wide–eyed, large–toothed smile quickly making an appearance as he stretched out the Y's ee sound.

Courtney shouted it was time to get in a little practice before the game, and Kevin agreed he should probably assemble the football team to go over plays. Joel said he was going to search for his clothes then go home to change for the game. Chad pouted. Joel kissed him. Chad smiled. Courtney dragged him away, rolling her eyes, and saying something about how ridiculous penises were.

Nine times out of ten, Ravenwood High's Homecoming game was against Chancellor. However, this year due to a scheduling conflict, it was against Hudson's Bay. They thought they had nothing to worry about, knowing Bay's reputation. They thought wrong. Nothing could prepare them for the team Bay had somehow built over the summer, except, of course, actual training against a good football team.

Chad spotted Joel sitting next to Nikki in the bleachers as they were in between cheers before turning back around and watching the game from the sidelines and waiting for a break in play. "Shit, we just might get our asses handed to us on a plate!" he told Courtney.

"You shut yo' fuckin' whore mouth, bitch!" Courtney shot back. "They ain't that good."

They watched as a tight end broke formation, ran towards the goal line, turning just in time to catch the ball the quarterback threw, and made the first touchdown mere seconds into the game.

"Never mind. We fucked," Courtney announced, giving in to defeat not even a minute into the first quarter.

"Listen, bitch," Jennifer piped in. "As head cheerleader, you need to get your shit together. Now."

Courtney smiled. "I love it when the Asian gets all feisty! We up," she said after Hudson's Bay scored the extra point. Or points, since Bay opted to run it in for two.

Eight to zero: Hudson's Bay in the lead.

Right before the football teams took their places, Courtney gathered the cheer team to cheer them on.

"Ravenwood offense! [clap clap clapclapclap]

Let's get to it!

Get to it

And we will,

Break, break, break

Break through it!

Run that ball [stomp stomp]

Catch that throw [clap clap]

Let's get to it!
Get to it
And we will,
Break, break, break
Break through it!"

They whooped and hollered and the crowd went wild. Ravenwood managed an easy first down, then stumbled and made no ground for the rest of the plays. With the ball in Hudson's Bay's court, the Bay cheerleaders took their turn.

"Eagles!
Take that ball, take that ball, take that ball away
And score!"

"That was probably the worst cheer I've ever heard in my entire life," Chad said, feeling pity for the Bay cheerleading squad and their tiny little pathetic excuse for a cheer.

Andrea Cox tackled the Bay player with the ball because, you know, as a linebacker it's her job. The ball flew from his hand, landed in one of Ravenwood's, and he took off towards the goal line, easily gaining forty yards before getting tackled. He knew how to hold a ball.

"Let's show those Eagles how we do this," Courtney said, her face in full bitch mode, giving the Ravenwood crowd a single look that made them all stand up and start cheering from the bleachers. She simply stood by with her finger pointed towards the crowd.

"Purple Power
Go RHS!
We got the ball,
We got the ball,
Ravenwood, go, go!
C–R–O–W–S
Crows [clap clap] are the Best!"

Courtney gave a quick head nod with her arms stretched out and shouted towards the Hudson's Bay's cheerleaders, "We so good we ain't even got to do nothin'!"

Chad whispered, "You shouldn't gloat."

"That ain't gloatin'. That be truth," Courtney told him, as they all bounced up and down over the fact that their team stole the ball and now in great position for a touchdown.

The next play got them an easy touchdown.

Cheers exploded.

Ravenwood ran in the ball.

Tied.

More cheers.

Chad turned back around to give Joel a smile and wave, and saw that Mr. and Mrs. Hollins, his mother, and Joel's dad were all together with him and Nikki. Mrs. Hollins and his mother were busy chatting away about something, and

Mr. Hollins was chatting with Mr. Talzan about something, but Mr. Hollins—his dad—still managed a wave back when he caught Chad's eye. Even Kayla and Nikki looked like they were attempting a conversation. Joel, on the other hand, looked bored.

"Courtney, I need to have cheer sex with Joel," Chad told her, serious as a beaver gnawing wood.

She looked at him with preposterous eyes. "You know that ain't a real thing, right?"

"I don't care," he told her. "Let's pretend. I totally want to be Kirsten Dunst to Joel's Jesse Bradford."

"I can't believe I'm allowin' this. Listen up, hoes," Courtney said, huddling the team.

Nobody had to be told what to do. Joel laughed when he realized what was happening. Then Joel became embarrassed at how long it went on. Then Joel finally sat back down, letting Chad know it was time to stop. It worked. Bay scored nothing and the ball was back in Ravenwood's hand.

At halftime, the score was sixteen to fifteen with Hudson's Bay in the lead.

After the third quarter, it was twenty-six to fifteen with Hudson's Bay in the lead.

With only thirty-two seconds on the clock, and the score thirty-three to twenty-nine with Hudson's Bay still in the lead, Ravenwood had little hope they could win the game, especially since Bay had the ball in their hands. Everyone expected them to just hold onto it until the game clock ran down, but when the quarterback threw the ball practically at Andrea, she barely moved towards it, caught it, and ran down the field so fast towards their goal that when she made the touchdown, Bay was still trying to figure out which one of their players had the ball.

She danced.

The team erupted.

The crowd went ballistic.

The Ravenwood cheerleaders waved their pom poms and hollered.

The game clock buzzed signaling the game was over.

Ravenwood won because of a bad play.

Chad ran up the steps and over to Joel and kissed him. "Oh my gawd! That was so awesome!"

"Yeah," Joel managed, his enthusiasm obviously faked. "Sorry, I just don't understand it."

"I'll explain it to you later. We won!" Chad shouted gleefully.

Kayla was down on the field making out with Courtney, Kevin was making out with Nathan, and a few players on the opposing team were gawking at these open displays of affection and probably would have said something, but Kevin's parents were right by his side while this was happening, and they were all scared to death of Courtney because she looked so badass and might cut them with nothing more than a glare. When Andrea took her helmet off to reveal the beauty queen underneath as she shook her hair back and forth, their disdain turned to gloom. The Eagles's coach, on the other hand, told them to buck up and congratulate the Crows on their win, told them they played really well and should be proud of themselves, and told them winning isn't everything but how they played the game. Their attitude markedly improved after that.

As the teams walked past each other and slapped hands and told each other, "Good game," the rivalry slowly dissipated. A few even hugged. The coaches chatted wildly about how great each other's teams played, with Bay's complimenting the fact that Ravenwood had a gay guy and a girl on their team who obviously, and I quote, "Know their shit!"

September 20, 2002

Princess Diarrhea,

The Homecoming game was the most awesome game ever! I don't know how long it's been since we went up against a team as equally matched as we were against Hudson's Bay, but Sweet Lawd Geezus! that was an amazing thing to witness. One day I will have to explain it to Joel who is standing over my shoulder right now shaking his head. One day, but not today. Tonight, we are going to celebrate our victory! Mom's letting me throw a party here while she's at the Hollinses with Joel's dad. Shit, I need to stop referring to them as the Hollinses and start referring to them as my dad's real family or something dramatic like that.

GRRRRR!!!

Why does life have to be so confusing to my poor adolescent brain? Who cares! Party time!

< < <   > > >

"Were you two having sex?" Kevin asked loudly as he spotted Chad and Joel walking down the stairs together.

"Maybe," Joel responded, cocking an eyebrow.

Chad rolled his eyes and shook his head. "Okay, so the only rule Mom left me with is don't break shit. Hopefully we can manage that."

A loud clatter in the kitchen indicated the one and only rule had already been broken. "Sorry!" Jennifer yelled. "Nothing broke!"

Upon further investigation, it appeared that Jennifer merely dropped a vegetable tray onto the floor that had somehow managed to keep itself intact. Chad picked it up and put it on the counter between the kitchen and dining room. She smiled her thanks as she hurriedly put out plastic cups and two–liter bottles of soda with Sheree. Within twenty minutes, the house was packed, mostly with cheerleaders and football players. And Angie.

"Hi, Angie! I didn't know you were coming!" Chad asked far more enthusiastically than he normally would towards her, especially since they never got along.

She rolled her eyes, and said with her arms folded across her chest, "Kevin made me come." She shook her head.

"You don't always have to do everything Kevin asks you to, you know," Chad told her.

Angie looked at him with her face scrunched up, wrinkling her nose and chin and somehow even her ears which made Chad realize she was going to be one scary–ass old woman as he spotted a slick sheen on her neck that looked like dried mayonnaise. "I know! But he's like my best friend."

"Still…" Chad said, not sure where he was planning on going with that so he just stopped.

"Still, Kev said there'd be hot guys here, but the only hot guys I see are all into guys themselves. Fuck my life," Angie said. Her arms remained ever over her breasts as if she was guarding them from an invasion, or she was in an invisible straight jacket.

"True," Chad said back. "I mean, look at me?" His cheesy Prince Charming grin sure to melt the Ice Queen. It didn't.

"Ugh." Angie walked off.

Chad shook his head.

The door opened and Mr. Hollins walked inside holding a large paper bag from the bottom. "Chad!"

Hearing his name, something he trained himself to do both with and without his hearing aids, Chad looked around to see who called him, unable to recognize the voice from the sea of voices. Mr. Hollins walked towards the kitchen.

"Hey, thought you might want something stronger than pop for this party," he told him, revealing the contents of the bag and smiling big goofy smile that eerily reminded him of his own.

"Really, Dad? Supplying alcohol to minors?" Chad said, tilting his head.

"I'm letting my son imbibe under my supervision, only I won't be around to supervise," Mr. Hollins said.

"Mom's going to kill me," Chad said. "You should take it back to your house."

"Your mother only asked to make sure anyone who drinks has a designated driver or stays over until they're sober," Mr. Hollins said, his face showing no signs of false advertising.

Someone grabbed Mr. Hollins's ass and said, "Hi, hot stuff! You go to college here?"

Mr. Hollins shook his head and turned around. Chad saw Angie's perky face and covered his own as he said, "This is my dad, Angie."

"Shut the fuck up! Ugh, my life is ruined!" she shouted, finding her way back towards Kevin and Nathan.

"Sorry about that," Chad told Mr. Hollins.

"You know, I'm tired of being objectified, but at the same time, the wife loves it because I'm all hers, so there you go," Mr. Hollins told Chad.

"Thanks for the beer, Dad," Chad said, giving him a hug.

"Anytime. Just don't let the word get around, okay? And make sure your sisters don't get too wasted," Mr. Hollins said before letting go and walking out, making eye contact with Sheree and Kayla before leaving.

He'd barely gotten halfway down the driveway when the chanting began. "DILF! DILF! DILF! DILF!"

Chad walked up to Sheree and Kayla and said, "Is it always like this?"

"Every time, Chad," Sheree said.

Kayla concurred. "Every. Time."

Courtney opened the door and shouted, "Ya'll need to shut the fuck up, bitches!"

They did.

"Now, where's the beer?" Courtney shouted before spotting Kayla and beginning the first of many slobbery make out sessions of the night.

"Has anyone seen Joel?" Chad asked, wondering where his boyfriend disappeared.

An arm reached around and grabbed his chest as a body thrust itself from behind him, dry humping his ass briefly. "Right here, hot stuff," Joel said. He licked Chad's ear, carefully avoiding the hearing aid. Chad turned around to see Joel with an open bottle of the same thick dark beer his father drank. "For you." He handed the bottle to Chad who gladly accepted it.

"Thanks," he said after taking a swig, waiting for the bite to dwindle. "You want one?"

"Nah. Don't want to become a statistic," Joel said. He was serious.

"I don't have to drink it!" Chad said, about ready to give it away.

"No. Your dad brought it over for you. Besides, with you wasted, I can take advantage of you," Joel told him, a mischievous grin on his face that reminded him of The Grinch, or more accurately, Tim Curry in *Home Alone: Lost in New York* when the credit card got declined as stolen.

"You know you can take advantage of me any time you want, Joel. No alcohol required," Chad said, raising and lowering his eyebrows quickly a couple times.

"I know," Joel said. He pulled him in, kissed him hard on the mouth while holding Chad's ass cheeks. "Now let's have some fun."

"Agreed!" Chad said.

Now, the theory was to have fun. However, Chad found himself being a babysitter all night; shooing people out of his bedroom; catching some guy he'd never seen before at the most inopportune time possible sitting on his mother's bed getting a blowjob from Angie while she kneeled in front of him; cleaning up after the blowjob (because Angie was not a spitter or a swallower but a pull–out–handjob–finish kind of girl) with rubber gloves and paper towels and Lysol and curses; unclogging the toilet from an obscene amount of poop that could not have possibly come from just one person, and if it did, they needed to see a doctor immediately. By the time he was ready to give up and deal with the disasters in the morning, his beer was warm. He drank it anyway. It actually tasted better.

A few hours later as he sat on the sofa with Joel's head in his lap, Sheree and Jennifer sharing the rest of the couch with them, he looked around at the remaining people. Kevin and Nathan cuddled up in a chair; Angie looking bored as always as she stared at herself in a compact mirror redoing her makeup again; Courtney and Kayla sitting in the loveseat, sprawled out and kissing. "Where's Nikki?" he asked, suddenly aware she wasn't in sight.

"Didn't come. You invite her?" Courtney said, peaking her head out from underneath Kayla's strawberry blonde veil.

"Fuck," Chad said, realizing that no, he hadn't. "Goddammit Chad, why are you such an asshole?"

"Chad needs to stop talkin' to himself in the third person," Courtney told him. "Besides, girl said she prolly won't make it. You know how uptight her mama is."

"True dat," Chad said.

"Mm hmm," Courtney said.

"Damn straight," Jennifer chimed in, causing Chad and Courtney to wince.

"Oh honey, noooooo," both Chad and Courtney said at the same time.

"What the hell?" Jennifer shouted. "Why not?"

"Cuz you ain't black, girl," Chad told her, sassy as could be.

"Oh, Fat Buddha, Chad! Neither are you!" Jennifer said, pouting.

"Don't be hatin'! I only white on the outside!" Chad said, bobbing his head back and forth.

Nathan grunted something incomprehensible.

Kevin asked, "Mind if we crash here? I don't think I can drive."

"Son of a bitch!" Angie shouted, dropping her compact into her handbag. "Seriously?"

"Seriously," Kevin repeated before sing-songing, "Had too many porters."

"Never!" Nathan said, sounding pirate–ish before losing consciousness.

Talking into Chad's crotch with his eyes closed, Joel said, "Isn't it weird that the gays outnumber the straights right now?"

"Fuck my life," Angie said. "Two to one."

"Hey! You do know math!" Kevin teased, patting her on the back and almost dropping a passed out Nathan from his lap.

< < <   > > >

September 21, 2002

Princess Diarrhea,

Jesus fucking Christ, I am never having a party ever again. Should I tell Mom about the cum stain I couldn't get out of her comforter, or let her assume it's Jeff's? Oh gawd, I'm going to throw up. Nope. False alarm. Holy shitballs. Kevin and Nathan are still passed out on the floor downstairs and Angie's on the couch with Bride of Frankenstein hair and Joel's still asleep in my bed where he should be. Ugh. I should wake everyone up. We have to get ready for that goddamned parade in a couple hours. Fuck. Please for the love of all things sacred and holy, tell me there isn't a marching band in front of our float?

< < <   > > >

Arriving at the starting point of the parade route just south of downtown, Chad had the sudden realization that his fears were justified. The middle school marching band would indeed be in front of them. Kevin's dad smiled and waved at them as they piled onto the stacked straw bales decked out with Ravenwood High School pennants, and banners on either side of the trailer. He looked the epitome of a redneck dairy farmer who also just happened to be co–president of the local PFLAG chapter; dirty old hat, overalls, red flannel shirt, and a face that would never come clean.

Chad lifted Angie up onto the trailer to take her place. They may not have liked each other very much, but that was no reason they couldn't be cordial. Seeing as they were the last two to arrive of the Queen's Court, they had no choice but to be next to one another. At least the ninety percent chance of showers was holding onto the remaining ten percent.

"Sorry about hitting on your dad last night," Angie said, checking her makeup one last time. Her hair had miraculously been transformed since this morning. Praise Jesus.

"It's cool. I mean, I know he's hot and he says he's used to it," Chad said, flashing her a smile.

"And sorry about random blowjob guy. He made quite the mess, didn't he?" Angie said, chuckling afterwards.

"Yeah, must not have blown his load in weeks!" Chad said louder than he meant to, causing Courtney's ears to perk up.

"Or at the game last night when I gave him the first one," Angie admitted, giving him what looked like an involuntary wink or a facial tic that hinted she might be having a stroke. He wasn't sure which.

"Sweet Lawd Geezus! Really?" Chad said, dropping his lower jaw.

"Yeah. Seriously. Wish I knew his name. He's kinda cute," Angie said, suddenly looking depressed.

"Oh my gawd, Angie. You are such…" Chad started.

"Don't you dare say it, asshole," Angie said sharply, her eyes wide, lips pursed, and body language ready for a fist fight.

"What? That you are such an independent modern woman who knows what she wants and isn't afraid to go after it no matter what people might say behind her back?" Chad said.

Angie's demeanor shifted. "Thank you. For a second I thought you were going to call me a whore like my mother does."

"For liking sex? Bullshit. Whore's do get paid, however, so, you know, they kinda got one up on us, right?" Chad said, pushing his lips to one side of his face as he nodded his head up and down.

"That is insane troll logic," Angie said.

"Fuck. The parade is about to start and I haven't seen Joel yet," Chad said, searching for his boyfriend in a sea of both familiar and foreign faces that looked like a big beige blur as he scanned.

Just then, Angie's face went blank as she stared behind Chad. "Oh. My. Gawd."

"Oh Jesus, what is it?" Chad asked, trying to find what Angie had focused on.

Then he spotted it. Or rather, them.

"Oh my Lawd!" Courtney cried. She cackled one of her loud trademark laughs. "Girls, you best be lookin' at this shit!"

Chad shook his head as the entire King's Court, all the Princes, walked up to the Queen's Court float with all the Princesses wearing nothing but purple underwear, Straw cowboy hats with a crow on the front, and cowboy boots. When Joel got close enough, Chad asked him, "How the hell did they convince you to do this?"

Joel smiled. "I convinced them. Of course, it didn't take much for Nathan. The other guys took a little more. And, those two over there,"—Joel pointed towards the pair in question—"are skinny as rails and paler than fresh snow. They demanded cowboy boots and hats."

Chad leaned down and kissed Joel. "Thanks for giving me an awkward boner."

"You're welcome," Joel said, then smiled a wide toothless grin.

The principal started walking up to them, face red as roses. Nathan met him and said something that quickly cooled him off. He even laughed before taking his place on the sidelines with his wife and kids and a few other school officials and their families.

The first dozen or so groups were already walking or driving the parade route, which really just consisted of Main Street for about a mile to the high school. When the middle school marching band started playing, all the Princesses plastered on their fake smiles and prepared their waving arms for battle of the elbow–elbow–wrist–wrist variety. Chad reluctantly played along with a brain–splitting headache and Joel just feet away getting ogled by onlookers. He decided to take Mrs. Hollins's approach, and let them look, knowing that at the end of the day, Joel belonged to him and him alone. Well, not possessively, but relationship–wise, because people should not own other people.

With a jerk that nearly toppled the uppermost stack that Courtney and one of the boring girls perched upon, their float started moving. The Princes in Purple Panties Platoon flanked them on all sides, Nathan taking the front which left a wide space between them and the middle schoolers who played their instruments in such a way it reminded Chad of a cat in heat getting gang–raped by a whole neighborhood of toms.

Chad spotted a face in the crowd. "Joel! Get that guy's name and number!" he said, pointing towards a tall guy with a black leather jacket.

"Really? What the hell?" Joel asked, motioning his hands all over his mostly naked body. "This not enough for you?"

"No! It is, trust me it is and I'd get up myself but Jesus I already am thanks to your sexy body on display. For Angie," Chad said.

"Oh, isn't that they guy she was blowing last night?" Joel asked.

"Yep. Name and number. Hurry!"

Joel obliged, though it took a little convincing, and a finger pointed towards Angie on the float for the guy to give up the information. He waved at her. She waved back like a regular person before switching back to Princess Mode. He jogged back. "Here's Abe's number."

"Oh my gawd, his name is Abe?" Angie said, her facial expression somewhere between disgust and intrigue.

"Abraham Alexander Aadlund the third," Joel recited from recent memory.

"He's my triple A!" Angie squealed, holding the piece of torn paper and not even bothering to wave at the crowd.

"I don't get it," Chad said.

"Yeah, neither do I," Joel said, realizing cowboy boots were not made for walking and definitely not for jogging as his toes started swelling. That or he probably shouldn't have worn his dad's since they were a size too small for his feet.

"Kayla told me! She read my palm at Stacey Hill's party and said I'd fall in love with Triple A, and I told her she was a crazy cunt. Shit, how did she know?" Angie asked.

"She's a witch," Chad said, still smiling his fake smile and waving his Princess wave.

"Shut the fuck up. Seriously?" Angie asked, slack–jawed.

"Yep." Chad was still on point.

"Cool. Thanks for doing that Joel. I owe you one," Angie said, even sounding like she meant it.

Joel smiled, then faced his body front, waving at the crowd with his head slightly in their direction. Middle–aged divorced women could barely contain themselves over the orgy of underage boy–meat on display. Jennifer's mom started throwing dollar bills into the street as they passed, causing Jennifer to nearly die of embarrassment as she stood next to her.

Then, without warning, the float jerked to a stop, making Courtney have to steady herself once again. Suddenly the middle school band stopped playing, and Billy Ray Cyrus's "Achy Breaky Heart" started blasting from hidden speakers in the straw bales. Nothing could prepare Chad for the following scene.

Joel winked at Chad, then started line dancing with the rest of the Princes, making their way around all four sides of the float to a cheering crowd gone wild. Courtney got up, somehow dancing on a straw bale in heels, defying the laws of physics just like her fabulous hair.

"Great, now I'm going to have wet dreams of your boyfriend and my best friend's boyfriend doing that forever. Fuck my life," Angie said, unable to take her eyes off the six purple asses.

"I know, right?" Chad said nervously.

When the song was over, the King's Court took their places and the marching band started up again with its low guttural growl and the float started moving and Chad was thankful that they were already halfway through the route.

"You don't have anymore of those stunts planned, do you?" Chad asked Joel as they resumed course.

"Nope. That was all for you." Joel winked at him, making his heart flutter.

"When did you even have the time to come up with that?" Chad asked, breaking Princess Mode.

Joel smiled. "We all have our secrets. Now, elbow–elbow–wrist–wrist, Chadwick!"

Chad glared at Joel with menacing eyes full of playful vengeance. At least his erection finally went away before they pulled into the high school's parking lot to disembark. He turned to Courtney to ask, "Need any help setting up for the dance tonight?"

"Fool?!" Courtney said, making her scrunchy face that practically disappears into her hair. "Done and done."

"How do you have the time?" Chad asked, offering his arm for her to take as she made her way down the pile of straw bales.

"Years o' practice, and a assload of helpuhs! Ha HA!" Courtney said, letting go of his arm as she jumped onto the pavement in heels. She wiped her rear of any stray straw, then twerked for good measure in case she missed any.

Chad leapt off the trailer after the rest of the Princesses, ran up to Joel, spun him around, kissed him passionately, then whispered into his ear, "I need to take advantage of you right now. It's important."

"Okay," Joel said. "My car's right here."

"Where are your keys?" Chad asked, noticing a lack of hiding places for just about anything Joel was wearing.

"In the car. Left them in my pants," Joel said, opening the driver's side door.

"You are under no circumstances going to put those pants on."

"Yes, master."

< < <   > > >

September 21, 2002

Dear Princess Diarrhea,

Joel in purple underwear and cowboy boots and hat are totally at the top of my list of hottest attire ever. Sweet Lawd Geezus!

The parade was way better than I thought it would be. The middle school kids need to stop playing or start practicing a lot. Fuck, they were awful. So bad, I feel sorry for their parents. Maybe I shouldn't be so tough on them, after all, the school year just started a few weeks ago and they probably just started practicing for this, and half of them had probably never even picked up an instrument before the class, and I should probably stop saying how horrid the whole ordeal was to endure.

Probably.

So, the Homecoming dance is tonight, Joel's napping after our afternoon delight, and now that I've got purple underwear and shitty marching band stuff off my chest, I'm worried about Nikki and Meghan. I mean, they've both been dealt some pretty shitty hands, and my worry is for different reasons, but I can't help but feel like a useless lump of flesh when it comes to ways I can help them.

Chad stared at the computer monitor, entranced by the blinking cursor after the last word he typed until the phone rang, causing him to jump out of the chair just enough to startle the cat, make Squeakers scream bloody murder, resulting in Chad tripping over said cat, falling on his ass, and cry, "Jesus Fucking Christ!"

The phone's incessant ringing made him wish his mother had purchased an answering machine at some point during her life. "Goddammit, what?!"

"Why are you so angry all the time when I call lately, Chad?" Nikki asked, a quiet laugh indicating she may be partially joking.

"Sorry. Tripped over Squeaks and fell and now my ass is black and blue. How are you?" Chad asked, rubbing his sore bum and praying that the black and blue part was only pretend because he really didn't want a bruised bottom.

"Fine. Just saw a moving van pull up into your driveway and wondered if you needed help," Nikki told him.

"Shit!" Chad shouted. "Joel! Wake up! Your dad is here with the stuff! Sorry, Nik. I thought they were moving in tomorrow. Seriously. No, I don't think we need help, but if you want to come over and hang out for a couple hours before the dance, that'd be awesome. I just need to put on real clothes and make sure Joel isn't still naked."

"You don't have to," Nikki said playfully.

"Ha ha. See you soon?"

"Yeah."

CLICK

"Joel! Serious! Wake the fuck up!" Chad shouted, throwing on a shirt and shorts.

"What?" Joel said before pulling the covers over his head. "Go away."

"Your dad and Matthew are here," Chad told him, staring down into the driveway from his bedroom's bay window.

"Fuck. What happened to tomorrow?" Joel said, throwing the covers down to reveal his post–coital nakedness.

"I don't know."

"Dammit. Where are my pants?"

"Still in your car. Here, wear these," Chad said, tossing him one of his cheer practice shorts and a three–quarter sleeve T–shirt that had Captain Kirk's face screaming "KHHHAAAN!!!" on it. His favorite. "I'll be downstairs or outside carrying stuff in or..."

"Calm down, Chad," Joel said, putting the shirt on. It was tight against Joel's body, making Chad realize just how much more muscle tone Joel had compared to him.

"I am calm!" Chad shouted.

Joel kissed him. "This isn't anything to be worried about. So what if Dad bumped up moving in by a day?"

"So what?" Chad threw his hands in the air. "I've got to figure out how to make room for your bed and clothes and everything in the office because you refuse to share my room, and all you can say is 'So what?'"

"Yes," Joel said. "Now calm the fuck down. We don't have a lot. A better television than your shitty excuse for one, but still, most of our furniture will probably end up at

Goodwill." He kissed Chad again then slapped his ass. "Now get down there and help bring in my shit."

Chad had managed to include the word "Woman!" at the end of Joel's sentence in his head because the way he talked reminded him of a character on *Little House on the Prairie.*

"Dudes! Get the fuck down here and help!" Matthew shouted at them, holding a large box as he walked in the front door.

Chad opened the garage door, which would normally contain his mother's car, but for now would have to be storage central until the sorting party. The boxes piled up quickly as Nikki watched, every now and then taking one of the smaller ones and pretending to be a girl. Chad knew better, but didn't care. He was just glad she was there and not moping around her house getting all depressed that her dad couldn't be there because he had a crappy heart probably from eating his ex–wife's cooking for too many years.

As if on cue, Ms. Walker pulled up just as the last of the Talzan's stuff was unloaded from the U–Haul. "Had to stop by the store for some groceries. Wow! You move quick!" she said, holding two sacks in her hand as she exited the car.

Mr. Talzan smiled at her, gave her a sweaty kiss, and said, "Now get in there and make me a sandwich, woman!" as he slapped her ass.

Son of a bitch. Like father, like son, Chad thought, watching as his mother walked into the house being chased by Joel's dad.

Joel walked up behind him and said, "I swear to gawd, it's like we are the adults in this family sometimes."

"Tell me about it." Chad shook his head and Joel hugged him from behind.

"Invite me in. I need a drink," Nikki said.

"Yeah, don't be such dicks, fuckers!" Matthew said, before offering his hand to Nikki. "Come on, we don't need them."

Nikki took his hand, and walked inside with Matthew, turning her face around and giving Chad and Joel a "What the hell is happening?" look.

"Oh gawd, should I warn her?" Chad asked.

"I don't know," Joel said. "He's never dated a fat chick before."

"You think he's interested?" Chad asked.

"They kept staring at each other the entire time we were unloading stuff, so yes, I think it's safe to say he might have an interest in your ex–girlfriend," Joel told him.

"I don't know how I feel about that." Chad shuffled, not sure if he wanted to walk into the house, uncertain if he'd find his mom making out with Jeff, Matthew making out with Nikki, or worse, both.

Joel felt his unease, and opted to pull Chad into the garage to sit on the well–worn leather sofa that should have just been kept in the van to be donated. It felt like a cave, the boxes piled high and all around them. They stared at Joel's mattress leaning against the wall.

"We can leave that in here for now," Joel said, squeezing Chad's hand.

"No, I should move the computer out of the office and get all my other shit out so you can have your own space," Chad said, squeezing Joel's hand back. "But thanks."

"Maybe later. Leave the office the way it is for now," Joel said. "I insist, mostly because I don't want to unpack anything just yet. Well, except maybe some of my clothes."

Chad sighed. "Speaking of clothes, have any idea where your outfit for tonight is?"

He turned around and stared at the mountains of unmarked boxes. "Son of a bitch."

Walking into the main gymnasium (Ravenwood High had two other smaller ones), Chad and Joel stood in awe of the transformation from high school gym to decked out dance hall. It should also be noted that it looked like America threw up all over it. Patriotism abounded in red, white, and blue. A giant banner that read: AMERICA: UNITED WE STAND hung dead center over the punch table. It looked like Nikki's handiwork.

"Oh my gawd, Meghan!" Chad shouted, giving her a hug when he realized she was standing next to him in a dress that looked eerily similar to the one Courtney picked out for herself, though decidedly less revealing.

"Hi Chad, Joel," she said, smiling and looking a bit awkward.

"You look great, Meghan," Joel said.

"Thank you. Courtney obviously picked it out," Meghan said, shaking her head.

"Don't she look so cute?" Courtney asked, giving her little sister a side–hug. "I keep tellin' her to lose the glasses but she won't so I ain't pushin' it no mo' 'til next year anyway ha HA!"

Meghan rolled her eyes, but smiled anyway. The light's reflection scattered by the mirror ball had nothing on the glittery themed dresses as they sparkled everywhere except the chocolate leg peeking through the excessively high slit on Courtney's dress that revealed she either wasn't wearing underwear or had on a high–waisted thong.

Sheree, Kayla, and Jennifer all walked in with their coordinated dresses that made them look like the American flag, with Kayla being the stars on blue, and Sheree and Jennifer wearing red and white stripes, all three of them barely covering their asses but smothered in sequins. They looked gaudy. Courtney loved it.

"What up, bitches?!" Courtney shouted, strutting towards them in six–inch stilettos and arms in the air.

"What up, my nigga?!" Kayla said, being one of only two people who could get away with saying that and not getting punched in the throat. Chad was the other.

Courtney and Kayla kissed lighter than usual, just a peck really. One must not ruin her makeup before the photo op, after all.

Joel suddenly looked nervous.

"Hey? What is it?" Chad asked.

"What am I going to do if I get voted Homecoming King? No, it won't happen. Nobody knows me. Never mind. Nathan will get it. The pasty skinny guys won't because I can't even remember their names. Shit." Sweat started beading on Joel's forehead.

Chad kissed Joel. "Calm down. Or maybe you can calm me down because what if I end up being Homecoming Queen? Jesus Fucking Christ, imagine that?"

Joel laughed. "Thanks. You do have it worse than me."

"Thanks for your pep talk, asshole," Chad said.

"Fuck," Joel said, looking at the entrance.

"What? Oh gawd, is my mom drunk off her ass and stumbling into the gym in just her bra again?" Chad asked, unable to turn around.

"No, wait, what?" Joel asked, not sure if he heard Chad right.

"I'm just messing with you," Chad said. "Seriously, is it safe to turn around?"

"Maybe. It's Nikki," Joel said.

"Oh," Chad said, turning around. "And Matthew."

"Shit." Joel looked pale with a chance of vomit.

"Shit is right. He cleans up nice!" Chad said, nodding his head up and down.

They were holding hands. Then Nikki introduced Matthew to the girls. Then Nikki took him out to the dance floor and started grinding her ass against his crotch.

"I think it's fair to say she's moved on, Chad," Jennifer said as she watched the scene unfold. "I hate her even more now. I mean, who is he?"

Joel held his face in his hands. "My cousin who only thinks with his dick."

"Well, I think the dick is going to have a place to be inserted tonight," Jennifer said. "Got any more cousins who look like you guys?"

"One," Joel said.

"Yeah?" Jennifer asked, face lighting up.

"Married," Joel said.

"Shit," Jennifer said. "Where can a hot Asian girl like myself with an ass like a ten–year–old boy find a guy who isn't gay or taken?"

"You'll find him," Chad assured, rubbing her back and regretting it right after because rubbing sequins is one of the worst sensations his hands had ever encountered and wondered just how the girls could stand all that chaffing.

"I guess until then I will just be a chronic masturbator. Fuck my life. Oh, goddammit, Angie! Why does your vocab have to enter mine?" Jennifer stormed off, which was probably a good thing because neither Chad nor Joel wanted to listen to her possibly going into further detail about her masturbatory life.

Just when Chad and Joel were going make their way to the punch table to find out what flavor and if someone had already spiked it or not, Courtney stopped them and announced they all needed to get a group picture while they were still on point with their outfits and hair and makeup. Nikki and Matthew had to be dragged off the dance floor. Joel tried not to notice that Matthew actually looked happy, not the fake chauvinistic aura he usually put off. They decided to do a big group picture first before splitting off into pairs. The three single ladies—Sheree, Jennifer, and Meghan—grabbed American flag props and humorously pretended they were their dates.

Kevin walked up to Joel while he and Chad were at the punch table finally getting their non-alcoholic strawberry lemonade and 7-up beverages, and said, "That was so frickin' awesome today at the parade!" holding his hand out for a high-five that Joel spent a little longer than he should have to take.

"Thanks. Nathan said he had a plan in case any school officials got their titties in a twist," Joel said after they slapped hands. His still felt hot. Kevin didn't hold back.

"What'd you say to Principal Paulsen?" Chad asked Nathan, who looked absolutely adorable next to Kevin wearing a white tuxedo, red shirt, and blue bowtie.

"I told him we were bringing awareness to testicular cancer," Nathan said. "Had to find a reason to wear purple underwear, and my dad said something about orchid being the color for nut cancer, which, side note, now that I think of it is totally appropriate since orchid literally means testicles. I trust him since he lost a ball to it."

"Awesome!" Chad said, before quickly adding, "About the save, not the loss."

"No prob. Just spread the word about it so we can keep up appearances!" Nathan said before turning to Kevin and telling him, "We should get our picture taken!"

"Later, guys!" Kevin said as they disappeared into the crowd.

Holding their punch, Chad and Joel kept trying to dance, but the playlist left much to be desired. Chad figured Courtney must have delegated that task, until he noticed it was a deejay and she was having words with him at that moment. She did not look well pleased.

"Get readyyyyyyyyyyyyyyy!!!" Courtney said loudly as she strutted over to them.

DMX's "Party Up (Up in Here)" started playing, making the kids holler, and Chad's face light up. "Yay! Come on!"

"You can't be serious?" Joel asked, but the look in Chad's eyes told him otherwise.

"Ya'll gonna make me lose my mind, up in here, up in here!" Chad sang, pulling Joel out onto the dance floor.

The song list had markedly improved after Courtney's chat with the deejay. Before they knew it, the principal had gathered the Homecoming Court to the front where in just moments they would find out who had been voted King and

Queen. He asked for a drumroll, however, without actual drums available, the audience either slapped their thighs or stomped their feet.

"Joel Tarzan!" Mr. Paulsen announced, to which Courtney corrected him with, "Talzan, fool!" and he said, "Sorry, Joel Talzan!"

Even hearing his name a second time wasn't enough to make Joel realize that his peers had somehow voted him as Homecoming King. Chad just laughed.

"Get yo' ass up there and get yo' crown, fool!" Courtney told him.

"Your speech must've made quite the impression!" Nathan joked with airquotes around "speech" before congratulating Joel as he pushed him towards the principal.

The assistant principal put a plastic crown on his head.

After Joel got over the shock that he'd just won Homecoming King, he took his place at the front of the gym that had magically been transformed into a dance hall next to a throne of sorts that was really just a high–backed red velvet chair. Not real magic, mind you, despite Kayla's offer to Courtney, but just Courtney magic that everyone was mystified by.

"And your Ravenwood Homecoming Queen for two–thousand–and–two is…"

The audience went silent, all waiting with anticipation and hoping their vote won. Chad found himself praying that he didn't win for selfish reasons that involved being called a queen by people he didn't even know. It took forever for the principal to open the envelope, and when he did, he just looked at the name and smiled, making the crowd unruly.

"Courtney Jones!" he shouted.

Of all the people there, Courtney looked the most shocked. She'd wanted this for four years, and year four she finally got it. Of course, she'd given up any hope of ever winning, so when she started crying tears of joy, they were genuinely happy tears. Kayla gave her a kiss on her lusciously plump red lips and pushed her up, clapping and cheering loudly. When the crown hit her Afro, nesting comfortably well above her skull, all she could do was smile. It was the one time in her life she was speechless.

"That's so awesome," Nikki said to Chad, still clapping as Matthew's hands held steady on her hips.

"It is. Weird that Joel's up there, but awesome nonetheless," Chad said back.

"Seriously, you didn't think having him up on stage practically naked wouldn't get him to win Homecoming King? That stunt probably made a lot of guys question their sexuality!" Nikki told him.

Matthew's ears perked up. "I must be told of this stunt."

"Perhaps I overshot when I told him to do it," Chad said, pushing out his lower lips at an angle and making his adorable face seem decidedly unattractive, then giving Matthew a look that he indeed would fill him in on the event.

"I'm going to get some punch for us, okay sweetie?" Matthew said to Nikki, flashing her a smile that made her swoon.

"Sounds great. Extra ice," she said back.

"Sweetie?" Chad asked after Matthew's distance made him out of earshot.

"Yeah," Nikki said. She looked positively radiant.

They watched Joel and Courtney dance to the King and Queen's Dance song, one that Courtney picked out because she got tired of it being a slow romantic song about love and filled with flowery nonsense. No, nothing like that. She chose John Mayer's "No Such Thing" because it totally represented high school, and now she would be the one to dance to it with her best friend's boyfriend. Chad realized his boyfriend could dance. Very well. Not the crap he was pulling during the DMX song. However, behind them, he and Nikki overheard an upper middle–aged man with a bad comb over tell another upper middle–aged man without anything to comb over, "Back in my day when I lived here, you'd never catch a salmon nigger and a coon in this school. They'd get lynched straight off."

Chad really hoped his hearing aids were playing tricks on him. People didn't still think like that, did they? Turning to Nikki, her face turning the familiar murderous shade of red, made him realize that yes, people still did.

She punched them both in the face and told them, "Get the hell out of here, assholes!"

Their nostrils flooded over their shirts and bolos, leaving a trail of blood as they exited the gym.

"I love you, Nik!" Chad said, hugging her round body.

Her demeanor changed instantly. "I love you, Chad! I hate ignorant assholes like those two bastards. What the fuck is wrong with people?"

"Well, their noses are wrong with them now!" Chad said. "I mean, that was impressive the way you swung back both your arms and let them fly into their faces like a slingshot."

Nikki laughed. "Thanks. Too bad I haven't worn my butterfly ring since we broke up, or the guy on the right would've needed stitches too." She seemed genuinely disappointed in herself.

Matthew returned with punch. "Do I need to finish those guys off?" he asked, handing the extra ice one to Nikki.

"Nope. Pretty sure I took care of it," Nikki told him, kissing him on the mouth and making Chad irrationally uncomfortable.

"Awesome Possum," Matthew said when their lips unhinged.

They started being a little too couple–ish for Chad's comfort level, so he casually took a few steps away from them. He spotted Meghan chatting with a few of the Prayer Circle kids, who all were hugging her or holding her hands, so he figured she must have told them at least some of what has been going on. Despite the obvious pain she felt, she had a smile on her face and looked genuinely happy. He just hoped that pain never manifested itself into depression and then transformed into thoughts of worthlessness before those thoughts poisoned her mind into suicide. He'd already lost a friend to that, and one was too many.

Someone grabbed his hand.

"Dance with me," Joel said, pulling him onto the dance floor.

"As you wish."

September 21, 2002

Dear Princess Diarrhea,

Some people wear their race like a badge of honor. Others wear it like a badge of shame. The same is true for sexuality, where societal pressures demand openness about the subject, but then force you to wear this scarlet letter brazenly across your chest because they feel they have the right to know. Fuck that. I'm glad I don't live in that society. I'm glad I live in a town where people embrace diversity. I won't be made to feel ashamed because I don't match. Because I am white on the outside, black on the inside, and gay all over. I am me! I am unique! I am loved!

<   <   <   >   >   >

"You are," Joel said, putting his arms around Chad's neck from behind, who reached up to wrap his own arms over Joel's. "Now get out of my room."

"Your room? I thought we were sharing mine?" Chad asked, eyes full of hurt.

"I've got too much stuff," Joel said, arms folded across his chest, but the smile over his face revealing he might be joking.

Chad decided to play along. "But I like having two rooms."

"Greedy little bastard."

"Maybe I can get my mom to let you turn the nursery next to their room into a storage room for us."

His mom overheard and said, "Not going to happen."

"Why not?" Chad asked.

His mother looked hesitant, a look she rarely had. "Well, because we're going to need it?"

"Really? For what? Your wine collection?" Chad said, letting his head fall like it barely dangled from his neck.

"A nursery?" she said.

Chad did not look amused. "Don't fuck with me, Mom."

"Surprise, Chad and Joel! You're going to have a half–sibling!" she announced, all smiles.

Chad turned to Joel who was already looking in his direction. "Just when things seem to be going great, the universe decides to throw us some more shit."

"I don't know, I think having a little brother or sister would be cool." Joel said. "Of course, we'd have some explaining to do when said sibling asks why we're brother–fuckers."

"I can't wait."

18 days

Author Bio

Cory Blystone lives in Vancouver, Washington with his husband Greg, their dogs Chuck and Sunny, cat Dexter, and their flock of chickens named after *Buffy the Vampire Slayer* characters. When not in school and doing homework, he enjoys writing, drawing, painting, reading, quilting, gardening, making absurd videos for YouTube, reading, rapping, cooking, baking, oh, and reading. He also was the Managing Editor for Clark College's award winning art and literature magazine, *Phoenix*, for the 2015 edition where his hand can be seen on nearly every page. Literally. He drew or wrote every title, and wrote all of the writer's statements for the literary works by hand to give the magazine a personal journal feel. You can check it out at ClarkPhoenix.com.

Also by Cory Blystone

Deadly Rhymes

Deadly Rhymes Trilogy Book 1

Ravenwood Series #1

Deadlier Rhymes

Deadly Rhymes Trilogy Book 2

Ravenwood Series #2

Deadliest Rhymes

Deadly Rhymes Trilogy Book 3

Ravenwood Series #3